# The Weight of Fearsome Things

## Book Two Of The Camino Family Trilogy

### K.D. Field

SANTIAGA
MANO

*For my friend, Leigh*
*True Blue – Partner in Crime*
*We Ride at Dawn*

# Author's Note

I began writing this story after our move to our farm on the Camino Francés in 2021. This book is the first in *The Camino Family Trilogy* written while living on the Camino.

After concluding *The Grief of Goodbye*, I knew that John and Javier's story was not over. The two men had unfinished business and stories to tell. And so did the wonderful Ines and Pen and Mateo. So many readers reached out to offer suggestions of where the story should go, but I wanted to treat John and Javier with the respect their backstories deserved. This book is about grief. But it is also about healing and our power to recognize our own humanity. And to learn to love ourselves despite our many flaws. In most families, secrets are woven across time. Our modern world doesn't have a corner on deception. But if we can learn to look past those things and treat each other's pain with the grace it deserves, we can begin to heal ourselves in the process.

Please enjoy *Book 2: The Weight of Fearsome Things*. The story of the Sullivan and Silva families continues. May you find healing in reading the story as I did writing it.

# Part I

## The Promise

# ONE

## PROMISES KEPT

The weather was warm for a Spring Day in Madrid. John Sullivan kissed and hugged his daughter, Pen, before she went upstairs in the house near Alphonso Martinez Square to prepare for her big day, trailed by her gaggle of fussing bride's maids. It was uncomfortable being here. John couldn't deny it, sitting in Javier Silva's home, preparing for Pen's wedding to Mateo. But he wouldn't have missed it for the world.

Pen was happier than he had ever seen her. Mateo was a good man and a fully qualified doctor. The two had been through a lot together in the past ten years, and their similar life experiences would mean they could weather the storms that would inevitably come. He was sure this was a marriage that would last.

John rubbed his hands together and rose to look out the window into a courtyard filled with potted palm trees and a bubbling fountain—a cool, shady place to spend a sunny afternoon. He would need to get upstairs soon to put on his tuxedo. This event was a very formal affair. They told him Spanish weddings could have five hundred people at the reception, and all dressed the nines. The drinking, eating, fireworks, and dancing would last until the wee hours.

Pen and Mateo had taken care of the civil ceremony the day before. They would have another reception at a winery somewhere in Northern Spain in a few weeks, thrown by relatives of Mateo's father, Javier. John would miss it and be safely back in the US, away from the discomfort of this whole situation.

A door opened, and he turned to see a linen-clad Javier enter the great room lined with books and stunning art. The space was large enough for several collections of sofas. An oversized hand-carved mahogany desk dominated the space, and this is where Javier headed. He was looking for something, rifling through the papers stacked on the top; it was a moment before he noticed John was there.

'Ah.' he said, holding up a folder. 'I was just looking for a patient's record. I'd misplaced it somewhere. I need to get back to them, and my nurse is busy fussing about the wedding.' Stopping. He smiled. John didn't care what he was doing.

John looked at this man who had loved his wife, body, and soul. He had to admit the guy was handsome. After all these years, Javier still reminded John of that guy on the 1970s TV show *Fantasy Island*. Very suave. Very sophisticated. Very Spanish. He reached up and touched his own greying hair. Neither of them was young anymore.

'Would you like a drink?' Javier offered. 'I imagine being the *Father of the Bride* is stressful.'

John chuckled.

'Not half as stressful as being the groom. I saw Mateo a little bit ago. He looked terrified. You guys do know how to throw a wedding.'

'In Spain, it's one of our superpowers.' Javier smiled.

Mateo's grandmother had handled most of the arrangements, grudgingly accommodating Pen's American touches into the ceremony and reception. The woman scared John a little.

Javier crossed the room. He opened a bottle of something, poured two glasses, and handed one to John.

'Sláinte.' said John, raising his glass.

'Salud.' said Javier, and they both drank.

'This is quite a room. The art is incredible. It looks to have been painted by the same artist.' John was restless, rising to stand in front of the painting closest to him. 'Not what I think of when I think of Spanish painters like Goya or Dali. This is light. It makes me happy to look at it.'

Javier smiled.

'My wife, Alejandra, painted all of these. She was a very happy person. Full of light.'

John sat back down, feeling like he'd crossed an invisible line; he struggled to find his footing. Javier stepped in to fill the void.

'We have never really spoken much, you and me, since that day in the village before León. We have been to countless parties for this marriage, but we have never talked about anything of consequence.' observed Javier.

'No.' said John, gazing down into the liquid he held.

'It must be strange for you to sit here with me. *The other man.*'

John hesitated. This man was fearless and direct.

'You were, and you weren't. I gave Tess my permission.' He said. 'My blessing, actually. So, you didn't do anything wrong. Either of you.'

'That's very generous.' Javier smiled. 'You are a better man than I.'

'Oh, I'm certain of that.' said John wryly. Smiling, he took another sip.

Javier chuckled. 'She was an amazing woman. Tess would have loved all this. She liked celebrating, and she would be so happy to see Pen so happy. And she loved Mateo.'

John swallowed hard. It was strange to hear this man speak about his wife of more than 25 years when he had only known her briefly.

'She was amazing.' He agreed. John could still see her face in his dreams, even though he could no longer conjure that vision while awake. 'I have loved only one woman in my life. My wife.'

Javier appeared thoughtful.

'I have only loved two women. My wife,' he hesitated, 'and yours.' Drinking deeply from his glass.

They sat in silence for a few moments, contemplating what that meant.

'Did you know I saw you there?' John glanced up at him. A look of anguish hovered in his eyes.

'Where did you see me?' Javier frowned.

'At the hospital. They told me it wouldn't be long. I didn't want Tess to be alone, so I got up in the middle of the night and headed there. I saw you in her room, holding her hand and kissing her forehead. I saw how she looked at you.' John gulped more of the drink than he meant to and coughed. 'I came early in the morning one day, and you were still asleep in the chair beside her bed. I went down to the cafeteria to wait for you to leave.'

Javier held his breath. 'Why did you say nothing?' He whispered.

'I didn't want her to be alone. I would be with her all day if you were with her at night. Tess was surrounded by love until the end.' John struggled to control his emotions.

Javier held his breath.

'Tess gave her doctor permission to keep me informed on her condition. After she went back to the US, she never contacted me again. It was how it needed to be. We both knew that. She was going back to you and your family. And she was going back to fight the disease. She needed to focus on all of that. But I wanted to know how she was, and one day before she left, she told me she had emailed her oncologist and asked her to keep me informed at critical points. I am a doctor, after all.'

'Yes.' John conceded.

'I got a call that she was near the end. Mateo was finishing exams, but I canceled all my appointments and got on a plane. I went to be with her. She was still conscious when I arrived, and we had good conversations before the last day. I didn't know how I would handle it after losing my wife the same way. *If* I could handle it at all. But I am glad I went, and I got to see her the night before she passed. The doctor called me at my hotel the next afternoon to tell me that she was surrounded by family when she slipped away. I flew home the following day.'

Both men had tears in their eyes—the grief still with them ten years later.

'We were there, Pen and me. We got to be with her at that moment. Pen rubbed her feet with her favorite lotion. The smell of lavender always reminds me of it. And I read *Pride and Prejudice* to her and held her hand. It was a beautiful and terrifying moment, letting her go. I don't think we've ever been the same.'

Javier stared into his glass without speaking.

'The next year, Pen came to you guys here for her year abroad. My pride told me I should fight it, but it was strangely comforting, knowing she would be with people she knew so well. That Tess knew so well. You would take care of her. I knew that. As you had on the Camino.'

Javier gathered himself.

'Pen looks more and more like her mother. Sometimes, I find it hard to look at her if she catches the light just right.' Javier appeared ashamed of this admission. 'Again, I don't know if I could have done it in your position.'

'Oh, I think you would have.' John stopped. 'She talked about you. Did you know that? Towards the end. She told me a lot of things about you.' He shook his head at the concern on Javier's face. 'Not the specifics of the other stuff. Just about who you were. How you helped her to live those weeks over here.'

Javier stopped breathing. When he looked up at John, it was with tears streaming down his face. His reaction took John off guard, and he struggled once again for control.

'I never asked you where she is buried. If I'm ever in the US, I would like to visit her grave.' whispered Javier, examining his glass.

'She was cremated.' John told him. 'She's in an urn in my house. I couldn't bear to think of her alone in a marble niche somewhere with strangers. She asked to be sprinkled at the places in the world that she loved visiting. I'm afraid I haven't done that yet, either. Still trying to let go, I guess.' He hesitated before whispering. 'A few of them are along the Camino.'

Javier looked up.

'I think I probably know where they are.'

'I'm sure you do.' John conceded.

They both thought about what that meant.

'Listen, John. When Mateo and I walked with Tess and Pen, it was in honor of my wife, Alejandra. She was an extraordinary person and deserved a pilgrimage of her own.'

John nodded. 'Tess told me at the time. I thought it was extraordinary.'

'Yes, but not unusual for those in Europe.' Javier chose his words carefully. 'I feel strange suggesting it, but perhaps you and I could walk it.

Together. In Tess's honor. You could fulfill some of her last wishes and visit the places Tess loved along the Way.' He stopped and waited.

John shook his head.

'I don't know. That sounds odd; her husband and her lover?'

'On the Camino, you will hear stranger stories.' Javier chuckled. 'Believe me.'

John was retired now. This suggestion was far outside his comfort zone, yet it felt oddly comforting.

'When would we go?' he asked without thinking.

John's quick reaction took Javier by surprise. This man had written the selfless letter that had set all their lives in a different direction—a man who didn't let his fears stop him.

'I am winding down my patient list. Mateo is taking over the practice. I could go in the autumn.'

John thought about it for less than a minute.

'I can make that work.'

The door opened from the hall, and Ines, Javier's housekeeper, entered the room.

'Apologies, but you both need to get ready if we're going to stay on schedule and avoid the wrath of Pen.'

She'd broken the spell, and both men finished their drinks in one gulp and stood. John surprised himself by reaching out to shake Javier's hand. 'In the Fall.'

Javier nodded and clasped his hand. 'The Fall.'

Then they went off to get ready to see their children marry. Secure in the thought that Tess was smiling wherever she was.

# TWO

## A DECADE OF WOUNDS

Her coughing woke Javier, sleeping in the chair by her hospital bed. As a doctor, the sound was one he had heard a hundred times before. Tess didn't have long to live. Javier wiped the sleep from his chocolate-brown eyes and ran his hand through his salt-and-pepper hair. He rose from the chair and stretched, reaching for the plastic water pitcher on the bedside table. Then he held the cup to Tess's lips so she could clear her throat.

The machines beeping and whirring only the day before were gone from the grey hospital room. Just the IV was left in her right hand to administer the pain medication, keeping her comfortable. The woman in the bed was a shell of the person he had met the year before when they walked 800 kilometers across northern Spain on the Camino de Santiago with their children. Today, Tess resembled a shriveled leaf poised to blow away in a gust of wind. An ugly floral headscarf soaked with sweat clung to her skull, and the purple circles surrounding her eyes had spread like a flowering bruise beneath her skin to the rest of her face and arms. Javier resisted snatching the dirty fabric away from this woman who had lived her life with such style. Only the blue lapis butterfly necklace with wings edged in gold, lying at her throat, was familiar—his gift to her a year before. As with his wife, Alejandra, he could do nothing to save another woman he loved.

The morning sun peeked through the beige hospital blinds. Javier needed to leave shortly. John, Tess's husband, and Pen, her daughter, would arrive soon. He split the blinds to peer across the desolate landscape of Phoenix, Arizona. Madrid was hot in summer, but this place was like an oven. The red rocks and dusty brown sky lay in sharp contrast to what he was used to. When it was time for him to fly home to Spain, he hoped never to return to this place.

'I need you to make me a promise.' Tess whispered, then coughed, struggling to strengthen her voice.

Javier leaned closer as she reached up with her bird-like fingers and stroked his cheek.

'Of course, *mi amor.*' he assured her. 'Anything.'

'I don't have long, but you know that.' she smiled. 'After today, we might not see each other again.'

Javier knew it was true, but hearing her say the words caused a lump to form in his throat. He smiled but didn't contradict her, kissing her frail hand.

'This is going to be so hard on John and Pen. Too many losses in their lives.' She took a sudden intake of breath. 'But life isn't fair. We both know that.'

Tess swallowed hard.

'More water.' she rasped.

Javier held the cup, and she guided his hand, taking small sips before pushing it away and clearing her throat.

'Pen trusts you. She will need you, Mateo, and Ines.'

Javier tried to smile reassuringly. 'Do not worry. Pen and Mateo are constantly texting each other. Sometimes, I hear Ines laugh at the jokes and pictures Pen sends to her while she cooks dinner in the kitchen.'

Pen sent Javier a photo on the anniversary of their arrival in *Obradoiro Square* in Santiago de Compostela at the end of their Camino the previous year. Tess, himself, Pen, and Javier's son, Mateo, smiled up at him from the selfie Pen had taken of them. They were still wearing their backpacks and holding their walking poles in the air. In the photo, Tess's face was tanned and healthy. The disease that would kill her remained hidden beneath the surface. Only a couple of hours after that photo was taken, while sitting in the Cathedral, Tess had told her Pen about her cancer. It was hard to believe it had been just 12 months.

'I know you will wrap your arms around her—all of you. But I'm concerned about John.' Tears fell as she spoke, but she didn't wipe them away. 'John is an orphan. Did you know that? Pen is all he has left. My death will take him down in ways that make me afraid, Javier. So, I need you to promise me you will help him, too.'

Javier held his breath. He didn't want to refuse her, but he had no idea what she might expect of him. He and her husband didn't speak. It's not as if they were best friends sharing confidences while watching her fade away. Even coming to see her before she passed was done in secret. Her doctor had phoned him the previous week to tell him the end was near. He flew from Madrid the following day and came to the hospital at night while John and Pen were at home asleep, doing everything to avoid making things more difficult for them.

'You know how the Camino helped me.' whispered Tess. 'It helped you and Mateo, too. And it saved Pen's life. John will need the same kind of help to process his grief. He doesn't know that yet, but he will in time. And he'll require someone to guide him. I have left John a list, Javier. Of all the places I want my ashes sprinkled. Places whose memories have brought me joy during the darkest times in the past year. There are locations on that list he will need your guidance to find. A couple of them are on the Camino.' Tess coughed, wiping her mouth with the back of her hand. Blood dotted her purple skin a bright red, and she wiped it on her gown. 'I need you to promise me that you will help him find his way so he can heal and move on. So he won't be alone. Promise me you will do this for me.'

Javier took a deep breath, closing his eyes. He had no idea how to fulfill this promise, and he said so. But Tess just smiled.

'You will find a way when the time is right. I know you, and I know him. John will not let me down in fulfilling my wishes. When he comes to ask, I need you both to do this for me. Together.'

Ten years later, the memory of that horrible day so long ago still shook Javier. It felt like a lifetime, and it had taken John ten years to mention Tess's list to him. Longer than he would have thought when she extracted that promise from him all those years ago. Javier assumed John had ignored

Tess's wishes, and she lay buried in Arizona. But no one knew better than him that grief had its own timeline. It refused to be rushed. And now, it seemed John was ready to let go of his wife and begin fulfilling her wishes.

Maybe the spring wedding of their children, Pen and Mateo, pushed John to decide. But, when he mentioned it to Javier before the wedding, Javier did his part to move the idea forward. Yet, now, Javier had second thoughts. Suggesting this trip had been done on the spur of the moment. An unplanned folly Javier hadn't expected John to accept. Perhaps, if he was honest with himself, he hoped John would refuse the offer.

The day after the wedding, Javier confided their agreement to Ines, his housekeeper and confidant of many years. She was making lunch when he sat at the kitchen table and confessed what he had done.

'This is good.' she said, her wise smile confirming her opinion as she stirred the pot on the stove.

'You think so?' he scowled.

'Yes. Tess wanted this. It's healing for the two of you to go and walk a Camino for her. John has some unfinished business. And so do you, I think.'

Javier remained unconvinced.

'It's the last thing I thought I would have to do when she made me promise. Maybe I was a little drunk.' he said, plopping some of Ines's famous bread and olive oil into his mouth.

But Ines was having none of it.

'No. I saw you before the wedding. You were not drunk. I think you sensed that John is still in pain and thought to ease it. You have something in common, the two of you. Grieving the same person. You will help each other.'

Javier nodded. Perhaps Ines was right.

'A lot can happen on the Camino.' she walked behind his chair, patting his shoulder. 'No one should know that better than you.'

# THREE

## THE ENDING IS THE BEGINNING

John boarded the rail car at the massive *Gare Montparnasse* station in Paris. Train travel was welcome after a bumpy flight across the North Atlantic. John hated flying. With a daughter now living in Spain, it was a necessary evil. He didn't know how Tess had done it for work all those years.

The train wound past grey housing blocks and miles of graffiti. This view was not his favorite of the City of Light as the packed TGV high-speed headed south toward the French border with Spain. The rail service assigned him a seat at a table with two other passengers facing him opposite. In the stained grey seats across the table sat a woman a bit older than himself and a thin boy about seven years old, dressed in well-worn beige cotton shorts and a grey t-shirt that likely fit him the year before. It surprised John to see a child on a mid-day train, as the school year had already begun on this sunny September day.

The boy with mud-colored hair fidgeted and bit his dirty fingernails while stealing glances at this curious-looking, tall, grey-haired giant. Caught, the boy's large black eyes quickly looked away. John smiled at him before returning his attention to his phone after connecting to the train's wifi and checking his email and messages. He scrolled through, secretly hoping that Javier would have to cancel and John would be off the hook. He could arrange to visit Madrid to see Pen and avoid this uncomfortable mess. But there were no messages from his daughter's father-in-law.

John looked up when he heard the boy say something to the older woman traveling with him, and she answered him in French, pointing to the front of the car. The boy hopped out of his seat and disappeared. John smiled at the woman, and she shrugged.

'I hope he is not disturbing you.' She said in heavily accented English.

How did she know he wasn't French?

John shook his head. 'Not at all. I remember traveling with my children when they were young. He is handling a long train ride very well.'

The woman nodded, then pointed to the front of the train where the boy had gone. 'Julian has had a great deal of change in the last week. My grandson. I don't think he knows quite what to make of me yet.'

John smiled.

'Is he coming to stay with you for a holiday?' he asked.

Sadness filled the woman's smile.

'Julian is coming to live with me forever.' she said. 'My daughter passed away last week. And there was never a father in the picture. We are all each other has left.'

John's heart fell into his stomach as Julian returned from the lavatory. The boy's sallow face was like peering into an old mirror.

'Does he speak English?' he asked her.

'No,' she said. 'I do not believe Julian has attended proper schooling in Paris. And if he went to school at all, it wasn't on a regular basis.'

John bit his lip and rubbed his chin.

'Does he like to play games?'

The woman offered another Gallic shrug. This grandmother and grandson were still getting to know each other. He reached into his backpack on the seat beside him and pulled out a small wooden box held shut by a thick blue rubber band. John removed the lid and the tiny chess pieces inside, setting them carefully on the table between them. Then, he unfolded the compact chess board and smoothed it flat. John's Grandpa Charlie taught him to play on the Iowa farm where John grew up. As an adult, he carried this small set for as long as he could remember, teaching his son, Charlie, and then his daughter, Pen, to play when they were little. It kept them occupied on family trips. John had no idea if Javier knew how to play chess, but it made him feel better packing the small set for the Camino.

As soon as the board flattened out, John and the woman watched in amazement as the boy reached over and placed each piece correctly.

'I guess he knows how to play chess,' John smiled.

The woman chuckled while questioning her grandson. 'He says the old man across the hall often watched him when his mother went out at night or was away for a few days. He taught Julian to play. Julian says his favorite place to play chess is in the park.'

Paris is well known as a chess mecca throughout the parks of the capital. The boy selected two pieces, one black and one white, and hid them behind his back. Then he held his fists out to John. *Choose*, he said to John in French. Chess is a universal language. John smiled and tapped the boy's right hand. Julian opened his palm to reveal a black pawn.

'*Tu passes en deuxième*.' said the boy, with focus, no longer a fidgeting seven-year-old but a competitor. He spun the board so the black pieces sat before John.

'My name is John Sullivan.' said John, holding out his hand as the boy reached out with his pale, pencil-thin arm and shook it.

'Julian.' he offered—no last name.

Julian got down to business immediately, making his opening move.

'*Bon*.' he said to himself. Satisfied. Then looked up, rewarding John with a gap-toothed smile.

They played their way from the north of France to the southwest coast on the Bay of Biscay. The two barely noticed when the train stopped at towns and cities on their route. Julian rubbed his chin before every move, frowning as he studied the board. When it was John's turn, the boy chewed his worn-down nails, his only tell.

Taught by a chess master, Julian gave John a run for his money. As they approached the station in Bayonne, an announcement encouraged travelers to gather their belongings. John and Julian sighed, disappointed their match was cut short.

As John folded the board and secured the lid of the wooden box with a thick blue rubber band, Julian gazed out the window at his new home. John knew exactly how he felt as the boy's grandmother pointed toward places she thought might interest her grandson. Her enthusiasm didn't appear to register with the lad, who had grown increasingly quiet.

At the station, the three of them disembarked the carriage together. John helped the woman with her grandson's dirty pink canvas suitcase with a missing wheel until they reached the station's interior. He had a tight connection to Saint-Jean-Pied-de-Port, where Javier awaited him.

'Thank you for keeping Julian occupied.' said his grandmother. 'I wasn't sure how the train ride would go, but you made it very pleasant.'

John smiled down at the thin boy holding onto his grandmother's hand. He held out the wooden box and presented the compact chess set to Julian.

'Would you like this?' asked John.

The boy looked up at his grandmother, who nodded. Then, he reached out and took the small box from John, hugging it to himself like a treasure.

'Mercì, John Sulivan.' said the boy.

'Thank you very much,' his grandmother smiled at John.

'Thank you for the game and the conversation.' John waved goodbye, watching them until the crowd swallowed the boy and his old chess set. His eyes filled with tears, but he didn't know why he felt so sad. Turning toward the reader board, John found his train to Saint-Jean and settled into his seat just as the doors closed. Jet lag caught up with him as the train left the station, and John closed his eyes, allowing the train's rocking to lull him to sleep.

# FOUR

## A BIT OF MADNESS

'Why would you do this?' Pen asked when her father phoned her in Madrid after her return from their honeymoon. 'With Javier, of all people?'

'We discussed it on the morning of your wedding and agreed,' he told her. 'Your mother deserves her own pilgrimage. She asked me to sprinkle her ashes at a few different spots, some of which are along the Camino. I've waited a long time but am ready to do it now. Javier is going to help me complete it.'

'Seriously, Dad?' sighed Pen. 'Don't get me wrong. I love Javier. He's always been very good to me. But it feels wrong for the two of you to do this together. Like crossing a line somehow.'

Pen covered the receiver and told her husband, Mateo – Javier's son — what was happening. Mateo's reaction told her Javier had already informed his son of their plans. Pen wasn't pleased she was the last to know.

'Who suggested it?' she asked, returning to their call.

'What do you mean?'

'One of you suggested doing this walk, and the other agreed. Who suggested it first?'

'Javier. I told him about your Mom's wishes. He offered to help me.'

'Ah.'

Her dad took a deep breath.

'Look. I know this is kind of unusual. But there is a lot of unusual stuff in our families. You're married to his son, for god's sake. I love Mateo like a son, but it's already weird. Doing this with Javier is in the same vein and not completely out of the ordinary, considering everything that's happened. Anyway, maybe things won't be so awkward between us by the end of it.'

He was right. Their families did have an unusual relationship. When Tess and Pen got back from their Camino, fighting her cancer was the sole focus. Pen had come to terms with all of it. But this walk with Javier bothered Pen.

'When are you planning on going?'

'September.'

Her mind reeled. That wasn't far away.

'Are you doing the whole thing?'

'Yes. We'll start in Saint-Jean and then sprinkle Mom at certain places on her list.'

Pen would know where they were.

'Can I see the list?'

'Yes. I can forward you a copy.'

'If I decided to come and join you at one or two places when you sprinkle her ashes, would you be okay with that?'

'Of course.' said her dad. 'I want you there if you want to be.'

'Okay.' Pen agreed. 'But promise to keep me posted on where you are. I'll meet you so we can do it together.'

'I will.' Promised her dad.

The line went silent.

'I love you, Dad.'

'I love you too, my Lucky Penny.'

# FIVE

## NO COLLEGE STUDENT

J ohn woke with a start as the car lurched. Not entirely sure where he was, it was a moment before John realized he was on the train from Bayonne to Saint-Jean-Pied-de-Port, nestled at the base of the Pyrenees in southern France. Exhausted from the jet lag, John sighed. Pen was right. What was he doing here?

John rubbed his tired eyes as the September scenery passed them by on the border between Spain and France. The engine was slowing down and gliding into the station. At 63, John was not a young man to be backpacking through Spain like it was a college gap year. He assumed Javier was a bit younger but still not a teenager. The five-hundred-mile walk to Santiago de Compostela was over mountains and across long stretches exposed to the elements. Accounts of the trek said it could be brutal. Pilgrims died attempting it. Every mile would be physically challenging. Let's face it: emotionally tricky. John shook his head. It's true what they said. *There is no fool like an old fool.*

He should have driven to these places. Javier could have helped him find some of those described in the list Tess gave to him in the weeks before she passed away. They could have completed her requests for Spain in under a week, then gone their separate ways. But Javier suggested Tess deserved a pilgrimage, as John allowed his competitive nature to kick in. If Javier could do this, then he could, too.

Standing on the station platform with his backpack, he looked around. Saint-Jean-Pied-de-Port is an ancient village in the Pyrenees mountains of Basque France, filled with timbered stone buildings. He had the information for the hotel where Javier had arrived the day before. In his pack were the pilgrim credentials his daughter, Pen, had sent him a month before. John learned he would need the document to stay in *albergues* or hostels all along the route. His daughter had already walked the Camino with her mother. Their pilgrimage is how all this started in the first place.

But, John didn't care about the Compostela pilgrims received when they reached Santiago de Compostela, 500 miles from where he now stood. He wasn't doing this walk to get a certificate. Sister Bernadette's face from elementary school flashed before him, but John pushed the image away. He wasn't doing this trek for a religion he no longer believed in, nor a God who had abandoned him long ago. John had made a promise a decade before, and he would do this for Tess alone.

He gathered up his pack from the platform and tried to orient himself. Holding up his phone, he waited until he had mobile service before opening the app directing him to his hotel. With a route map guiding his way, John confidently set off through the cobbled streets to meet up with Javier. This Camino had begun.

# SIX

## ANOTHER ROAD

Javier arrived in Saint-Jean the day before John. He stayed in a comfortable hotel in the town and enjoyed dinner with other pilgrims who left that morning. Tonight was the last night of comfort for the next several weeks, as John would arrive soon, and they would have dinner together. Javier's stomach was in knots, and his feet felt heavy as he marched down the hill in his hiking sandals toward the restaurant to make dinner reservations for him and John.

He was unsure how they would cope with the task ahead, not physically but emotionally. If they became sick or injured, they could stop walking. They were older, and this wasn't an impossibility. Javier wasn't wishing them illness, but he wasn't naïve. This Camino could be over before it began.

Returning to the hotel, he entered just as John completed the check-in process at reception. John turned around, clothed in his new hiking clothes and a tattered blue baseball cap. The American seemed surprised to see Javier standing behind him in the lobby. The other man's height always struck Javier. At 6ft 3in, John towered over the Spaniard's 5 feet 11 inch frame.

'Hey.' said John, clearly tired from the long, 24-hour journey from the US. And the time difference.

'Buenos tardes. I see you've checked in. Have you gone to the pilgrim office to get your credentials?'

'I didn't need to.' said John, holding up his pilgrim passport. 'Pen sent it to me. They just stamped it for me here.'

Javier nodded.

'Get settled. Maybe you want to take a shower. We can meet here in a half hour and get some dinner.'

Javier walked to the bar next door, sat at one of the outdoor tables, and ordered a beer while trying and failing to control his rising anxiety. Their complicated relationship made it more than strange to be here with John. While the other man was acclimating to the time zone and the idea of walking the Camino with his wife's lover, Javier needed a few moments to do the same.

Looking around, smiling pilgrims made their way out of their albergues. They looked excited, if a bit disoriented. Eating a good meal in anticipation of the climb over the Pyrenees the following day was essential. Javier had done this trek before and knew what to expect. Most of these people, including John, had no idea what they were in for. Blissfully ignorant, they smiled and ordered another bottle of wine. Javier was sure he and John would see them on the trail in the coming days.

Taking a final pull on his beer, he stood and stretched, then returned to the hotel. Javier found John sitting in the lobby, fumbling through a small day pack. His grey hair was still wet from the shower, and he wore fraying shorts and a faded yellow t-shirt from some long-ago 10k race he had run as a much younger man. The condition of the shirt said it was decades old. John's eyes told the story of his long journey to Saint-Jean.

'If you're hungry, I found a good place to eat. We want to leave before sunrise to avoid the heat, so we can go there now and make it an early night.'

John nodded, barely acknowledging Javier had spoken. He was zipping up his red day pack when Javier spotted the plastic bag. It wasn't large, but it looked heavy and covered in strips of colorful plastic tape. A moment passed before Javier realized what it was—Tess's ashes. John looked up in time to see him watching. Javier swallowed hard. Tess would be at dinner with them.

The two men walked down the cobbled street to a small restaurant by the river and spoke to the French proprietor, who led them to a table on the water. Wine and bread quickly arrived.

'You speak French, as well.' observed John.

Javier nodded. 'Ouì.'

John craned his head at the sun-kissed buildings, delaying conversation between them.

'This is a very old town.' observed John.

'Yes. It was founded nearly a thousand years ago. Some of the buildings appear to be from back then. But most are from the Middle Ages or later.'

'The Middle Ages? You say that like it was last week. We don't have anything in the US from the Middle Ages. It's interesting that this place is still so small, considering it's the starting point for the Camino.'

'It is just one of the starting points.' said Javier. 'There are many Caminos all over Europe – even in other places in the world. This one, the Francés, is the most popular. It's also one of the most challenging in terms of physical difficulty right at the beginning. But tens of thousands of *peregrinos* pass through here every year. The town relies on them to survive. Looking around, you'll see people smiling and happy to have reached the starting point. Most have no idea what is in store for them in the next 48 hours. Let alone the next month. For them, just getting here is part of their Camino.'

Other diners in the restaurant were dressed in hiking clothes, ready to start their journey. And, like John, just getting here had been an adventure unto itself.

'What *is* in store for us in the next 48 hours?' John asked with concern, 'I've read about it, but I don't know what it's really like.'

Javier wanted to prepare John but not scare him.

'It will be difficult at first. We will climb and climb, we will rest, and then climb some more. You will begin to wonder if the mountains ever end.'

Javier had seen Tess's list. He could have suggested they skip it.

'Do not worry.' Javier smiled. 'You will do fine. We can take it slow. It's been more than ten years since I walked the Camino. I don't have anything to prove, and neither do you. We can go as slow as we need to.' he said, drinking his wine. 'I booked us in at Orisson tomorrow night. It's just 8km from here. Many pilgrims injure themselves by walking too fast or trying to put in too many kilometers in the first week. We don't need to do that. It is not a race.'

He watched as the blood returned to John's tired face and smiled. The first day was always the hardest.

# Seven

## Another Bit of Madness

Neither of the men slept well, and it seemed like minutes, not hours, when John's alarm buzzed on his phone. John forgot where he was and nearly fell out of bed. Then it hit him. He would be climbing a mountain today. Rubbing his blue eyes and scratching his rapidly greying head, he padded into the bathroom.

After a long shower, returning to the bedroom to repack his stuff and tie his boots, John donned his heavy pack. Fatigue washed over him, and he sat down hard on the bed. Suddenly, he didn't want to do this. He didn't want to walk with this guy and make small talk. He didn't want to talk to anyone about anything. An introvert, John wanted to find a closet, climb inside, and close the door to be alone with his thoughts, just like he used to do when he was small in his room at the Iowa farmhouse where he grew up. But John wasn't seven years old anymore. He had made a promise to Tess.

Sighing, he stood and stretched. After fastening the multitude of buckles on his pack, John tried to get comfortable with the unnatural weight on his back. It was time to go. Heavy sigh. He grabbed his poles and slowly descended the dark wooden staircase as it groaned in protest under his weight. Javier was already in the lobby waiting for him.

Javier sat thumbing through the guidebook as John emerged into the lobby. He wasn't reading it exactly, just appearing to be. A useful prop he could hide behind during this trek.

The bags under John's eyes and his giant yawn screamed exhaustion. They would go slow today.

'Coffee?' asked Javier.

'Coffee.'

It was a dark, foggy morning, lending an air of mystery to the start of their journey as Javier led them to the cafe next door. He ordered two cafes au lait for them, which they drank in relative silence as John peered through the fog toward the invisible mountains. Other pilgrims walked past them, packs on their backs and poles in their hands, laughing and talking. Neither Javier nor John exuded the joy the others seemed to be experiencing.

John held his phone out to Javier.

'Can you take a picture of me? I need to send it to Pen. Let her know I'm okay and that I'm actually doing this.'

Javier took the phone and snapped a photo of a tired, smiling John giving his daughter the thumbs up. Then he handed it back.

He watched as John sent the photo to his daughter, then reluctantly rose out of his chair, stretched, and yawned again.

'Shall we?' Javier said with a sigh.

'I guess so. No time like the present.'

They slid into their packs and buckled up. Then Javier handed John his poles. They both took a deep breath and started in the direction the others had gone. Their adventure was beginning.

The march out of town seemed easy until they hit the first hill. An hour later, already winded, they arrived at the start of the climb uphill toward Honto.

We're both tired and not used to this much walking so we will take this very slow. One step at a time.' offered Javier as the sunrise peaked through the clouds over Saint-Jean.

Others passed them, but they didn't care. They knew their limits. The speed didn't matter. If they kept going, they would get there eventually.

It took them nearly four hours to get from Saint-Jean to *Refugio Oris-son*—four grueling hours with countless stops to rest. When the albergue came into view, it appeared to be floating above the fog, still blanketing the valley below. They just needed a bed for the night in the stone building they could see around the bend in the road. The two men were like Jack of Beanstalk fame. Hopefully, there wasn't a giant waiting for them.

Favoring breathing over small talk, they spoke very little on the trek to Orrison. After checking into the *refugio* and receiving their bunk assign-ments, they cleaned up and rested, then went for a beer and lunch in the pub on the main floor. The lodge was cozy, with a large stone fireplace. Soon, it would close for the winter snows.

'Did you and Tess stay here?' John asked him.

It was the first time John made reference to Javier and Tess's relationship since he arrived the day before. Javier blew out the breath he had been holding, waiting for this question. In some ways, it was good it came out on the first day. He didn't try to dodge it and pledged to be honest with John.

'No. I believe Tess and Pen stayed here. We hadn't met them yet. Mateo and I started early from Saint-Jean the following day and walked the entire way to Roncesvalles in Spain. It was a long and tiring day, and we met Pen on the trail. She entertained us, and she was walking far ahead of her mother. I didn't meet Tess until the next day on the road to Zubiri. We met by chance at a cafe. Pen was walking ahead with Mateo.'

Jealousy is an ugly thing, thought Javier. It eats at its victims from the side. Tess and Pen had stayed in this place before meeting Javier and Mateo. He watched John do the math. Things were still pure here at the top of the mountain. At this point in her Camino, Tess was thinking only of her husband. John wanted his wife for himself, but he wrote her a letter to live freely on her Camino. He knew what that meant, and so had she. Still, when her affair with Javier began, it shook John to his foundation. Javier suspected he was unprepared for how that would make him feel.

As they drank their beer, pilgrims from around the world joined them at their table. September is later in the walking season, and they would finish in Santiago in the rapidly chilling late October of rainy Galicia. However, the weather in Camino in early fall was less extreme than in other seasons.

'Why are you walking.' A pilgrim from Argentina asked John.

'I am walking for my wife. She died of cancer a decade ago, and I'll be sprinkling her ashes at places all along the way where she asked me to.'

The Argentinian pilgrim nodded, then turned to Javier.

'And you? Why are you walking the Way?'

Javier took a deep breath.

'I am also walking in honor of John's wife, Tess. She was my friend, and she helped me overcome the grief of my wife's death from cancer. My son and I walked in my wife's honor back then, and we completed the Way with Tess and her daughter, Pen. Today, my son is married to Pen. So, the Camino holds great significance for me.'

Javier spoke eloquently and truthfully. He had thought long and hard about why he was doing this. This walk wasn't just about John but also what Tess had meant to him.

John coughed, then excused himself to return to their room. Javier watched him go but didn't offer to join him.

Unlike the rest of Spain, on the Camino, dinner is served like in the US — around 7 pm so that pilgrims can get to bed before sunset. Most *peregrinos* leave their albergues early to avoid walking in the mid-day heat. Although, at this time of year in the Pyrenees, it was less of an issue.

Later, John returned to the bar for the meal, where large trestle tables accommodated everyone staying at the *refugio*. Javier waved to him, having saved a spot directly opposite. John took his seat just as the owner gave them a speech he'd given thousands of times before.

'Everyone. We thank you for staying with us. We are just the first stop on a long journey for all of you. But we are honored you have chosen to spend your first night out of Saint-Jean with us. We hope you like the simple meal enjoyed by many pilgrims over the centuries. First, there is vegetable soup. Then meat and vegetables. And finally, a simple Santiago cake. Please join me in thanking our chef for this fine meal.'

He gestured to the gentleman on his left, and the room erupted in applause. The man acknowledged their thanks with a slight bow.

'Now, there is wine and water. Drink a lot of water, and not too much wine, because tomorrow will be another long day. Enjoy!'

Served family-style, pilgrims at the table began dishing up plates of food. John handed his bowl over as a Belgian pilgrim ladled soup and handed it back. Javier filled his wine glass as he did for the others around them. The woman to his left asked if they had checked the weather.

'There is a big storm coming in tonight. The temperature is going to drop close to freezing. And there might even be a little snow.'

Javier had provided John with a list of must-haves to pack. John hoped The weather would hold until they got down the other side to Roncesvalles in Spain.

The diners dug into the hearty meal. Santiago cake followed. Songs broke out, and pilgrims were encouraged to stand, give their names, and say where they were from.

'This feels like summer camp when I was a kid.' remarked John.

'I have heard that before.' smiled Javier. 'But it is a tradition here. We won't encounter it often further along on the Camino. You will find that we will see the same people again and again. Some people in this room will be in Santiago when we finish, even if we walk slower than most. You will discover those who take rest days or get injured and are forced to stay in one town or another for a few days. Time bends on the Camino. It's just how it goes.'

The meal in the pub was loud, and pilgrims enjoyed the camaraderie as the wine and music flowed.

They each did their turn under the spotlight. John's shyness showed, and he felt uncomfortable as all eyes turned to him. To his right was a Buddhist monk. The man favored the vegetables and avoided the meat while sporting a radiant smile.

'I'm John.' he said, holding out his hand. 'I'm sorry, I didn't get your name when you stood.'

'Hy Yung.' said the monk, adjusting his robes. 'It is nice to meet you.'

'Nice to meet you.' nodded John

'You are probably wondering why a Buddhist from Korea is walking the way of Saint James.' The bald man's eyes twinkled in his scarlet and gold robes.

'I was, yes. Just a little.'

'Are you a religious man, John?'

'No. I was raised Catholic, but I am not religious at all.'

'And yet you are walking the Way of St. James, too.' he observed

'Yes. I am, but not as a religious pilgrimage. I am walking in honor of my wife. She died, and she wanted her ashes placed at certain locations along the Camino.'

'A noble journey.' observed the monk. 'A knight on a quest.'

John pulled a face.

'Oh. I don't know about that. If I am a knight, I am an old and tired one.' he said, changing the subject. 'Why are you walking it? You're not Catholic, and I don't think you are walking it in honor of your wife.'

The monk laughed.

'No. I don't have a wife.'

John smiled.

'You don't have to tell me if you don't want to.' offered John, 'It's none of my business.'

'This is true. It is none of your business.' The monk wasn't smiling anymore. He appeared deadly serious. 'But do you really know why you are walking, John?'

John frowned. The monk had suddenly closed himself off.

'I don't know what you mean.'

The monk chuckled to himself. 'I think you do.'

John's smile faded, as well. He turned away and drank deeply from his wine. He could feel the monk watching him with interest, but he didn't turn back. John closed his eyes and wondered if he would ever find peace on this journey. Or just a moment when he didn't feel uncomfortable. Like the odd man out.

'Are you ready to go up and get ready for bed?' Javier asked from across the table, forcing John out of his funk. 'We will have another early start because we want to be in Roncesvalles tomorrow before it gets dark and the weather turns bad.'

Rising from the communal bench, John winced from sore muscles. He glanced at the monk, who was still watching him. The man's face was an unreadable mask.

The bunks were uncomfortable. But the pilgrims were tired from the climb and did not care if it felt like a cement slab, and the men were asleep in less than five minutes.

In the morning, John felt a hand shaking him awake. Looking up, he saw Javier fully dressed, with his pack at his feet. The rest of the beds in the dorm were empty; their previous inhabitants were in various states of preparing to depart.

'I let you sleep as long as possible. But we need to eat breakfast and get going.'

John sat up and hit his head on the bunk above. He rubbed the bump.

'Why didn't you wake me sooner?' he asked.

'You were in a deep sleep. And the competition for the bathroom was fierce. Now you can go right in. I'll meet you downstairs when you're ready.' Javier picked up his pack and left the room.

John hated lagging behind the others or judged as if he couldn't keep up. But it wasn't Javier's fault. He should have set an alarm on his phone and put it under this pillow. Last night, he was tired and forgot.

Returning to his bunk after his shower, John bent to gather his sleeping bag when he noticed something. A slip of dark green paper lay on his bunk, weighted down by a beaded wooden bracelet with a shiny green stone engraved with gold symbols. John picked up the slip of paper and read the unusual gold script.

*You can not pour from an empty cup. Your quest is noble, and you are worthy. To discover your worthiness, you must embrace the beauty in imperfection. You must feel the pain buried in the truth. May you find compassion for yourself and others on your journey, John. And may you discover peace.*

John examined the bracelet and the single emerald-colored stone bead with the gold writing. The monk from the dinner was wearing one just like it. Why had he given it to John when he became so distant? John slid the jewelry over his left wrist and stuffed the note into his pocket. He reached into his pack, pulled out his dad's faded blue *Cubs* baseball cap and put it on, then went in search of Javier.

The valley was, again, covered in fog. The icy wind hit John in the face, and as he left the warmth of the bunkhouse, the ominous skies threatened. Upon entering the main building, the roaring fire welcomed him as Javier waved him over. Two women John remembered from the night before sat at the table— Americans from Virginia. John put his pack down and gathered breakfast and some coffee.

When he returned to the group, the women's laughter echoed over a story Javier had just told them. John's eyes narrowed as he watched Javier bask in the female adoration. They seemed enamored with his Spanish good looks. He ate his breakfast in silence, then went back for more coffee.

After John finished eating, the group reluctantly rose to leave the warmth of the stone building perched on the mountainside, zipping up their jackets and donning hats and gloves as they walked outside together. Other pilgrims were heading out, and a trail of hikers snaked up the mountainside, winding around the corner up ahead. Javier ran back inside and returned with John's poles. He handed them to John with a smile but didn't receive one in return.

'So, Javier tells us you're an American, too.' the dark-haired woman said to John. 'From Phoenix.'

'Yes, I just decided last week to walk the Camino. And here I am.'

'No, you didn't.' her eyes narrowed. 'You're here working out something. Something big, I think.'

His mood made him uncharitable.

'Well, as a wise monk once told me – it's really none of your business.'

John turned away from the group and set off alone, leaving a surprised Javier to run and catch up.

The men walked in silence for the first hour, climbing higher and higher. John's anger was a slow burn. It didn't seem to worsen, but it didn't subside either. He was rude to that woman in front of the *refugio*, and he was never like this—the guy who cut people down or lashed out at someone trying to be nice to him. John was the guy everyone described as *a nice guy*. The good guy. Steady. Dependable. If he was out of sorts, he went for a run to clear his head. Blaming others wasn't his style.

When his wife was still alive, he was the one who did the school drop-offs and pickups. Ensuring the kids completed their science projects and topped up their lunch accounts at school. *My Steady Eddie*, Tess called him. Though he had a successful career of his own, John kept everything running at home while his wife had her high-flying career. And he never complained, never resented her for it. Well, almost never. She spent half of their life together in another city, another state. Sometimes, another country. But he'd been proud of her and wanted her to succeed. He was a good husband until he wasn't. But he loved her. Truly.

Supporting her decision to walk the Camino with Pen, he'd given his blessing for her to do what she needed to do. But that decision had burned up two months of precious treatment time — time better spent fighting the cancer. A slim window of removing the tumors, ensuring that the cancer didn't return. A very aggressive form of the disease; she had come home and learned it had spread. The doctors told them Tess had missed the critical window.

They tried everything: every known treatment and some experimental ones. Tess flew to clinics throughout the country to join the best cutting-edge studies. But in the end, it was not enough. Her time on the Camino had taken her from him. The precious time she had spent where he was standing now with Javier. Suddenly, John hated this place. And she had the nerve to ask him to spread her ashes along this fucking trail. Why? Why was it so important to her? Was it because of Javier?

With his long stride, John picked up his pace. Javier would just have to keep up.

# EIGHT

## NO PAIN, NO GAIN

In a curious silence, Javier walked beside John over the Pyrenees. He had heard the exchange between John and the American woman. This version was not the man he knew. Or at least the person who had been described to him by Tess and Pen. Something was bothering the American this morning. Perhaps being on the Camino sparked it. Maybe John just needed to get it out.

The two men flew past other pilgrims as John stabbed his poles into the road like he was picking up trash in the park. People stared at them like they were crazy, going at an unsustainable pace. Soon, they arrived at the coffee truck parked at the top of a ridge. Javier suggested they take a break and rest over a coffee. John grunted, perched on a boulder, and turned away from the group of laughing pilgrims gathered there. He didn't remove his pack or get in line for a cafe latte. Javier purchased two of them and brought him one.

'Merci.' Came the terse, sarcastic reply.

The Frenchman operating the food truck made a potent brew. Javier offered sugar, but the other man waved it away. Like the Italians, John grasped the paper cup and threw it back in one gulp. Their pit stop didn't last long, and they were on their way past the last herds of sheep that had yet to be moved to lower pastures as the weather turned cold. The two men blew by a stone Celtic cross and through the gap in the rockface, concealing an ancient shepherd's hut before crossing the border into Spain.

'These stone huts are essential here. Even though the Roncesvaux Pass will close soon for the winter, some pilgrims attempt this crossing all year.

And those who live and work in the mountains are up here year-round and know the weather is unpredictable. Getting caught in the Pyrenees can be deadly. These huts have sheltered pilgrims and shepherds for over a thousand years.'

'Thanks for the history lesson.' Said John sarcastically. 'Anyway, I hope we won't need it. I plan on having a hot shower and a beer at the end of today.'

'That sounds good to me.'

They marched on. Some of the earlier tension had dissipated. Ignoring John's mood, Javier continued filling him in on the history of this part of the Camino—the Moors and Charlemagne's legendary exploits—whether he was interested or not. Soon, the two men were ready to make their final descent to Roncesvalles. The weather had turned ugly, with sleet raining down on the already treacherous path. The wind had picked up, and ice and heavy snow fell as they slowly descended toward the valley below.

At a certain point, they held onto each other to stay upright. Then, as they reached the copse of trees, John suddenly slipped on the slick mud and fell backward. His pack broke his fall, but pain twisted his features as he let out a wail.

Javier bent down immediately and attempted to help his friend to his feet, but John cried out, begging him to stop. Standing back and assessing the situation, Javier's mind raced. He needed a plan to get John out of this weather.

'What are we going do?' asked John, wincing from pain. 'We can't stay out here.' as hail pummeled them both. 'And I can't get up with this much pain.'

'I know.' agreed Javier. 'Let me extract your rain poncho from your pack, and I'll cover you with it. I'll put mine on, too, to keep the heat in. Then we'll see how you feel after a bit.'

The wind swirled around them, making it more difficult for Javier to pull the rain gear from John's pack while he lay on top of it. With great effort and more wincing from John, Javier freed the red plastic and draped it over John's prone body, then got into his own pack and put it on. By that time, they were already wet and cold. It was not a circumstance in which either could survive for long. They needed help as John was quickly losing body heat. A condition that could prove fatal if allowed to progress.

The doctor held up his mobile phone and waited for even one bar to appear, but the screen continued to clock, searching for a signal. Luckily, they were close enough to Roncesvalles. A bit more than a kilometer as the crow flies—more than two kilometers on the trail that zig-zagged down the mountainside. Javier was deciding whether to leave John and go alone to get help in the village when he heard an American female voice.

'Are you okay?'

Javier looked up, and there were the two American pilgrims from breakfast. After a day of practically running over the Pyrenees, the two women weren't that far behind them. Relief washed over him.

'John fell. He's in a lot of pain. I was trying to decide what we should do.'

'Do you want us to go to the village and send help?' asked Polly

John spoke up for the first time. 'No. Please,' he grimaced. 'Just help me up. I think I can make it. My back isn't spasming quite as bad right now.'

Javier was afraid to move him and said so, but John was insistent. First, they rolled him on his side and took off his pack as he moaned. Javier knew pain on a patient's face when he saw it. When they got John to a sitting position, Polly and Lucy put John's arms over their shoulders, supporting him as he slowly stood upright.

'I think if we stay with him like this on the way down and go slowly, we can all make it.' offered Polly, the pilgrim with the dark ponytail. 'Javier, can you take his pack?'

'Yes, of course.' he said, concerned about his friend.

Because of the weather, they took their time. It was slick, but after walking more than an hour, for what should have taken them twenty minutes, they made it to the monastery. Easing a shivering John down on a bench in the hall, Javier left to secure beds for all four of them. The American woman John insulted earlier in the day stayed with him.

'Look.' said John. 'I'm sorry about this morning. I don't know why I was so rude. I'm not usually like that. I was having a bad day and took it out on you. And then, it got worse. I can't thank you enough for helping me get down here. I wouldn't have made it if you and your friend hadn't come along.'

She smiled.

'We have names, you know.'

'I'm sorry. I'm being rude again. John.' he said, holding out his hand.

'Yes, I know. I heard you introduce yourself last night at dinner.' she took the hand he offered. 'I'm Polly. Lucy is the blond one getting us beds with Javier.'

'Nice to meet you. Again.'

Polly nodded.

'You wanted to know why I'm walking the Camino. If you had asked me last night, I would have told you it was for my wife. She died of cancer, and I started this in her honor. Spreading her ashes at all the spots she asked me to. But I think you're right. I have some big things of my own to work out.' The monk's bracelet was still on his wrist. 'I didn't understand that until today.'

'Okay, John from Phoenix.' smiled Polly. 'I get it. It seems you're on your way.'

After receiving bed assignments for the group, Javier and Lucy returned. Javier bent down and removed John's boots. Then he left them in the boot room with his poles. He gathered up John's pack while the ladies helped John to his feet and up the stairs to their bunks. They set John down on the lower bunk, and Javier helped to strip off his clothes until he was left in his underwear and began to shiver violently.

'I need to get you into a warm shower to get your body temperature up and keep you from going into shock. The pain is making it worse. That means I'm going to have to shower with you. If we didn't know each other before, we will in about 10 minutes.' Javier laughed uncomfortably, holding up his hands in surrender.

Polly and Lucy helped get John to the door of the men's shower. Other male pilgrims saw their dilemma and took over, doing their part to position John into the shower stall. Javier hung their towels up, then got into the cubicle with John, naked, keeping him upright under the steaming hot water.

'This is just what I needed.' said John gratefully as he began to warm up.

'Somehow, I don't think you mean what you just said.' laughed Javier.

John smiled, then grimaced as pain shot through him.

'The hot water will help your body recover and loosen the muscles. I want to examine you when we get you back to the bunk to make sure you don't have any other more serious injuries. If not, I have some meds to relax the muscles and help you sleep.'

John laughed again at their ridiculous situation, wincing in pain again from the effort.

'What's so funny?' asked Javier.

'Seriously? We are standing together naked in a shower. In your wildest dreams, did you ever think *you and I* would shower with each other? After everything we've been through?'

Javier smiled. 'Well. No. I did not have had this high on my list of life goals.'

John chuckled. 'I have a feeling my Bingo card will need to be completely rewritten by the end of this trip.'

'Bingo card?' asked Javier

John laughed. 'I'll explain it later.'

The shower timer turned off the water, and after uncomfortably drying John's entire body, Javier dressed him and then solicited the assistance of others to help them return to the bunks. He laid John down and determined he had likely pulled some muscles in his back during the fall but didn't believe he had fractured or broken anything.

'I think you should rest. I'll go see if I can get you some food. With the meds, I hope you'll be asleep long before the pilgrim meal.'

'Sure.' teased John. 'You just want the ladies all to yourself.'

Javier pulled a face.

'Seriously, though.' said John. 'Thank you for helping me. I'd still be laying out there if it weren't for you, Polly, and Lucy.'

'You're welcome.' said Javier. 'But I hope that is the last shower you and I ever take together.'

'I'd already forgotten that part. Thanks for the reminder.'

Javier chuckled.

'I'll be right back.

Javier found an open bar and purchased a *bocadillo*, a salami sandwich on hard, tooth-splitting bread. And a bag of potato chips and a coke. Then he came back and waited while John ate all of it.

'Your blood sugar is low, and you're stressed.' handing John the food he'd gathered. 'This is a good way to get the level up.,' setting the Coca-Cola beside his bed. 'The salt in the potato chips will help keep you from dehydrating, and the protein in the *bocadillo* will balance the carbs from the bread. You will take the meds and be asleep in half an hour. Your body wants to recover. We need to give it the right tools to do so.'

'Thank you for dinner.' John smiled gratefully, taking the food. 'What happened to my wet clothes?'

'Polly and Lucy took them down to have them laundered. I'll check on them before I go to bed.'

Everyone had pitched in, unbidden, to help the grumpy American, even after John's earlier rudeness. John swallowed the meds Javier gave him and ate his makeshift meal. He was asleep shortly afterward.

Javier walked alone to the pilgrim's mass in the ancient church beside the monastery. He received the blessing on behalf of both he and John. The Spaniard wasn't sure if any of it would make a difference, but he lit a candle for John and said a small prayer. While on his knees in the church, he spoke to Tess.

'Hello, my love. We're here. Just like you and I talked about at the hospital. I didn't think he would agree, but you were right. John isn't like other men. But he's struggling, Tess. We're going to need a bit of your magic on this trip, I'm afraid.'

Something was brewing with Tess's husband. Javier wasn't sure what it was or how it would work itself out, but he hoped John would find what he was looking for as the weeks progressed. Javier rose and lit a candle for Tess. In the past ten years, it had become a habit he hadn't bothered to break.

When he returned to the bunks, John was asleep. As he climbed up onto his bunk, he heard John mumbling and moaning in his sleep, wrestling with demons Javier couldn't yet imagine.

# NINE

## STORY OF THE KNIGHT

The scuffed toes of the small black shoes teetered on the grave's edge. The boy's toes pressed against the end of the thin, protesting leather. His dark suit hadn't fit him properly for more than a year as the wind licked at his bare ankles. At seven years old, he didn't have many occasions to dress up.

Johnny Sullivan felt faint as the priest droned on about life, death, and the kingdom of heaven while clasping the unfamiliar, calloused hand that held him to the spot. It was the only thing keeping him from falling into the deep hole that encased his parents in the polished rectangular oak boxes far below. Suddenly, the coffins were sucked into the earth, so he could no longer see them. Crying out, he had to refuse the urge to jump in after them.

*Ashes to Ashes,* the voice droned on.

One by one, people he didn't know took up small handfuls of dirt and threw them into the hole where Johnny's mom and dad had gone. After which, they patted him on the shoulder or ruffled his white-blond hair while uttering words he would never remember. His parents were dead. They were not coming back, no matter what anyone said.

*Dust to Dust,* said the voice.

The sky was like the slate-colored screen on his red *Etch-a-Sketch*, now packed into a box in the back of the old rusty truck with the peeling blue paint parked nearby. He stared upward as if someone in heaven might write something any moment explaining all this. But no message appeared, no matter how long he stared at the looming rain clouds. Some things have no explanation.

Johnny felt the big, calloused hand tighten around his yet again. He looked up into the weathered face of the old man.

'You can call me Grandpa Charlie.' The man told him in his thick Irish brogue when he'd arrived at the neighbor's apartment just a few days before. The day after the policeman appeared without warning in the principal's office, where Sister Bernadette escorted him from his first-grade class. The policeman told him his parents were dead.

The policeman said his grandpa was coming, but it was the first he'd heard of this man who had been father to his dad. Grandpa?

'I don't have a grandpa.' said Johnny.

Suddenly, the dream changed, and Johnny was backstage, peaking out behind heavy curtains, watching his parents on the stage. Then, his mother woke him up after falling asleep on a stained, smelly sofa in her dressing room. His mom always said they were circus folk. When one show ended, they moved on to the next.

'It's just us three.' his dad whispered as they ran out of the theater towards home. The sky turned black, and Johnny stood alone on the sidewalk outside their red-brick apartment building. Suddenly, Grandpa Charlie stood next to him. They packed his clothes in a suitcase, some mementos, and his favorite books in boxes. Johnny took his mother's pink chenille bathrobe off the back of the bathroom door, burying his face in the fabric to memorize her smell, then hiding it in the bottom of a box. He wrapped his dad's copy of *O Henry's* short stories in his father's *Chicago Cubs* jersey and folded it in his suitcase. Johnny and his dad were baseball fans, and *The Cubs* were their favorite team. He rolled the baseball cap his dad always wore and stuffed it in his coat pocket, wrapping his hand around it at the graveside.

He could hear the crack of a baseball bat and the crowd cheering at Wrigley Field. They snuck away to an afternoon game—just the two of them. Then, his dad's voice read him *The Ransom of Red Chief*. Johnny loved listening to stories his dad made up. But *O Henry's* stories were his favorites.

As the sky grew darker and the priest departed, Grandpa Charlie and Johnny stood alone as the gravediggers did their work.

'I think it's time for us to say goodbye to them. We need to head for home.'

*Home,* thought Johnny. All he had left in the world was under a stained canvas tarp, crisscrossed with old rope, in the bed of the battered blue truck Grandpa Charlie drove from his Iowa farm. *Home* was a place he had never been andcouldn't yet imagine. Would it feel safe, or would monsters be waiting for him there?

Like an endless grey ribbon, the roads pointing west went on forever as they drove away, and the skyscrapers of Chicago receded in the distance. The sky grew darker as the rain made it difficult for the wipers to keep up. He and his grandfather could barely see out the window. An increasing wind buffeted them, and Johnny wondered if it was the ghost of his parents, angry with him for leaving them in Chicago. Mad at Grandpa Charlie for taking him away.

As they approached the town near where the farm stood, the boiling dark clouds split and turned a shade of green. To outrun the gathering storm, Johnny felt the truck lurch as his grandfather shifted gears and stepped on the gas. This moment was the place in the dream where he always began to sweat.

'Tornado weather.' said Grandpa Charlie, without elaborating, steering the rusty truck off the highway and down a dirt road lined by grey wooden fence posts and rusty barbed wire. The tall corn stalks blocked Johnny's view of the horizon as they skidded to a stop in front of a large white clapboard house with neatly painted green shutters and a wrap-around porch. Still, the storm rocked the truck.

'Now, you do what I say.' shouted Grandpa Charlie over the wind. 'And we'll be alright.' His Irish brogue became thicker in times of trouble.

The older man opened the driver's side door as the wind roared. Hopping out, he beckoned Johnny to follow him, then grabbed hold of him so he wouldn't blow away. Wind and flying debris beat down on them, and dust blew into Johnny's eyes so he could barely see. Grandpa Charlie carried him to a slanted pair of old wooden doors set into the house's foundation. It took all his grandfather's strength to hold onto him to open the door to the stairs of the root cellar hidden below. He deposited Johnny on the top step and told him to go down inside, as a cat came out of nowhere and ran past him down the stairs into the darkness. Johnny heard a great *crack!* as the oak tree in the front yard split. Half of it fell on the truck they had just exited. He needed no more encouragement to run into the darkness, tripping on the bottom step and falling face-first on the dirt floor. Grandpa Charlie squeezed inside, closing out the light while fitting a bar through the worn leather loops attached to the inside of the cellar doors.

The smell of earth and something chemical overwhelmed Johnny in the pitch-black room as the cat meowed her displeasure before the hiss of a match and a kerosene lamp lit the space. Grandpa Charlie held up the lamp in front of his face. The light and shadows made him appear like the monster Johnny feared at the cemetery. Johnny got his first glimpse of the root cellar. Wooden shelves lined the brick walls with glass jars of fruit and vegetables suspended in clear liquid. A bin of potatoes sat on the floor next to a dirty burlap sack of onions. An ancient wooden rocking chair with peeling yellow paint was barely visible behind a brick pillar holding up the floor of the house shaking above them. A chess set sat ready on a crate as if Grandpa Charlie knew the tornado was coming. In the corner, covered in a green moth-eaten army blanket with a yellowing-stained pillow, sat an army cot. The blanket looked scratchy, but the cat didn't seem to mind and was already sitting on it, staring at him with interest.

'It's okay, kid. We have to wait down here until the storm passes. It shouldn't betoo long.,' the cat assured him.

Johnny gulped. Did she really talk to *him*?

'Nothing to worry about.' said Grandpa Charlie. 'A few hours, maybe. In the meantime, we have water, and there is the cot you can share with Rags.'

Johnny examined the cat's long fur in black, orange, and white patches. It did look a little like rags. He sat down next to the cat, who began to purr but said nothing more when it hit Johnny all at once. Burying his parents that morning and leaving everything and everyone he knew behind. Thinking of their home in Chicago and about moving to this strange place with storms that kill people. With someone he didn't know about even the week before. And now, he was sitting in a hole under a house, petting a talking cat in the dark, hoping a tornado didn't come for him. The tears poured down his cheeks as he looked down at his scuffed shoes for the hundredth time that day, trying to stem the tears. It was a moment before his grandfather noticed.

'Hey now.' said Grandpa Charlie, in his sing-songy voice, bending down and ruffling his blond hair. 'I know it's been a bad day for both of us. And there is nothing we can do about it. Not a single thing. So, I think you should rest.' he grasped Johnny's heels. 'Off with these shoes that don't fit. We'll head into town tomorrow and get you some that do. But, for now, you need to stay warm. Rags can help. And I can tell you one of my stories. One that I used to tell your Da when he was a wee one.'

Johnny wiggled his toes to restore the feeling. His big toe peeked through a hole in his black sock as Johnny burrowed beneath the scratchy army blanket and curled into a ball. Rags settled on the musty old pillow above his head, purring.

'There now. Okay. Let me think.' Grandpa pulled the rocking their over to the cot and took a deep breath, tucking in the blanket around Johnny.

'Now, once there was a young boy who lived in a castle, the youngest of five strong boys in his family.' Grandpa Charlie told him. 'By some coincidence, Johnny, he looked much like yourself.'

'His wealthy father had recently passed, and the fighting amongst his cruel brothers had begun almost immediately. The boy knew it would not go well for him in the end. Nothing was set aside for the youngest son, whose eldest and meanest brother was now in charge of the family and the castle where they lived. In a rush to find his own glory, and before his father's belongings were distributed amongst the elder brothers, he stole his father's armor in the wee hours of a foggy morning. Then, he set out to do battle with his father's enemies—to fight the good fight.

'In the castle stable, the boy required the groom's help as he lifted the sword into the sheath and mounted the large steed.'

'Riding down a muddy lane through the nearby village, he left the castle and everyone he knew behind. Upon hearing the horse's hooves, the villagers emerged from their doorways, shouting and laughing at him. His father's armor was three sizes too big, and the helmet slipped down over his eyes. The boy could barely see. The chainmail hung below his fingertips, and the breastplate cut into histhighs as he rode his father's horse out of town.'

"You'll never make it.' they jeered. 'They'll kill ye before ye swing the first blow."

'But the boy was undeterred, setting off on his own to find glory. It was many years before he returned to that part of the country. So many that the villagers had forgotten all about him. They had troubles of their own.'

'One day, he rode into the village square on his father's horse. Back to the place where he was born. By this time, the boy had grown into a man. The armor fit him as if it were made for him, and he could wield the sword with the force and precision of the knight that he was.'

'The villagers poured out of their homes to see the warrior riding into their town. When they realized who it was, the news spread quickly.'

"When you left here all those years ago, we thought, surely ye would be dead in days. But ye look strong and healthy," they told the knight.'

'The boy, now a man, bowed his head in deference to their remarks.' Grandpa bowed his own.

"Tellus the stories of your many battles and how ye slew your enemies." begged the butcher in bloody breeches.'

'The knight smiled down from his trusty steed.'

"I fought in one war after another. Demons and liars, you can only imagine in your worst nightmares. All wielding swords and weapons from which I could not escape. And sorcery that nearly did me in. But I never gave up, and because of it, I am the man before you today."

Johnny's eyes widened. His earlier tears had dried as his grandpa continued his tale.

'The villagers gaped in awe.'

"Name the battles and on whose fields ye fought. For which great kings did ye draw your sword, and what riches have ye brought back from these victories." shouted the baker covered in flour.'

'The knight smiled. "I never drew my father's sword.' he replied. 'Against any man.'

'The villagers seemed surprised by this.' said Grandpa Charlie. 'The man they saw before them was big and strong. The epitome of a knight in every story they had ever been told as children.'

"If ye never fought in great battles or collected riches from your enemies, where have ye been all these years?" insisted the fishwife in the dirty apron.'

'The knight shook his head.'

"I have fought great battles and collected many riches along my journey." he said.'

'The eyes of those gathered narrowed skeptically.' said Grandpa, squinting.

"Where are these riches?" they asked, looking towards the humble bags that hung from the war horse's saddle.'

'The knight just smiled. "I battled the demons of my own creation. For every man, these are the hardest to conquer. There were days I thought they would take me, but I was stronger than they were. A man who can fight and defeat his own demons will never be fooled into fighting another's."

'A hush descended upon those assembled.' whispered Grandpa

"But ye spoke of riches." the poor villagers observed with disappointment.'

"Aman who truly knows himself is rich beyond understanding." said the knight. "For he can never be led astray by another."

'Murmurs rippled throughout the crowd.'

"But why did ye come back here with nothing?" asked the village cobbler wheedling a hammer. "Ye could have gone anywhere."

'The knight stopped and considered the question. "Because I needed to see just how far I had come. Thank you for reminding me."

'Then he turned and rode back out of town.' smiled Grandpa down at Johnny.

# TEN

## LEARNING TO WALK

John thrashed in his sleep before rolling over and opening his eyes. Julian, the boy on the train, flashed into his mind. Perhaps he had delivered the familiar dream this time—a child so much like himself. On the bunk opposite, Javier sat dressed, ready to head out.

'How are you feeling?' asked a concerned Javier.

John moved a bit but didn't feel the pain he had the previous evening.

'I've been riding a horse in my sleep and outrunning a tornado all night. So, you'd think I'd be sore, but I feel okay.' Rubbing his eyes and smiling at Javier's surprised reaction. A psychologist would have a field day with his recurring dreams. 'No back spasms when I move. That's a good sign, right?'

'Yes.' agreed Javier, 'But let me examine you.'

The doctor lifted John's t-shirt and ran his hands along his spine—poking in critical places, waiting for John to cry out. When he didn't, Javier nodded and pulled the shirt down.

'No visible damage from last night. No bruising is good. But I would say that if you want to walk today, we must take it very easy, and you should ship your pack.'

'Ship my pack?' asked John.

'Yes. There are shipping services on the Camino for pilgrims and their packs. You can ship your pack for a day or every day for the entire way to Santiago. Today, we will take advantage of that service. I will ship mine as well because if you have a problem, I want to make sure I am not carrying anything but you.'

'How do we do that?' asked John.

Javier held up a couple of envelopes.

'Like everything else in Spain, by filling out forms and spending a few euros.'

They gathered their gear together and left their packs in the lobby office. Afterward, they went in search of breakfast at a local bar, ordering coffee and *tortillas*—egg and potato omelets. Walking without his heavy pack felt strange to John; like he was missing something, but John had brought his day pack with Tess's ashes. He wasn't going to chance her getting lost with the bag service.

'Did you bring,' Javier swallowed, 'all of her on this trip?'

John coughed and took a sip of his coffee before responding.

'Yes. I couldn't bring myself to separate any part of Tess. Besides, which part would I bring with me to Spain? Her heart? Her blue eyes? No.' he said, patting his red day pack. 'She's here with me. All of her.'

Javier nodded.

'I imagine the sack is heavy.' he said, pointing to John's red daypack. 'You don't have to carry her all by yourself, you know. I can share the weight along the way.'

John tightened his grip on the pack.

'She's not a burden.' said John, quietly. 'And besides, she is mine to carry.' He wiped his mouth. 'I made a commitment to Tess. I might be late in carrying it out, but I'll see it through.'

John watched Javier fumble uncomfortably with his guidebook, redirecting the conversation toward the route for the day. They would walk to Zubiri. The path down the mountain was treacherous, and Javier would assess whether John could make it the entire distance when they arrived at the village of Espiñal. He could call a taxi if he needed to.

The two men finished their breakfast, and John donned his father's old *Cubs* cap and carefully shrugged into the daypack. They walked past the famous road sign telling them they had only 790 kilometers left before reaching Santiago. After the events of the previous two days, John couldn't imagine how they would ever get that far.

The start of the trail was flat, but it became increasingly hilly as the morning progressed. Javier and John crossed streams and pastures filled with cows and horses. The conversation between them felt forced and stilted. Maybe it was showering naked together the day before. Or perhaps they were still adjusting to spending so much time in each other's presence. Stopping for a mid-morning coffee in Viscaret-Guerendiain allowed Javier to assess yet again how well John might fare on the rocky Roman road, pitting the steep downhill into Zubiri.

'The next part will be much more difficult. We will be subjected to several kilometers downhill on treacherous paths in mid-summer.' Looking at the sky. 'Let alone if it starts to rain. I am warning you because if you fall again, you could seriously injure yourself.'

'What's my alternative?' asked John.

'We could take a taxi from here. Pilgrims do it all the time when they are injured from crossing the Pyrenees. You have nothing to prove to anyone. Everyone walks their own Camino. If we hadn't shipped our packs, I would suggest we stay here and rest for another day, but we must get to Zubiri one way or the other to meet up with our things.'

Only days before, John had considered driving to all the places on his wife's list, but now, it seemed like cheating to take a taxi. Then again, he could be laid up for a week or more if he fell again.

'Alright. Let's take a taxi for the last few kilometers. According to Tess's instructions, I don't need to deposit any of her ashes in this stretch. No reason to risk getting injured.'

Javier made a call. The taxi was there in a half hour, and they were in Zubiri 20 minutes later. It was still early, and the albergue where they shipped their packs wasn't open until one o'clock. They sat at a corner bar and ordered a beer and chorizo.

'I feel a little strange drinking beer before noon. Not something we typically do in the US unless you have a problem with alcohol.' observed John.

'Well, you're in Spain now. You can drink whenever you like without your neighbors judging you.' he smiled.

John raised his glass. Javier's tablets had done their job the night before, and John had slept well for the first time since he left the US. Only soreness remained from a couple of hours of walking.

They checked into their albergue and went through the new routine, sleeping early and rising at sunrise.

'Do you think you can carry your pack today?' asked Javier. 'It will be a long walk to Pamplona. It's relatively flat along the river, but we won't arrive until the afternoon.'

'I think I can do it.' offered John. 'My back is feeling much better. I got lucky the back injury wasn't more serious.'

Javier agreed. It could have been much worse.

They set out along the river, through the canopy of leafy trees, walking through old stone villages where the gravel path snaked up the hilly bank.

'Did you walk with Tess here?' asked John.

Javier held his breath. Gauging John's mood was becoming a habit.

'Yes. I met Tess the day before at a cafe. The same one where you and I stopped yesterday. If I remember correctly, she asked if she could share my table. It was then we discovered that our children were walking together. We both needed to get to Zubiri, so I suggested we walk together.' Javier remembered. 'She seemed lonely. Pen had chosen not to walk with her.'

'I know she was.' agreed John, 'She wanted to get closer to Pen on the trip, but Pen wasn't cooperating at that stage.'

'No, she wasn't. In the albergue in Zubiri, I found a bottle of Tess's cancer medication on the bathroom floor. She dropped it. I knew what it was for and put it back in her pack, but I didn't confront her. It wasn't my business, and I just met her. But I knew she was ill at this stage on the Camino.'

John remained silent as they walked for the next kilometer.

'As a doctor, did you ever try to talk her into quitting? To go home and to start treatment sooner?'

Javier took a deep breath.

'I was not her doctor. She said she didn't need me to be. Something was driving her to walk the Camino. After thinking about it for over a decade, I'm unsure I ever really understood what that was, except perhaps Pen's issues. But there was something more. I could feel it. It was a few days further from this point when she told me about her cancer. When she showed me the letter you had written to her. It was at that point I told her if she were my wife, I would insist she stay home and start treatment. That I couldn't have let her come on this trek.'

John stopped in his tracks, squaring off with Javier. His words cut.

'So, you think I should have forbidden this trip before she left? Did you know Tess at all? No one had that power over her. From the moment she mentioned it, she would do this thing come hell or high water. I wrote her that letter to give her my blessing. To ease her burdens somehow, I wanted her to know I was in her corner, no matter what.'

Javier blanched.

'So, you couldn't stop her, but you are telling me I should have, as a doctor, a relative stranger. I barely knew her back then, as you point out. I saw how much this meant to her, and I tried my best to help her accomplish her goal and be as healthy as possible while she was in Spain – to be her friend. When she became ill, I helped her. You know this. I would never have hurt her or encouraged Tess to do anything she didn't want to do.'

Javier closed his eyes, struggling with the memory.

'Anyway,' Javier grumbled. 'I had a different perspective then. Different than either of you. At that time, I had already lost my wife to cancer. I knew what that felt like. You didn't. Not yet.'

The river ran past them as the sun peaked from behind the clouds. The two men stood in silence, almost daring each other to do or say something more. Each was looking for answers that would never come—the prison of, *if only* is a lonely, solitary place was filled with regrets and recriminations. Neither man wanted to stay there.

'We should get going.' suggested John. The tense moment had passed.

'Yes. We can change nothing by rehashing what we might have done. It is easier to see clearly with the benefit of hindsight. I wish Tess were here as much as you do.,' said Javier.

John snorted.

'I don't think you have a clue how much I wish she were here.' he said, his lips quivering, his cheeks red with anger. He marched ahead of Javier with no idea what lay ahead.

# Eleven

## One Last Shot

The trek into Pamplona took hours. The heat climbed as they walked from the city's edge to the old town. John's back told him it was a good thing they stopped when they did. He was sore as they cleaned up, then left to look for food.

The restaurants in the old town of Pamplona still accommodated outside seating as they neared the end of their summer tourist season. Javier chose a place to enjoy a drink and decide where they might like to eat dinner. The men were finishing a bottle of wine when Polly and Lucy, the two Americans who helped John in Roncesvalles, walked past. John had drunk most of the bottle of wine while Javier watched silently.

'¡Hola Pilgrims!' shouted John, waving.

Polly and Lucy turned when they heard John's voice.

'¡Hola, señor! What are you two doing here? Did you take a bus?'

'Nope, we walked. My back is much better, thanks to you two.' Intentionally ignoring the part Javier's expertise had played in his recovery.

'When we left Roncesvalles, you were asleep. I didn't think you'd be walking yesterday.' said Lucy.

'We shipped our packs, and the good doctor's muscle relaxers fixed me right up.'

'I hope you're not taking them and drinking wine.' cautioned Polly.

'Nope. I'm off the meds, and now I'm off the chain. I can have as much wine as I like tonight.'

Polly smiled. It was clear to everyone in the restaurant John had already consumed more than enough. 'Well, after your fall, I guess you deserve it.'

Javier pulled out a chair.

'Join us, please.'

The women sat down, and the waiter came over. Two more glasses arrived, and another bottle of wine appeared with them. Javier spoke to the waiter, and pinchos began to blanket the table. As each one came out, Javier encouraged the others to try them. John waved the food away and poured himself more wine. Then, he ordered another bottle before turning back to the group.

'So. Tell me, Polly. What do you do back in the US?' asked John.

'I'm an FBI agent.' said the American with the dark-haired ponytail.

'Really? I bet you have some interesting stories.'

'I do, but if I told you, I'd have to kill you.' she smirked.

They all laughed.

'What do you do when you're not walking the Camino, Lucy?' asked Javier.

A smile spread across Lucy's rosy cheeks. 'I'm a painter.'

'Wow.' Javier's eyes widened. 'What do you paint?'

'Abstracts. People mostly.' said the blond, pixie-haired pilgrim.

'Do you have photos of your work?'

Lucy pulled out her phone and passed photos around for John and Javier to see.

'I'm not a qualified art critic, but your paintings are beautiful.' offered Javier.

'So, you like art?' she asked Javier.

'Oh yes. My wife was an artist. She painted every day. Her hands always smelled like a solvent, and paint was forever under her fingernails at bedtime.'

Lucy smiled across the table at her FBI agent partner, who chuckled.

'Oh yes. You haven't heard about Javier's love of art and wives.' declared John loudly.

The women tensed as Javier blanched.

'You see, Javier loves everything about women. It's probably because he's Spanish. And we all know women can't resist a suave Spanish doctor. Especially my wife.'

The others looked pensive and held their collective breath.

'I think you've had quite enough to drink.' Javier stood, reaching across the table to grasp the nearly empty third bottle. At that moment, John's clenched fist connected with his right eye. Javier fell back, and the chairs around the table scattered as he went down. The waiter came out to see what was happening, but Javier waved him away, telling him he had fallen.

Lucy helped Javier off the ground as Polly approached John.

'Let's get you back to the albergue.' she offered quietly, in a voice trained to defuse violent situations.

Hitting Javier had sobered John instantly. How could he have just done that? John struggled to find words to explain. Like a naughty child, he let Polly lead him down the warren of streets in the old town, and they sat on the bench in front of where he and Javier were staying.

'So. You and the good doctor have a bit of a history, huh?' asked the tall, athletic FBI agent.

John closed his eyes. 'Yes.' he whispered.

'If that's the case, why are you walking this with him?' she asked, confused.

John struggled to collect his thoughts.

'I need to locate the places my wife wants her ashes to be scattered. Javier knows where those places are.' He sounded like a lost little boy, even to himself.

She shook her head, clicking her tongue.

'Dude, I'm not sure this is so healthy for you. Since Saint-Jean, bad things have happened to you. Maybe you're meant to listen to what the universe is trying to tell you and leave it until another time.'

John choked up, burying his face in his hands. Polly put her arm around his shoulders.

'Tess wanted me to walk it.' he cried. 'I promised her ten years ago on her deathbed.'

Polly sighed.

'Yeah, well, I don't think Tess would have wanted you guys to kill each other.'

John hung his head in shame. 'What the fuck am I doing here?' he asked no one in particular. 'I'm a 63-year-old retired engineer. I just hit my wife's lover, my daughter's father-in-law, in the face on a street in Spain. Like I'm some drunken teenage backpacker. I've officially lost it.'

Polly smiled sympathetically.

'Maybe you're becoming yourself again. Rebirth is a painful process. Believe me when I say if you're going to walk this whole thing, it will get harder before it gets easier. It will help if you prepare for that, or you should do it another time. The Camino does weird things to those who walk it. Your entire life before the Camino is probably filled with people who have written your story from *their* perspective. But, on the Camino, you get to write that story for yourself without all the expectations of your family, friends, or boss. It's just you. I think that's why people come here — to write their own stories for the first time in their lives. The truth of who they truly are. A process that can only happen with strangers who expect nothing from them.'

'How do you know?' asked John, wiping his cheeks.

'I've walked this before. It's when I finally got real with myself about being a lesbian and living life on my terms.'

'You're a lesbian?' asked John, surprised.

Polly sighed and rolled her eyes.

'Yes. Jesus, you *are* a 63-year-old retiree.'

'No.' said John, 'I don't care if you're gay. When I walked into the bar in Orrison that morning, I heard you and Lucy laughing with Javier. It seemed like you were flirting with him. I don't know why, but it pissed me off. I wondered, was every woman on the planet attracted to this man?'

Polly laughed.

'Well, if I wasn't gay, and I wasn't with Lucy, I might be attracted to him. He is charming, and he has a certain appeal. But no, neither of us has the hots for Dr Javier.'

'Lucy is your partner?'

'Yup.' smiled Polly proudly.

Somehow, this made John feel a little better.

'Your left hand is swelling up nicely.' said Polly, nodding towards his fist resting on his lap. 'You broke the skin. Let's get you some ice and make sure it isn't broken.'

At the mention of his hand, the pain finally cut through all the adrenalin coursing through him. John agreed he needed to tend to his hand, but there were other pressing concerns.

'What am I going to say to Javier?'

'*I'm sorry* might be a good start.'

'Yeah.' whispered John. 'It might.'

Lucy and John found an open *farmacia*. The pharmacist examined John's hand and had him wiggle his fingers. It hurt, but the pharmacist said a break was unlikely since he could still move it. He sold them an ice pack and told John to take anti-inflammatories. The duo stopped and bought water before walking back to the albergue.

' Thank you for the talk, Polly, and for helping me so much over the last few days—even when I didn't know how to ask for it or even deserve it. Especially when I treated you so poorly.'

She squeezed John's arm.

'That's what the Camino does. We help each other, whether deserved or not. We get to bestow grace on others, and in doing so, hopefully, we learn to give it to ourselves. But I plan on walking some long days from now on to get far ahead of you guys. I can't swoop in and save the day every time.' She said it with a smile, but he knew he had been more than a little trying, even to himself. 'You got a lot of drama surrounding you, my friend. Maybe take a look at that.'

John returned to their bunks, but Javier was not there. He lay down, and it wasn't long before the wine caught up with him, and he was asleep. He didn't wake up when Javier came in.

The following morning, John rose and got ready as Javier exited the bathroom, fully dressed, picked up his pack, and left without a word.

John knew he deserved the silent treatment. He finished packing and was surprised to find Javier sitting on the bench out front, waiting for him.

'Oh.' said John, surprised. 'I thought you had already left.'

'I considered it. But we need to talk.'

'Yes, we do.,' he agreed.

'Too much has happened between you and me, even before the last few days. Our children are married to each other, and we cannot have bad blood between us. It will tear apart the people we love the most, and I think we both want invitations to our grandchildren's birthday parties.'

John nodded in agreement while Javier continued.

'First, I owe you an apology. I have owed it to you for a long time. I didn't just sleep with Tess. I fell in love with her. I knew she was married and shouldn't have allowed it to happen. Do I regret my time with her?' he shook his head. 'No. I didn't just help her when she was ill. She helped me see I could heal and live again after losing Alejandra. I needed that, for both mine and Mateo's sake. Except that it haunts you, and the pain created by my relationship with Tess has continued throughout the years. I regret the hurt I caused you.'

John looked down at this guy who admitted his mistakes. He had treated Javier poorly on the Camino.

'I told you. I gave Tess my permission.'

'Stop!' Javier put his hand up. 'This doesn't matter to your heart. It might absolve her of some transgression in your mind, but it doesn't take the hurt away. Tess wasn't a saint. She was a human being in a great deal of pain for many reasons, grabbing at the last threads of her life before it completely unraveled. She came here, and she did what she did with me. And she had her talks with Pen. I imagine that was two months you wish Tess had spent with you. Two months sooner, she would have entered treatment, but also, two more months where you would have been with her. I think you're very hurt and perhaps, based on what I have seen, a little angry about it. Maybe that is what you're finally admitting to yourself.'

John was silent.

'It's OK to be angry.' Javier offered. 'But don't hit me again. Next time, I promise you, I'll hit back.' Javier smiled up at John with a swollen black eye. 'At least I still have all my teeth.'

John smiled, too.

'I'm sorry for hitting you.' he said sincerely.

Javier held out his hand, and John took it, wincing in pain, pulling him to his feet.

'Maybe now we can be friends.'

'I think I could use one right about now.' agreed John as they set off together through the warren of cobbled streets toward the next climb.

# Part II

# A Trail of Lies

# Twelve

## Alto de Perdon

The two men walked out of Pamplona side by side until Javier pulled ahead on the dusty trail, snaking its way westward up and over the foothills outside of the city. John watched the doctor's back while huffing and puffing up every incline toward Alto de Perdon. Javier was far off in the distance as John passed through the village of Zariquiegui, perched above the city of Pamplona. Tired, John entered the *Iglesia de San Andrés* church and sat down in the candlelit darkness, head throbbing and a little hung over. Staring up at the altarpiece, he had the place to himself among the musty wooden pews.

Over the centuries, the burning incense embedded in this building's walls triggered a memory somewhere deep inside, transporting him back in time. After the death of his parents, his grandfather raised John Catholic, but John did not attend church as an adult. The smell of incense reminded John of his first months in Iowa after his parents died. The memories rushed toward him of sitting beside his Grandpa Charlie, with his legs dangling from the bench every Sunday morning as the priest delivered the mass in Latin. More than half a century later, John wasn't sure what he believed anymore. But, back then, the mass was predictable — something he could count on. After such a profound loss, he needed that.

John removed his pack. Setting down the heavy weight onto the wooden pew beside him, he removed his wallet from the zippered pocket in his hip belt. Pulling out the yellowed column of newsprint, he sat down and unfolded it—Tess's obituary. John had read it so many times the velum was covered in clear tape to keep it from falling apart. He really should make a copy, or soon, he wouldn't be able to read the words—her words. Tess had insisted upon writing her own obituary. She wanted the last word before she passed. As organized as she was, she sealed it in an envelope, already addressed to the local newspaper with a stamp—an actual stamp. It sat on the table by her bedside. She hadn't asked him to mail it, so he wasn't sure who posted the letter and how it ended up in the newspaper. But he received an email confirming the receipt with the publication date just days after her passing. John didn't subscribe to the newspaper but bought one, cut it out, and kept it in his wallet like a talisman. Tess was still with him. He could read her take on what her life had meant whenever he needed to.

Holding the obituary, he got to his knees, took off his dad's *Cubs* cap out of habit and respect, bowed his head, and prayed. After he finished talking to God, he spoke aloud to Tess.

'I'm doing this thing for you like I promised. The bad news is it's not going very well. I've managed to piss off everyone I've met, including a monk.' John shook his head. 'Yup. A Buddhist monk. That's who I am now—the guy who enrages the most peaceful people in the world. And I punched Javier in the face for doing nothing except loving you, probably better than I ever did. So, I'm pretty much the biggest douchebag out here. Ticking all the boxes. Making you proud.' he said sarcastically, his eyes swelling with tears and profound shame.

John dug into a compartment of his pack for tissues when the bracelet given to him by the monk fell to the floor. He picked it up, examining it. The gift was a kind gesture without expectation—a symbol of peace. John slid the beads over his left hand, wondering about the mysterious engraving on the emerald and gold bead.

'Why did you want me to come here?' pleaded John to the cavernous space. 'Why did I agree to do this?'

He sat in silence as his words bounced around the echoing chamber. Tears poured down his cheeks.

'It's been ten years, but I'm lonelier than on that first day. Do you know that? Will it ever get easier? Will it ever go away? I hope you have Charlie with you to keep you company, but Pen lives thousands of miles away from me. These days, I spend my time trying to think of things to do.,' he sniffed. 'Sometimes, I can go for a week only speaking to that crazy guy across the street—the one with all the political signs and flags in his yard. You remember him. Or the checker at the grocery store.'

'I miss you, Tess. I miss feeling your foot in bed. I miss the silly made-up songs you sang in the morning when you were getting ready for work. The ones that never rhymed.'

John smiled at the memory while wiping the tears on his cheeks.

'Humming to fake it when you couldn't think of the right rhyme.' he chuckled. 'You were a terrible singer. You really were.' he admitted. 'I can barely remember your face anymore, but I still remember those stupid songs. You, dancing in the kitchen with your coffee.'

John blew his nose.

'But that was before Charlie died when your singing stopped. That's how I knew your smiles weren't real. Pen and I knew it because you stopped singing and dancing.' his tears flowed, and he didn't try to stop them. 'I was lonely long before you died, Tess. But now, it's crushing me. I read somewhere that people who have a pet live longer. So, I thought about getting a dog. But then, visiting Pen would be more difficult. And it wouldn't be fair to the dog.'

John pulled on the bracelet with the green bead, fidgeting.

'I'm rambling. I know. None of this makes sense.' John wiped his eyes with the back of his hand. 'But I don't know what else to do. People tried to set me up with their friends or sister-in-law who just got divorced, but I couldn't do it.' he sniffed. 'Well, I did go on one date a long time ago — Jim's wife's friend from work. But it was so awful. She talked about her cats. And about her ex-husband. I just sat there. I hardly said a word. Talking about you seemed like a betrayal, somehow. So, I told her I had an early meeting and left. I don't want anyone else, Tess. I just want you.' he cried. 'Except you're gone, so where does that leave me?'

John wiped his nose.

'I know it, so you don't have to tell me. I'm broken. Seriously. Something is wrong with me. The people I love tend to die. Is it their proximity to me? Should I just become a hermit? Pen lives safely on the other side of the world, far away from me. But do I die of loneliness, eventually? Or do I become that weird guy who talks to strangers at the store and has nothing important to say?'

Unsurprisingly, Tess didn't answer his questions.

'So far, on the Camino, I am the craziest person out here. Javier will confirm it if you ask him. So will an FBI agent I just met.' John rolled his eyes. 'Don't ask.'

He wiped his tears again.

'I don't know what I expect you to do for me. I guess I just need you to know what I'm up against. Maybe you have some pull up there, and there is some sort of angel you can send my way who can help me figure this out.' he sighed. 'Should I quit and do this later? At a better time when I'm not such a mess?'

John sniffed.

'Who am I kidding? When would that be?'

He wiped his eyes again. 'All I know is I love you, Tess. I haven't forgotten you for one moment, but maybe I need to find a way to think about you a little bit less. Maybe I need to stop being the sad widower and learn how to be a little more normal. After all this time, like a habit, I don't know how.'

John kissed his fingers and held them up to the vaulted medieval ceiling. To whom, he wasn't sure. Just then, two laughing pilgrims entered the sanctuary. John rose from the kneeler, still sore from days of walking over mountains. His hand throbbed from hitting Javier the previous day as he quickly gathered his pack and poles and exited the church. Entering the bright sunshine to rejoin the trail, he knew Javier would wonder where he was.

As expected, Javier beat John to the top of Alto de Perdon, where he sat across from the oxidized, windblown iron statues of pilgrims walking the Way. Waiting. John huffed and puffed his way up the last stretch and stood looking out over the valley back toward Pamplona with his hands on his hips, stretching his back and catching his breath. Then, he turned to Javier.

'Listen. I'm sorry for hitting you.'

Javier held up a hand to stop him from continuing.

'No, really. None of this is your fault.' John sighed, 'How I'm feeling and my behavior back in Pamplona. I don't have a right to be angry with you. And, if I think about it, I'm not angry with you. Or even with Tess. I know that might seem ridiculous.'

John wiped the sweat on his lip with the back of his hand as the white windmills spun in the distance.

'This weight I'm still carrying seems ridiculous, even to me, because it's been ten years since she passed. Why do I still feel like it was yesterday?'

Looking out over the valley, John sought the answers that would never come.

'It was horrible the first year. All the anniversaries. Tess' birthday. Christmas. All the firsts. And then, the second year seemed even harder. People stopped asking about her or how I was doing. Like she never existed. But, for me, she was still right there. I could smell her scent in the house – even though her shampoo wasn't in the shower anymore.'

John's tears flowed for the second time that day, and Javier didn't interrupt him.

'I lived with a ghost I talked to out loud on a regular basis. Sometimes, I had whole conversations with Tess in the car after work on the way home. Some days, I would wait until I got in the door. I could actually hear her voice expressing her opinion about something or other.'

He looked down at Javier sitting on the monument across from the sculptures. Sure that the other man thought him insane.

'You probably think I'm nuts. But I would ask Tess for advice on the stupidest things and usually hear the answer. As if she were right there.'

He sniffed, dabbing his nose with the back of his hand.

'But, over time, Tess started to fade. Her voice wasn't as readily available to me anymore. I watched a bunch of our old family movies. Pen's soccer games from when she was in kindergarten. Charlie learning to snowboard. Tess on a beach with the kids, building a sandcastle. Her laugh was the soundtrack of our lives. And, for a while, it was like I could reload the sound of her voice. But, eventually, even that wouldn't do it. Too much time had passed. Too many things had happened since she died, and she wasn't a part of them. I switched jobs, and she didn't know my new boss—the people in my office. I bought a new car she had never ridden in. It took me five years and prodding from Pen before I cleaned all her stuff from our closet. I used to smell her clothes and slept with her bathrobe for over a year.'

It was a moment before John noticed Javier was crying, too.

'I don't think you are crazy, John.' he whispered, barely audible over the wind on the ridge. 'I know exactly what you have been through because I did the same with Alejandra. I never washed her pillow. And I know all about talking to someone who isn't there. You're afraid to stop talking because you think they will disappear forever if you do. It is as if the sound of your voice is what is keeping them close. You can't accept that their thread to this life is broken forever, and they're already gone. I believe that when Alejandra and Tess died, they went straight to heaven. It's us who are trapped in hell without them.'

John choked up, sobbing like a baby. He covered his face with his hands. Javier stood, and the two men embraced, crying as other pilgrims walked up the trail and passed them. It was a moment before they broke apart, each man wiping his own tears. Javier bent down to grab John's poles from the dirt.

'We need to get going. It's a rough walk down from here and worse if we're crying.' Javier smiled reassuringly.

John nodded. He wasn't ready to tell Javier everything yet. Maybe he never would. John took the poles Javier offered, and silently, they walked toward Puenta la Reina and a bed for the night.

# Thirteen

## The Unraveling

John and Javier fell into a regular cadence. Only the elevation changed, lending degrees of difficulty with which John was slowly becoming comfortable. They walked all morning and checked into an albergue or pension each afternoon in a small village or a hill town. Cleaning up after a sweaty day, they ventured out to find food. Later, they fell into a deep sleep only to awaken the following day and do it all over again. After the emotional exchange in Alto de Perdon, their conversations veered purposefully from the subject of Tess. Neither man seemed to want to tempt the detente that had settled between them.

After an exhausting day on a stretch of pine forests known as *the knee wrecker* for its steep climbs and treacherous descents, John and Javier ended the day climbing up to the hill town of Viana. The small pueblo dates to a third-century Roman settlement, but the Moors built the castle on the hilltop. Its position on the Camino Francés made it an important center of culture for pilgrims in the Middle Ages, and stone architecture from that period remains on full display.

Their albergue sat amongst the medieval buildings in the old town, and upon arrival, they were hot and tired, ready for dinner. But the restaurants were still closed for siesta, so the vending machines in the lobby would have to suffice. The two men sat on threadbare sofas, downing potato chips and protein bars. A bookshelf held stacks of well-thumbed paperbacks in a variety of languages. Board games piled haphazardly on the bottom shelf had pieces tumbling out of broken cardboard lids. John spotted a box with

*Chess* written on it, bending down to extract it from the pile. He dusted it off, then held it up.

'Do you know how to play chess?' he asked Javier enthusiastically.

Javier nodded, popping another chip into his mouth as he cleared the coffee table before them.

'We can put the board here.'

John smoothed out the bent gameboard and placed the pieces in the correct squares. He reached into the box for the last remaining white knight, but it wasn't there.

'It doesn't matter.' offered Javier. 'We can play anyway.'

John shook his head. 'That's not how chess works. Chess is like life. You can't play unless you have all the correct pieces. Otherwise, what is the point?' he asked with disappointment.

His earlier enthusiasm disappeared at the lost prospect of playing the familiar game he loved. John returned the board and pieces to the box, replaced it on the shelf and returned to his bunk. Rolling over, he thought of young Julian in Bayonne and wondered if he had found a new chess partner to play the set John had given him. He prayed the boy didn't feel so alone anymore.

The following day, John and Javier made their way along the río Ebro towards the medieval Puente de Piedra bridge leading into the city of Logroño.

'We will arrive at my family's winery tomorrow. I let Mateo know where we were a few days ago and our pace. He said you had spoken to Pen, and they will meet us there tomorrow afternoon. We can decide with them when to go to the rose garden on the sheep farm and deposit some of Tess's ashes.'

Crossing the bridge, they made their way into the old town of the honey-colored stone city. A fiesta was in full swing and the inhabitants of the town and countless tourists seemed to be out on the streets barricaded from car traffic. John asked what was happening.

'I forgot about *Las Fiestas de San Mateo*.'

'What is that?' asked John.

'They're festivals that celebrate the harvest of the wine in the La Rioja region. These are the festivals of Thanksgiving. People used to make offerings to the saints for the harvest. There will be processions and grape stomping called *pisado de la uva*.'

'They're still crushing grapes by stomping on them?' John's eyes widened as they clicked their poles along the cobbled square in front of the Cathedral.

'It's mostly just for fun. The wineries use machines to do that now.'

Weaving through the crowds, the two men received some *Buen Camino* blessings from people on the street. Locating the hotel where they had planned to stay, they heard Javier's name called out as they reached the entrance. Turning around, John saw a tall, long-legged woman waving at them, hurrying across the street. She was beautiful with long dark hair shot with grey, worn in waves down her back, and a white floral sundress that hugged her curvaceous figure. She kissed Javier on both cheeks with bright red lips and smiled at John.

'*Buenos días.*' she said.

John smiled back.

'This is my cousin, Isabela. She has the neighboring vineyard down from my aunt and uncle.' Javier explained. 'This is John Sullivan. Pen's father.' he told his cousin.

John nodded. '*Buenos días.*'

Isabela laughed.

'Good afternoon. I speak English, so we will be safe from your Spanish.'

Her direct approach surprised John. He wanted to defend himself but thought better of it. Isabela was correct. His Spanish was crap.

'What are you doing here?' she asked Javier.

'We're staying tonight in Logroño and heading to the vineyard tomorrow to meet Pen and Mateo. Are you in town for the festivities?'

'I am.' she smiled, pointing back in the direction from where they'd come. 'We are sponsoring the grape stomp today. I have some of my guys setting it up now. We begin the stomp at 4 pm.'

Javier turned to John. 'Let's get cleaned up, and we can go and watch.' Then to Isabela, 'Where are you setting up?'

'Near the cathedral in Calle Portales'

'OK. We'll meet you there by 4 o'clock.'

John wanted to see the grape stomping, but he wasn't sure he craved an evening with Javier's cousin. She was prickly and seemed to find amusement in teasing him. He was done with feeling the odd man out on this trip.

Later, the two men backtracked down the wide pedestrian mall to the cathedral, where a large wooden tub stood. Three winery workers had just finished constructing it. Tall columns of crates full of grapes were stacked up, ready to fill the tub. Isabela stood off to the side, gesturing as if conducting an orchestra while furiously talking on her mobile.

Javier approached one of the men, who smiled and shook his hand. They chatted briefly, and Javier told John he had volunteered to help fill the tub with grapes.

'I think you should not lift these boxes. Let's make sure your back holds out for the Camino.'

Javier was right. He should avoid lifting anything for a few more days. Isabela got off the phone as the men finished filling the tub. Crowds had begun to gather as a marching band played music nearby, lending to the circus-like atmosphere.

Like a seasoned performer, Isabela took up a portable microphone and announced to everyone in the crowd what they could expect as the grape stomping got underway. The workers from her winery sold tickets to those gathered. All the proceeds would go to charities associated with the cathedral behind them. A line formed as people scrambled to purchase the opportunity to stomp grapes, and Isabela appeared pleased with the turnout. She walked over to where John and Javier stood.

'It's time to get into the tub to whip up more excitement and to encourage people to open their wallets.' she grabbed John's hand. 'Come on. You will help me stomp.'

John tried to resist.

'Oh no. I am not getting into that tub. I've never stomped grapes before.' he said, horrified at the prospect.

'Perfect! You can show the inexperienced that it's easy and they have nothing to fear. Maybe you can get American tourists to remove their shoes and empty some of the euros they can not take home into the baskets we will pass around during the show.'

Turning to Javier for help, his friend only held up his hands and shrugged. He, too, was no match for his cousin.

John allowed himself to be led to the vat before removing his shoes. They stepped up a ladder onto a platform and into the mounds of fresh grapes. Dressed in shorts, he shivered as the ripe, fragrant purple grapes squished between his toes. Isabela reached between her legs and grabbed the edge of her long sundress. She tucked it in the belt around her waist and tightened it before joining him in the tub.

Isabela started on the outside, using the side of the wooden vat as support while going around in a circle. John followed her lead as he struggled to stay upright. Soon, she stomped more vigorously across the middle, whipping up the crowd and encouraging ticket sales like an experienced carnival performer.

'For those of you who are a little nervous. Look at him!' pointing to John as a visual aide while speaking into the portable microphone.

'Sir, have you ever stomped grapes before?' she asked in Spanish and then English.

John leaned into the microphone, grasping her shoulders for support. 'No'.

His response required no translation as the crowd laughed and clapped.

'And how are you finding the experience?' again in both languages.

John looked out at the crowd. They were enjoying watching him make a fool of himself. The absurdity of the situation had him laughing, as well. He couldn't remember the last time he smiled this hard. Javier recorded a video with his phone—more evidence of his humiliation. Mateo would undoubtedly share it with Pen. John bent down, picked up two handfuls of grapes, and threw them at Isabela. She responded with a scathing look but quickly recovered.

'It's a lot of fun!' shouted John. 'You should all try it! Especially any Americans out there!'

*FOMO*, the fear of missing out, kicked in hard. More people came out of the crowd and bought tickets for a chance to stomp and post the videos on social media. Baskets passed through the crowd for additional donations from the less adventurous.

Isabela grasped both of John's hands, and they danced in the vat to the claps and cheers of the assembly as a group of wandering musicians provided the soundtrack to their performance. Finally, it was time to relinquish their spot to paying ticket holders, and Isabela and John climbed out of the tub. John descended first, helping Isabela by lifting her out of the vat. Not thinking about his back, John flung her over his shoulder as the crowd cheered. She screeched and kicked her legs, imploring him to release her. John turned her around, setting her on her feet as the pain gripped him, and he nearly dropped Javier's cousin.

'What's wrong?' she asked, bending down as John fell to his knees.

'It's my chest. The pain.' he told her through gritted teeth. 'I can't breathe.'

Isabela eased John onto the stone cobbles, then looked up, frantically searching the crowd for Javier while shouting his name. The doctor ran to where John lay on the ground. Javier asked people in the crowd to lift John's legs while he examined his friend. John's face was a grimace while Isabela clasped his hand and held his head.

Javier stood. 'I'm calling an ambulance.'

Soon, the sound of the siren grew louder as the crew arrived. They quickly loaded John into the yellow van with the blue flashing lights, and Javier followed.

'I'll tell you where we are and what's happening.' he told his cousin. Then, he turned to focus on John, who was clutching his chest as the doors closed and the ambulance pulled away.

# FOURTEEN

## A BROKEN HEART

The hospital emergency room stood full of patients and families as Javier waited amongst them, pacing the floor, anxious for news of John's condition. After an hour without a word, he looked up as Isabela swept through the automatic doors, clutching her handbag with her phone glued to her ear.

'How is he?' she asked, hanging up.

'I don't know.' said Javier. 'I'm debating whether to call Pen. I had just sent her a video of her father stomping grapes when I heard you call my name. I don't want to worry her, but I don't want her to believe I wouldn't tell her that her father had a heart attack. It will take them time to get here, and I think it is the right thing to do.'

Isabela nodded. 'Maybe wait until we know a bit more. Pen and Mateo are coming tomorrow, correct?'

Javier nodded, frowning, and returned to pacing under the fluorescent lights.

Another hour ticked by. Finally, a nurse emerged in the waiting area and called Javier's name. The two cousins stood, searching the person's blank face for news of their friend, but none was forthcoming.

'Please, come with me.' The uniformed person instructed as she escorted Javier back to the emergency department, turning right into a private cubicle.

'How are you feeling?' he asked John after they pulled back the curtain, concerned when he saw his friend appeared pale and drawn. Wires attached to machines blinked, and beeping dominated the room. Oxygen flowed into his nose via a tube.

'They don't have all the results back yet, but they gave me some stuff for the chest pain, and I think it's helping.'

'Do they believe it was a heart attack?' asked Javier, sure that John's Camino was at an end.

'They aren't sure. The doctor said he would know more soon. That I should rest.'

Javier nodded.

'Isabela is in the waiting room. She showed up an hour ago.'

'I hope I didn't ruin her fundraising.' said John. 'It's not a great advertisement for grape stomping when the first stooge of the entire operation falls over.'

'I wouldn't worry about that. People will give out of pity.' He teased with a wink.

John laughed, then held his chest. 'Isabela can come in here if she wants.'

'I think she would like that. It will reassure her. She's very worried about you.'

Javier left and returned with his cousin, who rushed ahead, barreling into the room. She grasped John's hand and squeezed, stroking his forehead. It had been a long time since a woman had gotten that close.

'John, you have a whole church and the priest praying for you. I made sure of it before I came. And I went inside myself on my way to my car to pray to Saint Rita to intercede on your behalf. She is the patron saint of hopeless cases.' Isabela assured him. 'I think you qualify.'

John smiled. 'Well, thank you for that, I think. I have been eligible for her intervention for a very long time.'

The Spanish beauty smiled.

'Don't worry,' she told him. 'We have a special relationship, Saint Rita and me. She's helped me through dark days. I take her roses on her feast day every year in May. She always answers my prayers. Sometimes, maybe not how I expect, but she comes through when I need her. She will intercede on your behalf.'

It was nearly midnight when the emergency doctor returned to the room to give John his results. Javier sent Isabela home an hour earlier, promising to call her if John's condition changed.

'Well.' the doctor smiled. 'I have some good news. It is not a heart attack.'

John let out a sigh of relief.

'Have you had unusual stress lately?' he asked.

John laughed. 'You mean, other than walking a hundred miles across Spain in this heat?'

'Yes.' chuckled the doctor. 'While exercise is healthy, moderation is key. I also wonder if anything else in your life has been unusually stressful.'

'Why do you ask?' John frowned.

'Because I believe you had a panic attack. Your blood work is perfect—no signs of heart problems in the EKG or ultrasound. A panic attack mimics a heart attack in many ways. Symptom for symptom, except the heart and vascular system damage. What were you doing at the time you first felt the pain.'

He had Isabela over his shoulder after the grape stomp. At that moment, John felt light for the first time in over a decade. More like a twenty-year-old college student than a sixty-three-year-old widower. And then the pain struck.

The doctor listened and wrote a few notes.

'Are you married, John?'

John hesitated.

'I was.' he whispered. 'I've been widowed for ten years. My friend,' he pointed to Javier. 'is helping me to distribute my wife's ashes in some of the places she asked me to while I walk.'

'On the Camino?' asked the physician.

'Yes, well, sort of. Nearby.'

The doctor nodded.

'Perhaps this is taking more of an emotional toll on your body than you might have presumed. The Camino is a long, arduous walk for people not on an emotional mission such as yours. Your body is telling you to take it easy. But I think your heart is saying something, as well. Listen to it. Rest more. Take care of yourself.' said the doctor, patting John's shoulder. 'Is there anyone special in your life? Since the passing of your wife?'

The question surprised him.

'No.' John said. 'No one since. My daughter is married to Javier's son. She lives in Madrid at their family home. I live in Arizona in the US.'

'So, you are alone,' stated the doctor matter-of-factly. 'No family nearby.'

John hesitated.

'I am alone.' he finally admitted. 'I have held on to my wife's ashes for ten years. It's time to let her go.' he said, tears sprang to his eyes.

'Yes. And yet it can be difficult.' observed the emergency physician sympathetically, 'But it is necessary. You need a support system. After the loss of a spouse, outcomes are better for those aging who have a healthy support system.'

John knew he was right but hadn't dated anyone after Tess. He owed her that somehow—after everything.

The doctor wrapped up his diagnosis and completed his notes.

'You can get dressed and go. But I am giving you some pills for anxiety. Take them when you need them. Try some deep breathing techniques. You can look this up on YouTube – under *Mindfulness*. It will help. And I would like to see you rest for a few days—no walking for a little bit. Then, I see no physical reason you cannot continue your journey. But you must seek medical attention immediately if you have any further issues. Just because this was not a heart attack doesn't mean the next one isn't.'

Javier was waiting for John when he exited the emergency room doors.

'I spoke to the doctor,' said Javier. 'I hope you don't mind.'

John pulled on the sweatshirt Javier had brought for him.

'No. I don't mind.' John looked around. 'Where is Isabela? Did she go home?'

'Yes. Several hours ago. You don't remember?'

It was all a blur for John. He was exhausted and embarrassed. A panic attack. Did they think he was faking a heart attack? He wondered if he should stop the Camino now. He could still drive to all the places on Tess's list, finish quickly, and be safely home in a week.

'I figured we could go back to the hotel. Or we can take a taxi to my family's house outside Navarrete.'

John didn't feel like being around more of *la familia Silva* at that moment. He needed to gather his thoughts and decide what he wanted to do. And he didn't need to see Javier while he did it.

'Let's go to the hotel. I need a good night's rest.'

Javier called them a taxi, and they rode the ten minutes to a hotel.

'I'm glad Isabela went home. It was kind of her to come.' said John, absentmindedly watching out the window as the city flew past.

'You don't know her well, but she is a good person. She can be prickly, but she has a big heart.'

'Where is her husband?' asked John, 'Does she have kids?'

'No husband. Not anymore. She married an American professor. He was not faithful, and they divorced before she moved back here to take over her parent's vineyard. They never had children.'

John nodded. 'She's a strong person. Fierce, even.'

Javier chuckled.

'Fierce is an apt description. I know it was a tough time for Isabela, and it soured her on the institution of marriage. She likes to do things her way and is savvy and well-respected in the winemaking business—an excellent businesswoman.'

John returned to watching the city. The woman probably intimidated her competition. He could relate because Isabela scared the hell out of him.

# FIFTEEN

## LA BRUJA

Dressed in a dark grey suit and an emerald blouse, Pen stood at her desk in the cubicles amongst the junior curators in the museum where she worked in Madrid. Looking down at her phone, she sighed. Javier sent a video to their family group chat of her father stomping grapes with Isabela in Logroño. She responded with a heart emoji but nothing more. Pen wasn't sure what she wanted to say or what she should say. *Hilarious! Marveloso!* Or maybe *Be careful!* None seemed right, so she deleted each one and remained silent. She would see her dad the following day, but she felt uneasy. She wasn't sure why.

After her mom died, her dad was all she had left. Well, she had Mateo, too. But her dad was the last of her family. Mom and Dad, Charlie and Pen. The original four. She worried about her father every day. While still in high school, Pen was constantly concerned about what he ate or if he took too long to come home from the store. She couldn't lose her father, too.

Pen teared up, remembering the constant vigilance she kept after the memorial for her mom. Her dad never knew the tabs she kept on him.

It wasn't a mystery why she felt this way. In those early years, she was afraid that if something happened to him, she might end up in a place she had no intention of going. Pen remembered sitting in her bedroom after her mom died and making long lists—contingency plans so she wouldn't end up with her grandmother if the worst-case scenario came to pass. Her dad didn't know it, but Pen kept a go-bag packed in her closet and cash on hand, including her passport. She made sure she had a bank balance high enough to cover an international plane ticket. If anything happened to her dad while she was under 18, Pen would have fled to Madrid, to the house near Alphonso Martinez Square, to people she knew would protect her. Pen wasn't being paranoid. She needed to defend herself.

After her mother's memorial service, she and her dad hosted a reception at his golf club for those who had come to pay their respects. Her mom's parents never came to see their daughter when she was dying. They said it was too far to fly, and her grandma insisted they were too old to make the 1700-mile trip. But she called Pen on her cell once to 'see how you are doing.'

Pen said her mom wasn't doing well, and she cried, telling her grandma she was worried Tess would die. But her grandmother pushed it aside.

'Oh, honey. I've spoken to everyone in our family, and nobody here is even worried about your mom. We're just worried about you. How are *you* doing?'

After that telephone conversation, Pen ran into her bathroom and threw up. Her grandmother didn't care at all about her own daughter.

To Pen and her dad's surprise, her grandparents showed up at their daughter's memorial service, crying loudly and making a scene. A performance meant to soak up the condolences of those in attendance. All while looking theatrically devastated at the loss of the person they refused to support during her illness. Pen didn't understand why they bothered since they didn't come to see her mom when she was alive.

After such an emotional day, Pen was in the ladies' room at the golf club, washing her hands and catching her breath away from everyone. Suddenly, she felt a claw encircle her upper arm as pointed, frosted-pink nails dug into her flesh. Looking up at the gold-framed mirror, Pen saw her grandmother's grey-haired reflection like a specter behind her. The woman looked frantic. Pen's heart raced.

'Now, Penelope, I've been looking for you.' said her grandmother sweetly, but her words cut like steel as her eyes narrowed. 'I need you to talk to your father.'

Pen scowled. 'Talk to him about what?'

'Well.' said her grandma calmly. 'I have just spoken with him, but he's being unreasonable.'

'Unreasonable?' said Pen, confused. Her dad was never unreasonable.

'Well, yes.' the woman cooed, feigning innocence. 'I just think we all need to be realistic and settle things before your grandpa and I fly home this afternoon. So, we can get things ready.'

'Ready for what?' asked Pen, frowning down into the face of the shrunken woman.

'For you to come live with us, of course.' said the old woman with icy cheerfulness.

The blood drained from Pen's face, and she suddenly felt faint. 'What are you talking about?' asked Pen, pulling her arm from her grandmother's grasp and then rubbing the area where the fingers left a mark. She could tell her grandma didn't like it.

'You need a firm hand and a *real* mother. God knows, your own was never around to teach you anything. Now that she's dead, your father will want to start dating soon, and it's better for him if he doesn't have a child around. Women don't like that sort of thing in a man they're dating—another woman's child. Anyway, your grandpa and I have talked about it, and we think you coming to live with us is best for everyone.'

She picked some invisible lint from the shoulder of Pen's dress with her sharp nails.

'Not for free, of course. Your dad will have to cover the expenses. The one thing your mother was good at was making money, so he has plenty to pay for whatever you'll need – food and such. And to cover the increase in things like our water bill and gas in the car to drive you around. Of course, the costs associated with the general inconvenience to us of raising you. But I am willing to make the sacrifice.' Laying on the martyrdom thick.

Pen's mouth hung open. Speechless. This woman was her mom's mother, yet she avoided speaking her daughter's name. And she wanted money to take care of her own granddaughter? Fear shot through her as the tears Pen had wiped away earlier began to well up again. Pen had never considered living with her grandparents. Suddenly, something dark bubbled up in her.

'My mother's name is Tess, you know. And this is the day of her memorial. A day when I have to say goodbye to her.' Pen's bottom lip quivered with anger in response to her grandma's words and intense longing for her mom. 'Do you really think it's appropriate to talk to me like this on the day of my mother's memorial?' she asked.

The woman pursed her lips and made a face. 'Of course, her name was Tess.' she said, exasperated. 'I named her – don't you forget that. An ungrateful child, if there ever was one. You remind me of her sometimes. Do you know that? *A little bitch.*' She muttered under her breath as though Pen couldn't hear. 'Anyway, I just spoke to your father, and he's not thinking clearly. I'm sure we will speak again when he's had a chance to think about it and sees that what I'm offering is best for everyone.' she reached up to stroke her granddaughter's cheek as Pen recoiled at the touch of the cold, wrinkled hand. 'I just wanted to ensure you and I are on the same side.' her grandmother purred.

Pen glowered at the old lady in the cream-colored vintage Saint John bouclé suit. It didn't fit her anymore, but she wore it like a snake that refused to shed its skin.

'I'm never coming to live with you.' Pen said quietly. 'As a matter of fact, I will never visit you. Ever again. Please, leave me and my dad alone!'

Pen ran from the restroom. She found a quiet corner in the banquet room to hide behind a potted palm and tried to calm down. Pen had never felt so alone. Grasping for her phone in the pocket of her black skirt, she texted Mateo for support.

Pen: *you will never fucking believe what just happened at my mom's memorial reception*

Mateo: *????*

Pen: *my grandma wants me to go live with her so my dad can find a new wife*

Mateo: *no way!*

Pen: *yup! I swear it is like she is the witch in a fairy tale or something – the kind that eats children. I'm Gretel, so that makes you Hansel. When she touched my arm, it felt evil or something—ice cold. I can't explain it.*

Mateo: *what did your dad say?*

Pen: *haven't found him yet.*

Mateo: *find him. See what he says. Then call me*

Pen searched the room. She spotted her grandparents hurriedly gathering their things from the coat check as her grandmother pushed her grandfather toward the door while chastising the old man with the cane for being too slow. Scanning the crowd assembled, Pen finally found her dad on the far side of the mahogany bar overlooking the golf course. He stared out the large window, alone, lost in thought. Pen wasn't sure what she should do. Should she bother him with this now or wait? But this was important.

Fidgeting, twisting the paper towel she'd carried from the bathroom, Pen waited until she saw her grandparents were out the door. Then, she made a beeline for her dad just as he looked up, frowning.

'What's wrong?' he asked, on the alert, searching his daughter's face as she approached. 'Are you okay?'

Tears poured down Pen's cheeks. She swallowed hard and wiped them away.

'I was just in the bathroom. Grandma came in,'

Her dad's face switched from concern to fury. He took a drink of the amber liquid in his hand and wiped the corners of his mouth.

'What did that...what did she say to you?' he asked through gritted teeth.

Pen gulped, trying to catch her breath.

'She said she told you that I should go live with her. You would want to find a new wife, and I should get out of the way. She said mom wasn't a real mom and that I needed a *firm hand*.' Pen sobbed as John wrapped his arms around her while she cried. When she pulled back, her dad offered her his handkerchief.

'She said mom was ungrateful and that sometimes I was like her. She called both of us *little bitches*. Grandma wants money, so raising me doesn't cost her anything. Dad, I don't want to go live with her. Please tell me I won't have to do that. I won't get in the way if you want to date someone. If you find someone who loves you, it's fine. You can do what you want.'

Her dad closed his eyes, visibly struggling to compose himself.

'Listen to me,' he said, setting down his drink and cupping her face with his hands. 'You are my daughter. After everything, we are still a family. Especially now. You are not going anywhere without me. It's just us now, Pen. That woman will never get her claws into you while I draw breath. What she did to your mom is enough for me to keep you far from her grasp.'

Pen gulped. 'But what if something happens to you? First, we lost Charlie. Now, Mom. What if I'm left alone?' she cried.

Her dad shook his head.

'I'm not going anywhere. Do you hear me? We can discuss a backup plan another time, but you will never have to deal with that woman again.'

Ten years after her mother's death, the seeds of fear her grandmother planted that day never went away. The idea that she might be left alone to fend for herself. Pen shook her head, willing the feeling away.

'You're in Madrid.' she whispered to herself as reassurance. 'You have Mateo.'

She stood in the office in the Reina Sofia, grasping the blue lapis butterfly necklace nestled at her throat—the one that used to belong to her mother. After landing her dream job, she and Mateo were no longer teenagers but husband and wife. When she messaged him these days, he was across town, not seven thousand miles away on the other side of the world. Their most pressing decisions ran to when they would meet up for dinner. He and his father, Javier, and their housekeeper, Ines, were part of her family now. There was comfort in that.

Pen was honest that day when she told her dad she would be happy for him if he ever found love again. And yet he remained alone all these years.

Today, his loneliness worried her. Her father was out walking the Camino with Javier. He could fall or have a heart attack. Things like that happened all the time on the Camino. Who knew all the possible hazards? Pen looked down at her phone and the photo of her dad smiling in Saint-Jean. He'd sent it to her more than a week before. She offered up a little prayer for his safety. *Please don't let me lose another one.*

# Sixteen
## Just One More Step

The following morning, on the doctor's orders, they skipped the walk and took a taxi to Javier's family home in a vineyard on the other side of Navarrete. John watched as the taxi passed through the small town. Navarrete is a picturesque hill town with a famous cathedral he had planned to visit, but he didn't ask to stop to see it. The night before, he requested that Javier not tell Pen and Mateo about his panic attack. John didn't want to worry his daughter. She would think he wasn't up for this adventure, and he didn't want to admit she might be right.

Soon, they turned down a dirt trek in the vines that led to a large stone house surrounded by a high stone wall. A creaky iron gate swung open, and a swarm of relatives of all ages greeted them, including two gigantic blond Mastin sheepdogs. John found himself embraced and spoken to in languages he hadn't mastered. Someone picked up his bag and made off with it. A grey truck coming over the ridge kicked up dust as they turned and watched it approach. When the vehicle reached them, the layer of grit disguised its blue color, making it appear a dusty grey. The driver-side door opened, and Isabela emerged. She wore an old straw hat, and a thick, black braid threaded with grey ran down her back. Dressed in jeans, cowboy boots, and a well-loved red plaid shirt with western snaps, if he didn't know where he was, John would have thought they were standing in California and not a winery in Northern Spain.

Isabela smiled at John as rapid Spanish mixed with kisses and hugs enveloped her.

'Are you staying for lunch?' Javier asked her.

'Yes. *Tio* called me. So, I came.'

To John, she apologized. 'I didn't have a chance to change. We have been in the vines finishing the harvest. Tomorrow, we begin the crush.'

The crush is the first step of many in winemaking. It determines the outcome of how the wine tastes. The skins, seeds, sugar content, and how they play together are married during this crucial time. The crush starts that process.

'If you're here tomorrow, you're welcome to watch. We like to have a little party to celebrate. Nothing big. Some lamb from the farm,' her chin pointed to some point in the distant north. 'and, of course, vegetables from my garden, our wine, and a bonfire. You can taste autumn in the air. The leaves will start to change soon, and the nights are already getting cooler, so bring a jacket.'

John was relieved she hadn't brought up the medical incident with the Silva family. He was self-conscious enough as it was.

'Let's go inside.' Javier led the way while petting a dog. 'Pen and Mateo will be here soon.'

They went into the big house and out to the courtyard in the center, surrounded by potted plants and trees. A table groaned with food, and John watched as everyone grabbed chairs and began chatting loudly and simultaneously. Javier motioned for him to take a seat.

'Muchas gracias.' was all John could think to say, over and over.

Finally, the assault on the senses ended as those assembled dug into the bounty before them. Still stunned, John began eating, even though he was more tired than hungry. Cousin Isabela was seated to his left, and as he turned her way with a mouth full of something undeniably delicious, he saw her smiling at him. She laughed.

'You look overwhelmed by our humble lunch.'

He swallowed before answering.

'In the US, this would stretch the bounds of a large Christmas dinner.'

Isabela smiled a knowing smile.

'I was a professor of chemistry at an American university. I spent more than one Christmas in the US, invited to the homes of colleagues. I know how it works there. In Madrid, perhaps lunches aren't so large, but here, since we're all family and working on our farms, it's normal.' she shrugged.

John was surprised that a chemistry professor would be working in the fields of a winery, and he said so.

'I thought you were more carnival barker or gypsy than a professor.' Isabela smirked.

'I guess I should thank you.' she said sheepishly, 'Last night, we raised double the money for charity than we thought we would. You were invaluable in getting the tourists and the expats to cough up the cash.'

'Nothing like drama to loosen the purse strings, eh?' he smiled. 'I'm glad I could help.'

She lifted her glass and drank her wine, then leaned over and whispered in his ear.

'How are you feeling?'

'I feel fine. Maybe a little embarrassed.' John admitted.

Isabela put her hand over his and squeezed reassuringly. 'Don't be. It's an emotional thing you are doing. It's bound to cause you some pain. Maybe you need a massage.' her eyes twinkled. 'A spa day.'

John laughed. 'Maybe.'

'Anyway,' she said, changing to a subject that wasn't so uncomfortable for John, 'as to how I came to be in the wine business, my mother inherited the winery before she married my father. When they passed away, it came to me as their only child.'

'So, you left your career in academia to become a winemaker.'

'Actually,' Isabela replied proudly. 'I was born a winemaker, left the vineyard, and became a chemist. Winemaking is chemistry.' She took a drink of the wine in her glass and held it up like a visual aide. 'And, if I am completely honest, alchemy. We are at the mercy of the gods—soil, water, weather, hot days, cool nights.  It all contributes. Then, we take what is given to us and see what happens. Like life.'

John studied Isabela as she spoke. Her face wasn't young, but it wasn't old either. Maybe early 50s. Isabela's eyes twinkled with mischief, which surprised him, especially after yesterday—flirting, even. It was a long time since a beautiful woman had flirted with him. As John smiled back, Isabela looked away. He returned to his lunch, and Javier asked him how he had enjoyed the food and wine.

'Very much. I'll need a nap after the meal.'

'Lucky for you, you are in Navarrete.' he said, lifting his glass to his friend. 'You're right at home with family.'

They finished up, and Javier led John upstairs to a room. He took a shower, laid down, and was asleep quickly. He awoke a few hours later when his daughter, Pen, jumped on his bed.

'Wake up! Dad.'

John opened one groggy eye, and upon seeing his daughter, he sat up and hugged her like a life preserver.

'I'm so glad you're here.'

'Me, too. Mateo and I got delayed by the train, but we made it. Finally. Want to go for a walk? I know the vineyards pretty well by now.'

'Let me get my shoes on.' said John, pulling back the duvet.

Pen led them up a dusty road to the top of a hill overlooking the valley.

'You didn't have any trouble getting up this hill. I guess you're a true pilgrim now.' she teased.

'I don't know about that, but I know I'm in better shape than I was a few weeks ago.'

Pen smiled and squeezed his arm.

'You're tan. More so than when I was in Phoenix last time.'

'Well, I walk 6 or 7 hours a day in the sun.' he reminded her. 'It was bound to happen.'

Pen kicked the dirt.

'Are you enjoying it?' she asked, concern marring her face as she scanned his for information.

John considered the question.

'Yes, I am. I like the freedom on the Camino and the simple life. I don't have much, but I don't need much. I am concerned with water, food, and a place to sleep. That's it. And I hope I don't stink too badly.'

Pen laughed.

'You're fine. You can do some laundry while you're at the house. That will help reset all the hand washing you've probably been doing.'

They walked through the vineyard arm in arm to the top of the ridgeline.

'How do you feel about tomorrow?' he asked her.

Pen sighed.

'I don't know. I know Mom wanted it, so I think that's good. It's important to honor that. But at the same time, it feels like I have to let her go all over again.' Pen sniffed. 'And I don't like that part.'

She looked up at John with tears that matched his own. John reached over and embraced his daughter. Looking out over the vines as the sun set, lost to their own thoughts.

'I think it's time we let her go.' he told his daughter. 'Let her be at peace. You have a big life ahead of you. She would be so proud of you.' He scanned the valley below. 'I'm so proud of you. I think this walk is helping me let go, too. Maybe not 100% yet, but I'm getting there.'

Pen nodded and wiped her nose on her sleeve. She wrapped her arms around her dad's waist as they slowly walked back to the house.

The following day, John, Pen, and Mateo piled into an estate truck and made their way down the dirt road and out to the highway with Javier at the wheel. The group was heading for a sheep farm Javier inherited from his uncle, who passed away the year before. John held Tess's ashes on his lap in his red day pack, thinking about the last time his wife had been there.

When they arrived at the property, a weathered man in a navy blue cardigan and a black beret greeted them.

'This is Manuel. He is the manager of the farm.'

Javier explained to Manuel who they were and what they would be doing. The man smiled, waved them off with his stick, and left.

'My uncle operated this farm when Tess was here helping with the lambing. He passed away, and Manuel runs it for me. I will spend more time here now that I am retired.' Javier unlocked the door to the farmhouse. 'Shall we?'

John ducked down as they filed through the door with a low stone lintel and into the small kitchen with a timbered ceiling. It had been in the Silva family for a long time.

'Would anyone like something to drink before we get started? Coffee or something else?'

They all shook their heads.

'Okay.' Javier took a deep breath. 'John, you have what Tess wrote down. Please tell us her wishes.'

John removed the envelope containing the wrinkled sheet of paper from his pack, put on his glasses, and read aloud the entire letter she had written. He stopped periodically to catch his breath and wipe his eyes.

*My Dearest John*

*I have been blessed with such a wonderful life filled with adventures. You have been with me for most of them, and I carry all of them in my heart. Memories that I dream about and that haunt me in the middle of the night while here in the hospital. Sometimes, it's a smell or the light falling just right to take me back to times I can't forget. Won't ever forget, even when I'm gone from this world.*

*My intention is not to be a burden, my love, but I need you to do me a favor and make sure that I get to revisit some of these places one last time. So, I can leave a little piece of myself as an offering of thanks to the gods who blessed me with such a good life. The list isn't short, and some might not make sense. But please do this for me because I cannot do it myself. Pen might also help decipher some of it. But it's important to me. So here goes:*

- *Seattle – Leave a little bit of me with Charlie so we can keep each other company. I never liked the idea of him being all alone up there.*

- *From our Honeymoon – The Giant's Causeway in Northern Ireland. The surf is so violent and seems to be a place of creation. Beginnings and Endings. Maybe I'll come back as a faerie.*

- *Edinburgh, Scotland – Climb to the top of Arthur's Seat. Remember when we took the kids there? I want to have some of me find the wind and blow out over Edinburgh.*

- *Greece – Take me to Paros. We took that boat out so the kids could play on the white sand and swim. I want to be sprinkled in the sea there. In the blue water, floating to the white sandy bottom.*

- *Cyprus – I want to go to Aia Napa. You can sprinkle me in the water or on the beach. And toast me with some ouzo in the square where all the college kids party.*

- *The San Juan Islands – take me out in a boat, maybe to where the orcas are, and place me on the water. Listen to the seagulls. I'll be there. If you can't find a boat, you can take the ferry to Orcas Island and pitch me off the back. I'll be just as happy.*

- *Aix en Provence, France – With a thousand ancient fountains and the honey color light. No wonder Cezanne was so inspired to paint it. Find a Roman fountain in which to place me on Cours Mirabeau. And light a candle for me in Paroisse Cathedrale Saint Sauveur. It's a place of great significance. When you go, you will feel it and understand.*

- *A sheep farm in The Basque Country – Spain – I can't tell you how to get there, but Pen might be able to help you find it. I want to be sprinkled in the most beautiful rose garden I have ever smelled beneath the lavender roses.*

- *Castrojeriz, Spain. – I don't have a good reason for this, but I loved that place. It is something special.*

- *The courtyard in the home of Mateo and Javier Silva in Madrid – I was happy there. I want a bit of me to rest there. The exact spot doesn't matter.*

*Whatever is left, you can do what you want with me. But know that after you do these things, I will be at peace, And, my darling, I hope you will be at peace, too. You gave me everything with your whole, flawed heart, and I forgive you as I pray you forgive me. I was loved, and I loved. That is all we can ask for in this life. I'll be with you as you travel to these places – giving you strength.*

*All my Love*
*~Tess*

John broke down, and when he looked up, the others were crying, too. Javier embraced him. Perhaps it should have felt weird, but they had been through a lot in the last two weeks and were slowly learning to trust each other.

Mateo had his arm around Pen as she wiped her eyes.

'So, the rose garden then.' she said bravely to the group. 'Let's go.'

They filed out silently as Javier led them around the back and through the protesting iron gate in the ancient stone wall into a well-tended rose garden cultivated over many years. The verdant roses were at the end of the season, but the vines had remaining blooms.

'My uncle loved this garden. He spent a lot of time cross-developing different varieties. There are roses here that grow nowhere else in the world.'

He turned to Pen.

'Some of the flowers from your and Mateo's wedding party at the winery came from here. *Tio* Diego would have been very proud to have supplied them. He bred them for beauty, but more than that, he bred them for fragrance. Even so late in the season, their fragrance hangs in the air.'

John walked to a lavender rose that was still in full bloom. Tess loved lavender. He bent down to smell it, and the scent was like a basket of ripe raspberries. Javier watched him as he closed his eyes as if to memorize the smell—the perfect place to put Tess, a person unlike any other.

He turned to invite the others to enjoy it. They each did so in turn and agreed it was the right spot. John pulled the bag of ashes from his pack and opened the top. He set it on the ground and took out a small handful.

'I want to say something.' said Pen.

She took a deep breath.

'Mom. We know you're here with us today. After dragging me to Spain as a grumpy teenager, you fell in love with this country and made me fall in love with it, too. It changed my life, and I never thought of thanking you for all you did for me. Even when I didn't make it easy for you, if it weren't for you, I wouldn't have the life I have. I wouldn't have Mateo. After all this time, your hand reaches me. I know you're here guiding me, and I'm grateful. But it's time for you to go and be at peace. Little by little, we are letting you go. It won't happen all at once, but I know it will happen.'

Tears poured down her face, and her bottom lip quivered as Mateo squeezed her hand.

'Don't worry, we will never forget you and Charlie. Ever. Take care of each other up there. Know that Dad and I are doing okay down here.'

She turned and buried her face in Mateo's chest. Tears ran down his face as he wrapped his arms around his wife. John stood with a small handful of ashes.

'Tess. Your list is long, and I know I'm starting in the middle, but I guess I needed some support to begin the process. You would not believe who I'm doing this with.' he stopped and wiped his eyes. 'Okay, maybe you would. You know me pretty well. I made it to the sheep farm you described. I'm not sure how, but we're in the garden where you wanted me to go. And we've found a flower that pretty much sums you up. It is one of a kind, and it even smells good, just like you. There hasn't been a day that has passed that I haven't thought of you. A morning in the last ten years that I haven't woken up and rolled over for a moment believing you would be there. But Pen is right. It's time we let you go. You're not of this world anymore, and we need to let you fly away.' John choked up. 'I will love you to the end of time with every fiber of my being, my darling girl.'

John bent down, placing her ashes at the base of the rose bush, then standing up. Just then, a blue butterfly landed on a petal. It sat there for a moment, its wings opening and closing. Then it flew away. Javier wiped his tears. A sign, if there ever was one, that she was ready to be on her way.

Pen reached over and hugged her dad. Then she turned to Javier and hugged him, too. He smiled when she pulled away with her hand on the blue butterfly necklace she'd worn every day since her mother's passing — the *something blue* from her wedding day.

'I think we should have a glass of wine and a toast in the garden before we go back to the vineyard.' offered Javier. 'I will get a bottle. Everyone, have a seat.'

The group found chairs and sat down. Javier returned with a bottle of rosé and glasses. After handing them out, he poured the wine, then joined them, looking out over the valley.

'To Tess.' he said, raising his glass.

'To Tess.' they replied in unison as sheep bleated in the background, joining in on their toast—the music of a farm.

'It's beautiful here. Will you retire to the farm?' John asked.

'Not full-time. I'm going to be here a lot more often, though. Manuel has done a good job, but I don't want to be an absent farmer. And my uncle could use some help at the winery. He is nearly too old to run the place.'

'It's a nice life.' said John. 'Peaceful.'

'I don't know if I would call it peaceful. It's hectic at times, but it's got a predictable cadence, like the tides. You know when it will be busy and when it will be quiet, like now. The lambing is over here, and it's not the shearing season. We milk regularly and contribute to a co-op that makes cheese from sheep milk, but that's just the daily business of running the farm.'

John swirled the pink liquid in his glass.

'Is this your wine from the vineyard? I like it.'

'Yes. It is my family's wine. Later, we will walk down to Isabela's, and you will have a treat. Her vineyard is small, but they make very, very good wine sought after by collectors. It is limited in production, so the prices are quite high. Sometimes, she graces me with a bottle, and I save it for special occasions. But we will have the rare opportunity to drink it tonight at the harvest party.'

The group discussed Pen's new job at the museum in Madrid. And how Mateo was getting on taking over Javier's practice. After turning the discussion to the mundane, Pen composed herself and suggested they return to the winery. John picked up the daypack containing Tess's ashes and walked over to the lavender rose bush, bending to take in the scent for a final time. Then he turned silently and made his way out the gate. Pen took her time and was the last to leave the garden. When she returned to the truck, she carried a lavender rose cut from the bush where her mother rested.

They rode back in silence. Lunch was ready when they arrived, but John excused himself and climbed the stairs. His broken heart ached like an open wound. The emergency room doctor in Logroño was right. How could he continue on the Camino?

# SEVENTEEN
## TO NEW BEGINNINGS

It was early evening before a knock at the door awakened him. Javier stood in the door frame.

'Is everything alright?' he asked John. 'Can I do anything for you?'

'No. I'm fine. I was sleeping. I just needed some time alone.'

'I understand,' Javier assured him. 'We are going to walk down to Isabela's. You can come now, or you can stay here. It's up to you.'

John sat up, running his hand through his gray hair, smoothing it down, then rubbing his prickly chin.

'Do I need to get myself scrubbed up for this party? I haven't shaved in a while, and maybe I should change my clothes.'

'This isn't that type of party.' said Javier. 'No changing clothes or shaving is required.' He ran his hand over his own grey stubble.

'Okay.' sighed John. 'Can you give me 15 minutes?'

'How about a half hour?' offered Javier. 'That should give you plenty of time. I have something I wanted to do before we go.'

'Perfect.' said John, pushing back the duvet. 'I'll meet you guys downstairs in a half hour.'

Javier shut the door. John closed his eyes and lay back down. Today was almost more than he could bear, but after the nap, he felt better. Placing the first handful of Tess in the rose garden and checking off one of the places on her list broke the dam of his inertia. The first step was always the hardest, and John had taken it. He was moving forward. Slowly, yes, but forward, nonetheless.

Sometimes, the hardest things to do are the right things to do, but it takes courage. John was glad Pen and Mateo had come with him. And even Javier. He wasn't alone in his grief and didn't have to do this by himself. Rolling over, John felt the daypack lying next to him. He had clung to it since leaving Arizona, never letting it out of his sight. But part of Tess wasn't there anymore. And tonight, he would attend the party without it.

In the bathroom, John ran water over his hair. He decided to change his shirt, even though Javier said it wasn't necessary. John was sitting outside when the others arrived, ready to depart.

His tall daughter looked lovely. Pen wore her light brown hair in a loose bun. Her robin's egg blue sundress complimented the blue eyes she inherited from her mother. He saw she was barefoot, carrying sandals. She smiled at his surprise.

'I'll wear rubber boots and then change. It will be dusty on the walk down.'

John had chosen to wear his hiking sandals. He was tired of the boots he wore every day on the trail, and this change of pace was welcome.

The sun made its way over the horizon, casting long shadows as they went. Like Isabela, John could almost taste fall in the air. Something that didn't happen in the desert where he lived.

'Where do Isabela's grapes start and the other vineyard's end?' asked John.

'A little bit over that rise.' pointed Pen. 'Then we'll head down towards the house.'

They walked for 15 minutes more, cresting a hill with a view of Isabela's property. John saw a more extensive operation than he had expected. Nearby sat a stone house with a tiled roof and a large patio surrounded by a wall. From their spot on the hill, he could see over and into the courtyard, where a collection of comfortable chairs circled a large fire pit. It was shaded in the afternoon sun by olive trees planted near the house in large pots. In anticipation of the evening festivities, long wooden trestle tables were placed on the terrace and covered with white tablecloths. The staff brought out chairs and dishes for the harvest celebration.

To the right of the house were buildings nestled into the hillside. He had seen this before in Napa Valley, using the earth as a natural temperature-controlled environment for aging wine. These would be cool caves filled with barrels.

Behind the house sat large barns and outbuildings, housing tanks to hold the young grape juice as Isabela looked to get the chemistry just right before transferring it to the oak barrels for aging. This area was a hive of activity that would probably continue over the next several weeks.

They walked down the hill through the vines and entered the large iron gate in the wall. Javier led them through formidable wooden doors and into the cool interior of the house, with flagstone floors and vaulted-timbered ceilings. Isabela's unexpected house was decorated in a casual California style. It had a decidedly American vibe with overstuffed grey-blue sofas framing tall windows overlooking the vineyard. A large stone fireplace dominated the room and, combined with the sofas, would make it a nice place to read a book on a cold winter day.

'Ah!.' said Isabela, appearing from nowhere, clapping her hands together. 'You have come at last.'

John turned to see their hostess emerge from the back of the house. Isabela wore a sleeveless white cotton sheath dress that poured over her knees. Around her neck were draped turquoise strands that shone against her mocha skin. Gladiator sandals zig-zagged up her tanned calves, and her salt and pepper hair fell in loose curls down her back, with waves framing her face.

She kissed Javier and Mateo on both cheeks and hugged Pen. Then she turned to John and smiled, reaching out her hand to squeeze his as she had done by his bedside in the hospital a few days before.

'You're most welcome to our little get-together. I like celebrating accomplishments, and the harvest is always the year's biggest accomplishment. Everyone is coming in the next hour or so, but we can enjoy a drink before they arrive.'

She led them to the other side of the house and out through a pair of French doors to a large stone patio. Groupings of comfortable outdoor sofas and chairs with fluffy white cushions dotted the flagstones, along with a drinks cart positioned off to the side.

'This is my favorite place. I get to keep my eye on the fields, and in the morning, I can greet the sunrise with my coffee. Please sit, and I will get us all something to drink.'

Isabela rummaged in the drinks cart, pulling a bottle from the back covered in dust. She wiped it off with a dishcloth, holding it up, when Javier gasped.

'You are going to open *that* bottle?' he said, eyebrows raised.

John wasn't sure what they were talking about. The bottle looked old, and the label cracked and yellowed. He couldn't read the writing, but it looked like a hand-written script. The neck of the bottle was sealed in the old way with dripping red wax.

'Why not?' said Isabels with enthusiasm. 'My forefathers made wine to be drunk — to enjoy it with family and friends. For what I am unsure, I have saved these for far too long. Since some of my favorite people are here, I think we should have some of the good stuff. Besides, you are all my family.' Then, she stopped and looked at John. 'And I hope I have made a new friend.'

John nodded, happy to be included in the group.

Isabela held the bottle out to Javier. 'Why don't you open it for us?'

Javier rose and, reverently, took the bottle. He held it gingerly, examining the label.

'I have drunk this wine before. Upon the occasion of my wedding to Alejandra and Mateo's christening at the church in Navarrete, he smiled at his cousin. 'Then, when Isabela's grandfather and father passed away. It is the flavor of some of the most important moments in my life. This,' he told the assembly, holding up the bottle, 'is a special bottle – an exceptional vintage for special occasions. We are fortunate to be drinking this.'

Javier chipped away the wax, uncorked, and decanted the wine, allowing it to breathe for a few minutes. Smelling the old cork, he handed it to Isabela. She did the same, closing her eyes and smiling. Then she walked to a seated John, gifting him the cork.

'You will keep this cork while you're walking. This wine is one of the first bottles ever produced on this land by my family. It is very, very old, but it has endured and improved with time, just like all of us. Your Camino is about enduring and becoming better. Like the best wine, you will not be the same at the end as you were in the beginning.'

John smelled the cork. Inhaling the yeast, blackberries, and current, he looked up at her, and she smiled. Then Isabela turned and presented a glass to each of them. Javier poured the wine.

Isabela held up her glass. 'To new beginnings.' They all toasted in unison. 'Now, everyone. Close your eyes and take a sip.'

John moaned as the garnet liquid hit his tongue.

'Mmm. That is amazing.' he took another small sip. 'I've never tasted anything like it.'

'That's because there is nothing else like it. Truly rare things are to be cherished and enjoyed. Then, we let them go. I have held on to this particular bottle for a very long time. We are enjoying it tonight, in this moment. And when it is finished, we will taste it on the tongue in our memory.'

She took another sip and looked directly at John. He wasn't sure she was talking about the wine. He wondered how much she knew about why he was here and what the four of them had done at the sheep farm earlier.

Isabela brought out a charcuterie board before the rest of the party arrived. The group was finishing the wine when noise from the court-yard reached them, beckoning them to join the newly arrived guests at the tables set up for the festivities. There would be over a hundred people for dinner, and children of the winery's workers wove in and out of the crowd, with Isabela embracing everyone she met.

John stood off to the side with Pen and Mateo until the two new-lyweds found themselves pulled into the fray with hugs and questions for the young doctor and his new American wife. John wondered if this was what their vineyard wedding reception had been like this summer. The one he thought he had escaped but now wished he had attended.

Everyone took seats around the tables, with roses, rosemary, and lavender dressing their length. John stuck close to those he knew and found a spot. Isabela took the seat across from him and smiled. She picked up a fork and used it as a gong against her wine glass to quiet the crowd. She spoke in Spanish and English to accommodate the languages understood by all the guests.

'Everyone. Thank you all for coming to our harvest celebration. This year presented some challenges with drought, but the grapes look very good, and I think the sugar content is higher than normal, so my hopes are high. I want to thank Ricardo,' she inclined her head. 'who managed many things with grace and poise this season. I would be lost without you.'

A cheer went up, and the crowd turned to a man with tanned, leathery skin who was kissed vigorously on the cheek by a woman beside him.

'I hope you all enjoy the meal and the wine you have produced over the years as a thank you from me. We have more work ahead of us to put this vintage to bed. But we can take a little time right now to smell the roses. Muchas Gracias. Eskerrik Asko. Thank you very much.'

They all raised their glasses. 'Salud' was exchanged as glasses *clinked* against each other. John drank from his and was pleasantly surprised at the wine. It wasn't the rarest ambrosia they had drunk on the back patio. But it was still excellent. This must be the wine they sold commercially, he thought. All these people worked throughout the year to produce the nectar of the gods. They deserved to enjoy it.

Platter after platter made its way outside from the kitchen. The smells were heavenly, and the food was unlike any that John had ever tasted. He was not a fan of lamb, but the meat was perfectly seasoned, the grilled vegetables equally mouthwatering, and the wine improved even more as the evening wore on.

Eventually, someone pulled out a harmonica and an accordion, and they sang songs everyone seemed to know. Well after dark, a guitar emerged, and the dancing started. The raw emotion of the dancers and the music were intoxicating. Perhaps the wine was going to his head. John was engrossed when he felt a tap on his shoulder.

'Dad'

He turned to see Pen and Mateo.

'Sorry. I was watching the dancers. Is everything alright?'

'We're going to walk back to the house. I'm not feeling well, and I'm tired.'

'Do you want me to come with you?' he asked, concerned about his daughter.

'No. Stay and enjoy tonight.' Pen leaned down and kissed his cheek. 'We will see you in the morning.'

His daughter and her husband walk off into the night as a wave of melancholy overtook him. She wasn't his to take care of anymore. That was Mateo's job now.

John turned to find Isabela topping off his glass, smiling.

'What is it?' he asked.

'I like watching you. You seemed very engrossed in the music and the dance before.'

'I've never seen this type of dancing. The guy on the guitar is talented.'

'He is the brother of my estate manager. He's a professional, actually, and is well-known in the area. He likes to come to these gatherings for the wine, so he sings for his supper at our harvest celebration every year.'

John surveyed the crowd.

'I haven't seen Javier in a while. Do you know where he is?'

'He left to take our Aunt and Uncle home. They didn't want to drive in the dark.'

John looked out into the darkness. 'Is he coming back?'

'I don't know. Perhaps. But you can stay for our bonfire. We will be lighting it soon. I always think of it as a pagan offering to the gods for a good harvest.'

Drinking wine since early evening, John felt the effects. He wouldn't try to return on his own to the big house until he sobered up.

The workers lit the bonfire, and the dancing ended. Now, it was just the guitar player and the fire. A chill descended in the night air, and families with small children faded into the shadows to get them to bed. Only a few people remained. They chatted and smoked, enjoying the last of the wine. John found the combination of the flames and the guitar haunting and intoxicating. The wine didn't hurt.

Isabela sat on one of the oversized garden chairs wrapped in a blanket.

'So how did you like our little dinner?' she asked, taking another sip of wine.

'Little dinner' is not what that was. A banquet fit for a king.'

Isabela chuckled. 'This is small compared to Pen and Mateo's wedding reception. I didn't see you at their party here in June.'

'That is because I didn't go.' said John sheepishly. 'I had other commitments in the US. But, I went to the wedding and the reception in Madrid.'

'Yes. I know. I saw you there. You looked happy and proud during the ceremony. But very uncomfortable at the party. Almost sad. I watched you.' she whispered. 'I'm not sure why.'

Isabela's admission made John uneasy — as if he were an exhibit in a zoo. This woman had no idea who he was. She had no clue what he had been through and how much it had taken for him to go to Madrid and sleep in Javier's house. John raised a glass at their reception after the ceremony, pretending it didn't bother him. All for his daughter's happiness. It took everything he had. But that was behind him now.

'I was just out of my element as one of the only non-Spanish-speaking people there. Maybe it was the language barrier. I think most fathers feel a little sad when their daughter marries.'

'Hmm. Perhaps.' a beat or two passed. 'Would you like to see my caves?'

'Excuse me?' said John, taken aback.

'Where we store the barrels and the wine. Would you like to see it?'

'Okay. Sure. I imagine it's impressive.'

'It is.' she held out her hand. 'Come.'

They rose. Isabela said something to the remaining guests. He wasn't sure what it was, but it wasn't the usual 'Buenas noches.' They walked silently together in the dark, leaving the lights of the gardens around the house. John had no idea where he was going, but he assumed Isabela knew the way by heart. Suddenly, he tripped on a tree root, and she reached to steady him by grasping his hand. He righted himself, but she didn't let go, leading him to the door of the first building.

'My great-grandfather built these buildings. The caves are natural, and while he was poor and had limited building materials, he would change his and his family's fortunes by tripling the size for storing wine by utilizing what the caves provided. The perfect synergy between man and nature. We are grateful to him.'

She unlocked the large wooden door, opened the iron cage that marked the entrance, and turned on the lights. They entered a room containing racks of wine bottles with a large table running down the center. With another flip of a switch, the lights came on deeper inside the hill. Stone arches held the ceiling aloft, supported by pillars like a cathedral. The walls and floors were covered in mortared stones. Indirect lighting made it appear as if it came from deep inside the earth and perfectly illuminated the space. As an engineer, John found the structure ingenious.

Isabela walked further into the hillside, and John followed. The caves were cool but not cold. The earth controlled the temperature perfectly. Eventually, they emerged into a much larger room filled with barrel racks. It smelled wonderfully musty – chemistry in action. The marriage of the oak barrels, yeast, and grape juice. The alchemy she had spoken of before.

'It's impressive. If your great-grandfather built this, he did it with rudimentary tools and without modern engineering. I'm a structural engineer. I can't imagine undertaking something like this without everything I have at my disposal today. Amazing.'

Isabela smiled as she ran her long fingers along the wall, and John followed her. 'Sometimes, experience triumphs over education.' She walked to a barrel and patted it.

'I never had children, but each year, the wine is my baby. These barrels are the incubators of the dreams I have with every harvest. Some are realized, and some are not. Potential is just that. Nothing until it blossoms into reality.'

She turned back to John.

'Why are you walking the Camino?' she asked quietly.

John frowned, taken aback by the abrupt change in the conversation.

'What do you mean?' he asked, playing with the bracelet the monk had left for him in the Pyrenees. 'I just decided to walk it.'

She shook her head.

'No one *just walks* the Camino. Everyone has a reason. I am very interested in yours.'

John closed his eyes. It had been an emotional morning. Maybe he had drunk too much. Hell, he had a glass of wine in his hand right now.

'I am walking for my wife: my late wife, Tess. Pen's mother.' he corrected himself. It was a term he had never used. 'She passed away ten years ago from cancer and asked that her ashes be spread in different places around the world. Some of them were on the Camino. Javier agreed to help me find them. I'm walking for her.'

Isabela studied him.

'Hmm.' she acknowledged. 'A noble thing. A quest of sorts. I met her once. Did you know that? When they were here – she and Pen.'

John held his breath. He knew that this was where the affair had started. He wasn't sure what Isabela knew.

'And why does my cousin have a hint of a black eye?'

'What?' asked John, unready to discuss his bad behavior.

'My cousin is walking with you to help you spread your wife's ashes. You are both the fathers of Mateo and Pen, so this is plausible. But why does Javier have a black eye? I imagine how he got it, perhaps as far back as Pamplona, was something serious.'

John blanched. Was she a gypsy? What was she playing at?

'Did you ask him?'

'Yes.' she said. 'But now I'm asking you.'

He took a deep breath.

'I hit him.' whispered John.

'Oh, I know you did.' she smiled.

'Did he tell you that?'

'No. But I would know anyway. Your left hand still has bruises. You are left-handed.'

She's clever – he thought.

'I had too much to drink. And I was upset about something. I took it out on Javier.'

Isabela looked at him with an uncomfortable intensity as she weighed his words.

'And what were you upset about?'

'It was nothing.' dismissed John, searching the cave for something to change the subject.

Isabels stared at John like she could see through him, running her index finger absentmindedly over a barrel.

'You see, you strike me as a man who doesn't give in to reckless impulses. You are measured. Controlled. A bit of an enigma, if I am honest. A man not easily bated into a fight. And I see that you don't have a mark on your face. My cousin is younger than you. He could have struck back, but he didn't.' She waited for him to fill in the blanks.

'My wife, Tess.' he stopped and closed his eyes. 'My wife slept with Javier when they walked the Camino together.'

John had never spoken the words out loud before. It was like a dam broke, and he exhaled the breath he had held for over ten years. He had finally said it. Tears rolled down his face, but Isabela stayed where she was. She didn't attempt to comfort him.

'So, ten years later, you are walking the Camino to deposit the ashes of your wife with her lover? Wow.' Her face registered surprise. 'I have heard of evolved men, but you are one of a kind. I want to say it's because you're American, but when I was there, I found they were no different than Spanish men. Perhaps worse, actually. Because so many pretended not to be. *Machismo* is everywhere.'

He laughed, whipping his tears with his shirt. Then, he took a long pull on his wine.

'Maybe you knew the wrong men.'

'Come here.' she whispered.

He hesitated, then walked over to her, afraid as she cupped his face.

'You are a brave man, John Sullivan.' she kissed his lips lightly. 'Tonight, you will stay with me.'

He didn't resist as she led him out of the building and shut the door. When they returned to the house, the rest of the guests were gone, but the front door hung open. She led him inside and up the stairs to a large bedroom overlooking the terrace.

'Listen.' said John. 'This has been an emotional day. It's been so long, I don't even know if I'm up for this anymore.'

Isabela laughed.

'We are not going to have sex tonight, John. Sleeping with a woman isn't always about sex. Lay down and rest.' A shadow passed across her face. 'You aren't alone, you know, in heartbreak.'

John removed his shirt and pants, then lay under the duvet as he watched Isabela slowly remove her jewelry and unlace her sandals from her tanned calves. She pulled her dress over her head, and she unlatched her bra before sliding in next to him and laying her head on his chest.

'I wouldn't have sex with you tonight, even if you wanted to.' she declared.

John laughed, a bit nervous at this unpredictable woman. Laying in this bed with a topless Isabela was the closest he had come to another woman since Tess's death.

'The doctor said you need to take it easy. Besides, you'd required more strength to handle me.' she teased, smiling up at him.

John chuckled. He had no doubt.

'I didn't think you liked me after Logroño.' admitted John. 'After I picked you up at the grape stomping.'

He left out the part about being rushed to the hospital.

'Well, now you know that I like you very much.'

'I do.,' he whispered, 'And I like you, too.'

She smiled, lifting herself and kissing him.

'It's late. Go to sleep and rest. Doctor's orders.'

John slept like he hadn't in years. When he awoke and rolled over, Isabela sat on the edge of the bed as the sun peeked through the curtains.

'Good morning.'

'Mmm. Good morning.' John lifted his arm, and she snuggled in. 'How did you sleep?'

'I have been awake since before sunrise.' said Isabela

'Is it hard to sleep with a strange man in your bed?' asked John.

'No. I find that strange men are the perfect sleep aid.'

'Ah.'

'I'm joking.' she laughed. 'I don't have many strange men in my bed these days. Just American *peregrinos* who are looking for a roll in the hay.'

John studied the ceiling, unsure how he ended up in Isabela's house — in her bed. Even with all the interventions of well-meaning friends, John was as celibate as a monk. Not out of any planned abstinence, it was something he slipped into. And then, it stuck. He just hadn't met someone he wanted to get close to. Or maybe he had never allowed himself to try.

After Tess's death, John had Pen to think about. And he plunged into his work. But, now that Pen lived in Madrid, John didn't see his daughter much anymore. Since retiring last Fall, he had been at loose ends.  He'd played some golf and gone to his college reunion. But life had moved on. After Pen's wedding, he had prepared for and regretted agreeing to this trip. And now he was in bed with this beautiful Spanish winemaking chemist.

'What are you thinking about?'

He took a deep breath before attempting to explain.

'I'm wondering how I ended up here. Yesterday, we gathered at the sheep farm in the rose garden. We sprinkled some of my wife's ashes at the roots of a beautiful lavender rose.' He looked down at Isabela. 'If you had asked me at breakfast where I would be today, I wouldn't have said I would be in the bed of a beautiful woman.'

Isabela smiled.

'Unexpected miracles happen on the Camino. Are you glad you're here? With me?' she asked.

'Yes. I am.' John kissed her hair. 'My head wants me to feel guilty about it. But, somehow, I don't.'

'Then it doesn't matter how it happened. Just that it did.' She tightened her arm around him. 'My mobile has several messages on it. I think perhaps *La Casa Grande* is looking for you, their lost lamb. Would you like to call them?'

John rubbed his eyes.

'Can we have coffee first? I'm not sure how to face my daughter this morning. Yesterday was emotional, and she wasn't feeling well last night. I think because of it.'

'Okay. You get up. There are fresh towels in the bathroom. I will meet you on the terrace with coffee.'

Isabela rose on one arm, leaned over, and kissed John. Then, she got out of bed, knotting her brightly colored silk robe, and disappeared.

John went into the bathroom and closed the door. He almost didn't recognize the person staring back. The man in the mirror had a smile on his face. He looked happy and tanned. For the first time in over a decade, he felt more like himself.

After showering, John found his way down the stairs, passing an aproned girl pushing a noisy vacuum who didn't meet his gaze. It had been years since he'd taken a walk of shame, but it was fun in his 60s to do it without caring who might judge him.

Isabela sat on the terrace, still in her robe, when he emerged fully dressed. As promised, she had a table set with coffee and breakfast.

'Wow.' he said, surprised. 'You are fast.'

'I have someone who cooks for me. She was waiting to do all this when I came down. I am a better farmer and chemist than a cook. According to my mother, the domestic arts were one of my weaknesses.' She crossed herself and kissed the tips of her fingers.

'You have other talents.' he smiled.

She raised her coffee cup.

'As you say, I hope they still work.'

John put some sugar in his coffee and tucked into the meal in front of him. Then, he called Pen.

'Where are you?' she asked in a frantic voice. 'We've been looking for you everywhere and called Isabela a hundred times with no answer. I've been worried sick.'

'I stayed at Isabela's last night. There was no way I could find my way home in the dark after all that wine.'

His daughter sniffed.

'I'm outside her front door right now, so we can speak in person.' she said, playing the angry parent.

John gulped. 'Alright. We're on the back terrace eating breakfast. Come through.'

A moment later, Pen and Mateo stood next to the table. Pen's arms crossed in front of her.

'What's going on?' she asked.

'Nothing. I'm eating. Want some coffee?'

John offered Pen a seat at the table.

'I had coffee up at the house.'

'Mateo?' John asked his son-in-law.

'Sure.' This response got him a glare from Pen. 'I'll text my father and let him know we found you.'

Isabela tried to intervene.

'I'm so sorry. I slept in this morning and didn't see your texts and calls until a few minutes ago. That's why your father didn't call you back. We all had a late night and, perhaps, a little more wine than we should.'

Pen turned back to her dad.

'Javier thought you guys were leaving today. He was up and ready to go, but we couldn't find you when I checked your room, and you hadn't slept in your bed.'

'I stayed for the bonfire.' Taking another drink of his café con leche to delay telling the lie he would inevitably have to tell. 'Unless I was willing to allow Isabela to drive drunk or wander lost in the vines, I figured I should stay here. She was gracious enough to host me.' he smiled at her, and she beamed back at him. Their exchange seemed to unnerve Pen.

'I am a little surprised, that's all.' Pen lifted her chin defiantly. 'I wouldn't have thought you would be up for partying so late after depositing Mom's ashes in the rose garden yesterday. But I guess I was wrong.'

Her words stung John. He closed his eyes, and Isabela instinctively reached over and squeezed his hand.

'I had too much to drink. Perhaps I shouldn't have, but I did. It was a hard day yesterday for both of us.' John rose, wrapping his arms around Pen. She hugged him back and pulled away with a quivering bottom lip.

'Now sit down and have some coffee.' he said, pointing to his cup, 'This is the best coffee I've had so far in Spain. You need to enjoy it. And eat something. You look like you could use it.'

'What are you now?' asked Pen, finally smiling back. 'A Spanish grandmother?'

Isabela went to the kitchen and returned with two more cafes con leche. Pen did little more than sip hers. Finally, Mateo took it from her and drank the rest. She appeared miserable when he handed her a croissant.

Javier arrived as they were finishing up.

'I guess we will not be walking today.' observed the doctor, 'That is fine with me. I'm glad you found a place to sleep.' Looking over at Isabela, who turned away conveniently, 'We were worried you became lost among the vines.'

'Nope.' said John, 'I am healthy and rested. I haven't slept that well in years. Must be the Camino and the fresh air out here.'

'Must be.' said Isabela into her coffee cup.

The bruise around Javier's eye was barely visible today. When she arrived from Madrid, Pen asked her dad what happened to her father-in-law, but he wasn't ready to admit what he'd done. The earlier tension had eased after they had spread some of Tess's ashes.

'So, what is on the agenda for today?' asked Javier, rubbing his hands together.

'I have the crush.' Isabela declared. 'So, if you will excuse me, I must shower and get out to the sheds. If anyone wants to watch, they're welcome.'

She left them to their breakfast.

'Well, I don't know about anyone else, but that sounds like fun. I've never witnessed the crush before. Learn something new every day.' John rose and went to clear his plate, but Isabela's cook met him at the door.

'I'm in, too.' said Javier, 'It's been a long time since I participated in crushing the grapes. Isabela will need all the help she can get. Mateo? Pen?'

Mateo spoke up. 'Pen isn't feeling well. I'll come with you, though.'

The three men made their way out of the house and down to the sheds. Isabela strode down to the main barn shortly after them, her hair in a braid and her old straw hat perched on her head. The operation had been underway since early morning, and her foreman, Ricardo, appeared to have everything in hand. As the crew fed the grapes into the de-stemmer, Isabela tasted some fruit.

'What can we do to help?' Javier and John wanted to know.

'I need to meet with Ricardo to map out the day. Can you please help keep this all going? The two guys who are feeding the grapes need a break. They've been at it since sunrise. I'll be back after I've gone over everything with Ricardo.'

Javier explained to the two men that they could get a coffee and take a break. Mateo climbed up on the truck and began filling the plastic tubs the men were using. He handed them down to Javier and John, and they filled the machines that were running side by side. They made good progress before Isabela came out.

'I have a problem with a couple of the tanks. I need one of the guys who was feeding the de-stemmer to work on the tanks. Ricardo wants the other one to punch. Luckily, you are here, and if you don't mind, I can use your help today.'

'Of course.' said John. 'Whatever you need us to do.'

Isabela squeezed his arm.

'I'm glad you didn't walk the Camino today.'

'Me too.' he smiled down at her.

A look passed between Javier and Mateo, but they said nothing. The three men kept at it and unloaded another trailer of grapes after they had finished the first. It was after 2 pm before they realized they hadn't eaten lunch. Isabela came by to remedy it.

'The tables are set up in the courtyard. I've asked everyone to stop and have something to eat. Come up and join us. It's simple food, but it will keep us going for the rest of the day.'

They walked up to the house and found the tables in the shade, crowded with some of the people they met last night. It surprised John to learn that many of the winery workers were from other European countries and had come to Spain to look for work during the harvest. It wasn't just his imagination or the wine the previous night that the words he heard weren't languages he was familiar with. No matter. Each person was as valuable as the next on a farm.

The meal of hard, crusty bread, a stew of vegetables, and the leftover lamb from the previous night filled their bellies. No wine was served with lunch, as they worked on machinery that could take off a hand. But by the end of lunch, they were ready for the afternoon. Before returning to work, Isabela asked if John might help her lift something.

'Sure. Lead the way.'

She led him back to the barrel house they had gone in the night before. She shut the door behind them.

'I wish you were not leaving tomorrow. I would like to have you stay here with me. At least for a little while. I think you need to rest.'

'I wish there were more time, but I have to go.' he told her regretfully. 'There are some things to take care of. Important things. But I've enjoyed the time we've spent together.'

John gazed into her melted chocolate-brown eyes. When they met just a few days before, he found her instantly attractive but intimidating. She was strong in a vulnerable way. A contradiction he couldn't explain.

'Will you come back here, do you think?' she asked.

'To the winery? I don't know. Do you want me to?'

Isabela nodded. 'Yes. I would.'

She reached up and stroked his cheek. Then, she got on her tiptoes and lightly kissed him. The kiss deepened before she pulled away.

'Let's see what the Camino holds.' said John, unconsciously touching his lips where hers had just been. 'I have no idea what the next month looks like. I'm like a leaf in the wind right now.'

Isabela took his hand and led him outside. They locked the door behind them, returning to the barns where Javier and Mateo were still loading grapes into the machine. Isabela clasped his hand until they were in sight of the sheds.

'I'll see you later. Come to the house before you go. I want to be able to say goodbye.'

John agreed, swallowing the lump that formed in his throat. He walked back down and began pitching the grapes into the de-stemmer again. But not before catching a glimpse of Isabela walking back up to the house.

By early evening, the men were exhausted. They had done several truck-loads and needed a shower and a good night's rest. Fully aware he had ignored the doctor's advice, his back began to let him know he'd overdone it.

Javier and Mateo sat in the chairs in the courtyard with stained hands and clothes as John knocked on the door to the house to let Isabela know they were heading over the hill. Isabela opened the door, removing her glasses as she waved him inside.

'So, you are heading back.'

'Yes. It's been a very long day.' he smiled. 'But we need to get cleaned up. We're on the trail tomorrow.'

Isabela scanned his face. For what he was unsure.

'Well then, I'll wish you *Buen Camino* now. Stay safe.'

She got on her tiptoes and kissed him. John wrapped his arms around her, smiling like a teenager.

'I will. Good luck with the crush.' Said John, heading for the door.

'John.'

He turned back.

'When you get to Santiago, perhaps we can see each other again. If there is time before you go back home.'

He smiled. 'Perhaps.'

Isabela followed him outside to give Javier and Mateo a hug.

'Come see me when you are here next time checking on the farm. I would like to hear how you fared on the trail.'

'Noski' – of course.

'Thank you for all your help today,' she told them.

They waved, marching back up the hill. When they got to the ridge, John turned around and saw Isabela still there, arms wrapped around herself, waiting for them to disappear.

# Eighteen

## Dirty Laundry

The house in Madrid was quiet without Pen, Javier, and Mateo as Ines made her way down the dark hallway on the second floor. Dressed in her worn plaid cotton apron, in her arms, she held a wicker basket of clean laundry nearly as tall as she was. At 75, climbing the giant mahogany staircase with such a load was becoming more challenging, but she wasn't ready to admit it to herself or her employers just yet.

After depositing clean laundry in Mateo and Pen's bedroom, Ines nudged the door open to Javier's room and set her basket of folded clothes on the carpet. The colorful Moroccan rugs matched the heavy bed curtains, which she noticed needed to be sent out and cleaned. Was Inez losing her touch? Or perhaps she just needed to wear the glasses the eye doctor prescribed. Vanity, she chuckled—the downfall of more than one gray-haired old woman.

Ines had known Javier since he was a boy. First as housekeeper to his parents, Doña María and Don Eduardo, and then to Javier and his wife, Alejandra. In all that time, Ines had seen Javier's calm demeanor rattled only a few times. But in the days before he left, Javier was unsettled about his Camino with John.

After the death of his wife, Alejandra, their relationship as employer and employee fell away entirely as she took care of him and his son, Mateo. Until they healed, their unrelenting grief made for a heart-breaking few years. But Javier and Mateo finally found their way back to each other after they walked together from France to Santiago de Compostela. The two men were her family as much as if they shared the same blood.

Ines took the clothes from the basket and put them in their proper place in the armoire. She had been there since he was a child for every stage of Javier's life, starting when he played with toy cars in the nursery of his parents' enormous penthouse on the other side of town. A quiet boy, he was no trouble back then. Inez often made him her special sweets, cleaning cuts and bruises when he returned home from school with skinned knees and more than a few tears. Years later, she listened when Javier's heart broke for the first time over a girl in high school. Ines remembered it like it was yesterday. That afternoon, she was standing in the kitchen cooking when he came through the door. The skinny teenager opened every cupboard and the refrigerator, distracted.

Meanwhile, Ines remained silent, stirring the pot on the stove, pretending nothing was amiss. She knew Javier would speak when he was ready. Finally, it all came tumbling out.

It happened again one year on the Christmas holidays when Javier was home from university and fell in love with Alejandra, but he was afraid to tell his mother. Ines smiled at the memory and the irony that their son, Mateo, would grow up with a temperament precisely like his father's. Even as a youngster, Javier was kind, taking Ines's son, Antonio, under his wing and treating him like a little brother.

This time, Javier needed Ines's ear again before leaving on his latest Camino with John. Like that day in the kitchen so long ago, Ines knew the best thing to do was to remain quiet while pretending to be otherwise occupied. Eventually, he would fill the silence.

'I'm sorry, Ines.' Javier sighed while standing in this very room, packing for his trip. 'I don't know what's wrong with me.'

Ines raised a grey eyebrow but said nothing.

'Alright.' he admitted, 'Maybe I do know.'

Ines pretended not to hear him and continued folding the laundry on his bed as he packed his backpack.

'Why am I doing this? Am I crazy?' he called out to the ceiling.

Ines finished folding a t-shirt he would need for his trek. 'You know why you're going on this trip.' she reminded him. 'Tess asked you to, and you will go for her.'

Javier sighed.

'I know.' he said quietly, 'But I don't see how this will end well. John doesn't like me very much, and I understand why. What good is going to come from this?'

Ines pursed her lips.

'It should have taken place long ago.' she reminded him. 'That's what Tess wanted. But things happen at the right time, not always when we wish. I believe that. Besides, you and John are family now.'

Javier didn't appear convinced, gazing out the window at the long shadows cast by the plane trees planted on the sidewalk.

'I'm worried it will tear our family apart.' he said thoughtfully. 'If I were a psychologist, I would use this as an example of psychosis or masochism.'

Ines continued her work in silence.

'I could offer to drive him.' as if he were negotiating with himself. 'We could complete this in just a few days, or even a week, and still fulfill Tess' wish.'

The housekeeper shook her head. 'That is not what she wanted. She asked you to promise to walk with John. Tess knew he would need the Camino to heal after her death. Now, the time is right.'

Javier cleared his throat. 'And what about Pen and Mateo? Neither of them thinks this is a good idea.'

Ines hesitated before responding.

'I don't mean to seem unfeeling, but it isn't up to them. You and John are grown men. I've known you since you were in short pants, Javier. You are a good man. An honest man. You know the right thing to do. You are leaving on the train tomorrow, and John will meet you in France. The wheels are in motion. The Camino has secrets to reveal. For you both.'

# NINETEEN

## CHESS IS LIFE

The following morning before sunrise, Javier and John were awake and ready to head out. Pen and Mateo, still in their pajamas, woke up to see them off. John donned his tattered baseball hat before hugging his daughter longer than usual.

'Thank you both for coming.' John said gratefully. 'You made it easier.'

Her mood lighter; Pen playfully punched her dad's shoulder.

'Of course, we came. It was important. For all of us.' Pen reached up and tugged on her father's old cap. 'Your dad's *Cubs* hat. Bet you're the only one on the Camino with one of those.'

John reached up for the bill like a touchstone.

'It brings me luck, I think.'

'I still have Charlie's.' she said quietly.

Pen looked from her father to Javier and back like a mother bear and wagged her finger.

'Be safe on the trail. And keep me up-to-date on where you are. I know there are other places you'll be putting Mom's ashes. I can't be there, but take a picture and send it to me. Or, better yet, a video.'

'I will.' he kissed her cheek, and with a wave, they set off to meet back up with the Camino.

The men walked silently in the dark, awaiting the sunrise. John thought about Isabela. She looked like a lost child when he left her at the door the day before. The winemaker was fiery and didn't strike him as someone who needed anyone. But with her, he felt a tug. After grape stomping in Logroño, he was sure she disliked him, but she had come to the hospital and was friendly when they got to the vineyard. At the party, she was *more* than friendly. The lovely Isabela was a complicated woman.

'It was good to see Pen and Mateo these past few days.' observed Javier, breaking John from his musings.

'I didn't realize how much I missed her until I saw Pen. Being on the Camino in the same country makes me feel like she isn't so far away. But it is hard being in the US and not a part of her day-to-day.'

'I can imagine.' Javier sympathized. 'Perhaps you can spend more time with her at our home.' he offered. 'I know she is still settling into life in Madrid. And a new job. It might be good for her to have you close by.'

'Maybe. I just don't want Pen to think I am interfering. She's a grown woman with a husband. I don't want her to feel like I'm hovering over her.'

They walked further down the trail.

'I understand.' said Javier, 'I guess we think of things differently here. We aren't as concerned about *interfering* as you are in America. But it is an adjustment for both of you—her new life in a new country. And you being retired and without family close by. Pen still needs you, John. And I think you need her.'

John shifted his pack uncomfortably.

'Is there something you are trying to say?' John asked him.

Javier took a deep breath.

'No. I just want to make sure everyone is doing well. And that you feel you can come and visit whenever you like. We are perfectly happy to have you for as long as you wish.'

John kept up the pace.

'I appreciate that. How do you think Pen is doing with her new job?' asked John. Pen's illness over the previous few days nagged at him.

'I think it can be an adjustment to make friends and a career for yourself in a new culture. Cultural idiosyncrasies that you are not as familiar with can be a barrier. I have never lived in another country, but I can imagine that it comes with unique challenges. I am unsure if Pen is comfortable discussing such things with us. Perhaps she would feel more inclined to talk to her father about it.'

'Noted.' John frowned. 'Are you saying Pen is having a hard time?'

Javier shook his head.

'No. I am not saying that. Pen hasn't said anything to me about it. I just want to make sure she feels supported.'

This topic was uncomfortable for both of them. Javier went in a different direction as the lights from the village came into view.

'Anyway, we are almost to Ventosa. I must check on a house Ines, my housekeeper, inherited from her parents. She asked if I would make sure that it was still unoccupied. *Okupas*, squatters, are a big problem in Spain. Especially for empty rural houses.'

'That's fine.' said John. 'I wouldn't mind getting another coffee there, too. Today is rougher than I thought it would be. I'm beat.'

After helping at the winery the day before, a weary Javier agreed.

They arrived at Ventosa as the sun broke over the horizon, and Javier made a couple of wrong turns before locating the right street in the small village. At first, he tried to open the next-door neighbor's front door, but when the old lady came out, she asked him what he wanted.

'Buenos dias. I'm sorry. I am looking for the home of Ines Ybarra. Since we are passing, she asked me to check on the house for her.'

'Buenos dias.' The older woman smiled, wrapping her pink robe tightly against the morning chill. 'I know who you are.'

Javier pulled a face, registering surprise.

'You look just like your brother.' The woman said, 'Or maybe he looks like you.'

'I'm sorry.' Javier scowled. 'You must be mistaken. I don't have a brother.'

The woman shook her grey-haloed head. 'Ines's son. You look a lot like each other. Like your father, I guess.'

The blood drained from Javier's face.

'I don't know what you mean.' Javier said, stunned.

She tapped the side of her nose. 'I think you do.'

Then she pointed next door, turned, and shut her front door. Javier stood frozen in the spot.

'Is everything OK?' John asked, confused. 'You look like you've seen a ghost.'

Javier's hand covered his mouth. As if remembering John was standing there, Javier straightened and coughed.

'Yes. I'm fine. The next house is Ines's.'

But he wasn't fine. Javier had the key Ines had given him and unlocked the door. They entered the home with barred windows on the narrow village street. The small space was like a time capsule with shutters blocking the light. The decor was frozen somewhere in the 1960s. Javier flicked on the fluorescent kitchen light, which flashed in protest as he set his pack down and sank into the kitchen chair.

'Okay. I know something is wrong.' said John. 'What did that woman say to you?'

Javier sat silent as if in a trance. The woman had taken him off guard. His life flashed before his eyes. He was playing with Ines's son, Antonio, in the playroom at the penthouse in Madrid. When she was his parent's housekeeper, Ines would bring Antonio with her on days he didn't have school. Javier teaching Antonio how to ride a bicycle in *El Retiro*—and helping Antonio with his studies when Javier was home from university for the holidays. While Javier studied medicine in Barcelona, Antonio visited him to check out the university. They had gone sailing together. All of his friends asked if this was his 'little brother.'

The story that the boy's father was dead was the only one Javier knew. Antonio's mother, Ines, needed to work to support her son. He felt sorry for Antonio and had taken him under his wing. Javier remembered when his father offered to pay the boy's school fees, 'but only if he keeps up with his studies.' For some reason, this condition hadn't struck Javier as anything unusual. His father was a wealthy doctor, and Ines and her son were like family, at least to him and his father. Ines was just *the help* to Javier's mother, María. The housekeeper's son was an inconvenience, and María tolerated his presence only if he stayed quiet and out of her way when he was in her house.

When his father died, Javier's mother had her son handle all the financial arrangements. María was too distraught, dramatically taking to her bed for days—even weeks, while Javier met with the lawyer about the will. It was in order, but his father had a few unusual bequests. One was for Antonio's schooling and an allowance to pay for expenses. But there was nothing explicitly mentioned for Ines.

Javier hadn't thought about it in a long time. He arranged to have the school fees paid and the allowance deposited for Antonio so he could comfortably finish university. The amount hardly made a dent in the fortune his father had amassed through his work, connections, and investments. Javier never mentioned it to his mother. There was no reason to.

But this? This revelation wasn't anything Javier had ever considered. He knew his father liked Ines. She was good to them. Always very attentive. She ensured Eduardo ate when he became too engrossed in his work. Javier had caught Ines reading his father's medical journals, and after his father's heart attack, she strictly controlled his diet—even the amount of wine he had with dinner. All this, as Javier's mother seemed oblivious, preoccupied as she was in her social circle. But then, maybe Javier had been preoccupied, as well.

'The woman next door mistook me for Ines's son, Antonio.'

'I see.' said John. 'Is he near your age?'

'No. Antonio is much younger than I am.' he explained.

'Well, that lady is old. Maybe her eyesight is going.'

Javier chewed on his bottom lip.

'She said something curious. That it was because Antonio and I are brothers. We both look like our father.'

'I don't understand.' said John, confused.

Javier played with the saltshaker on the table without seeing it.

'I think she was saying that my father is his father.'

John's eyes widened. 'Is that possible?'

'I don't know.' he whispered, distracted. 'I understood his father was dead. It's why Ines worked for us. She needed to support her son. I always knew she came from up here. I know her family from all the times I've come here to visit mine. Sometimes, they would send Antonio with me on the train. We both helped with the grape harvest and occasionally on the sheep farm. My aunts and uncles would spoil us both. His grandparents adored him.'

'Well, that is a bombshell.' John agreed.

'Yes. Quite. I need to think about it before I approach Ines. I want to understand the whole picture and not upset her unnecessarily. If it's true, I wonder if Antonio knows.'

John whistled. 'This is big. Are you alright? Should we stay here tonight?'

Javier bit his lip. 'No. I don't need to stay here. I want to go to the cafe for coffee before we get going.'

They locked up and walked through the warren of narrow streets to the only open cafe. Javier ordered coffee for them both. The elderly bartender asked them where they were from.

'My friend is American. I'm from Madrid.' he said at first. 'Well, actually, my father's family is from here.'

The older man's eyes narrowed.

'You are Eduardo Silva's son. Yes? You look like him and your uncles.' observed the bald man behind the counter.

'You knew my father?'

'Oh yes. It is a small village. Everyone here knows your family — uncles, aunts, grandparents. After your father moved to Madrid, he sometimes had a weekend surgery at the local clinic. He was very useful to the community. He helped my mother's gout and even did a little dentistry.'

The bartender pulled back his wrinkled cheek, and they saw a space where a tooth used to sit. The man smiled.

'Your father was a good man. Popular here. But he got busy in Madrid, and the surgery closed. We were disappointed, but we understood that his reputation and high profile in Madrid kept him there.'

Javier considered the man's description of his father's activities.

'Do you remember Ines Ybarra?'

The man whistled.

'Of course. Ines was a beauty in the village. Everyone thought she would marry one of the local boys, but she went to Madrid. They say she got married there and had a son. I met the child here a few times when he visited his grandparents. He seemed like a good boy. Very handsome.'

Something about the way the man said it made him shudder.

'Do you remember exactly when the surgery shut down?'

'Well.' the man rubbed his chin. 'It was more than 40 years ago. Come to think of it. It was right about the same time that Ines moved to Madrid. I remember because that was the year we had terrible fires here. The smoke was so thick that the doctor said she should move for her health, and he advised her family. Ines had some breathing problems, I think. The next year, your father became too busy with his practice in Madrid to make it up here to open the clinic.'

'Do you still have a clinic?' asked Javier. 'Did another doctor take over?'

The man shook his head.

'No. The building is still there, but we never got another doctor. I know your grandfather had always hoped his son would go to medical school and return to the area to practice medicine. I remember there was someone people thought he would marry, but he didn't. So I don't think anyone was more disappointed than his parents when he stopped coming here to help the people in the village.'

John and Javier finished their coffee and tried to pay the man, but he held up his hands.

'How can I take money from you? Your father never took money from any of his patients. Your coffee here will always be on the house.' he held his hand to his heart. Javier thanked him as they donned their packs and returned to the trail. The road was rocky up ahead, and they had to climb over boulders as they ascended the hill.

'Did the bartender have any insight?' asked John, watching where he placed his feet.

'Yes. More than I would have thought.' Javier reiterated the conversation in English.

'Do you remember your father coming up here to do clinics in the village?'

'I don't know. I would usually be at one of the farms. I rarely came into Ventosa. But if I did, I was with my family. I never went to a clinic here.'

'Do you think your dad was trying to keep it from you?'

Javier frowned. 'I don't know. It seems strange that my father came up here for years to help people, but suddenly, he stopped.'

'It is curious.' agreed John. 'Especially, as the old man said, right at the same time when Ines moved to Madrid upon your father's recommendation.'

'Mmm. Well, the plot thickens. When we get back home, I will ask Ines about it. After discussing this with the man in the bar, I think there is enough to seek some answers, at least.'

John nodded in agreement. 'What is Antonio like?'

'He's a chemical engineer. He works for a company in Léon. I planned to call him when we got close to see if we might have dinner. I haven't seen him and his family in a while. He's married, and his children are in high school. Antonio is a wine connoisseur with an enviable cellar and some rare vintages. My uncles taught Antonio all about wine. Never having a son of his own, my uncle, Isabela's father, took a liking to him, and Antonio nearly went to apprentice at the vineyard. However, my father encouraged him to attend university and get an education. That was a couple of years before he died.'

'Maybe you can fish around a bit.' offered John. 'See if Antonio knows anything. We can tell him we came through the village to check on the house for his mother. That might help spark a conversation.'

Javier thought about what John was suggesting when speaking to Antonio. His mind reeled. He didn't want to be dishonest but didn't want to accuse anyone without evidence. This situation was the last thing he expected when he awoke this morning, and it wasn't yet noon.

They had lunch in Najera, then walked all afternoon, arriving at Santo Domingo when the sun was setting. Javier was troubled by what he had learned. He had barely spoken since Najera, leaving the hotel selection to John.

At dinner, Javier picked at his food.

'Would it be so bad if you discovered Antonio was your brother?' John asked

Javier took a large swig of wine.

'Did I wish for siblings growing up? Yes. Often. I never considered that I was anything other than an only child. But my existence in our house was sometimes lonely. When Alejandra and I married, we hoped for a house full of children. But it wasn't to be. We were happy with Mateo, but I yearned for a large family and wanted my son to benefit from a brother or a sister.'

John nodded.

'As an only child, I understand. But from what you describe, Antonio was around your house a lot when you were growing up. Even traveling with you up here during school breaks. It was like you had a brother, whether he turns out to be one in shared DNA or not.'

'That's true.' admitted Javier, 'We were close. I looked out for him. We have a shared history. Growing up, he asked me for advice on girls and other things. He still does, from time to time, like when he took this job in Léon. He was concerned about moving so far away from his mother, but it was a good opportunity. I told him not to worry. She would have us to look after her, of course.' Javier was thoughtful for a moment. 'I was the best man at his wedding, and I'm godfather to his children.'

'So, whether he is your father's son or not doesn't really matter.' Observed John, 'You've been family all along.'

Javier sighed.

'It's true. We have. And Ines has always been more of a mother to me than my own. She was there for me and Mateo when Alejandra was ill. Ines took care of everything when my wife died and made sure the transition to the apartment I bought was smooth when I moved us out of the house in Alphonso Martines Square. She has been a confidant to Mateo and myself. Ines never bullied me or pushed me with an agenda. She's is there when

I need her, and she helps to guide me.' His eyebrows narrowed, scowling. 'But I hate lies. I need to find out the truth.'

John knew all about lies.

'I understand. I think we start with Antonio and then speak to Ines when we finish here.'

Javier took a drink of his wine.

'Please do not tell Pen.' pleaded Javier. 'I don't want to upset Mateo for nothing.'

'Of course not.' John assured him. 'There is nothing to tell. We only have the rantings of an old lady and the cloudy recollections of an ancient cafe owner. We need more information and real evidence.'

Javier nodded. 'Exactly.' he took another drink of his wine. 'I'm glad you're here. That I didn't learn about all this alone makes it easier.'

John smiled sheepishly, 'I know I punched you in the face a few towns back, but I think we're friends now. I'm glad I'm here, too. Let me know what I can do.'

They finished up and returned to the hotel. The bombshells of the day had worn them both out.

Over the next few days, the two men often walked on their own. Javier had a lot on his mind and seemed in a hurry to get somewhere in the distance. John found the hours of solitude a meditation. They were nearly two weeks into their Camino, yet so much had already happened. John thought back to his time with Isabela. The butterflies in his stomach were those of a teenager rather than a retiree. Should he feel guilty? He didn't want to. The beautiful Spanish winemaker wasn't someone he could easily forget.

As his trekking poles clicked like a metronome, John cast his mind back to when Tess was ill. Toward the end, when the doctors were exhausting the last of her treatment options. One morning, he left Pen with her mom in the hospital room and went to the cafeteria for a coffee, taking a break. But, when he returned, he stopped outside and listened to the conversation between his wife and daughter. Tess's words to Pen rang through him on the Camino like a distant bell.

'When your heart is broken early and often, it's easy to believe that's the normal state of things — the natural way of the world. I believed this for a long time. But I learned that it isn't so. It's not normal to always be sad, Pen. To mistrust the world and to be skeptical of love and friendship. To love takes tremendous courage. The bravest people take the risk of heartbreak again and again so they can have a chance at forever.'

Through a crack in the grey blinds of the window in the hall, he watched as Tess tucked back a wayward strand from Pen's ponytail behind her ear.

'And I'm not just talking about romantic heartbreak. Life is not fair. Our hearts get broken for so many reasons. Both big and small. Families hurt each other far too often, sometimes without even understanding how. I know I am guilty of this myself. But you're too grown up to lie to, my girl. To pretend that my treatment is working. So I'll tell it to you straight — I won't be here to see you through difficult things. To hold you when the tears fall. Nor will I have the opportunity to cheer for your greatest triumphs. But, I'll be watching from where I am – just on the other side of the veil that separates us.'

John saw Pen's tears wet her cheeks as Tess tried her hardest to smile. Swallowing hard, Tess struggled to keep her composure.

'Losing Charlie and now me,' she whispered, 'is hard. It isn't fair, and you shouldn't have to go through it. This kind of loss can either harden or soften you – but only you can decide. I hope you choose to let all your heartbreak soften you. To open you up. To make you more willing to risk it all for the life you want because, Pen, you know more than anyone that life is fleeting. It can fly away in an instant when you aren't paying attention, so you have to grab ahold of it and refuse to let go.'

He watched Pen nod as Tess wiped their daughter's tears.

'It would break my heart to know all the sadness you've experienced in your young life had caused you to close yourself off and set you on a path of bitterness. Cynicism is the easy way—the choice of too many people. Never forget, you get to fall down, Pen, as often as it takes, but you don't get to break.'

Pen lay down beside her mom as Tess stroked her hair.

'You are a remarkable person, my beautiful daughter, but you don't always have to be remarkable—the top of your class or the best player on the team. You can be ordinary whenever you want. Lazy and grumpy, spending a weekend in bed eating barbeque potato chips and ice cream.' Tess smiled down at her daughter, who gazed up into her mother's face. 'I know you know how to do that.' They both smiled. 'But, when you're ready to shine, make it count. And when you're ready to love, jump in with both feet. It's worth it. You're worth it.'

John wiped the tears pouring down his face. Then he sniffed, took some deep breaths, and straightened up, smiling as he entered the room.

'All good?' he asked his wife and daughter as they pulled back from their embrace.

Tess nodded, wiping her face, as John turned to Pen.

'Yeah,' she told her dad.

But it wasn't good. Tess would be gone in a flash. It happened so fast that it took his breath away. Pen spent every moment she could with Tess as those last lucid days slipped by. And then, they just held her hand and waited for the final deep intake of breath. And, nothing.

Remembering those heartbreaking days, John cried on the trail, keeping his head down as other pilgrims passed him. He wasn't interested in swapping stories about why he was walking the Camino or sharing a laugh. John needed to process everything that had happened. He needed to remember his wife and his son. His parents. On the Camino, he allowed himself to grieve for them without distraction while letting the tears flow out in the open, learning to say goodbye so he could move forward. People he knew had given him advice over the years on healing from grief, but John knew better that there were different kinds of grief. The loss of his son was not the same as the loss of his wife. None of those people knew what he had done. After two weeks on the Camino, John knew that letting go of Tess was more than just grieving. After over a decade, he somehow needed to learn to forgive himself.

# Part III

## The Breadcrumbs

# Twenty

## The Wrong Foot

A few days later, they entered Burgos after hours of walking that never seemed to end. Javier didn't suggest they stay at the Parador, as he had with Tess. John knew where they were because he had made Tess and Pen's reservations for that night, but he didn't bring it up. The men walked through the city and checked into the large municipal albergue. It had an elevator—something they had not yet encountered on the Camino. John laughed, riding it to the top floor instead of walking his tired legs up the stairs. After only a few weeks on the trail, simple pleasures were like gifts from the gods.

It was a Sunday, and John wanted to go to the cathedral. He needed to light a candle and spend some quiet time in the space. Javier told him to go ahead. He would see him later, so John walked to mass by himself.

The world-famous cathedral in Burgos is enormous, and he knew it held the relics of saints. After lighting his candles and talking to God, John reached into his wallet to pull out Tess's obituary, as was his habit on the Camino. He peeled back the leather and checked every compartment. Then, he checked again. The yellowed newsprint was gone. John's heart raced. He looked around, then checked his pockets. It wasn't there. Closing his eyes, he tried to calm down. The words Tess had written about herself were something he could recite from memory. But the paper it was written on was his sacred relic from the days after her passing. Irreplaceable. John didn't know what to do without it.

Just then, his phone buzzed. *Pen*. He looked at the screen as he rose from the kneeler to quickly exit the church.

'Hey.' said John, happy to hear his daughter's voice.

'Hey, Dad. How's it going?'

'It's good.' he swallowed hard.

'Where are you?'

'I'm in Burgos. I just left the cathedral.'

'Is Javier with you?'

'No. I decided to go to the church, and he's doing his own thing. We've spent every day together for weeks, so a little space is good.'

'Church, huh? I wanted to see how you're feeling after spreading Mom's ashes.'

John considered the question. He'd had days to process what it meant to him.

'I feel better, somehow. I'm not sure why spreading a handful of her ashes makes such a difference, but it seems to.'

'I feel the same way.' Pen admitted. 'But, it made me miss her more. Especially right now. I don't know why.'

John closed his eyes, taking a deep breath to control his emotions. He missed Tess, too.

'I wish you were here with me, Pen. Your mom was lucky she got to walk this with you.'

Pen laughed. 'I'm not so sure you would have felt that way if you'd been there. I kind of went off the rails in Burgos.'

John remembered the incident.

'Still,' he told her, 'I would love to have you here.'

'Are you okay, Dad?' said Pen, sounding worried.

'Yeah. I'm just a little, I don't know, melancholy today. Feeling far away from you. Even though we're closer than we usually are – geographically.'

'I'm glad you're in Spain. I wish you lived here. I need my dad.'

John wasn't sure what kept him in their Arizona house or even the US. Was it Tess? They only lived in that house together for a few years before she passed. He didn't think of that as their family home. No longer a fixture on his mantlepiece, part of his wife would be all over Spain and the world.

John reached behind him for his daypack and realized he had left her ashes at the alberge.

After the Camino, he needed to think about his next chapter. His final chapter. Pen was living in Europe. Even though his Spanish was terrible, being near his daughter and future grandchildren was something to consider. One thing he knew for sure was that living life as a hermit was killing him. He needed it to end.

They said their goodbyes as John walked back through the old city's cobbled streets to the albergue, so deep in thought he wasn't sure how he managed to find it.

'Look who I found!' came a shout from a local cafe.

It had been just five days since John's last glimpse of Isabela standing outside her house. He wasn't sure when or if he would see her again, but here she was in a pair of skinny jeans and a black leather jacket, her dark hair flowing down her back, sitting next to Javier at the cafe across the road.

'Hi.' He said, grinning.

'¡Hola!' said Isabela, her smile beaming from her late summer tan.

'What are you doing here?'

'It's Sunday. I felt like a drive.'

'That's quite a drive.' said John, surprised

'No. Only an hour. It's not too far when you're on four wheels. I thought I would see how you two were getting along on your journey west.'

'We're doing great.' John said, smiling. 'I think I'll remain a pilgrim from now on and roam around the world aimlessly. Like Peter Pan.'

Isabela tut-tutted at this and rolled her eyes.

'Peter Pan never grew up. I prefer mature men.'

John raised an eyebrow.

'Are we hungry?' asked Javier, changing the subject.

'I'm starving after such a *long* drive.' teased Isabela.

Javier rubbed his hands together as John checked his phone for the second time since arriving at the cafe.

'What's going on?' asked Javier.

John shook his head.

'I just got off the phone with Pen.' said John. 'We're both learning to let go, I guess.'

Isabela stood and wrapped her arms around John. He hugged her back, surprised that having her close was just what he needed. It wasn't until the night at the vineyard that John realized how little touch he experienced since Tess's death. Other than a handshake from a friend or a hug from one of their wives, he went untouched by another person for years. Isabela's arms felt good.

'Do you want to get something to eat, or do you need some time alone, John?' offered Javier

John shook his head.

'No. Now that I think about it, I'm actually pretty hungry. And Isabela drove all this way on her Sunday drive. I don't want to waste it brooding. Besides, I can't do anything except feel how I feel. And it's the same for Pen. She knows I'm here when she needs me.' he held out his hand. 'so lead the way.'

They walked to a restaurant nearby. It was a crisp, sunny autumn day. Javier and Isabela debated the right wine and ordered food to go with it. Thinking about Pen, John left them to it. The bustle of the old city was a good distraction for him. Around every corner was a building or piece of architecture from another century. The streets were packed with families enjoying the last gasp of summer sun.

'We shouldn't have too much wine.' said Javier, 'You have to drive back to the vineyard.' he reminded his cousin.

'Well, perhaps if I have too much, I'll get a room and stay here for the night.'

Javier laughed. 'That is one solution.'

Isabela smiled at John.'Yes, it is.' Then, changing the subject. 'What adventures have you two had since I saw you? No more black eyes, I hope.'

'I think we're past black eyes.' John smiled. 'We've moved on.'

Javier confirmed they had.

'It is true. We are past that.' agreed Javier. 'But we have come across a bit of a mystery. Maybe you can help shed some light on it.'

Javier recounted the incident with Ines's neighbor in Ventosa. Then, he reiterated the conversation with the man in the cafe regarding his father and Ines. His cousin was quiet for a moment before taking a deep breath.

'Well.' admitted Isabela, 'There have always been rumors about your father and Ines.' Holding up her hand as Javier blanched. 'My parents dismissed them and refused to let anyone talk about it in our house. Especially my father, being his brother. But I heard them in other places. It was curious, they said, that Ines left so suddenly with an illness she had never had before. They said it was due to the smoke from forest fires. I understood that no one had ever heard of a husband or her getting married in Madrid, including her parents. The village is small. People talk.'

'It's strange, don't you think? I never remember my father having a clinic in the village.' said Javier, 'Conducting weekend surgeries and helping the local families.'

'I don't remember any of it, either. I was too small. I just remember when Antonio started coming to help on the farm. When you would come up for a holiday, he was usually there, too. My father took a liking to him, and my mother used to bake him sweets. It was like he was a little brother. After I discovered America, I think my father hoped to turn Antonio into a winemaker.' Isabela took a sip from her glass. 'But, before he died, *Tio* Eduardo pushed him to go to university to study engineering, and he was the one paying for it. So, we didn't see Antonio much after that. If you remember, Antonio came to the wedding reception for Mateo and Pen at the vineyard. With his wife and kids. And Ines. But, before that, I hadn't seen him in years.'

'Ines was so proud of Mateo that day.' said Javier with a faraway look in his eye as he struggled with the new revelations. 'She cried during the speeches; I remember.'

'It's possible that he is your brother, I suppose.' said Isabela, plopping something into her mouth and wiping her hands on her napkin. 'Based on what I've heard over the years. Do you want me to see what else I can find out? Clearly, there are people in the village who remember the situation back then, and there is also *Tio* Diego. He might have some information he'd be willing to part with now that he is old and his brothers are all gone. Nowadays, a secret like this isn't as shocking as it would have been nearly 50 years ago.'

Javier sighed.

'If you can do it without creating a dust cloud, then yes, see what you can find out.'

Isabela agreed to be careful.

'If it's true, do you think your mother knows?' she asked her cousin.

'Never.' said Javier without hesitation. 'If María had known, Ines would have been gone years ago. Disappeared if my mother had anything to say about it.'

Javier's mother, María, was a force of nature. The tiny black-haired woman frightened everyone, including John.

'Would she have divorced your father over it?' asked John.

Javier made a face. 'No way. Divorce means a scandal. And scandal means lower social standing. My mother would never have sacrificed that. Being the society queen means more to her than almost anything. Although, no one cares about any of that anymore. And most of her friends are dead. I think she's only alive to spite the rest of the world. María will win the prize for living longer than any in her social circle.'

'Okay. Let's say your dad is Antonio's father.' said John. 'He took a significant risk acknowledging the child and moving Ines to Madrid, then allowing her to work in his house near the lion's den. I think he must have loved her very much to do that. And Antonio, too.'

Javier frowned.

'My father knew my mother better than anyone. He knew what she was capable of. Eduardo must have lived in fear of her finding out every day of his life when Ines began working there.' Javier shook his head. 'Anyway, we don't know if it's true.'

Isabela acknowledged they needed more definitive proof.

'I'm going to see what Antonio knows when we get to León.' said Javier, 'I'll keep you posted on what we learn.'

Javier yawned and stretched.

'I think I'm going to make it an early night. All this family drama has made me tired.' he signaled to the waiter for the check. 'This dinner is on me, but don't feel like you two need to leave on my account.'

He paid the bill and kissed Isabela's cheek.

'Safe drive home.' Javier winked at John and left.

'Well, that was subtle.' said John.

Isabela smiled, reached across, and squeezed his hand.

'Javier knows I like you.'

'What else does he know?'

'He's a man. He can read the signs. I'm not sure he knew what to make of it when you stayed at my house overnight.'

'I don't think my daughter understood it, either.' said John sheepishly.

'Then let's not try to fool anyone. Let's have fun like two adults that enjoy spending time together.'

John liked the sound of that. No pressure. No drama. He picked up her hand, kissing her palm and her endearing callouses. The woman sitting before him was no shrinking violet. She knew her own mind, and she had driven 60 miles to see him, no matter what she said about a Sunday drive.

'Are you staying the night?' he asked.

'Shame on you.' she said, with mock offense. 'Did you assume that I had this all planned out?'

Her feigned shock made him chuckle.

'Perish the thought.'

'I have a room at the Parador.' Isabel winked. The look in her eyes was pure huntress.

John wasn't sure what exactly he wanted to happen. The five days they'd spent apart gave him plenty of time to think about her. But he didn't know if he was ready for what she had in mind.

'I'm up for a nightcap.'

Isabela smiled as they rose and walked out into the crisp evening air. They strolled to the hotel in an uncomfortable silence until John's discomfort boiled over.

'We are leaving early tomorrow to continue our Camino.' John reminded her, fidgeting with the wooden bracelet from the monk, like a teenager on a first date.

'That's okay.' she said, 'I have to leave very early. We are still in the middle of the crush. I want to be home by 7 am.'

With her busy schedule, John was surprised she made the drive.

'Wow, alright. Are you sure you want to stay the night here?'

She looked over and grinned.

'I've thought of nothing else for the last five days.' sliding her arm through his. 'My knight in shining armor.'

He bowed with mock gallantry.

'Then I'm at your service.'

They arrived at her room, and Isabela had a bottle of wine waiting for them. It felt like months since John had stayed in a place with such comfortable surroundings.

'Do you mind if I take a shower?' asked John. 'The one I had at the albergue this afternoon was unsatisfying and short. It only gave me two minutes of hot water. *Bracing* is the only way to describe the final three minutes under the trickle.'

'My shower is your shower.'

Turning on the water in the marble bathroom was glorious. The spray from the showerhead was strong, and the room filled with steam almost instantly. John stripped down and stood under the water for a few minutes before he felt arms reaching around him. Electricity coursed through him. Turning, Isabela smiled up at him.

Pushing back her hair from her face, he bent down and found her lips. Isabela wrapped her arms around his neck and deepened the kiss. John had heard people say 'The Camino provides,' but knew they didn't mean a night at the Parador in Burgos with a beautiful winemaker. Or maybe that was precisely what they meant.

Isabela's body felt good. Over the past week, John had thought about her as he lay on his hard bunk in one albergue or another. She was passionate and uninhibited. Isabela was a rare woman who didn't care what anybody thought of her, and best of all, she was intelligent and easy to like. The combination was intoxicating.

Isabela edged under the water, and John rubbed her shoulders and back. Then, he reached around and cupped her breasts. She backed into him and arched her back. It had been a long time since he had done anything like this, and he wasn't sure he could do it anymore – whether, at his age, his body would respond without some chemical assistance. He gathered some of the body wash and massaged her. She leaned back and let him touch her wherever he wanted.

He went lower, and she moaned when he found the right spot. Encouraged, he played for a while until she was begging him.

'Please, don't tease me.'

John moved her over to the wall of the shower, and he entered her from behind. He had prolonged it enough, didn't want to wait, and rode her fast and hard. Isabela moaned while he went deeper and held on to her hips for leverage. She cried out, and John met her there with a mixture of release and remembered bliss.

Afterward, still dizzy, John held onto the shower wall for support. A strange guilt washed over him, but he knew he had done nothing of which to feel ashamed. It had taken him more than ten years and one moment in the shower with Isabela to realize he wasn't married anymore as she turned around and kissed him.

'I knew driving 100 km was worth it.' she smiled.

'I aim to please.' he said, with a tinge of sadness.

'Are you alright?' she asked with concern.

John nodded but didn't elaborate on the knot in his stomach. After rinsing off, he gently dried her with a bath towel. Then they crawled into bed, and Isabela laid her head on John's chest.

'I could get used to sleeping next to you.' smiled Isabela.

'Mmm. It is nice.' John said into her hair. 'I like waking up and seeing your face.'

Isabela rose onto her elbow.

'You should come up to the winery after you finish your Camino. I'm sure Javier will need to check on the sheep farm. It will be after the crush, so I will have a long, lonely, cold winter ahead of me.' she said, running her hands through the grey hair on his chest.

'You have survived many long winters without me in the past.' John reminded her.

'Yes, but lately I don't want to.' her tone changed from playfulness. 'I am being serious now. I hope you come up. Stay a few weeks. Do you have something pressing back in the States?'

John hesitated.

'I don't know yet.' he admitted. Rushing home to *what* was the question. But home was familiar, and with all the discomfort of the Camino, John still craved the comfort of the known, no matter how lonely that existence might be. Isabela was aware of his list for placing Tess's ashes. And Javier was trying to solve the mystery of his father and Ines. Each of them had distractions. She lay down and snuggled further into the crook of John's arm.

'We haven't had the wine.' said John.

'You do the honors.'

John rose from the bed and opened the bottle with the expertise of a man who knew his way around wine as Isabela watched him. He was not young but was fit from walking and kept himself in shape, even before the Camino, running a few times a week.

'Why are you smiling at me?' he asked, looking up from pouring the wine.

'I don't know. I like you. I like looking at you. You're a good man, John. I can tell.'

John sighed.

'I don't know about that. I punched your cousin in the face. And before that, I was rude to two women who only tried to be nice to me and saved me in the Pyrenees. Then there was that Buddhist monk...' he said, holding up the bracelet on his wrist.

'Oh.' Isabela clicked her tongue. 'These are serious crimes. You're right; you are awful, and I would like you to leave.' she scowled, pointing at the door to the room. 'Anyway, if they convicted me of every tantrum or outburst, I would be in jail for a very long time. I was nasty to you when you picked me up from the grape vat in Logroño.'

'As I recall, you were *very* angry with me.' He reminded her.

'I was.' she said, rolling over and looking at the ceiling. 'I'm not sure why. Maybe it's because I don't appreciate being told what to do. And I didn't know you or the kind of person you are.'

'Hmm.' John pondered the question. He wasn't sure what he thought of himself anymore. 'What did you think I was going to do?'

'I don't know. I just panicked.'

John handed her the wine glass and got back in bed.

'To making new friends.' he said, holding up his glass.

Isabela inclined her head and touched her glass to his. 'Salud.'

John took a sip. 'So, Javier tells me you were married before. I was surprised that I wasn't your first.' he teased.

Setting her glass down on the nightstand, Isabela readjusted the pillows. She's stalling for time, thought John. Sitting back, she took a deep breath.

'My ex-husband is a brilliant man. He is the dean at a University in the US, and I was a visiting professor. We had a whirlwind romance, and we got married in Mexico. My parents were upset because I didn't come back here to get married, and I didn't tell anyone in advance. After my parents met him, they didn't like him at all. In their defense, he was, *is* an ass. But I didn't see it.'

'In the beginning, it was small things to humiliate me in front of the other faculty. I brushed it off as joking or a language thing and left it at that. Then, my husband began having affairs with some of my graduate students. It was blatant, as if he wanted me to find out. Finally, he brought one of them home and had sex with her in our bed. When I walked in and discovered them, he didn't even stop what he was doing. He just looked me in the face and finished. I didn't know anyone could be that cruel.'

The lingering pain in her eyes cut John to the core.

'People do things, awful things sometimes.' whispered John. 'Maybe, even he didn't know why he did that to you.'

'You don't have to make excuses for him. After that, I packed up and left him. I got a position at a Madrid university and spent time with Javier and his wife before she got sick. I even lived with them for a while. It worked out because I was closer to my parents before they passed away, spending more and more time up here. Eventually, when my father could no longer keep up after he became ill, I took over the operation.'

Not only had her heart broken, but it had also been crushed underfoot by a man who was supposed to love her. He put down his glass and wrapped his arms around her, burying his lips in her hair.

'I'm not perfect. I have stories of my own, too. But I promise I would not do anything like that to you.'

She pulled back and smiled up at him.

'I know. That's what I like most about you. You're a kind man.'

His smile was tinged with sadness.

'It's easy to be kind to you. You've treated me well since we met.'

'Because I ravaged your body?' teased Isabela.

'No. Because you've shown me how much you care.' a lump formed in John's throat. 'It's been a long time since someone cared for me like that. It's been a long time since I felt I was enough.'

'Since your wife died?' she asked.

'Even before.' he whispered.

John blew out a big breath as tears came to his eyes. The feeling was so unexpected it caught him off guard. He hadn't realized that he had felt that way, but the words slipped out of his mouth, and he knew it was true.

'You're more than enough. You are a person any woman would feel lucky to have in her life.'

Isabela kissed him lightly, and he held on to her.

'This is like a dream being here with you.' admitted John, 'This is not like me at all, and you'll have to forgive me, but it's been a long time. I don't know how to do this. To talk to someone other than Tess about this kind of stuff.'

Isabela nodded.

'I understand. But you must forgive me if I don't want it to stop. In the meantime, I have a vineyard to run and a vintage to put to bed. And you have some personal business you need to finish. You know where to find me. I'll be there. Waiting.'

They held each other. John could hear Isabela's breathing become regular. She snored a little, and it made him smile. Isabela was real, afterall. Sadly, sleep didn't find him until much later. Too many thoughts swirled in his head. He could see his wife clearly and honestly, and John saw himself. The things he had done. Things he wasn't proud of. Tess hadn't been perfect either, but goddammit, he had loved her. And he knew she loved him. John had held onto her and her memory for so long. Without it was like being out in the cold without a blanket. But she was slowly slipping away. He looked over at Isabela and smiled. For the first time, John could see a future where he might be happy again.

# TWENTY-ONE

## BEYOND BURGOS

John's alarm went off at 5:30 am, startling them both. He walked with her through the empty streets to see Isabela safely delivered to her car. She opened the door, then turned to John, burying her head in his chest and wrapping her arms tightly around his waist. He hugged her back until she pulled away.

'Time to go back to real life.' she said.

'It often works out that way. I don't live on the Camino, so I'll be delaying the 'real life' part for a little longer.' he smiled. 'But, before I forget, I lost something and wondered if you might have found it at your house.'

'What is it?' she asked.

'It's an old newspaper article.'

Isabela shook her head.

'I don't think so, but I can ask my housekeeper. It's in English, I presume. And important?'

'Yes. If not, don't worry. It's not a big deal.' But it was. 'I was just hoping you might have found it. Maybe I lost it somewhere else.'

John didn't elaborate further.

Isabela got in the car and started it up. Then, she rolled down the window as John leaned in to kiss her.

'Text me so I know you got home okay.'

A wide smile spread across her face.

'It's been a long time since I had someone to text when I got home safely.'

'You have someone now.'

Isabela put the sporty white Audi A1 in gear, then waved out the window as she picked up speed down the wet, cobblestone street.

'Drive safe.' he whispered, watching her car disappear.

John looked around, hoping to find his way back to the albergue where Javier and his pack were waiting.

Only the streetlights illuminated the wet cobblestones through the warren of empty alleys in the old city. The nearly full moon of the night before was setting. After several missed turns, John found his way up a set of narrow steps where the municipal albergue sat at the top. Lights from the cafe across the street spilled onto the pavement. Through the window, John could see Javier thumbing through his guidebook—Javier's pack and his own sat at his feet.

'Ah. There you are.' said Javier, removing his glasses as John walked through the door. 'I was wondering when I might see you this morning.'

John looked appropriately contrite, grinning sheepishly like a teenager coming home well past curfew. 'Go ahead. You can say it.'

'Say what? I assume you and my cousin enjoyed each other's company, and you both slept well. And now you are ready to walk the Camino for the next six hours. At least.'

John smiled. Son-of-a-bitch. But he laughed.

'That's exactly what we did. Warm milk and tucked in by 8 o'clock.'

'Just as I thought.' Javier chuckled. 'Would you like a coffee or two? Have a seat, and I'll go and get us some.'

The morning was chilly as John dug through his pack and pulled out his fleece. He zipped the bottoms of his convertible pants back on and put on his stocking cap, finishing dressing just as Javier came back with the coffee and the tortilla.

Javier's guidebook sat on the table, open to their route. They could probably make it to Arroyo San Bol, he offered, but if John was too tired, they could stay in Hornillos del Camino. John listened as the Spaniard read the points of interest and the elevation while eating breakfast. When he finished eating, they headed out past the remains of an old fortress.

The sun didn't rise behind them until they were well outside the city. The path was easy and flat, and they walked in silence until Javier interjected.

'I've never seen Isabela so taken with someone. I didn't know her husband or spend time with them together, but it means something for her to drive all this way to see you.'

John was uncomfortable discussing his relationship with Isabela, especially with Javier.

'I don't know. I think we enjoy each other's company.'

Javier chuckled.

'Well, that is true enough. Have you dated many women since Tess passed away?'

'No. I haven't dated anyone. I told you that. Isabela is the first person I have been with since Tess.'

He knew his response sounded harsher than he had meant to, but it wasn't any of Javier's business.

'What about you? Have you had sex with anyone since having sex with my wife?'

Javier visibly grimaced.

'Tess was the first person I was with after Alejandra died. That was five years later. So, believe me, I understand about going a long time without meeting anyone who can live up to what you lost. But part of what Tess showed me was that my life could go on. The suspended animation I lived in with Mateo didn't need to last forever. It isn't lost on me that someone who was losing her life helped to give me back my own.'

Shame washed over John.

'I'm sorry I said that. I know you understand what I've gone through losing Tess, probably better than anyone, because you lost her too. And you understand what it is that made Tess so special.'

'Yes, I did. I loved Tess.' Javier admitted, 'But after she left Spain and passed away, I knew that my life would go on. She would have insisted upon it. I haven't dated anyone seriously since then. But I have been out with people and made love to several women. One of my good friends, she and I, we meet. We have dinner. And sometimes, we have coffee in the morning.'

It sounded so tame. So civilized. John didn't have friends like that.

'I didn't know what to do for years.' said John, 'I just worked, and after Pen went off to college, I worked even more. I never looked at other women. I just wasn't attracted to anyone. Honestly, I wondered if that part of my life was over. There was nothing wrong from the outside, but inside, it was dead. It shocks me to say it, but at 53, I felt numb inside. Like that all disappeared with Tess.'

John felt weird telling Javier all this, but he needed to talk to someone.

'So, no one was more surprised than me when I found myself in bed with Isabela at the winery that night. After last night, it turns out all the equipment still works. She's wonderful. And I feel great when I'm with her. Like I woke up from a long nap, and there she was. She's so feisty but also a smart, passionate person I admire.'

Javier smiled. 'I'm glad. You two seem like a good fit. Both of you need someone who has as much integrity as the other. When I saw her yesterday, I was surprised. But when I thought about it, I shouldn't have been. Not really. I'm glad you found each other.'

'It's not weird for you that it's your cousin and me?' asked John

'We are well past judging what is *weird* in our family, John. I think you wait and see what happens.'

John smiled.

'That's exactly what I intend to do.' as he picked up the pace.

# Twenty-Two

## Ashes to Ashes

The following afternoon, the two men walked into Castrojeriz, hot and sweaty from a long, dusty day on the trail. The heat was brutal in the Meseta in late September, and the elevation changes didn't help. They checked into an albergue recommended by Javier. Since this hill town was another location on Tess's list, the two men would need to choose a location to sprinkle Tess's ashes.

'Is this another one of the places you all stayed?' asked John

'Yes. It is one of the best places. They separate men and women if they can. And the dinner is excellent.'

After scrubbing up, they went for a beer at a cafe in the square before dinner. John brought his backpack and Tess's ashes, hoping the perfect spot would present itself. A gathering of rowdy pilgrims sat on the terrace around the tables near the fountain, singing as the wine flowed. The other pilgrims welcomed John and Javier to join in as they graciously accepted, and glasses and food passed their way. A fellow American pilgrim sat next to John. She was young and rosy-cheeked, with a blond ponytail covered by a green bandana. At the start of it all, he thought.

'I think I saw you a few days ago in Burgos.' the young American pilgrim observed.

'Maybe.' said John. 'We're walking together in honor of my wife. She passed away from cancer ten years ago. We are laying her ashes at spots on her list.'

The girl's eyes widened.

'Wow! That's so cool. Like, where did she want to be sprinkled?'

'A couple of different places, but this is one of them. Somewhere in this square, I think.' John said, looking around.

'Seriously? Here?' the young woman's eyes widened.

'Yeah. We'll enjoy a drink with you guys, and then we need to figure out where we will do it.' said John.

'I think you should put her at the base of the fountain. It's beautiful. Her ashes will flow from there out into the valley.' the girl looked out at the sun setting over the hill. 'That's what I would want.'

'That sounds nice, actually.' agreed John.

Unbidden, the girl stood up and quieted everyone by whistling loudly.

'Hey! You guys! This is,' she turned back to John, 'what's your name?'

'John.'

'This is John.' she pointed at him. 'He's walking the Camino with his friend…' Again, she turned to John.

'Javier'

'With his friend, Javier, in honor of his wife who died. She asked to be sprinkled in this square, and we decided to do that near the fountain. We're going to go over there now. If you wanna come, join us and say a prayer, or recite a poem, or something, that would be cool.'

She sat down and drank the last of her wine. John and Javier looked at each other. They hadn't planned to announce their intentions to the group or ask anyone to join them. Just then, the blond American girl stood again.

'Come on. Let's go.' said the peppy pilgrim.

As if following the Pied Piper, everyone rose in unison, walking to the fountain together. The two men were the last to join them. John set his pack on the stone cobbles, removed the ashes, and stood before the ancient stone fountain. The motley crew of smelly pilgrims stood silent, but the American girl encouraged them to hold hands in a circle while they waited.

John gathered a small handful of ashes and went up to the trough. He stood with his eyes closed momentarily and said a silent prayer, then bent down and laid her at the stone base. As he opened his eyes, the girl broke into a pitch-perfect rendition of 'Amazing Grace.' It was the most beautiful music John had ever heard. After the first verse, others joined until the group from around the world sang the centuries-old hymn together.

John stood inside the circle until the singing ended. Starting with the American girl, each person approached him as if in church, blessing him with *Peace, Namasté,* or *Buen Camino.* Then, they each embraced Javier. When it was over, the two men stood alone, stunned.

'That was unexpected.' said John.

'That is what I would expect on the Camino.' whispered Javier

Javier put his arm around John's shoulder, and they walked back to the table to join the others, where John raised a glass.

'Thank you all for making this moment so special. Tess would have loved this. To Tess!'

The group raised their glasses 'To Tess.'

One of the other pilgrims had recorded the entire proceeding and offered it to John. He happily sent it to Pen so she could feel a part of laying her mom's ashes on the Camino.

That night, John slept hard. He didn't dream but woke up thoroughly rested and thinking of Isabela. They packed up before sunrise and climbed Alto de Mostaelares to catch the sun as it broke over the horizon. Just a week from León, he wondered how Javier was doing, thinking about his upcoming conversation with Ines's son, Antonio. John and Javier were nearly halfway on their Camino, and while John was feeling better about why he was there, he knew Javier was wrestling with what he had learned, and the tension was rising the closer they got to León. With each step, they inched toward the end of the Camino and the prospect of returning to Madrid. The place where the whole truth lay with the only person alive who knew it. Ines.

# TWENTY-THREE
## GETTING TO THE BOTTOM

Three days later, they crossed the halfway point. The men celebrated with wine at their albergue in Bercianos del Real Camino.

'We made it.' John smiled, taking a sip. 'It's all downhill from here.'

'Yes.' agreed Javier. 'It will seem like it goes much faster now. Every day, you'll begin to feel like it's winding down because it is. But we still have some big mountains yet to climb.'

Both literally and figuratively.

'Yeah, I saw that in the app.' said John, looking at his phone. 'There are more than a few big elevation changes after León.'

'We have almost completed the Meseta, which most people find difficult because it is long and hot. But this late in the year, it hasn't been so bad.' said Javier.

'No. It's been great. I think the scenery here is beautiful.' John broached the subject Javier had avoided for days. 'So, we'll be in León in a couple of days. Have you decided how you're going to approach Antonio?'

'I'm still working on that. I sent him a message, and he's free the day we arrive. We'll go to his house and have dinner with his family.'

'If you want to go alone, I'm fine with that. You don't have to feel the need to take me with you.' offered John.

'No. I want you there. This situation is going to be tricky. You can help me fill in the story that began with the neighbor in Ventosa.'

It was raining the day they arrived in León, and Javier suggested they go all out.

'Let's splurge.'

John made a face.

'You know what 'splurge' means?' asked John, surprised.

'Of course. It's a common American phrase, I believe. It means doing something special.' said Javier with confidence.

John chuckled. 'Okay – let's splurge.'

They checked into the Hotel Real Colegiata de San Isidoro, cleaned up, and then took a taxi to Antonio's family home. When the younger man opened the door, it was clear to John that they shared some DNA. Javier and Antonio had the same eyes—eyes John had seen in others at the vineyard.

After a warm welcome, the men were ushered into the house and almost immediately had wine in their hands. Luckily for John, everyone spoke English.

'So, you are walking another Camino.' said Antonio to Javier.

'Yes, this one in honor of John's wife. You know Pen is his daughter.'

'Of course.' said Antonio. 'I remember you from the wedding.'

Javier turned the conversation back towards Rioja.

'We stopped at Isabela's and helped with the crush.'

Antonio smiled.

'I have many fond memories of the crush. This year, I haven't been able to get away. Work has been demanding. And the girls have their activities. Cristiana will graduate from high school this year, and her sister is not far behind. Hard to believe they're growing up so fast.'

Javier and John agreed that raising children went by quickly.

'How is Pen?' Antonio asked John.

'She's doing well and working as a junior curator.'

How well Pen was doing was up for debate, but John knew Javier had other pressing matters and continued to steer the conversation, keeping them on track.

'Your mother asked if I would check on your grandparent's house in Ventosa while I was there. Everything seems fine. It looked like they had just stepped away. Nothing out of place.' he smiled. '*No okupas.*'

John frowned.

'Squatters.' Javier reminded him.

'Thanks for that.' said Antonio, taking another sip. 'As I said, I haven't been able to get over there in a while. I know the lady next door keeps an eye on it, too.'

'Yes, she came out and spoke to us.' said Javier. 'She thought I was you.'

Antonio laughed. 'She is nearly blind. So, I'm not sure what that says.'

'Well, she seemed very sure. Then she said something curious.'

'What was that?' asked Antonio

'She said that she had mistaken me for my brother. I told her I was an only child. She said we both looked like my father.'

The blood drained from Antonio's face.

'What did she mean?'

'I'm not sure.' said Javier quietly.

Antonio stood pensive, staring out the window. He rubbed his chin, momentarily lost in thought, before turning to Javier. 'What do *you* think she meant?'

Javier and John exchanged a look before he answered.

'I didn't want to jump to conclusions. We went to the local cafe to have coffee afterward. I spoke to the owner and learned things I didn't know before.'

'Like what things?' asked Antonio

'That Eduardo had a clinic in the village. When I was a small boy, he would come up from Madrid on weekends to run a surgery. He helped a lot of local people and took no payment for it. I never remembered him doing that.'

Antonio nodded. 'I remember, the lady next door told me that once.'

'The man in the cafe said the town was disappointed when he stopped coming, but they understood he was in demand in Madrid. The barman said it was the same year as the bad fires in La Rioja and Navarra. The same year, Ines moved to Madrid for her health.'

'What are you saying, Javier?' asked Antonio, his eyes narrowing. 'What are you saying about my mother?'

The tension in the room was thick.

'I don't know what I'm saying. I only know what the old lady said to me, and then the man running the cafe, when he realized who my father was.'

Antonio paced, then sat on the arm of the sofa next to his wife, staring at the carpet.

'It could just be the ramblings of two old people. Gossip in the village is like a sport.'

Just like Javier, he was struggling to explain it away.

'What do you know about your father?' asked John. 'Have you ever visited his family or relatives on that side?'

Antonio shook his head.

'No. My mother told me that he was an only child and that my grandparents passed away. I didn't question it.'

'How did he die?' asked John.

'She said he got sick. And that he died when I was little. She told me he was handsome and was very good to her. He left some money so she could keep the apartment where I grew up. She only had to go to work after I started school. That's when she came to work for your parents. I don't remember much before that.'

'I remember when she started working for us.' said Javier. 'Ines always baked cookies, so I had a treat after classes. And she would bring you when you weren't in school.'

Antonio smiled.

'I remember. Your house was very fancy, and I was afraid to touch anything. Your mother had a small dog that bit me one time, and when I cried, your father picked me up and took me into his office. He cleaned out the wound and bandaged it. He told me it was okay to cry and not to be ashamed. So I did, and he hugged me. Then he took me to the kitchen, to my mother, and they both sat with me until I calmed down. He was a good man.'

Javier nodded. He remembered the incident, as well.

'He came to all of my school functions and many of my sports games.' remembered Antonio, 'He took an interest and was there for the science fair each year and when I had to give a speech in front of the school for *La*

*Fiesta de la Comunidad de Madrid*. He helped me practice my speech and told me he would be there so I wouldn't be nervous. My mother once said he pulled strings to get me into the same school you had gone to. And he paid my school fees. Eduardo always told me I could be anything I wanted to be if I worked hard enough. I wanted to live up to his expectations.'

Javier listened intently before responding.

'You've always been family to me. So, I'm not saying this out of anything other than trying to find the truth. But who do you know pays for his housekeeper's son to attend an expensive school? Who would go to his housekeeper's son's school or sporting events? And send him on a train with his own son to stay with his family. When I think back, I see little distinction between you and me in my father's eyes. He even made provisions for you in his will.'

Javier took a deep breath before continuing.

'I know. It's a lot to think about, but until your grandparents' neighbor in Ventosa said the words to me, I was blind to the possibility, too. But I can't seem to come up with an answer other than the one that is staring me in the face.'

Antonio's wife returned from the kitchen and announced dinner was ready. Neither Javier nor Antonio appeared to have an appetite, but they gathered around the table. Javier changed the subject and asked his goddaughters about school, boys, and their friends — anything to lighten the mood in the room. Antonio's wife, Marta, seemed curious about the conversation before dinner but said nothing in front of her children. After the meal, the girls asked their mother if they could go out to see friends.

'OK. Tell me everything.' said Marta, sitting in the living room, having coffee.

The three men looked at each other. None of them wanted to be the first to speak. Finally, Javier explained the situation, and Marta's eyes grew round.

'That's quite a story. It is interesting how much your father was present in Antonio's life. But have you discussed this with Ines? She would be the person who would be able to confirm or deny what you all are speculating about.'

'Do you think it might be true?' Antonio asked his wife.

She sighed.

'I have always found it curious. This association between you, your mother, and the family she worked for. They were very prominent in Madrid society, almost like royalty. I knew that Javier's father paid for your schooling, even after he died. I don't think this is normal for an employer and employee. Especially a domestic servant.' she held up her hand, frowning. 'I'm not saying anything against your mother, but she's been that family's housekeeper for more than 40 years, either with Javier's parents or with Javier and Mateo. It's not typical.'

Antonio rose, pacing again. Suddenly, he seemed to come to a decision.

'She's right. It's not typical. So, what do we do now? What do I say to my mother?'

As an outsider, John interjected tentatively.

'You could do a DNA test. If it proves you're siblings, you have part of the answer.'

'But don't you want to understand the background? What happened, and why? Only Ines knows the whole story.' offered Marta

Javier agreed.

'Okay. I think we take a DNA test first. If it comes back that we don't share the same parent, then we don't need to bother Ines. If it goes the other way, then we speak to her. Together.'

Antonio frowned. 'What will change knowing this now? Will it just hurt my mother?'

Marta spoke up.

'Maybe it will be a relief to her. It might set her free.'

Antonio remained silent.

'Anyway, Ines doesn't have to cook and clean for us if she doesn't want to.' said Javier, 'We can make other arrangements.'

'I don't think she does it for the money.' said Antonio. 'She loves you and Mateo like family. Based on what my grandparents left her, she could have retired to Ventosa long ago. She didn't want to leave you.'

Javier smiled. 'We need to make sure to protect Ines in all this. But, first things first. Tomorrow, we are going to get a DNA test. It will take a couple of weeks for the results to come back. Then, we can figure out what to do next. John and I will finish the Camino by then, so the timing is right.'

They all agreed this was the best plan. John and Javier would take a rest day and hang out in León to arrange for the test. Later, Antonio walked them to the door.

'I'm sorry to drop all this on you, Antonio. I just wanted to be honest with you.'

Antonio patted his back.

'I would expect nothing less from you. I'll see you tomorrow.'

John's phone buzzed in the taxi back to the hotel. *Isabela*.

'Hey.' He said.

'¡Hola! How are you?'

'I'm in a taxi with Javier. We just left Antonio's house.'

'How did that go? 'she asked.

'It went fine. They're meeting up again tomorrow.'

'Good. Listen. I spoke to *Tio* Diego. Why don't the two of you call me when you get back to the hotel so we can exchange information? I learned a few things that will interest you.'

# TWENTY-FOUR
## THE PLOT THICKENS

At the hotel, John called Isabela and put her on speaker. 'Hi, Isabela.' said Javier anxiously.

'Hey, Javier. Okay. So I spoke to *Tio*. He brought me some pastries *Tia* made, and we spoke over coffee. At first, it was just niceties, but then I decided to go for it.'

'How did he respond?' asked Javier, visibly concerned about upsetting his elderly uncle.

'Initially, he said he hadn't heard any rumors about your father. That it was probably just some villagers making trouble. But after I told him more of the details and that you were looking into it, he opened up a bit.'

John grew impatient as this mystery grew.

'And...?' he asked, prodding her to get to the good part.

'*Tranquilo*. I'm getting to it.' she said, 'So, he told me that your father's marriage was on the rocks at one point. Your mother was more interested in her social life in Madrid, and his ambition didn't match hers. Diego said Eduardo regretted not returning after medical school and settling down here. Eduardo felt guilty about letting their parents down and began visiting Ventosa to run a weekend clinic. Your father would bring you with him because, and these are Diego's words, your mother didn't enjoy having you underfoot.'

Javier closed his eyes and sighed.

'I'm sorry, Javier. I'm just telling you what he told me.'

'I understand. I also know it's the truth.'

'Anyway. *Tio* said there were rumors that he had started a relationship with Ines. But the family never confronted him about it. Then, suddenly, he stopped coming up so often. He would send you on the train with a nanny or by yourself when you were older. Later, you would accompany Antonio, which we already knew. For *Tio* Diego, that confirmed what had happened. They treated Antonio like family because they assumed he was your father's son, but it was never spoken of openly. Even amongst the brothers. *Tio* saw Ines's parents in the village, but no one acknowledged it.'

'Was Diego upset by the conversation?' asked Javier. 'He's elderly. I don't want this to cause him any pain.'

'He seemed okay. Afterward, I told him I wouldn't discuss it with anyone but you. I wasn't trying to dig up old scandals. I just wanted to help you find out the truth.'

Javier sighed.

'I'll speak to him about it next time I am there. Tomorrow, Antonio and I are taking a DNA test. The results will take a couple of weeks.'

'Wow!' said Isabela, 'That was fast. What did Antonio say?'

'He is upset. But after hearing everything we have learned and talking it through, he wants to get to the truth, too.' said Javier. 'But he wants the DNA test results before he speaks to Ines.'

'Makes sense. If it comes back that you are not closely related, then it's all for nothing.'

'Exactly.' agreed Javier. 'If Antonio is my brother, I must determine what that means.'

The three of them silently contemplated this familial eruption before Isabela spoke.

'I think I've done what I can up here. Keep me updated on the results when you get them.'

'I will. Thank you, Isabela.' Javier hung up.

John whistled. 'Uff! This is a lot. Are you alright?'

'Yes. The evidence is stacking up. But the DNA test will be the deciding factor. I'm glad Antonio wants to do it.'

'Have you thought about what you will do if it is true?'

Javier considered the question.

'I believe Antonio would be entitled to a portion of my father's estate. After my mother passes, certainly. We would need to discuss that. You met my mother at the wedding. She's a dragon. If it is true, then we couldn't tell her. She's elderly, and I think it might kill her. I wouldn't do that, even to her.'

'It's a complicated situation.' admitted John.

'Yes.' Javier stood and stretched. 'I'm going to go to bed. I'll meet Antonio tomorrow to have the test and meet you back here afterward.'

'Sounds good.'

As John readied for bed in his room, his phone buzzed. *Pen.*

'Hey!'

'Hi, Dad.' said Pen, sounding down.

'What's going on?' he asked, concerned at the tone of her voice.

'Nothing. I just wanted to hear your voice and see how you are?'

'I'm in León.' John wasn't going to talk to Pen about Javier and Antonio. It wasn't his story to tell. And it involved her husband. 'What's going on with you?'

'Nothing. The new job is taking my mind off Mom a little bit. I've been having these terrible stomach aches. Mateo thinks it's just the stress from starting the new job. But I don't know.'

'How are you feeling about the job? Is it going well?'

'I think it is. Sometimes, though, I feel like I'll always be a foreigner. It's not that people aren't nice, but I know I will never be from here, and everyone else knows it too.'

John closed his eyes. Hearing the pain in her voice made him feel helpless. She wasn't five years old. He couldn't kiss her skinned knee and take the pain away.

'You're capable, Pen. I wonder if it's a little bit of imposter syndrome. Are you worried you aren't qualified for the job?'

'No. I know I'm qualified. It's not that. I have a master's degree. But it's like,' she stopped, perhaps searching for the right words, 'there are times when some curators look at me like, 'Who are you to tell us about a painter from our own country?' Even though I'm an expert on the subject. These days, I speak up less and less. Sometimes, it feels like I'm shrinking to fit whatever they're looking for. Like one of these days, I'll turn to dust.'

John could hear tears. Then, Pen sniffed.

'I'm worried about you, kid.' said John. And he was. The pain in her voice didn't seem like it was the new job. His daughter sounded depressed.

Pen sighed. 'Don't worry, Dad. I'll figure it out. I'm just venting. I love Mateo, but he doesn't know what it's like to live in a country that isn't his. He doesn't see what I see and experience what it's like not to belong anywhere anymore.'

John knew what she was talking about. He was uncomfortable every day on this trip. And while John loved walking in Spain, every interaction with a shopkeeper tested his rudimentary understanding of Spanish. And he had made too many cultural faux pas to count. It didn't take much for John to feel foolish. But then, he had an idea.

'You might call Isabela. She worked as a professor in the US for many years. She knows what it is to feel like a fish out of water — the one who doesn't belong at work. She might be able to help. Or at least she would commiserate with you.'

Pen agreed. 'I hadn't thought of that. But you're right. Isabela might understand. I'll call her on the weekend.'

John smiled. Both Isabela and Pen were capable women. They could support each other.

'In the meantime, please get the stomach pains checked out. Just to be sure. They can give you something for it until you get your feet under you at work.'

Father and daughter said their goodbyes and hung up. John lay in bed for a long time before sleep overtook him. He was sorry Pen was having such a difficult time, but he was happy she thought to call him for support. His daughter still needed him, and his being so far away was becoming a problem for them both.

The following day, with Javier off for the DNA test, John had a free morning. He walked around the old town. His phone rang as he was sitting down for lunch. Isabela's name flashed on the screen.

'Hi!' he said, smiling.

'Hello. I was taking a break from the activities around here today, and I thought I would give you a call.'

'Well, I'm glad you did. I was just having lunch while waiting for Javier to finish the test.'

'How is my cousin?' she asked, suddenly serious. 'Honestly, John.'

'I think it's a little overwhelming. The best way to describe his mood is *introspective*.'

'I bet. It has got to be hard.'

'I would imagine.' observed John. 'Every time Javier walks the Camino, it's filled with drama. This one is no different. But this situation has far-reaching implications for his family.'

'Yes, I'm afraid you're right. But we'll know the truth soon enough.'

John decided to change the subject.

'So, what's new at the vineyard?'

Isabela smiled on the other end. 'This vintage will soon be put to bed. Then it's a winter of repairing equipment and preparing for next spring. I'm thinking I might take a vacation. It's been a while, and I need some time off.'

'That sounds interesting.'

'Yes. There are many destination possibilities. Perhaps you can help me narrow it down to one or two.' she teased.

'I'm no travel agent, but maybe I can be of service.'

Isabela laughed. 'I knew I could count on you. Are you still on track to be in Santiago in two weeks?'

'I think so. It's starting to get chilly in the early mornings, and they say Galicia is wet and cold, so I'm hoping that we don't need to spend more time crossing the mountains that are coming up.'

'Well, if you need someone to warm you up, just call me. It's not that far.'

John smiled. 'I'll keep it in mind.'

'Good. Let me know when you're over O'Cebreiro and heading down. That will be the last major obstacle for you. The rest is just a long walk.'

'I will.' he said. 'I miss you. Does that surprise you? Because it surprises the hell out of me. I wish you were here.'

Isabela skipped a beat before responding.

'I wish I was there, too.' She whispered. 'As I said before, maybe we can spend some time together when you've finished walking, and I'm wrapped up here for the season.'

'I think I'd like that.'

'Good.' she said, 'Now, have your lunch. Tell my cousin if he needs anything, he can call me.'

'I will.'

John hung up. When the waiter delivered a beer, his phone buzzed yet again. It was Javier.

John: *Where are you?*

Javier: *at the hotel, where are you?*

John shared his location. Fifteen minutes later, they sat across from each other.

'So how was the testing?' asked John, digging into his salad. 'It seems like it took a while.'

'Actually, it took no time at all. But Antonio and I got lunch afterward. Neither of us slept well. I have been thinking about all this since Ventosa. He just learned about it last night, so he's in shock, I think.'

'Does he believe it's possible?'

'He thinks it might be true. That there is a good chance. He said his mother never talked about his father. He had vague memories of him when he was young. But other than that, he wouldn't recognize him if he saw him on the street. There were no photos of him in their house. Ines told him something about a flood where things became damaged. But they lived in a fourth-floor apartment, so that story seems flimsy now.'

'When will you have the results?' asked John

'By the time we get to Santiago.'

'That soon?'

'Yes. It's not so unusual these days.' Explained Javier. 'The lab said it's a simple test.'

'I guess you just have to sit back and wait.'

'Yes.' said Javier. 'In some ways, that's easier. Until then, there will be less detective work or other things that will cause upset. There is only one answer, and we have the test to give it to us.'

Javier's face darkened. He looked exhausted.

'What a mess. Why can't anything be easy? Why can't people do what they say they'll do? Do what they're supposed to do?' he sighed. 'I guess I'm disappointed in the two people I loved the most as a child.'

John told him to wait for the results.

Javier responded with a withering look. 'I already know the result. I pulled up photos of Antonio and me from family gatherings. And then, Mateo. We all have the same nose and mouth. Antonio has this unconscious gesture, just like my father. He clicks his nails in the same way when he is nervous. I saw it today.' he sighed. 'Why does that make me so angry?'

John wasn't sure if Javier wanted the answer to that question.

'Life is messy.' said John. 'You think things are one way, and then you find out they're not. When we are disappointed by others, anger is always the result.'

'Yeah, well, I don't like being lied to.' said Javier. 'Why did they do it? And how could they keep it a secret for so long? He practically moved her into our house. I trusted Ines more than anyone when I was growing up. And I looked up to my father like he was a god.'

John struggled to explain.

'In a world of pain, we're all just looking for happiness, Javier. You know that more than anyone. A bit of relief from the agony of living. And then, from the torment of our choices that hurt those we love the most.'

Javier's eyes narrowed. 'So, you think what they did was justified? All those years of misleading everyone. A lifetime of it.' he said, his voice cracking like a lost little boy.

John took a deep breath, trying to explain. 'Your marriage to your wife, Alejandra, that was pure. No one strayed. It sounds idyllic, but I think you know that's not the norm.'

'What do you mean? Because I,' he ran his hand through his greying hair again. 'Because of my relationship with Tess, I should understand what happened between my father and Ines. The lies they told. I never lied to you or anyone about what I did with Tess. But in their case, other people were involved—children's lives. I had a brother the entire time and didn't know it. I wasn't alone. Do you know how alone I felt growing up?' Javier's voice broke.

John closed his eyes, trying to decide how far he should go. 'Ironically, yes, I do. My parents died in a car accident when I was little. I had no brothers or sisters — just my Grandpa Charlie, whom I had never met before. He was a wonderful grandfather, and I should have been happy. Grateful, and I was. But, growing up, I often felt alone until I met Tess, and we had a family of our own. After we met, for more than twenty years I felt like I had hit the lottery. I had everything I dreamed of when I was little. Standing at the graves of my parents, I had asked God for a family. And he delivered. Then, slowly, like torture, the strings of my dream were pulled apart, one by one. First, my son Charlie.' John choked up, swallowing hard before continuing. 'Then the aftermath. Finally, when Tess died, I felt cursed. My friends thought I was crazy for letting Pen come to Spain for her year abroad because I had no one left at home. But there was a part of me that wondered if it was true. If I were cursed, she would be safer here than in the US. So, I understand the loneliness you speak of. To my core.'

When Javier didn't respond, John continued.

'I'm not saying you must understand what your father and Ines did. I'm saying that people do things all the time and don't stop to consider the consequences.' John rose from the table to put some distance between them and paced as Javier sat silently. Then he stopped. 'I cheated on Tess. Okay? And then, I don't know why, I made sure she knew about it.'

Javier's eyes widened in horror. As if by reflex, he stood to face John as the blood drained from his face. 'I don't understand.'

'It was two years after Charlie died.' John gulped as the words came rushing out. 'At the time, I thought it was the worst two years of my life. It brought back all the pain of losing my parents. I felt as if it couldn't get worse.' he snorted. 'I had no clue what was coming. Just how much worse it would get.'

Javier sat down hard, stunned, concentrating on a spot on the table, refusing to look at John.

John's story came out as if through a fog while digging into the muck of his most shameful memories.

'The first six months after we buried our son, we all clung together. The emotions were what you would expect. We would cry together sometimes. But slowly, that ended. I stopped crying in front of Tess. Thinking back, Pen stopped, too. Sometimes, I would catch our daughter looking out the window, lost in thought, but I never asked what she was thinking. And I didn't want to upset Tess and Pen with my continued grief. Somehow, I felt I wasn't entitled to keep showing the world how devastated I was. Maybe it was some misplaced idea of masculinity that I should be stronger. But Tess went a different way. She became a cheerleader at home—like a court jester, always trying to cheer us up. But that was her only setting. The spigot of her emotional range had completely shut off. Sealed away. It was as though she made it her mission to make us smile. She couldn't allow for our sadness. And the more she did it, the more we hated her for it. The more *I* hated her for it. She booked family trips for us like we had before Charlie died. Some weekend outings. The pumpkin patch. A Christmas tree farm. A local festival none of us cared about. I recently found photos on a flash drive in the back of a drawer in my office at home. She took photos of Pen and me, telling us to *smile*. We looked miserable, but she refused to see it.'

Javier sat horrified.

'After Charlie died, we stopped having sex altogether. Now, I know it's pretty normal. But it was as if neither of us could figure out how to restart that part of our relationship. The act was what had created our son, and he was gone. It was as if we had an unspoken agreement that its intimacy would break us both. Pleasure was no longer allowed. We went to bed each night and rolled away.' John continued with tears in his eyes. 'We never talked about it, but I missed her in that way. I missed being with her. The comfort of knowing her body and that we were still connected. We lay next to each other in the same bed, but the distance between us was the Grand Canyon.'

'Two years after the accident, I was at a conference with a colleague, and I had a little more to drink than I normally would. One thing led to another. I'm not proud of it. I didn't even enjoy it. Afterward, I went into the bathroom and threw up, crying into a hotel towel. It was something I could never take back. I wasn't being myself, the person I knew I was. But then, nothing had been normal since the death of my son.'

John's lip quivered, but he took a deep breath and continued. 'I went home and pretended like it didn't happen. I could never tell Tess. But then, she continued with the cheerleader thing, and I got angrier and angrier. How could she pretend like everything was okay? How could she expect us to behave like it was? So, the next time I traveled, I met up with the woman again. And this time, I left the receipts in plain sight. Not consciously, but I look back now and see how I couldn't go on. I needed something to change. You can call me a coward, and you would be right. I could have insisted we talk about our feelings. Go to counseling. But I didn't.'

'Why would you do that to her?' whispered Javier, shaking his head, then looking at John with such loathing it shocked him. 'She was hurting, too. I know she was.'

'I don't even know.' said John with tears streaming down his face, awash in shame. 'It wasn't a conscious thing. But I somehow needed to know she hadn't lost the ability to feel. To know that she didn't die in that car crash right along with Charlie. And that I wasn't alone in my inability to dig my way out of despair.'

John covered his face with his hands and sobbed before wiping his nose on his sleeve.

'I have experienced too much death in my life—too much grief. I am so tired of it, Javier. I can't carry it anymore. I'm not that strong.' he said, exhausted. 'Why? Why me? Am I being punished?

It was a moment before Javier finally spoke.

'What happened when Tess found out?' asked Javier.

John sniffed.

'I bought the woman a gift from a place that was obviously not a tire store. Something ridiculously cliché. And I left the receipt on my night table. I put it on our joint credit card – along with a hotel charge for a place I wasn't supposed to be. It didn't take a rocket scientist. And Tess was a smart woman.'

Javier waited. 'I bet she was devastated. And knowing Tess, very angry.'

John wiped his nose on his sleeve. He remembered back to that horrible day. Tess held out the receipts as he walked into the kitchen after work. She didn't speak a word. John looked over and noticed a nearly empty wine bottle on the counter. There was a cork but no glass. Then, she went into their bedroom and stripped down. Tess climbed into the shower and stood under the scalding hot water for a long time. John waited in the kitchen — for what he didn't know.

'I heard her crying, but it was the wailing that broke me—a keening. It came from a place deep inside her. As if every hurt she had ever felt was contained in that one sound. I entered the bathroom and found her sitting on the shower floor as the water rushed over her.' he cried. 'Like she didn't have the strength to stand. I turned off the water and picked her up. She was shivering and clung to me, ripping the buttons off the front of my shirt. My suit was soaking wet, but I didn't want her to let go because I knew we would be lost if she did.'

'We sat on the bed like that for a long time. I held her like a baby while she sobbed. We both did. And then, we made love for the first time in two years. You probably wouldn't expect that, after finding out I was unfaithful, she would want to do that, especially with me. But we needed to know we were still us. After all that had happened, we were still in this marriage. Together.'

'Did you ever talk about the affair?' asked Javier.

John nodded and ran his sleeve under his nose. 'Yes. Afterward, we lay there, and Tess asked me all the details. She wanted to know if I was in love with the woman. It was an easy answer. Absolutely not. More important to her, Tess asked me if I liked her. Were we friends? Did she make me laugh?'

Javier closed his eyes. 'It's a strange question. But I can hear Tess asking it.'

'That's what I thought,' said John. ' Tess said she would be more worried if I liked the woman because Tess and I had been best friends before we became a couple. We liked each other from the first moment and made each other laugh.'

Javier nodded.

'Things were better after that.' said John. 'But still not normal.'

'Did you ever see the woman again?' asked Javier. 'The one you had an affair with?'

'Once. At a meeting in New York for a project I was working on. It was awkward, but I had already told her it was over. Frankly, my heart wasn't in it, and she said she knew that from the beginning.'

Suddenly, the light went on for Javier.

'So, this is why you wrote that letter to Tess before she walked the Camino. I always wondered. Was it out of guilt?' he asked, frowning.

'Maybe a little.' said John. 'But, I wanted her to have the Camino she needed without constraints. I had no idea what this walk does to a person. How much you change while you do it. If I had known, I might not have written what I did.' he stopped to consider the question. 'But maybe I would have. I don't know. I loved her and was afraid of losing her — from cancer or grief – mine or hers. I did what I did. And now, I'm sitting here with you. I've never told anyone else. The secret, the shame, has eaten me alive, even though I thought it died with Tess.' John stopped and faced Javier. 'I am surprised Tess never told you. All the time you spent together.'

Javier shook his head. 'No. She said nothing negative about you except that you weren't perfect. After everything, she was loyal to you. She loved you, John, even after what you did to her. She told me that more than once. For her, you were *The One*.'

John fought to keep from crying out. 'I know she did.' he whispered. 'For so long, I felt like Tess was out of reach. She had taken herself off somewhere, emotionally, where I couldn't go. But I think she fought as hard as she could to find her way back to us. Maybe she fought harder than I did.'

Javier remained silent, not letting John off the hook.

'I can't undo what I did.' John wiped the tears on his shirt tail. 'No matter how much I wish I could. Regrets are pointless.'

'So, Pen never found out?' asked Javier.

'No. I don't think so. Tess wouldn't have told her, and I know I never did.'

'But she thinks her mom cheated on her dad.' Javier frowned. 'That's the impression left on Pen. One of the last experiences of spending time with her mom, and that is what she thinks.'

John shook his head. 'No. Pen knows about the letter. She knows that Tess wasn't cheating.'

'She was a teenager. They see everything as black and white. And she doesn't know why you wrote the letter.' Javier sighed. 'Family secrets, John. They eat away. The ghosts always find their way out to haunt us.'

John knew his mistakes were mixing with what Javier was going through. He also knew Javier was right. But telling Pen wasn't high on his priority list.

'All this time.' whispered Javier. 'You were *the selfless hero,* and I was *the villain.* Tess was *the villain,* too. For more than ten years. I don't know how to respond.'

John wiped his eyes. 'Not for me. I told you, I am not angry with either of you. I did this to myself. But maybe it's time to put *hero* and *villain* labels aside. Maybe the idea that things are always black and white should be retired, as well. Because of my gross imperfection, I try to look at people from multiple perspectives—even those who have hurt me. No one is all dark or light. They say *hurt people, hurt people,* and I know it's true. We especially hurt those we love the most. We disappoint them because they risk loving us. But it's not always intentional. Sometimes, we hurt them for fear that they will find out who we really are and reject us and our weaknesses. Our fears are what cut so deep. Ironically, our greatest fear is that the ones we love will no longer love us.'

John reached down and squeezed Javier's shoulder.

'Maybe this is why your father and Ines kept their secret from you and Antonio. It cost them dearly and must have been a terrible burden. But they tried to raise you and Antonio like the brothers you are. They gave you memories of each other in your day-to-day lives in Madrid and up at the farm, surrounded by family who loved you unconditionally. That's the best they could do. And they did it out of love, not malice. If you are right about all this, you have a brother now, a real one. And nieces. Mateo has cousins, not just aging grandparents and uncles. He has Pen, yes. But when you and Ines are gone, Mateo has a family who shares the blood that runs through his veins and those of his future children. Maybe I don't have the right to say this, but you can view it as a gift and accept it rather than ask for the 'why.' Because, in the end, does the 'why' really matter?'

Javier sat staring into his beer. He looked both angry and sad. They had been through a lot on this trek. A trek that was supposed to be all about Tess had turned into something neither man could have bargained for.

'Let me ask you something. Have you told my cousin all this? Does Isabela know how you treated your wife?' asked Javier, with a look of pure loathing.

John took a sharp breath, surprised by the question. 'No. We haven't had that conversation.'

'I didn't think so. Isabela's husband hurt her badly and did some of what you did. How do you think she would feel learning this?'

'I don't know.' whispered John. 'She told me about her ex-husband. I'm not entirely sure it's the same thing, but I'm tired of secrets. If this relationship goes any further, I will tell her.'

Javier nodded, then rose like he was carrying a boulder before declaring he needed space. He left John sitting at the cafe and walked away without a word.

John paid for the beer and his uneaten lunch, then found his way to the church beside their hotel. He remembered the appropriate motions, like muscle memory from attending church with his deeply faithful Grandpa Charlie. He and Tess decided to raise their kids without formal religion. They believed Charlie and Pen could be good people without dogma as their anchor. But, today, John took comfort in the known. He made his way to the front of the church, crossed himself, fell to his knees, and bowed his head.

'I can't take the weight of it all anymore. When can I put this down? Please, God, help me. I need peace. I need forgiveness. I need relief.' he begged. 'And I need love. Somehow, this can't be the end for me. Am I going to live the rest of my life alone as penance? Is this the sentence for my crime?' John cried. 'Please help me find my way. Help me know what to do. And please help me to help Javier.'

John rose to leave. As he made his way slowly up the aisle to the back of the church, he noticed Javier was there, too, head bowed, praying in a side chapel. Somehow, the two men had found themselves in the same place, searching for answers. John didn't disturb him as he returned to the hotel, leaving Javier to his conversation with God.

# Part IV

## Going It Alone

# TWENTY-FIVE
## ANOTHER MOUNTAIN TO CLIMB

John woke and texted Javier as he packed up. The warmth of the hotel room would be hard to leave on a wet, windy autumn day walking out of León. Used to living in the sun of Arizona, John faced the increasingly cold weather on the Camino with dread. But it was not just the weather; something had shifted between him and Javier. He hadn't seen Javier since their conversation the previous afternoon, but John felt it. After twenty minutes and no response, John put on his coat and pack, went down the hall to Javier's room, and knocked. Silence greeted him.

John walked downstairs to the lobby and sat on the sofa near the front desk. He waited before texting Javier again. When the other man finally appeared, he wasn't dressed to walk the Camino, and his pack was nowhere in sight.

'What's going on?' asked John, confused.

'I am sorry to tell you, but my Camino is ending here. You must complete the last weeks on your own.' said Javier, matter-of-factly.

'What?!' asked John, confused. 'Is this because of what I told you yesterday?'

Javier sighed. 'In truth, at the moment, I have too much going on in my life that requires my attention. Last night, I spoke with my family's lawyer. And I have some things to do before the DNA results come back. And before I speak to Ines. If I walk to Santiago with you, I will not have the time to prepare for what is coming.'

'Excuse me?' asked John.

'You know how to walk the Camino now.' Javier assured him. 'You can do this by yourself. Just follow the yellow arrows, like always. But I must return to the Basque Country and get my family's house in order. I'm not asking you to understand. But it's something I need to do. Now.'

John understood. Of course, he did. But he lacked the confidence Javier seemed to have in him. For the past three weeks, he had mindlessly followed Javier's lead on walking the right path on this Camino. Now, he would have to figure it out for himself. John picked up his pack and grabbed his poles.

'Buen Camino.' said Javier before turning back to the elevator and returning to his room.

The rain poured down in sheets past the window, and a river of water ran from the rooftop to the planters lining the courtyard. John walked out through the lobby doors and stood under the shelter of the former cloisters. Digging into his pack, he extracted his rain gear and put it on. Then, shrugging into his pack, he fastened the buckles and marched through the gate. Standing on the quiet cobbled street of the old historic center, John looked right, then left. There were no yellow arrows he could see. Maybe it was a sign. Like Javier, he could just rent a car and stop this madness. Take care of business as quickly as possible. Pen's face flashed in his head. His daughter needed him. He could feel it. Maybe the lack of arrows was a sign.

For weeks, yellow arrows seemed everywhere in every town and city they had walked through— on rocks, sidewalks, and buildings. Sometimes, large yellow arrows were inelegantly spray-painted into the middle of the road. But now, nothing. It was as if Javier had removed them all in the middle of the night to mock him. John decided to walk to the right, back toward the Cathedral. Surely, arrows were waiting for him and every other Pilgrim from there.

At the Cathedral he found his first arrow of the day before realizing it pointed him back from where he had just come. He was walking in circles.

'You're messing with me now.' he said to the gloomy skies pouring down upon him. John hunkered deeper into his rain gear and trudged back from where he had come.

The light peeked over the horizon as the city awakened. Cars splashed past him on the street, drenching John at low points in the road. So much water fell from the sky that John barely noticed the water coming up from below as a line of red taillights lit his path on his solitary march out of the city.

It seemed that León would never end as he followed the road, walking mainly on the sidewalk. John paid close attention to the Camino markers as he walked for the next two hours. On the lookout for other pilgrims to follow to confirm the right direction, he appeared to be the only one walking out of León that rainy morning in mid-October. All the other pilgrims, along with Javier, had vanished.

*Fucking Javier.* Why did he have to ditch John? They were supposed to be doing this together. That was their deal. But the guy abandoned him. John thought back to the afternoon before and their discussion at the cafe. He kicked himself for revealing his affair. It wasn't any of Javier's business anyway. John tried to make the man understand that sometimes, even good people do hurtful things. But this morning, it appeared that what Javier took from his admission was that John was a bad guy who had hurt Tess. And, by extension, Javier. John couldn't control how the other man felt, but he wished Javier could see past his actions and focus on what John was trying to say. The man's reaction cut too close to what John was already feeling. Javier's harsh judgment quickly triggered John's self-loathing on the most miserable day of his Camino.

Slogging for hours through the wet and wind, John eventually arrived at Hospital de Órbrigo. The stone town dates back to the 13th century when the townspeople blew up their bridge to stop Napoleon's army and their progress in conquering Spain. Despite his rain gear, John was wet and muddy to his skin. While walking across the famous bridge, his only thought was of a warm room with a hot shower, dry socks, and underwear.

Finally, clean and warm, John sat in his €50 room and surveyed his situation. He spent the day entirely alone—his first on this Camino. Usually comfortable with his own company, John had become used to Javier's interjections of Spanish history and local cultural anecdotes. The bridge he had just crossed was unlike anything he had ever seen. But he had no idea who built it or why. It would be up to him to look it up during his dinner. And dinner tonight would be a lonely affair. It seemed he was the only person staying in his pension.

John descended the stairs as the proprietor stood cleaning glasses at the bar out of habit rather than necessity. They acknowledged each other as John bundled up against the wet cold and left to find food in a more welcoming location. On the way, he thought about calling Isabela or Pen, but he didn't want to field questions about how Javier was doing. He had no idea where the man was at the moment, and he didn't want to have to lie.

In the end, his dinner was unremarkable. Three courses of the same *ensalada atún*, filleted chicken with French fries, and a dessert of Santiago cake. The pilgrim menu. It was calories and protein – the twin friends of any pilgrim. But after weeks, the familiar combination provided little culinary joy. Over coffee, John wondered yet again if he should continue his walk. He didn't need to finish. Tess hadn't required this of him in her letter. Just that he spread her ashes along the Camino, and he had done that in the places she specified. But the Camino flame that started in Saint-Jean burned a little brighter. He was closer to the end than the beginning. Javier was right. He needed to do this last bit on his own and finish what he started. Isabela's cork was still in his pocket, and he worried on it more and more, like a talisman. The monk's bracelet still adorned his wrist, and he fidgeted with it at coffee stops. John didn't believe in such things, but the combination of the two made him feel less alone.

Making his way back to the pension through the dark, wet streets of the historic town, John stopped to take in the quiet as the light from a street lamp spilled across the cobbles. He was in Spain, walking through places his wife and daughter had passed through a decade before. But John was no longer the same man as when they walked. Squeezing the cork, he knew Isabela was correct; he wasn't even the same man who started this journey more than three weeks ago. Maybe he wouldn't be the same man who walked into Santiago. Zipping his jacket up to the neck for warmth, John returned to his pension. A couple of mountains awaited him before he was home.

# Twenty-Six
## Digging in the Dirt

Javier navigated the rental car down the long gravel road leading to the sheep farm he inherited from his namesake, *Tio* Javier. His father's brother and closest confidant, the two men were best friends since childhood, growing up in the vineyards of La Rioja. The farm was where his nephew, Dr. Javier, would begin his search for the truth.

As he told John in the lobby, after their conversation at the cafe, Javier returned to the hotel and phoned his father's longtime solicitor in Madrid. After his father's death, Javier had taken over the family affairs as his mother, María, was in no fit state to unwind the complicated set of accounts set up by her husband in anticipation of his eventual demise. There were numerous bank accounts and charitable bequests—significant investments with dedicated income to maintain his mother's lifestyle. However, Maria was wealthy in her own right. She didn't need the money. Javier left much of the paperwork to the lawyer, Don Ruben Alcor Ortega, who explained that his father had thought of every scenario and that he should not be concerned about too many details. But now, the details mattered, and the lawyer was old. After repeated requests for answers, the older man finally revealed information he had previously withheld. Javier presumed this was out of loyalty to his client and friend. But loyalty had its limits. And Javier made sure the old *abogado* knew it.

Like his father, Javier was a patient man. He waited quietly on the line while the old gentleman swallowed a drink of whatever beverage he enjoyed in the evening. Finally, after a significant cough, the lawyer drew forth a secret that might be the key to the entire mystery.

'As you know, my obligation is to my client. Your father left strict instructions upon his death, and I followed them to the letter. Please do not imply that I violated the law, my friend, because I also followed the letter of the law as it was written at that time. Yes, perhaps things have changed now, but that is of no concern to me. As was my duty, I executed your father's last wishes and his final *testamento*.'

Javier sighed. 'I am not suggesting that you did anything illegal, Don Ruben. However, I need answers, and I need them quickly. I understand inheritance laws. I know what is required. I also know there are ways around them while a person still lives — the property or funds gifted away from the family. Perhaps set aside for one purpose or another. Money that finds its way elsewhere. Secrets that are quietly buried so as not to embarrass a family in good social standing when a person dies. Perhaps to ensure reputations remain intact. I don't care so much about property or money. What I need to know are the secrets.'

The older man coughed once more. Javier heard rustling, imaging the old lawyer in his wood-paneled library in Madrid, cloaked in his silk dressing gown, with a Cuban cigar burning in the ashtray, while rifling through papers in a cabinet. The solicitor returned to the phone.

'Okay, okay.' stalling, the raspy voice regained its familiar authoritative timber. 'Years ago, your father insisted I store some boxes for him in my office. I never looked inside. But they would be shipped to his brother upon his death.' more paper rustled. 'The address, if you could call it that, was in the Basque Country—some farm. I had to hire a service to deliver it there. It wasn't cheap. I don't believe even *Correos* or *Amazon* would deliver packages that far from nowhere. Even today.'

Javier held his breath. 'You sent my father's boxes to my *Tio* at the sheep farm?' he asked.

'Yes. I think that's the place. Anyway. I have no idea what happened to them after that, so don't ask me. I never heard from your uncle after I sent them. The signed receipt returned to me showed he took possession of them. It is in my files, so you can not accuse me of disposing of them by any other manner.'

'And you have no idea what was in these boxes?' asked a frustrated Javier. The man dealt out information like a locked vault. Waiting for Javier to ask the right questions.

'No. I do not. The boxes were the possessions of a client. I never looked inside. Come to think of it, they were like little coffins and were nailed shut. Each of them was very heavy. It took two men to take them away.'

Javier thought for a moment. 'So, the boxes were made of wood? Is there anything else you want to tell me?'

The old man breathed heavily into the receiver before answering as if considering his following words carefully. 'Go to the farm, Javier. See what you can find. Then, call me.' The line went dead.

Javier sat on the bed in the old convent hotel in León. His Camino was over.

# TWENTY-SEVEN
## IT'S NOT WHAT HE THOUGHT

The angry weather continued with torrential rain the following morning. John's gear was still damp from the day before, and there were puddles on the floor of his room as his fleece dripped throughout the night. Squeezing it out in the bathtub once more, he would not benefit from it on this cold, wet day walking toward Astorga.

Dragging his pack and poles down the dark staircase, John soon learned that his pension was not serving breakfast or even coffee. Strapping on his gaiters and putting on his pack, John struggled with his rain poncho alone. He left the room key on the bar and stepped out of the relative warmth of his now-previous accommodations. It was time to search for food before heading out of town. Who knew when his next opportunity for sustenance might present itself?

The early morning darkness made finding a cafe much easier as the fluorescent light spilled out from the windows of open establishments. A bar displaying a faded sign with food beckoned John as he entered and shrugged off his pack. Another pilgrim was enjoying a coffee at a nearby table, and John nodded her way. Then, he ordered one for himself, as he had heard Javier do a hundred times before. The barman grunted but turned to make the coffee and the ham and cheese croissant he requested.

As the other pilgrim greeted him, John turned around and waited for the coffee.

'Buenos dias.' she offered.

'Buenos dias.' said John. 'I apologize. I don't speak Spanish.'

'Don't worry.' said the woman. 'I don't speak it well either. I am French.'

John examined her more closely with her coffee-colored complexion and brown eyes. Like America, France is also a melting pot of cultures.

John grabbed his food and coffee and asked the pilgrim if her could join her. She nodded, then wiped her hands on a napkin and held one out after he'd set his dishes on the table.

'I am Gaelle. Nice to meet you.'

John smiled, shaking her hand. 'John the American. Nice to meet you.'

'Where did you start your Camino?' she asked

'Three weeks ago, in Saint-Jean. What about you?'

She swallowed her croissant. 'In Le Puy. 800km before Saint-Jean.'

John's eyes widened. 'Wow. That's a lot of walking.'

Gaelle's smile creased her freckled face. 'Yes. It has been a long journey. In just two weeks more, I will finish.'

John took a swig of his hot café con leche. 'Have you walked alone since Le Puy?'

Gaelle nodded. 'Yes and no. Sometimes, I walk with people for a few days. But then they stay in a place for an extra day, or I might stay somewhere else, too. And we lost track. But I have met lovely people on this trip. Sometimes, I see pilgrims more than once at different times. But this isn't so much about walking with other people but with myself. Listening to myself. Healing old wounds.'

John nodded. He hadn't had much of that on his Camino, having walked with Javier most of the way. Gaelle smiled.

'Why did you want to come to walk the Camino, John?'

John hadn't revealed his reasons for walking — his actual reasons. Yes, Tess wanted him to spread the ashes. But that wasn't why he was here. John still wasn't sure he understood what it was, but he knew he was closer to finding out now that he was alone.

'I'm not entirely sure.' he told Gaelle.

She smiled. 'Yet.'

'Excuse me?' said John, confused.

'You aren't quite sure *yet*. I think you will discover it very soon.'

'You sound like my friend, Javier.' he said. 'We walked together until León. But he had something important he needed to do and left yesterday. He said I needed to finish this alone.'

Gaelle was finished with her food and gathered her things to leave.

'Would you like some company today? he asked, like a lost puppy. 'On the walk to Astorga?'

Gaelle stopped and studied John. 'I don't think so. Your friend is right. It would be best if you spent some time alone. It's the only way to figure things out.'

Gaelle put on her gear and smiled at John as he finished his breakfast. 'Perhaps we will see each other on the way.' Then she left without another word.

John watched her go. What the hell? Was this his karma? In the end, he always found himself alone. Finishing his breakfast, John gathered his dishes, and set them on the bar, leaving the money for the coffee and croissant. He put on his pack, gathered his poles, and went to the door. Looking back, the barman was deep in conversation with the lone customer. Neither seemed to mark his departure. Right now, he didn't matter to anyone.

# Twenty-Eight
## They Must Be Here Somewhere

Javier searched in the house, tearing through cupboards and clearing under beds. It seemed his uncle had saved nearly everything he had ever possessed — every scrap of paper or paper clip. It was slow going as Javier read through old farm journals and ledgers. The old man was quite the Lothario in his younger years, as he kept a stash of letters tied with different colored ribbons from women with whom he had corresponded. One appeared to be the wife of a neighboring farmer who wrote to him with somewhat explicit regularity during the 1960s and 70s. Javier didn't have his uncle's side of the correspondence, but from the writer's references, it appeared *Tio* Javier was a prolific lover. If it was the woman he was thinking of, it challenged his imagination to think of her like that, having only seen her in rubber boots, a worn apron, and gray hair tucked underneath a scarf. Imagining his uncle in that way made Javier smile. Perhaps it ran in the family and was why his uncle didn't judge his father's indiscretions too harshly. Maybe this is why, for Eduardo, his brother's farm was the safest place to store the secret boxes.

Darkness fell as Javier stood in the bedroom his uncle had occupied for decades. His back hurt as he stretched and yawned. The old wooden floor creaked under his feet. Where could these boxes be? What did they even look like? And after he found them, what did they contain? Javier remembered the outbuildings on the property. There were ten or so that would need excavating. But tonight wasn't the time. He needed food and a good night's sleep before tackling the first of them.

The following morning, Javier chose the one nearest the house and spent the rest of the day pulling junk outside and spitting spider webs from his mouth. But, by nightfall, he was no closer to discovering the truth.

# Twenty-Nine

## Beyond Astorga

John stopped for lunch in Astorga but pushed on to Murias de Rechivaldo. He met other pilgrims in Astorga but ignored their advice to stay overnight and tour the cathedral and the Gaudi Museum. John wasn't in the mood to be a tourist. The French pilgrim assessment was correct, and so was Javier's. This part of his Camino required solitude.

For the first time in over three weeks, his feet began to give him trouble—as a large blister formed on his right heel. The rain and his wet socks ensured his misery continued. He limped into the small village, going to a local albergue and asking for their only private room. John was disappointed to learn that it had already been taken. His only choice would be a bed in the large room filled with bunk beds, or he could try another albergue. *Beggars can't be choosers*—he heard his grandpa's voice.

John secured a bed for the night. And enjoyed a five-minute hot shower and some warm, dry clothes.

'You are limping.' observed the host. 'Are you injured?'

John smiled. 'No. I have a blister from all the rain. Is there a pharmacy nearby?'

The woman shook her head. 'We do not have a *farmacia* in this village. But, even if we did, it is a holiday. They would not be open. Do you have bandages and alcohol to disinfect it?'

John shook his head. Javier had his first aid kit. John had forgotten to get it from him after announcing his shock departure from their Camino.

'Let me finish something. I can help in 15 minutes. Have a seat in the lounge.'

'Don't worry about it.' John tried to wave her away. 'I'm sure it will be okay. I will live.'

The woman pulled a face. 'Once you get a blister, it doesn't just 'get better'. Not in this weather. If you get an infection this far from Santiago, you will not finish. And, besides, you still have two mountains to climb. Sit in the lounge. I will bring what you need.'

John didn't like relying upon other people, but he did as she instructed, buying a beer from the vending machine and a bag of crisps. A futbol game blared from the television, and a couple of Danish pilgrims shouted at the screen. John didn't know one end of a futbol pitch from another. Even when Pen played soccer, he never understood anything except when they scored a goal. Baseball had been his and his dad's game. John went to Pen's matches to support his daughter, not because he loved the sport.

As promised, the albergue host arrived on time with a plastic bin filled with medical supplies. The woman removed John's flip-flops as she examined his foot.

'I was a nurse before I retired. It would be best if you threaded your blister with alcohol to sterilize it. Then, we will drain it and bandage it up.'

Her gloved-up, capable hands performed the task with efficiency as John watched her stab him with the sewing needle while trying not to flinch. Afterward, the woman seemed satisfied with her handiwork.

'There. You should begin to heal, and if you keep it taped over while walking, you will not have to worry about infection.'

John thanked her, but she waved it away. 'It is the end of the season. You are lucky I still had supplies left. You should pick up some at the *farmacia* in Rabanyal tomorrow. The conditions between here and there are difficult, and the path is brutal and rocky from Cruz de Ferro to Molinaseca. Trust me.'

The following day, John took her advice and stopped at the small farmacia in Rabanyal before limping on to Foncebadon and a room for the night. As he looked out the window at the snowfall, John didn't relish the thought of the icy hike down the mountain the following day from the Iron Cross.

# THIRTY

## COME OUT, COME OUT, WHEREVER YOU ARE

Javier was sore from excavating the old stone sheds on the property. He went through one after the other, and still, he had no luck locating the boxes his father's lawyer sent to his uncle. Where could *Tío* have put them?

After their tense exchange in the hotel lobby in León, John hadn't reached out to him, and Javier hadn't contacted him either. While rummaging through the sheds, Javier had time to reflect on their conversation at the café and regretted his reaction. John revealed his infidelity to Javier in an attempt to help him and to connect. He could see that telling the story was difficult for John. The man seemed tormented by what he had done, so much so that he had remained celibate for ten years following Tess's death. Javier felt sure he was being truthful about that. At this point, John had no reason to lie. So why had John's revelations triggered him so profoundly? Was it the need to protect Tess? But from what? Why was he angry with John for something that had happened long before Javier met Tess? Marriage is complicated. And their marriage was between John and Tess. It was none of his business.

Javier sat in the rose garden, watching the sunset while nursing a beer—the rose bush where they deposited Tess's ashes lay at his feet.

'Do you think I was too hard on John?' he asked the bush. 'Should I call him?'

Why was he surprised when no answer came? Of course not. Tess was gone, and he was on his own. But if he did call John, what would he say? Sorry, I abandoned you on a wild goose chase to find mysterious boxes belonging to my father that don't seem to exist.

'What do you think, my love? Where would you be if you were old wooden boxes filled with family secrets?'

Javier heard one of the dogs barking non-stop back toward the barn. Still carrying his beer, he marched from the house to the barn. It was a trek after a long day. Winter lambing season hadn't begun, and most of the work these days took place in the milking sheds. The barn was empty when he arrived, except for the giant yellow Mastin barking at a tiny, grey-striped kitten mewling from the roof of the barn shed piled with rusty farm implements. Javier petted the whining dog and then spoke to the kitten.

'How did you get there all by yourself? Did he chase you up there?'

An ancient, rickety wooden ladder leaned on the barn wall, and Javier propped it against the shed, testing the first step. Would it hold his weight? If he fell, there was no telling when someone would discover him. Checking his pocket for his mobile, he climbed up. At first, the kitten was skittish, hopping onto an old piece of equipment to hide. But she purred as if to encourage him closer. Javier lifted the flea-ridden mongrel into his arms, petting and soothing the frightened animal. He tucked her into his jacket and buttoned it up so she wouldn't fall on the climb down. Javier looked around as if for the first time. Old equipment and piles of junk littered the platform, making up the shed's roof. A stained tarp peeked out from under a pile of heavy chains. Javier pulled the end of one chain, and the rest fell at his feet, causing him to jump back, teetering on the roof's edge. He yanked on the end of the tarp to steady himself, and as if by magic, four old wooden boxes appeared.

# THIRTY-ONE
## A ROCKY PATH

In the early morning darkness, John walked up the mountain through the snow from Foncebadón to the Iron Cross. Millions of pilgrims have visited the site over the centuries. The snow-covered pile of stones rose through the fog as the sun came over the horizon. John laid his stone with the millions of others that formed a large mound, holding the tall cross in place. He marveled at all the offerings. Pictures of loved ones who had passed or were battling illness peeked out of the white fluff—rocks inscribed with messages of peace and hope or pleas of forgiveness. John stood for a moment and thought of Tess here—hoping and praying for healing. They didn't know they would need a miracle at that point. He wondered if she had asked for one for herself, would she still be with them now?

Other pilgrims had told him that this holy place did things to people; everyone completed the ritual in their own time. John stood and bowed his head, asking for help—or guidance. He craved forgiveness and relief from the constant ache for those he'd lost. Grief from the death of his son had twisted him into someone he didn't recognize, and his guilt about Tess was something he lived with every day. Regret was the worst punishment imaginable—like a permanent hairshirt until the wearer deems himself worthy to remove it. John knew he didn't deserve to suffer for the rest of his life because of one horrible choice. Tess understood that when she asked him to take this trek with Javier. After everything, his wife never judged him as harshly as he judged himself.

John walked down the mound, wiping tears from his frozen cheeks as he picked up his pack and readied for his solitary walk down the treacherous, wind-swept mountainside.

The path to El Acebo turned brutal as the weather went from bad to worse. Icy rain and wind battered him as he finally reached the village perched above the valley overlooking Ponferrada. John stopped at a cafe to dry out before continuing toward the city in the valley below. The cafe was part of a pension run by an American couple who appeared happy to chat with a fellow citizen over a beer. Just then, the door opened, and the Frenchwoman, Gaelle, entered soaked to the bone. She smiled when she saw John.

'Hey there.' said John.

'Halo.' she replied in sing-songy French-accented English while removing her wet gear. 'You beat me here.'

John stood up in the old timbered building to help her with her pack as she plopped down in the chair across from him, grateful for the opportunity to rest.

'Can I get you something?' asked John.

Gaelle sighed with weary.

'I could use a hot coffee. I'm freezing.' she shivered. 'It was brutal walking down from Cruz de Ferro.'

John ordered her a warm drink. He brought it back to the table, and she wrapped her red fingers around the cup before bringing it to her lips.

'It seems you have been ahead of me since I last saw you in Hospital de Órbigo.' She said. 'I'm surprised I caught up with you.'

John took a sip of the last of his beer. 'Yes. I didn't stop in Astorga or even Rabanyal. Yesterday, I went on to Foncebadon.'

'I felt a little guilty about not walking with you to Astorga. But, seeing your face, I think it was good for you.'

John smiled. 'Maybe.' unfolding his long legs and standing for a stretch. 'It's been a good walk so far.' Looking at his watch. 'But I need to get going. I've been here for over an hour, and my muscles are tightening.'

Gaelle frowned. 'You are leaving so soon?'

John put on his gear, then slid his rain poncho over himself and his pack. Finally, he grabbed his poles.

'I'd like to get to Ponferrada today. I want to do some laundry and sleep in a warm hotel room. Maybe have a meal that doesn't include the words *del dia.*' he laughed.

Gaelle smiled knowingly. 'I understand. Maybe I will see you on the trail.'

'Maybe.' said John, waving to the group from the door. He walked outside into the ominous sky and a treacherous trail down the mountain to Molineseca, nestled in the foggy valley below.

# Thirty-Two

## A Light in the Distance

Pen sat at the kitchen table drinking coffee in the home she shared with her husband, Mateo. Ines stood at the stove in her worn floral apron, making an omelet as Pen swallowed hard, trying to keep her café con leche down. She had a lot on her mind these days. The dream job at the museum was more challenging than Pen anticipated. Not because she was unqualified. No matter how many friendly invitations she made to her coworkers for a coffee or a drink after work, making friends with colleagues proved beyond her skill set. Even colleagues who didn't like each other liked Pen even less.

Pen's immediate boss didn't seem to warm to her, either. It took a few months, but recently, she discovered why. Mateo surprised her for lunch one day—upon seeing Mateo through the glass partition of her office, her boss, the woman who barely spoke to Pen and criticized everything she did, bounded through the door. Unbeknownst to Pen, this dragon went to school with Mateo from kindergarten through high school. And, from the look of it, she still had a crush on Pen's husband.

Rapid-fire Spanish peppered her, multiple cheek kisses, and memories reminisced—an interaction in which Pen was intentionally excluded, at least by her boss. But Mateo's face lit up, too, discussing *the old days*. It was as if she were invisible to her husband; he was some guy she barely knew.

'You remember Lola from our wedding?' Mateo asked Pen as if he just realized he had a wife. 'We have been friends for a very long time.'

No, she didn't remember this creature from their wedding. One of the five hundred guests, Lola wasn't remarkable enough to stand out on one of the happiest days of Pen's life. The retched Lola, who had made Pen's work a daily misery, put her arm through Mateo's and cooed.

'Well. I think we can qualify that a bit, don't you?' as Lola turned her 100-watt smile towards Pen for the first time ever. 'Mateo was my boyfriend in high school.'

Pen's face turned a bright red. *Boyfriend?!* This horrible woman was my husband's girlfriend?! The person who discounted her every idea. Her every contribution. And who made her feel like nothing, an outsider, by punctuating every sentence Pen uttered as if to apologize and dismiss her. 'You must excuse her. She's American.' A *guiri*. Forever a foreigner.

Pen had never heard Mateo speak about this person. Now sitting at their kitchen table, she asked herself *why*. Clearly, they were still in touch enough for Lola to end up on his side of the family's guest list. Granted, having their wedding in Spain meant Pen's guest list was decidedly shorter. But still.

Pen wanted to shout at her boss, 'I earned this spot! I'm more qualified than you imagine!' but she didn't dare. Besides, after that day, Pen wondered if it wasn't her CV but the family connection that had gotten her the job at one of the most prestigious museums in the world. Did Mateo have a word with the viper Lola? Pen closed her eyes as her confidence took yet another hit.

'How are you feeling?' asked Ines, placing the omelet before Pen. 'Do you feel up to eating something this morning?'

Pen shook her head. 'Thank you, Ines. But I think I will stick with coffee.'

And where was her dad? she wondered. Pen wanted to give him space on the Camino, but Mateo had been trying to reach Javier for the past few days, and his texts went unread. Pen worried something had happened to them, and no one knew where they were. She would call Isabela later. Maybe she knew what was going on.

Mateo's arrival in the kitchen shook Pen out of her worry over her father.

'Feeling any better?' he asked his wife while accepting the coffee Ines offered.

'Not really.' said Pen, miserable. 'I can't seem to shake this. I'm taking a sick day.'

'Do you think it's stress? You barely slept last night, tossing and turning. It was like sleeping next to a washing machine. Do you want me to examine you?'

'No!' pleaded Pen. 'I just need to rest.'

She rose to the sink to wash her cup and saucer.

'*Vale.*' Mateo frowned. 'Well, I will check on you later. But I have to run. I have an early appointment with my first patient.'

He quickly drank the rest of his coffee, kissed Pen's head, and thanked Ines before dashing out.

Ines took the cup from Pen, dried it on the dish towel, and placed it back in the cupboard.

'When will you tell him?'

'Tell him what?' whispered Pen, unconsciously placing a protective hand over her stomach while deliberately avoiding looking in Ines's direction.

Ines smiled, patting her shoulder, but said nothing.

'I haven't even taken a test yet.' she told the older woman.

Ines sighed. 'I have grocery shopping to do this morning.' Reaching into her apron and holding out a ginger candy. 'Suck on this. It will help with the nausea, and I will make you some ginger tea. While I am out, I will stop at the *farmacia* and pick up a test. Afterward, you can decide when to tell Mateo and your fathers.'

Pen nodded. She felt ten years old again. Pen loved and appreciated Ines, but this was when she needed her mother. The ache overwhelmed her, and the hole left by Tess's absence grew as nausea overcame her defenses, and she vomited into the sink. Ines held back her hair, then handed her the dish towel as Pen wiped her mouth.

She was already struggling at work, and the news of a baby would make things more difficult when Lola the dragon discovered the news. Pen wanted to talk to her dad about all this. She needed his calm perspective. Where was he on the Camino, and why hadn't he messaged her back?

# THIRTY-THREE
## ENOUGH TO FILL A LIBRARY

Javier found a rusty iron bar and slid it under the lip of the first box. Prying it open took all his strength as the nails groaned against the force. It was as if his father was warning him not to expose his secrets. Not to let what was inside see the sunlight. He peeled off the lid and set it aside. Stacks of black leather-bound books filled the interior. It weighed too much to carry down the old ladder. Selecting the first book, Javier cracked the old leather and discovered pages of writing in his father's hand. On the inside cover was a date: 9 January 1960.

Sifting through the stacks of black leather books, Javier discovered that his organized father had placed them inside by date. Like a time capsule, it was as if he was preparing for them to be unearthed sometime in the future, and Eduardo wanted to save the reader time. Javier pushed the first box aside, then opened the second the same way. More black books filled the space.

Javier tugged the third box from the small space where it had been hiding for decades. The kitten hidden in his shirt protested as he slipped against an old iron spring mattress.

'Sorry, *brujita*.' He said, patting the meowing lump in his shirt. 'We're almost done here.'

Gathering an armload of black books, taking care not to squish his new friend, Javier climbed down the old ladder, praying it would accommodate the extra weight. Then, he and the kitten marched back to the house.

Inside the kitchen, Javier laid the books on the table in the low-ceiling room. Then, he poured a saucer of milk and extracted the sleeping kitten from his shirt. She was none too happy about it until she discovered food waiting for her. Javier petted her as she purred like an airplane engine, glad for the company.

'You're my lucky charm, little witch. Without you, I would never have found the boxes. We have a lot of reading to do, *brujita*. Together, I think we're going to discover the truth.'

Javier poured himself a glass of wine, then sat down and opened the first of his father's journals, which began long before he was born.

# Thirty-Four

## The Grief of Goodbye

Reaching the city took over twice as long as he expected. After twisting his ankle a few times on slippery rocks, John gratefully finally made his way to the sidewalk that took him into Monlineseca and onto Ponferrada. The city's Templar castle sat nestled between the León, Cantabrian, and Lugo Mountain ranges in El Bierzo—an ancient kingdom with an almost mythical history.

At last, John sat inside a warm cafe in the *Plaza Virgen de la Encina*. The weather had become worse the further he went down the mountainside. The temperature was barely above freezing, and well-worn grooves in the pavement directed torrents of water from higher up the street as snow-laced rain poured from the sky.

After limping into the cafe and depositing his pack, John ordered a hot tea, hoping to warm himself up, before booking a hotel on his phone for the night. Flash floods were in the forecast, and he was glad to be high above the waters. John ordered another tea and took advantage of the cafe's heat for as long as possible.

More than an hour later, having eaten and drunk as much as seemed reasonable, he stood to gather his things. The hotel he booked was down a steep set of stairs and across the bridge to the new section of town. The weather would only worsen, so there was no reason to delay. Just then, out the window, he noticed a lone figure walking up the plaza. The pilgrim was dressed in a rain poncho but was weaving as if they had finished off a couple of bottles of *Mencia*, for which this region was so famous. It took a moment before John realized it was Gaelle. He ran outside and called her name, but she didn't respond. Then, he braved the deluge and approached her. She looked up but didn't appear to recognize him.

'Gaelle.' he shouted.

She allowed him to lead her back to the warmth of the cafe. John sat her down, then removed her rain poncho and pack. Her bare hands were bright red. Without the poncho, she began to shake uncontrollably. Fearing Gaelle's condition, John wished he had Javier's medical knowledge. Rubbing her hands, he reached up and touched her face.

'Gaelle. Do you recognize me?'

She nodded.

'What's my name?'

Her teeth chattered, but he made out a whisper. 'Jjjjohn.'

'That's right.' he said, vigorously rubbing her arms. 'Can you feel my hands holding your fingers?'

Gaelle shook her head.

John made a decision. Turning to the cafe owner, John used the limited Spanish he possessed.

'Nosotros necesitamos ambulancia.'

The proprietor had been watching them since John reentered the cafe with Gaelle. He picked up his mobile and dialed. A few minutes later, a siren grew louder in the distance as hot tea arrived on the table. John lifted it to his friend's lips, attempting to warm her before help arrived. But she never took a sip as John caught her as she fell to the floor.

# Thirty-Five
## The Next Generation

Mateo put his keys on the hall table in the foyer of his home and went in search of his wife. Pen had been sick intermittently over the last several weeks, but today, she was getting worse. In between patients, Mateo messaged her to check in, but he grew concerned as the hours ticked by, and he received no reply.

The young doctor checked the great room, which housed his father's hand-carved mahogany desk and where his mother's paintings still hung. He half expected his wife to be sitting on one of the sofas, reading a book or scrolling on her phone. But she wasn't there.

Entering the kitchen, Mateo was sure Ines would know where Pen was. Ines was the beating heart of their home, constantly feeding them and ensuring they stayed on track. He often thought of her as the wise Buddha who saw all but only dished out advice when asked. After the death of his mother, Ines was the anchor that held them together. And now, she was the same for Pen, who had lost her own mother and now lived far away from her father and where she grew up. Sometimes, Mateo forgot how difficult it must be to navigate life in a country that wasn't your own, How everything was different and required so much energy to understand. Lately, he noticed Pen was struggling but hoped it would pass. Maybe he needed to pay more attention.

Climbing the mahogany staircase in the 18th-century mansion, Mateo searched for the two women who dominated his life. He found them in the bedroom he shared with Pen. The room was just down the hall from his childhood bedroom, which still looked like he'd walked out of it the day before—a time capsule. Pen lay in bed against propped pillows as Ines spooned broth into her mouth.

.When Mateo left this morning, he didn't realize how unwell Pen had become. The dark circles under her eyes were getting worse.

'What's going on?' asked Mateo, frowning.

Ines rose, patting Pen's hand and setting the broth on the bedside table.

'I'll leave you two to chat.'

She smiled at Mateo, squeezing his arm as she passed.

Mateo sat down, smoothing the floral duvet and tucking it around his wife. He reached out and felt Pen's forehead.

'You don't feel feverish.' He declared. 'But you look ill.'

Pen sat up, pulling the duvet to her chin, exhausted.

'I'm not ill.' Offering a weak smile. 'I'm pregnant.'

Mateo's eyes widened in surprise. 'Already? But we weren't going to try yet.'

Pen shrugged, holding her stomach. 'Well, I guess this little person has other plans.'

'How do you know? Did you take a test?'

Pen nodded. 'This morning. Ines picked one up from the *farmacia* on the corner.'

Mateo chuckled. 'So, the whole neighborhood knows.'

'I guess they won't think it's for Ines.' said Pen, smiling weakly.

'Do you want me to examine you?' asked Mateo. 'To make sure everything is okay?'

Pen shook her head. 'No. I want you to sit with me and be the confused father and husband— nervous right along with me. I don't want you to be my doctor. I'm sure we can find someone else for that.'

Mateo hugged her as Pen choked up, tears falling down her cheeks.

'What is it?' he asked, frowning as he pulled back. 'Am I hurting you by hugging you?'

'No.' sniffed Pen. 'It's just that I miss my mom. I wish she were here. I don't know what she would do besides what Ines is doing, but I still wish she was here to talk to me. I've never had a baby before, but I know how it works in the US. In Spain, I don't know what they do. Are there birthing suites? Can you even be in the delivery room with me? Will they give me an epidural? I'm overwhelmed by doing this here.' she admitted, her lower lip quivering.

Mateo brushed the hair back from her face, tucking the stray strands behind her ear.

'We can do it however you want. I know people, and if you want to have an epidural, we'll have one. If you want a birthing suite with music, I'll find one. We have lots of time.'

Pen nodded, but the tears flowed.

'What's wrong?' asked Mateo. 'You seem sad. This is good news.'

Pen wiped her nose. 'What are they going to say at work? I just started my job there.'

'I'll call Lola.' offered Mateo, failing to understand this is the last thing Pen wanted.

'No!' she exclaimed a bit too forcefully. 'I might be pregnant, but I can fight my own battles.'

'Battles?' shaking his head in disbelief. 'Lola will understand. You won't have to fight anything.'

But Pen's face told a different story. She tightened her arms around her middle as if she needed to protect this baby with her life. At that moment, Mateo missed his mom, too.

# Thirty-Six

## Family Secrets

Javier stayed up all night reading his father's journals until his eyes drooped. At noon the following day, he awoke at the kitchen table surrounded by little black books, and a purring kitten snuggled beside his cheek. What a difference one day could make. Before yesterday, Javier would have told anyone who asked that he knew his father well. They were good friends by the time he passed. But now, Javier wasn't sure he ever truly knew the man.

He could hear his father's voice in the text. But it wasn't the sound of it that he found so uncomfortable. It was the thoughts themselves. Eduardo was a profoundly lonely man in Madrid. This revelation seemed a strange juxtaposition to the person Javier remembered—someone with a full social calendar who had won awards for his work. From the perspective of a child, his father appeared in high demand. *Important* as his mother constantly reminded him. Even decades after his death. But now, after reading his father's journals, he saw a man who never felt like he fit in. A farm boy at heart from La Rioja, Eduardo played the role expected of him by everyone. He ate fine food, drank the most expensive spirits, and dined with politicos of the time. But it was only when he returned to where he grew up he could be himself—a simple man who wanted to help people. Why didn't Eduardo return to Logroño after medical school?

So many memories flooded back. Evenings when Javier's parents dressed for the theater or a dinner party. Ines lifted Javier out of the bath and wrapped him in a soft terrycloth robe so he could say goodnight before they left, feeling his father's hand on his chin while smiling down, telling him to be good and not give Ines trouble.

Suddenly, he remembered his father's face when the train pulled out of the station in Logroño to return to Madrid after a weekend or holiday at the winery or the sheep farm. Javier always felt sad leaving the bustling kitchen of his *abuela* or running through the fields with the sheep. He could still feel the cookies in the sack pressed into his hands at the station and his childless *Tia* waving goodbye with tears in her eyes. But if Javier was sad, his father's face was bereft. He never understood why — until now. Finally, Javier read the key that unlocked his father's world just before sunrise. And himself in the process.

During his training, Eduardo was a young resident doctor in Madrid who was attached to a local hospital. He met María at a dance held by the head of the hospital. Girls from the best families were invited to mix with the young doctors. There, Eduardo met María Francisco Gomez, a girl from the best family of all. Dressed in a borrowed tuxedo, he nervously pulled at his too-tight collar as he spotted María across the ballroom, eyeing him with too much curiosity.

In those days, girls weren't supposed to be forward, especially in the 1960s in Franco's Spain. But María didn't care about the rules and marched across the dance floor, introducing herself before he could get a word out. Javier's mother's behavior as a young woman surprised him. She seemed to live and die by social norms and the opinions of others, at least as far back as he could remember. Of course, she was always a force to be reckoned with, but his father's description of her in his journal didn't match the woman he knew.

The journal ended at that point, requiring Javier to retrieve a flashlight from the kitchen drawer, march out to the barn for the second time, climb the ladder, and retrieve the next set of books. Like a bestselling novel, Javier was hooked. He needed to know what happened after his father met his mother.

# THIRTY-SEVEN
## A CLOSE CALL

After the emergency services wrapped her in blankets and loaded her in the van, John carried their packs to the ambulance and rode to the hospital with Gaelle. Afterward, he sat in yet another curtained hospital cubicle where machines buzzed, binged, and air whooshed, hoping this person, a virtual stranger whose hand he held so tightly, would recover. John didn't know Gaelle's last name, but he wanted nothing more in that moment than for her to be okay. The grey color in her cheeks worried him.

Profound exhaustion washed over him, remembering a similar bed in an emergency room thousands of miles away and fifteen years before. Except, back then, the room had grown strangely silent. The machines and wires and all the tubes disappeared. No medical personnel came in and out to check on the patient in the bed. Tess had already left to take 11-year-old Pen home as John sat alone with his son, waiting for the coroner to take him away.

The nurse patted his shoulder, assuring John they would look after Charlie, but John didn't want to leave him until the last moment. He stroked his son's sandy blond hair, remembering their trip to the barber shop two days before. Tess insisted they both have haircuts for the graduation photos, reaching up and scruffing her son's hair while standing in the kitchen. On the way, he and Charlie stopped to pick up mochas at a coffee drive-thru and laughed at a stupid dad joke as the stylist shaved Charlie's neck. John closed his eyes, remembering his son's first haircut as a toddler when he wailed at the sound of the clippers. They'd had their hair cut together each month ever since. But now, holding his son's glasses, that was over.

Charlie's face bore just a tiny cut on his chin. Other than that, there were no signs of the injuries that took his life. No bruises. The injuries he sustained were below the sheet covering him. Later, John would see the photos of the car that held the five boys in the crash. It looked like a small cube of jagged metal. No wonder there were no survivors. John stroked Charlie's cold face as tears poured down his cheeks, willing his son to wake up and tell him it was all a joke. That he was still here and they could go home together. But no matter how much he wished it to be so, his son remained where he was – his skin transparent and lifeless.

The nurse entered the room, touching his shoulder, and John flinched. The coroner was there to take Charlie away. John nodded, wiping his tears as the men entered the room. He leaned over and hugged his son for the final time, not wanting to let go. Then, the two faceless men positioned themselves at Charlie's shoulders and feet.

'On two.' heard John; then they lifted his son from the hospital bed to the gurney, pulling the sheet over his face.

John wanted to scream, *Don't do that! If you do that, it means he's really gone, and he can't be gone!* But he remained silent as he sobbed, watching them wheel his son away to a place he couldn't go. John's entire body shook as the nurse helped him to a chair.

'Would you like to speak to the hospital chaplain?' she'd asked kindly. 'He's right outside.'

John closed his eyes, hoping this day would be a nightmare he could wake up from, but the nurse was still there when he opened them. He sat in the hard plastic chair in the room he would never forget. It was the last place he would ever see his wonderful son. John nodded, and the nurse left before returning with the man in the black shirt with a white collar.

John attempted to gather himself as the reverend handed him some tissues.

'Why did this happen, Father? Why did a God, who is supposed to love us, take such a perfect soul? He didn't do anything to hurt anyone. Charlie is smart and would do great things. I know he would.' pleaded John—as if this man in a collar could intercede with a God John tried hard to believe in.

The tall, bearded priest took a deep breath, arranging his face in a sympathetic expression. 'I want to tell you I know why this happened. That there is a reason and that I know what it is. But I don't. I can sit and pray with you if you like. For as long as you need.'

Suddenly, John was more tired than he had ever been. The adrenaline of the past few hours had left his body, and it was all he could do to sit upright, let alone form a sentence. There wasn't anything more to say, anyway.

'Thank you, Father. I think I just need an Uber to go home.' Then, he rose and exited the Emergency Room like a zombie, barely able to work the app on his phone to arrange for a ride home to the two people he had left in this world – Tess and Pen—the only ones who understood how he felt. The three of them would need each other to get through this.

# THIRTY-EIGHT
## DOING THE RIGHT THING

Javier's days and nights became consumed with the journals as Eduardo's words unraveled family mysteries Javier hadn't even known to inquire about when his father was alive.

An exhausted Eduardo walked the halls of the hospital in Madrid. He rubbed his eyes as his 24-hour shift finally came to an end.

'Dr Silva?' he heard as a nurse held the phone aloft. 'Telephone call for you.'

Eduardo sighed. He dragged himself to the desk, accepting the receiver from the nurse.

'Dr Silva.' he stated, more abruptly than he intended.

'Buenos días.' said the hauty voice of a woman. 'This is María Francisco Gomez.'

When Eduardo failed to respond, the woman continued.

'From the party for the doctors a couple of months ago.'

The light dawned as Eduardo thought back to that evening. He had drunk more than he intended. This voice on the line belonged to the bold girl with the bright red lipstick who had attached herself to him that evening. As the night progressed, the fine spirits he had drunk transformed her into a beauty. At one point, they left the party for a stroll through her father's gardens. But the rest was a bit foggy.

'Yes.' said Eduardo. 'Of course, I remember. How are you?'

They hadn't seen each other since that night. He couldn't imagine why she was calling him months later.

'We need to meet.' said María.

Eduardo didn't have time for this, and he said so. He was a busy resident; sleeping, eating, and doing his laundry dominated his free time. Dating wasn't on his agenda, no matter how attractive or wealthy María and her family might be.

'I don't think it's optional.' she said. 'I'm pregnant.'

Eduardo's face fell. His earlier exhaustion drained from him in an instant.

'Excuse me.' he said, now thoroughly awake

'You heard me. I'm pregnant. And my father would like to meet you.'

Eduardo gulped, doing the math. His life flashed before his eyes. Logroño. Navarrete. The winery where his parents were probably sitting down for lunch. He needed to think.'

'When can we meet?' said the voice on the phone.

'With you or with your father?' he gulped

María chuckled. 'With me first, of course. And then, we can decide when to tell my parents.'

Eduardo knew María's father was a top official in Franco's government. He was a powerful man and very rich. He could ruin Eduardo's life and the lives of his family if he chose. In an instant. If María told her father, with one phone call, the people Eduardo loved most could be disappeared. And that included himself.

'I am finishing my shift at the hospital. I can meet you in an hour.'

María sounded giddy. 'Wonderful!' She gave him the address of a cafe near the hospital and hung up.

Eduardo stood at the nurse's station, holding the phone. Nothing around him would look the same ever again.

# THIRTY-NINE

## FORGING AHEAD

John awoke the following morning in the chair next to Gaelle's bed. He stretched, and she smiled.

'Your face has some color.' he told her. 'How do you feel?'

'Tired but much better. Thank you for taking quick action. It seems I wandered to the right cafe in Ponferrada.'

She didn't remember that he had gone out into the square to steer her there.

'I guess so.' John smiled. 'Do you need anything?'

Gaelle shook her head. 'No. The doctor should be here soon to tell me when I can leave. If they release me, I would prefer to stay in a hotel and recover.'

'I could help you find a hotel and get you there.' offered John.

Gaelle shook her head. 'You've already done enough. And I don't want to delay your Camino. Besides, I will need to rest for a few days before continuing. But I can't thank you enough, John. Without your help and quick thinking, it could have been very bad for me.'

'You scared me yesterday.' he sighed, 'Please wear warm clothes from now on. I know skin is waterproof, but it's getting cold on the Camino.

Gaelle promised she would as her expression turned serious.

'The doctor told me how close I came. You're my Camino angel.'

John pulled a face. 'Nonsense. You would have done the same for me.'

He stood and stretched again, looking around for his things. There was nothing to pack up because he slept in his clothes from the day before. John was ready to head out with his poles tied to his pack and his jacket draped over the chair he slept in.

'So, you'll continue your Camino?' he asked, donning his blue rain jacket. 'You're so close to Santiago, and you've walked so far. But you don't have to finish right now.'

Gaelle smiled.

'Of course I will. But I need some time. It will be a few days before I can return to the trail. But don't let me stop you.' Gaelle produced her phone. 'Can I get your details?'

John read off the numbers. Then, he shrugged into his pack and squeezed Gaelle's hand.

'Take care of yourself, *peregrina*.'

'The same to you, John the American.' she smiled. 'Buen Camino.'

For once, a trip to the hospital had ended positively. Maybe the Camino had cured his streak of back luck. Things were finally turning around.

# FORTY

## BOX N° 3

The pieces of Javier's life began to click into place. María's indifference toward him as he was growing up. The decided lack of warmth in his parent's long marriage. Based on the journals, his father had not entered the union willingly but out of an obligation for an unborn child and a fear for his own life. Yet, when Javier looked back, he saw his father's face and knew that while Eduardo was unprepared for his arrival, he loved the son who had changed the direction of his life.

Over the following days, Javier poured through his father's journals as the familiar voice spoke to him from the pages. After his marriage to María, Javier wasn't sure why his father took such a chance in continuing to record his true feelings until Javier arrived at the point when Ines entered the picture. His father's words became more animated, almost poetic, and it was clear that Eduardo was in love with Ines, a woman who represented home. She understood him in ways María never could. And she expected nothing from him except love and kindness.

*When I'm with her, I know I'm home. Even her hair smells like the earth from which the vines take life. Ines describes the taste of the lemon ice cream in Navarrete, and I sit in rapture. I don't have to explain my feelings to her. She's happy sitting quietly on a blanket and listening to the wind. A man can think with Ines nearby. She is so kind to the children and elderly in Ventosa, and I find that even the soil on her dress is precious. When a dust devil surprised us on a picnic by the river, I wiped the dirt from her cheeks with my handkerchief. I will never wash it.*

Javier read his father's words, and a great sadness washed over him. This man lived two lives. One where he performed precisely as expected in his work and his home life. And the other, where he could be who he truly was. Javier teared up. Sadly, the son was a part of his father's performance. He would never know the man his father would have been without him.

Javier shifted the kitten, curled up asleep in his lap. Setting down the completed journal, he returned to the barn and climbed the rickety ladder. The old yellow dog lifted his head from his afternoon nap in the straw but didn't stir. After a week, Javier became a predictable part of the animal's daily life.

The contents of the third box were different than the first two. It contained random artifacts of Eduardo's life. Digging through, he extracted the embroidered handkerchief referenced in his father's journal. True to his word, Eduardo had saved this piece of cloth so precious to him.

Inside, there were ledgers and paperwork organized into folders. It surprised Javier that many documents were in English and written on the letterhead of a bank in the United Kingdom. There were also letters from a solicitor in London to his father's *abogado* in Madrid. Based on the date, the letters and documents were forty years old.

Javier extracted a sheet of type-written paper from the plastic sleeve protecting it.

*Hackburn, Bolden & Grey LLP*
*34 Eton Garden Court*
*St. James's*
*London SW1Y*
*United Kingdom*

*Don Ruben Alcor Ortega*
*Alcor Abogados de los Reyes*
*C. de Camino viejo 27, 7º*
*Camberi, 28003, Madrid*
*España*

*8 September 1985*
*Trust Execution for Beneficiary: Ines Delores Ybarra Diaz*

*Dear Don Alcor Ortega*

*Enclosed, please find the executed documents we discussed. Per your request and that of your client, Don Eduardo Silva, a trust has been established with Barclays in Guernsey in the Channel Islands and is awaiting funds. Additionally, deposits can continue as you see fit. As the trustee, you have complete investment control over the account, and we will notify you when the account balance approaches any thresholds set by law. As explained in our earlier correspondence, other rules may be triggered regarding the allowable frequency of deposits and amounts of continued funding. Per the enclosed, withdrawals may be initiated by the beneficiary, Ines Delores Ybarra Diaz, or her heirs only after meeting the terms of the trust.*

*If your client has any further questions or would like to speak to us directly, he can do so at his convenience. We are at his service. Charles Lindford-Hearst at Barclays Guernsey is prepared to make himself available at any time. I enclose his card containing his private number should the need arise.*

*We are pleased your client has put his trust in us for this delicate matter, and we will endeavor to live up to the task. Please do not hesitate to contact me with the smallest of concerns. We await confirmation of the funds transfer from Madrid and remain at your service.*

*Sincerely,*
*Justin Highsmith-Jones*
*cc Henry Hackburn*
*Enc*

Javier couldn't breathe. He reread the letter before sitting upon a nearby piece of ancient farm equipment. Javier no longer needed the DNA test. The smoking gun as to the relationship between his father and Ines stared back at him from the single sheet of paper he held in his hand.

# Part V

## Divine Lessons

# FORTY-ONE
## A GAME OF CHESS

John woke early the following morning and headed through the vines between Cacabelos and Vilafranca del Bierzo. The red dust from the clay path coated his boots as he made his way up and down dirt roads traversed by both tractors and pilgrims alike. Rounding a bend, John stopped short. Before him was a mirage of such incongruity that he rubbed his eyes with the back of his gloved hands. But that didn't help.

In front of him sat a man on a kitchen chair at a beat-up wooden table on the side of the path. It seemed very sturdy, and John couldn't imagine how he had carried it to this spot by himself. The older gentleman with leathered skin wore a black beret and a navy cardigan over a plaid dress shirt. A chessboard was set out in front of him, awaiting another player.

'Buenos días.' said the weathered man, 'Por favor.' Indicating John should have a seat and join him in a game.

John looked back from where he had come, still unable to believe his eyes. He approached the man slowly.

'I'm sorry.' he said. 'I don't speak Spanish. Maybe there will be another Spanish pilgrim along who can play.' Making a move to continue on his way.

'Please, have a seat.' said the old man in perfect English.

The hair on the back of his neck prickled, but John's excuses melted in his mouth. John loved playing chess and missed it after he had gifted his old set to the boy, Julian, on the train a month before. This walk was one of the longest stretches he'd gone without playing since he was a boy. He unbuckled his pack, and his poles landed in the red dirt. The man turned the board so the white pieces sat before John.

'Please go first.' he said in clear English.

Surprised, John made one of his signature opening moves, then studied the old gentleman, who was focused on the board but looked up at John, tilting his head, curious.

They each moved in turn, quickly at first, then more deliberately, taking their time.

'Where are you from?' asked the man.

'I am an American.' said John,

'Yes.' said his opponent. 'But where are you from?'

John shook his head. 'I don't know what you mean.'

The man shifted in his seat. 'Who are you, John? Where do you come from?'

John didn't remember telling the man his name. What was this man playing at?

'I'm just John.' he held out his hand for the man to shake. 'I'm sorry. I didn't catch your name.'

The weathered face broke into a smile, but he ignored the gesture before John's hand dropped back into his lap.

'Oh, they call me many things. My name isn't important. I am more interested in you, John, so I am asking again. Where are you from?'

John held his breath before answering.

'Well,' he hesitated while considering how much to say to this odd stranger. On the Camino, people revealed intimate details of their lives to others. John had never done that before this walk. Stalling for time, he reached out and moved his rook.

'I live in Arizona, but these days, I am just a pilgrim on the Camino. My daughter, Pen, lives in Madrid, and I'm wondering why I live so far away from her.'

The older man rubbed his mocha-colored chin and nodded, select-ing another piece and making a bold move.

'But why are you *here*?' he asked, pointing to the red clay under their feet.

'In Spain?' asked John, a crease in his brow.

The man waved his weathered hand. 'Here. Why are you here on this path, playing chess with me?'

John frowned. 'You asked me to play with you.'

'Yes. But you accepted. Why?'

This was getting weird.

'I like to play chess. And you seemed like a nice person.' John moved his knight.

'Hmm.' the man rubbed his chin once again. 'So, you are just here, at this moment. Nowhere else.' he moved his other rook. 'Check.'

John studied the board, distracted by the question. 'I guess so.'

'Curious.' said the man, adjusting his beret, then moving his queen.

'Why is that curious?' asked John, making his next move.

The man chuckled. 'You haven't mentioned your wife or anything that has happened to you while walking your Camino. Don't you find that curious?'

John opened his mouth but stopped. The old man was right. Usually, he described himself as a widower and a retiree—*a lonely old man*. His reason for being on the Camino was about his wife, dead now for more than ten years. This description of himself faced the past, and he used words assigned to him by others. But now, he didn't think of himself as either of those things. John was himself. Not old nor young. Just John.

'Perhaps on this trek, you are learning that you matter. That you are worthy.'

John shifted in his seat. Why was this guy getting so personal? He swallowed hard.

'I have done things for which I am deeply ashamed. Let down those I love and was supposed to protect. I haven't loved myself for a long time.'

The man pursed his lips, and John braced himself for his harsh judgment.

'Yes. Perhaps it is because you define yourself by those actions but fail to see the love you have shared with those around you. The remarkable difference you have made in the lives of others.'

John held his breath.

'It is in the shadows where we find ourselves if we have the courage to look. Don't you think it is time to put down the shame you carry, John? And give yourself grace as you have bestowed grace on not just family but strangers. Give yourself the grace to be human amidst the darkness. To see your own worth.'

The old man reached out and made his final move. Rook-rolling John's king while he was distracted. 'Checkmate.'

The man rose, removing his flat cap and wiping his brow with a handkerchief from the pocket of his wide-whale brown corduroy trousers. The same ones Grandpa Charlie used to wear. He reached out and shook John's hand at last, smiling.

'Thank you for the match, John—the man who is now himself.' Then he turned and disappeared into the vines.

John stood frozen to the spot, watching the little man go as blood drained from his face. What just happened? He searched the vines where the man went but could see no one. A shiver ran down his spine as he picked up his pack, quickly fastened the buckles, and collected his poles from the dirt. The sun came out from behind the clouds as John walked 50 meters down the trail towards Villafranca del Bierzo before looking back to where they sat playing their game moments before. He opened his clenched fist. The white knight from their match sat in his palm. The missing piece from the set in Viana, weeks ago. And the only piece on the board allowed to jump over another. When John looked up, the table and chairs were gone.

# FORTY-TWO

## O CEBRIERO

John huffed and puffed his way up the mountainside from Las Herrias as he climbed toward the final peak on his Camino. It was all downhill from there, or so he read. So much had happened since this walk began a month before that John hardly recognized himself. That morning, he called and checked on Gaelle. She had regained her strength and hoped to continue the Camino in the next few days. John barely knew the woman but was fully invested in her recovery. That's what the Camino did to pilgrims. Strangers shared intimacies and became the closest of friends in a single day.

Just then, his phone buzzed. He took the opportunity to stop and catch his breath, pulling his phone from his pocket. Javier's name topped the notification. John waited. The man wasn't his favorite person right now. He had abandoned John in León and taken off for God-knows-where to do God-knows-what. And John had not heard from him since. Curiosity got the best of him, and he unlocked his phone and read the message.

Javier: *¡Hola! John. How are you?*

John shook his head. How am I? Fuck this guy. *I'm great!*—he wanted to type—*After you ditched me in León, I've walked alone for a week. I've walked through weather no one should be out in, twisted my ankle* (it still bothered him), *saved someone's life, battled nasty blisters, and relived some of the worst moments of the past 60 years. And I might have played chess with God in a vineyard. Right now, I'm climbing another fucking mountain!*

But he didn't say all that.

John: *Fine. How are you?*

*typing...*

Javier: *Where are you?*

Why does he care where I am?

John: *I'm almost to O'Cebreiro. Where are you?* (*Motherfucker* – he wanted
to add but didn't)

Javier: *I'm back in León.*

*typing...*

Javier: *Do you want some company for the last week walking to Santiago?*

The lush green mountains of Galicia spread out below John. Clouds
floated past, and it smelled like rain. John took a deep breath. Javier had
gotten him from Saint-Jean to León. The man deserved credit for that.
When Javier left him, John wondered how he would go on alone, but
after Astorga, John was confident he could do this. If Javier hadn't left,
John might have wondered if he could finish this on his own – if he were
truly capable. Through the trials he faced in the past week, he earned the
confidence that comes with overcoming physical and emotional pain. And
the Camino provided plenty of opportunities for it. John didn't require
handholding or coddling. He could make it to Santiago on his own. But
Javier was extending an olive branch. John knew it was essential for himself
and Pen to accept it—for their family.

John: *Sure. I'll be in Sarria in two days. Can you be there?*

*typing...*

Javier: *I'll be there. Dinner is on me.*

After a windy walk on a narrow path that skirted the ridgeline, John reached the top of the mountain. A blazing fire in the grate of his albergue in O Cebriero heated the common area as John stood and warmed his hands. Other grateful pilgrims walking late in the season stripped off their sodden gear to join him in front of the flames. John's phone rang once more.

'¡Hola!' said Isabela.

An even warmer feeling spread through John that had nothing to do with the fire. Like a familiar but distant memory—like coming home.

'Hi there,' he said. 'How are you?'

'I'm well. Happy to hear your voice.' said Isabela, rustling the covers. She was calling from her bed.

'It seems like a month since I've seen you.' said John.

He wasn't far off.

'Too long. You're almost done. Just a week more.'

'It's getting really cold and wet.' he told her. 'I'm ready to reach Santiago.'

John heard rustling as Isabela rolled over.

'What's the plan for after your Camino?' she asked.

John focused on walking. Every day was singular — with nothing beyond it. He had no plans except to meet Javier in Sarria. But this phone call confirmed what he suspected. Isabela had gotten under his skin. He wasn't sure how it happened, but his smile reached his eyes for the first time in a long time.

'Maybe we should talk about it.' he offered.

'I like the sound of that.' she agreed. 'Keep in touch and let me know when you're getting close to Santiago.'

John ended the call.

'I think I might have a girlfriend.' he whispered like a teenager. No one was more surprised than he was as he zipped up his jacket against the drafty room and headed to his bed for the night.

# FORTY-THREE
## THE REUNION

Two days later, John set out early in the dark. Walking in the rain, John thought of Tess. Could she see him? What would she think of him and how he had changed on this trek? Was this what she had wanted for him when she wrote her list more than ten years ago? He wanted to believe it was. As her love for him reached out and touched him across a decade, happy tears fell for the first time on this Camino. His intense grief had transformed into a dull ache. But his life was no longer behind him as he thought of Isabela and Pen. John had a lot to look forward to.

By the afternoon, he walked into Sarria. Sarria is the largest market town in the final 100 km of the Camino Francés, and as the rain poured down, John found the hotel where he agreed to meet Javier. Entering the warm lobby, John couldn't help but smile when he saw Javier's familiar face. Neither of them was the same man who had parted in León. Any bad blood between them dissolved as they embraced.

'How has it been without me?' asked Javier. 'I imagine you have some stories to tell.'

'As an FBI agent once told me in Pampñoma—if I told you, I'd have to kill you.' laughed John.

John put his pack down. He checked into his room and got cleaned up. Later, they met in the lobby for a drink.

'Are you ready to tell me why you left León so abruptly? And what you've been doing since then?' asked John, braver than he felt.

Javier took a deep breath.

'Where should I start? It's been a lot.' he took a swig of his beer. 'I returned to the farm and spent days digging through my uncle's house, searching for four boxes my father instructed his lawyer to send to my uncle after his death. By some miracle, I was about to give up when I found them stacked under a tarp at the top of the barn. Each box was filled with his journals and financial documents. A record of his entire adult life. And these boxes contained more pieces in the puzzle I have been trying to solve.'

'Interesting.' John frowned. 'What did the journals say?'

'Honestly, it painted a picture of my father I never knew. My mother was pregnant when they married. My father never loved my mother, and he was with her because of me.'

John blanched.

'That must be difficult to discover after all these years.'

Javier nodded. 'That wasn't the hardest part. Reading his life in his own words, my father was profoundly lonely for decades. He was heartbroken when he discovered my mother was pregnant and that he was unable to return to Navarrete. To his family. He never wanted the high-profile life in Madrid that my mother craved. And he hid his despair so that his son never knew.'

'I'm sorry.' said John, sincerely.

'Me too. But there is more. After reading through hours of his journals and barely eating or sleeping for a week, I found papers proving that my father and Ines are connected. He set up an account – a trust in the Channel Islands — to care for Ines after his death.'

John's eyes widened.

'Why wouldn't the lawyer have told you when your dad died?'

'That is a mystery. I think the lawyer thought he was keeping a secret for my father. All the documents were sent to my uncle for safekeeping. This complicates things. Not only do Antonio and I need to speak with Ines about his parentage, but we need to discuss the fact that she has a small fortune sitting in a bank on an island off the coast of France.'

John couldn't imagine how Javier felt. His own problems seemed to pale in comparison to the complexity of what Javier was facing.

'I don't know what to say. Like you said, secrets eat from the inside out. As painful as it is, in the end, maybe it is a good thing to get it all out.'

Javier shook his head. 'Perhaps.'

The following day, they awoke to pouring rain. But the weather wasn't an excuse to stop walking the Camino. They suited up in waterproof gear and headed out. Even in the foul weather, John still donned his dad's old *Cubs* baseball cap. There was a moment at an albergue weeks before when he thought he had lost it—his lowest point on the Camino. Reaching up, he rubbed the bill like a talisman and marched ahead.

The rain poured down on them as lightning flashed. They ducked into a small café to warm up and enjoy a second coffee of the day.

John wrapped his hands around his coffee cup as Javier drank his beer.

'Have you heard from Pen?' asked Javier.

'Not in the last week. Why?' asked John.

'No reason,' said Javier. 'I just wondered how she was feeling. In Burgos, you said she wasn't well. I've been thinking about her today. I should call Mateo and check in.'

At that moment, the picture of Pen lying on the bathroom floor after her drug overdose flashed into his mind. He rarely thought of that moment anymore, but her future could have been so different if Tess had not risked it all and brought her to Spain. His wife's gamble changed everything for his daughter and everything for him and Tess. Her risk secured the successes Pen now enjoyed. And his heartbreak. John shook his head. There was no more time for regrets. His daughter was safe.

Their arrival in Portomarin in a deluge meant they would stay put, as the forecast warned of worsening weather. Lightning and thunder moved in as if on cue, reinforcing their decision.

Before bed, John decided to take a walk and call Isabela.

'Hey, stranger.' She said when she answered. 'Where are you now?'

'I'm in Portomarin—only a few days to go.

'I heard Javier is up here at the farm. So, you're walking the rest of the way by yourself?'

'Javier is here with me, and he seems fine. His departure from the Camino was as abrupt as his return yesterday.' John didn't feel it was his place to reveal Javier's secrets. 'Maybe you should speak to him.'

'Hmmm.' offered Isabela. 'Something tells me you know more than you're saying, but I respect that you are keeping his confidence.'

John changed the subject to avoid saying more.

'I wish you could be in Santiago when we finish. I've missed you.'

'I've missed you too.' admitted Isabela. 'We are almost wrapped up here for the season.'

'When we get to Santiago, the DNA test results will be available from the lab, and Javier will get his answer. So, everything is winding down for everyone, I guess.'

'Yes. It seems so.' whispered Isabela. 'Where are you staying in Santiago?'

'I hadn't thought about it. I probably should. Are you familiar with the city? Any recommendations?'

'I'm not Galician, but let me ask around. I can make the reservation for you and send it to you.'

She had gotten past whatever was bothering her about her cousin. John smiled. 'That would be great. Perhaps check in with Javier before you finalize anything since he will probably have an opinion. Mateo and Pen will be there, too.

'OK. I'll call my cousin and see how he is. His visit to the sheep farm is a bit of a mystery. He was close by but didn't call. Someone told me they saw him. I've spoken to Pen. She said you told her to call me. She sounds down, John. I think it is good you will see her in a few days. Maybe having you to talk to will help her, too.'

Isabela's words nagged at him. Javier had brought up his concern for Pen earlier. Suddenly, getting to Santiago took on more urgency.

'What are you worried about with Pen?' he asked, wanting her opinion.

Isabela sighed. 'I don't know, precisely. She just seems off. We talked about the job and office politics. But I feel it is more than that, John. I can't put my finger on it.'

'I'll call her now.'

But Isabela offered another opinion. 'I don't know how much you'll get from her over the phone. She seems closed off. Lonely is the best way to describe how she sounds. Maybe I'm just overreacting, but that was the feeling I got when we spoke.'

They disconnected, and John dialed Pen. It rang, but she never picked up. John looked at the time. She was probably still at the office, maybe in a meeting. He would try again later.

John walked back to the albergue. It was nice to have someone to talk to about family matters and to have a confidant once again. On the Camino, he avoided examining his developing feelings for Isabela. Convincing himself, he was preoccupied with other things. Now, he had to admit he felt deeply for the winemaker. A closeness he wasn't sure he would ever feel again. She seemed to understand him in ways he didn't understand himself. John didn't know if that was love, but he knew he didn't want it to end. And yet, he hesitated. What would Isabela think of him if he revealed what he told Javier back in León? His infidelity. His betrayal of Tess was his greatest source of shame. Would she run away like her cousin? Would it be over before it even began?

John took a deep breath. His grief came back like a habit but was gone in a flash. Since starting this walk in Saint-Jean, Javier had become more than Tess's lover to him. John didn't want to see the man in pain. And he didn't want to cause Isabela pain, either. Threading the needle of his emotions would have to wait for another day.

# FORTY-FOUR
## THE HAPPINESS CAFE

They walked the muddy path up hills and down valleys in the unrelenting rain of Galicia. The only break in the weather came between Palas de Rei and Melide.

'Look!' said Javier, pointing through the gate on the road, a mirage stood before them. 'It's a food truck!'

John read the sign on the grey trailer with the symbol of a meditating Buddha. Still wearing his bracelet, he wondered where his monk friend from the Pyrenees was and if he had stopped there.

Javier read the menu aloud. 'O Cafe de Felicidade. The Happiness Cafe. They have tostada aguacate.'

John's mouth dropped.

'Avocado toast.' explained Javier, leading the way through the gate. 'We're eating here. My treat.'

John followed Javier to order breakfast, served nowhere else on the Camino.

The blond woman working the window spoke Spanish to Javier but perfect American English when she turned to John.

'How did you know I'm American?' he asked her.

She smiled.

'Takes one to know one.' she winked. 'It's a look and a certain walk.'

'Is there an American walk?' he asked.

'You'd be surprised.' she laughed.

John knew what she meant. He could usually spot other Americans on the trail.

'What will it be?' she asked him. 'Maybe a waffle with real Canadian maple syrup?'

John's mouth watered. 'No way! You're a culinary goddess.'

The American proprietor smiled again. 'You're not the first to tell me that. And you won't be the last. I serve what I craved on my own Camino. Have a seat. I'll bring it to you when it's ready.'

The hungry pilgrims ate until they were sick. Luckily, Melide was only six kilometers away.

The following day flew by. John and Javier rose early, heading out of Arzua on another cold, miserable morning before sunrise—their last full day on the Camino. The path was muddy under a tunnel of ancient oak trees.

Only a kilometer out of Arzua, they heard a loud rustling as a sounder of *jabalies* broke out of the brush and stood frozen in the middle of the trail. The pack of wild boars appeared startled to encounter pilgrims as John and Javier were to see them. If provoked, their curved tusks could savage them in a second. Javier placed his walking poles before them, halting their progress.

'Do not move.' he whispered. 'Be ready to defend yourself with your poles.'

Their headlamps blinded the boars as clouds of steam rose from the nostrils of the animals. Time stood still as the pilgrims stopped breathing. The adult boars encircled their young as they snorted warnings at those obscured behind the blinding light. The standoff lasted for several minutes before the females broke the tension by ushering their boarlets to the other side of the trail and through the bushes as the males stood guard. Then, the remaining *jabablies* joined the pack one by one and disappeared into the dark brush.

The two of them let out the collective breath they were holding.

'Holy shit!' said John. 'That was one of the scariest moments of my life. What were those things?'

'It was also one of the most dangerous moments of your life.' said Javier 'Jabalies. Those wild boars could have killed us. It happens here in Galicia. Not often, but it does happen. It was the headlamps that saved us. They were blinded and couldn't tell what we were or how many of us were behind the light.'

'Perhaps tomorrow we should start after sunrise.'

It would be the final day of their Camino. It was the smart thing to do.

# FORTY-FIVE
## RACING TOWARD THE FUTURE

Pen watched the high plains of Spain fly past. Mateo had given her his window seat on the early morning high-speed train from Madrid's Chamartín station to Santiago de Compostela. Her husband held her hand, but they had spoken few words since boarding.

Pen couldn't wait to see her father, but the prospect of returning to Santiago held memories for her. Memories of her own Camino with her mother the year before she died. Pen's hand went protectively to her stomach. This baby would never know Pen's mother, Tess — never understand how things might have been different for its mother. Speeding toward the northwest corner of Spain wasn't what bothered her. Pen had been to Galicia before to visit Mateo's grandmother, Sofia, when she moved there to be closer to her family after the passing of her husband, Sebastian. His grandmother lived near A Coruña on the Costa del Morte, more than an hour north of Santiago. Today would be the first time Pen set foot in Obradioro Square in front of the cathedral without her mother. Pen closed her eyes. After so long, why was the prospect of returning there so emotional?

Mateo squeezed her hand reassuringly.

'Are you okay?' he asked. 'Are you feeling alright? Do you want me to get you something?'

Pen shook her head and returned to the scenery, unsure why she felt so down. She needed her dad now that she was to be a mother. The phone calls and texts between Madrid and Phoenix would no longer suffice. She wanted him and his ever-calming presence close by. When she called him on the Camino, her dad seemed different. But that was the whole point of walking it, after all. She first noticed it at Isabela's the morning after the party. The way Isabela looked at her father unnerved Pen. She liked Javier's cousin, but the thought that her dad might return the feelings of the confident winemaker was a burr under Pen's skin — as if he was cheating on her mom after all these years. The thought was irrational, and she knew that. On the flip side, if her dad liked Isabela, he might consider moving to Spain.

Pen had to admit her dad's suggestion that she call Isabela for advice about navigating tricky politics at work was helpful. During their phone call, Isabela was a good sounding board on women and corporate culture in Spain. Offering Pen insight on how to fit in and what to avoid. More than anything, Isabela gave Pen the support she desperately needed the day she phoned her at the winery.

'Thank you, Isabela, for helping me with some perspective. It has been tough.' she said.

'Of course.' said Isabela. 'Any time. Moving to a new country and learning how to exist in a culture that isn't your own can be tricky. I remember it well. Honestly, Pen. You can call me whenever you want.'

Pen decided to step outside of her original reason for phoning Isabela.

'I think my dad likes you.' she said quietly.

Isabela didn't answer right away.

'I like John very much. Is that okay, Pen?' she asked respectfully.

Isabela wasn't her mom. She didn't have children of her own, so she couldn't advise Pen on how to raise a child. But she could be a friend.

'Of course, it's okay. You are both adults. And I will be happy if my dad is happy. Please don't hurt him.' she sniffed. 'I don't think I could take that. He's more fragile than he seems. I don't think he could take it either.'

'I won't.' said Isabela. 'I promise.'

With her pregnancy, Pen had no intention of quitting her job. But she wasn't naïve. Her tricky situation at the office would get even harder once the announcement of her pregnancy was made known and then again after the baby arrived.

Mateo let go of her hand and rose, heading to the cafe car. Pen shook her head when he asked again if she wanted anything. After he disappeared through the car door, Pen rubbed her stomach with her left hand and thought of her mom as her wedding ring reflected the sunlight. Is this how Tess felt when she was pregnant with Charlie? Based on what Pen knew, Tess had no support from her own mother, so she had to figure out mothering, just like Pen. How did Tess navigate it all? How did she know what to do and not do? How to keep him safe?

In the end, her mother couldn't keep her brother safe. He died young, and there was nothing her parents could do to stop it. The core of her greatest fear suddenly shone through. Once this child was born, it would be out in the world. There would be so many dangers she couldn't control. And so many opportunities for something to go wrong. This baby was coming, and time was short for discovering and neutralizing potential threats. Where should she start?

Mateo returned and set down a bottle of water and a bag of crackers on the tray before her, just in case her nausea returned. Pen knew he was trying his best. He seemed so happy about this baby. Not worried at all. Pen didn't share her fears with him. Like her mother, her job was to take care of everything regarding her child's welfare, and she would somehow figure out a way to rise to the challenge.

The train wound through tunnel after tunnel in the mountains of Galicia. The constant rocking of the carriage from Ourense to the train station in Santiago wreaked havoc on Pen's stomach. She got up, went to the bathroom, and ran her hands under cold water. The hormones of this little one were making her hot and cold at the same time. Pen looked in the mirror and wiped her face with a wet towel. The dark circles under her eyes required the application of more concealer from her bag. She didn't want Mateo or her dad to worry. In the next two hours, she would see her father again. It felt like she was swimming towards him against a strong current. Maybe seeing her father was all she needed to feel grounded again. To feel like she wasn't losing her mind. Pen brushed her hair and applied some lip gloss before taking a deep breath and opening the grey metal door.

Maeto rose to let her pass Pen pass.

'Everything okay?' he asked his wife, concerned. 'Are you feeling well?'

Pen smiled. His concern worried her.

'I'm fine. I can't wait to get off this rocking train and see my dad.' Pen teared up. 'I don't want to think about him returning to the US.'

'There is still time.' said Mateo. 'Do you want me to speak to him?'

'No. I don't know. I want him to *want* to stay in Spain. I just,' she closed her eyes as tears fell, and she wiped them away. 'If he goes back, I don't know when I'll see him again. What if there are complications? What if?' Pen shook her head. 'I don't even know.'

Mateo wrapped his arm around her, and she laid her head on his shoulder.

'I think your dad is just going through a lot, letting go of your mom. When he finishes the Camino, he might think differently. It would be best if you talked to him, Pen. And I think it would help if you talked to me. You need to tell me if you're worried about something so I can help. That's my job.'

But Pen believed her fears would come true if she said them out loud. And some of them weren't so easily identifiable. Anyway, Mateo might think she was crazy. Exhausted, she closed her eyes, more tired than she had ever been.

# FORTY-SIX

## NEVER THE SAME

The following morning, John and Javier arose for the final time on the trail. It was the day they would walk into Santiago, and their spirits ran high. After sunrise, they took their own advice and left their albergue in Santa Irena to avoid another wild boar encounter, walking through groves of giant eucalyptus trees.

'I'm looking forward to seeing Pen.' said John, smiling.

'I imagine it has been difficult for her to live in Europe while you're in the US.' said Javier.

'It has. When I was working, it wasn't quite so bad. I was distracted. But Pen has a life of her own now. She doesn't need me hanging around.'

Javier disagreed. 'I think she would prefer it if you lived close by. We're your family, John.'

John had never considered this before his Camino but thought about it daily on the trail. Pen's family was his family. He had people he could count on. Why was he so afraid to embrace them?

'What are your plans after the Camino, John?' asked Javier.

'I'm not quite sure yet. Isabela has invited me to spend some time at the winery in La Rioja. So, we'll see.'

Javier raised an eyebrow, smiling. 'Oh, yes?'

John avoided the question.

'But I also need to head back to the States at some point. I'm here to spread Tess's ashes at places she requested. Many of those are in the US, and I want to fulfill them all now that I've begun. This ritual has been wonderful, and when we get to Madrid, we'll put her in another of the places on her list. I didn't understand it before, but I do now. She wants to be at the endings and the beginnings of meaningful moments in people's lives. It's just like her to have found those places.' John coughed to clear the emotion from his throat. 'I loved her fiercely. But because of this Camino, I'm letting her go.'

It took them several hours to reach Monte de Gozo. From the top, they looked out over the city of Santiago. The two men stood with their arms over each other's shoulders, staring out across the city with the Cathedral at their feet.

John imagined what Tess felt at that moment— the thrill of completing the pilgrimage and the fear of what would come. At this point, Tess hadn't told Pen about her illness and, after a month of walking together, was still fighting to get closer to their daughter. But that would change at the cathedral in just a few hours.

Just then, John spotted the orange and red robes blowing in the wind. Hy Yung, the monk from Orrison, stood 50 meters from John, looking over the valley. Despite the cold, he still wore his sandals. John pulled at the bracelet on his wrist before calling out to the man, who turned to John with a radiant smile and a wave. John closed the distance between them, holding up his wrist so the monk could see that he still had the gift.

'How are you?' asked John.

'I am well.' said the monk. 'And you look well, John. I think you have done the work you came to do.'

'Indeed I have. Thank you for your understanding and blessing at the beginning of this journey. I am not sure I understood how this would change me and how it would help me heal. When I met you, I was still afraid.'

The monk smiled.

'We are all afraid at times, John. But we are resilient with courage. You have shown bravery in continuing your journey despite your fear. That is the lesson. I read something wonderful on this Camino by someone who knew that their death was imminent. And the words touched me deeply—her love of her family and her acceptance of the tragedies she experienced. But more than that, she embraced her flaws and accepted her death was just another transition. Ultimately surrendering to her humanity.'

The monk pulled out a slip of yellow paper from his robes.

'I found this obituary lying on the floor of a church. It is written in English, and I think the woman is American. But you can hear her voice when you read it.'

John held his breath. He reached out and took the folded newsprint he knew so well. Tears poured down his cheeks when he looked up at a confused Javier.

'This is my wife's obituary.' John said, choking up. 'I lost this on the Camino. I didn't know where, but I must have dropped it in that church.'

He wiped his eyes, then unfolded it like a sacred relic. 'I looked for it everywhere and thought it was lost forever.'

Javier peered around John's shoulder, reading Tess's final words.

'That is Tess in a nutshell.' whispered Javier, wiping his own tears. 'Surrender and acceptance.'

'I guess I was meant to carry this to you, John.' said Hy Yung. 'To return what you lost.'

John folded the paper, sliding it into his wallet. He thanked the monk, who waved it away.

'We are all connected, John. There is not a John Sullivan or a Hy Yung. We are the same from the same source, and there we will someday return. We don't lose anyone. They live inside us, and we inside them—energy flowing throughout time and spaces like a river. But, as you know, sometimes we get lost and need to take the time to find ourselves again.'

Hy Yung looked deeply into John's eyes and smiled.

'I believe you have used this time wisely to do just that. Congratulations. It is nice to meet you finally, John Sullivan.' Then, he turned in his colorful robes and made his way down the hill without another word.

An hour later, John and Javier entered the old town. The wail of the piper playing for pilgrims as they entered the square in front of the Cathedral was a melancholy sound that took John back to his childhood in an instant. His Irish grandfather played the pipes on special occasions at church when John was a boy. Memories of his and Tess's wedding when Grandpa Charlie had played for her as she walked down the aisle. The keening sound surfaced the last vestiges of grief, and he let his tears flow unchecked.

The sun came out from behind the clouds, and along with other pilgrims, the duo slowly descended stone stairs under the portico and entered the square before the Cathedral. It felt disorienting being at the endpoint. The two men hugged each other in congratulations and heard their names shouted as Pen, Mateo, and Isabela waved to them and ran to greet them.

'How do you feel?' asked Isabela, smiling as if John were the conquering hero.

'I feel great. And even better now that you're here.'

John turned to his daughter and hugged her, not wanting to let go. When they pulled away, he saw Pen wipe tears from her cheeks.

'I'm proud of you, Dad.'

John beamed. It was a long time since he had felt proud of himself.

'For weeks, yours is the face I've been waiting to see.' he told his wonderful daughter.

Mateo took their photo as they posed together in front of the Cathedral. John and Javier raised their poles with arms over each other's shoulders. Brothers.

The family made their way across the square to the hotel, and Pen and Mateo waited with Javier while John and Isabela checked him in.

'Is the room in my name?'

'The room is in my name. I saw no reason for the pretense of two rooms. You just need to register in my room and get another key.'

John smiled. 'Yes, ma'am.' Looking back to where his daughter stood with her husband. 'Pen is a grown-up, and I'm done trying to be perfect.'

'Staying with me is imperfect?' asked Isabela with a raised eyebrow.

'Not as far as I'm concerned.' John put his arm around her shoulder and kissed her hair as the others looked on.

'Anyway, I spoke to Pen. She said she just wants to see you happy.'

'You talked to Pen about us?' he frowned, taking the key from the agent.

'She brought it up. It was when she called me for advice on her job. I told her I like you a lot. She made me promise not to hurt you.'

'Ah.' said John. 'And you promised.'

'I did.' smiled Isabela.

After a long, hot shower, John shaved for the first time in over a week. His grey hair was longer than it had been in years. His cheeks had a sunkissed glow, and he felt healthier than in a decade. On the Camino, he was unconcerned about his appearance. Getting clean and warm was the priority, and he didn't have time to consider how others viewed him.

John emerged from the bathroom in his towel to Isabela sitting on the bed, waiting for him.

'Hello.' she smiled.

'Hi.' he said with unexpected shyness. 'You're an unexpected Santiago surprise.'

'I wanted to be here when you finished.'

She stood and encircled his neck.

'I'm not going to start anything because we need to meet the others, but you can count on me not giving you a break later.'

'I hope not.' John said before returning her kiss.

He texted Pen, and he and Isabela met the others at the hotel bar.

'There you are.' said Pen, smiling. 'I was wondering if you would ever leave the warmth of the shower.'

'It feels good to be clean and dry.' he leaned over and kissed the top of his daughter's head. 'I'm so glad you guys are here.'

The waiter arrived, and they ordered some wine—everyone except Pen.

'Are you still sick?' asked John, remembering that she had been ill at the house in La Rioja. And her condition hadn't improved when he'd spoken to her several times along the way. But he was more concerned about her mental health. These days, Pen seemed down.

Pen and Mateo smiled.

'Well, we wanted to wait until you were both here to tell you. Mateo and I are pregnant. We're going to have a baby in the Spring.'

Javier said something in Spanish and rose to hug them, and Mateo hugged his father back.

John rose and went to his daughter. He held her face, looking into her blue eyes, so like her mother's. He hugged her tightly and then shook Mateo's hand.

'Wonderful news. How are you feeling?' John asked her, concerned. For some reason, Pen didn't appear as excited as the news implied. 'Any better?'

'I am still sick in the mornings, but the nighttime isn't as bad as before. We don't know if it is a boy or a girl, but we can find out in December.'

'Girl or boy doesn't matter.' said Mateo, raising a glass. 'Healthy is what we want.'

'Of course.' said John, 'Healthy is all that matters. And with so many doctors in the family, it shouldn't be a problem.'

As the others threw out potential baby names, John removed his credentials from his pocket, turned the long passport in his hands, and reviewed all the stamps. So much had happened since those first steps in Saint-Jean, and as he looked at the places associated with each imprint, they flashed in his mind. He remembered how he felt at certain points on the trail and the people he met in albergues and cafes along the way. John wondered where Gaelle was and if she had fully recovered. The memories of his journey were surprisingly emotional.

Pen leaned over.

'I remember what that feels like.' she whispered.

'What do you mean?' he asked her.

Pen smiled. 'You can't believe you did it. You walked all that way. Because of it, you'll never be the same. Believe me.'

Pen was right. That was precisely how he felt. John folded his credentials and stood before announcing it was time to get his Compostela. Javier poured himself another glass of wine and waved off another credential. Pen and Isabela escorted John down the hill to the Pilgrim's office.

The electronic queue called his number, and John presented his passport to the clerk.

'Where did you start?'

'Saint-Jean-Pied-de-Port in France.' he said.

'And did you walk the whole way?'

'Yes, I did.' said John proudly.

'And why did you walk the Camino? Spiritual, religious, or for sport?

John thought about it for a moment.

'I walked in honor of my wife – who died from cancer.'

The woman's pen hovered over the paper, and she looked up.

'Did you know you can get the Compostela in honor of someone? It's called *Vicarie Pro* and is used to remember the person. Would you like to add that?'

John nodded, 'Please add her name. Tess Margaret Sullivan.'

Pen hugged Isabela as they watched John through the window as the clerk added her mother's name to John's Compostela and handed it to him.

'Would you like the mileage certificate? Proof that you walked 799 km on the Camino Francés?'

John shook his head.

'No. I know what I did. I don't need anyone to certify it.'

Afterward, the three of them walked back to the hotel.

John left Isabela and Pen in the lobby, asking for time alone in the Cathedral. He walked across the square, climbed the steps, and sat inside as scores of pilgrims milled around.

'OK, Tess. I made it. We're all here in Santiago.' he looked up into the vaulted medieval Cathedral. 'And Javier did it with me, mostly, so he's here, too. I hope, if you were here, you would be proud of me. It wasn't easy. I almost quit a hundred times.' he thought back to Logroño. 'And I have embarrassed myself a thousand times more. But I kept going like I did after you left us—one step at a time. That's it. Just one more step, and I made it here to this moment. I guess that's the whole point. It sounds easy, but you know more than anyone that taking another step is sometimes the hardest thing to do.'

He wiped his cheeks.

'Pen's here. I miss her so much, sweetheart. Every time I see her, I wonder why we live so far apart. But now I think maybe it's time to change that.

Maybe I need to rejoin the world and get a life.' he frowned. 'I'm worried about her. Something is off, but I can't put my finger on it. Perhaps I'll have a word with Mateo.'

John sniffed. 'But there is something else. You'll never believe it. Mateo and Pen just told us. Honey, you're going to be a grandma. Pen is pregnant—our family's future will arrive in the spring. You would have loved this. All of us would have loved having you here.'  John closed his eyes and tugged on the monk's beads encircling his wrist, hesitating. There was more.

'I met someone. After all this time, I'm not so alone anymore. Isabela isn't you, but I think that's okay. I didn't think it would be, but it is. And I have a new family – with Mateo and Javier. You don't have to worry about me anymore. And neither do I. On this long walk, I learned how to put it all down, Tess. The shame of what I did, how I hurt you. I know you forgave me long ago, but I had to learn to forgive myself. I'm not exactly sure when it happened – maybe it was somewhere between León and O Cebriero. But I'm done beating myself up for grieving Charlie the way I did. For almost tearing us apart. It's enough now.'

He wiped his eyes on his shirt tail.

'I added your name to my Compostela. You were the person who made me do this because you're wiser than I will ever be. Somehow, you knew I would need this experience with Javier to heal, so this is yours as much as mine.' he held up the tube as if the ghost of Tess could see what was inside. 'And it's just the beginning. Don't worry. Little by little, I'll finish every place on your list.' John wiped the tears from his cheeks yet again. 'I love you, Tess. No matter what happens, I will always love you.'

John rose and walked silently back to the hotel. In his pocket, he gripped the white knight and the old cork Isabela gave him that night of the party. She was right. He had changed, barely recognizing the man he was just a few weeks ago.

'How do you feel?' Isabela asked him when he returned to the room.

'It's getting easier to let her go. And my life feels more real. Like I'm awake again after a long sleep. I'm glad I started with this Camino before doing the other places on her list.'

Isabela smiled kindly. 'I'm glad I was here with you when you finished.'

'Me too.' he said, hugging her tightly.

Exhausted, John laid down on the bed and was snoring in minutes. Isabela covered him with a blanket and curled up beside him.

# FORTY-SEVEN
## THE RESULTS ARE IN

A few hours later, John's buzzing phone woke them. He rolled over and looked at the screen, and yawned. It was Javier.

'I apologize for waking you, but Antonio has the DNA test results. He wants to open them on the phone with me, and I want you and Isabela there. Can you come down to my room?'

John sat up and stretched.

'Of course. We'll be right there.' John turned to Isabela. 'The DNA results are back.'

She jumped up off the bed and straightened her hair.

'Let's go.'

Javier looked serious when he opened the door to his wood-paneled room.

'Are you alright?' asked Isabela, concerned for her cousin.

'Yes. I think I already know the truth, but I want it confirmed. Then, I have some other things to discuss with you two.'

Javier dialed Antonio, putting him on speaker.

'¡Hola!'

'¡Hola! – John is here with us.'

'Hello, John.' said Antonio.

'Hi, Antonio. Isabela is here too.'

'Marta is with me, as well.' Heavy sigh. 'OK, I'm opening the envelope with the results.'

They heard paper tearing and then silence before Antonio read the report.

'It seems we share a significant amount of DNA. About 27% of our DNA is the same. They use the phrase 'possible half-siblings.''

'Wow.' Isabela's eyes widened. 'That's pretty significant.'

'Yes.' agreed Antonio, 'There is other information here, but that is what we wanted to know. We know my mother isn't your mother, which means Eduardo gave us the same DNA.'

Javier closed his eyes, and Isabela waited for her cousin's reaction.

'Alright. Now we know.' Javier said at last. 'We are brothers.'

The line was quiet.

'Yes. We are. There is no doubt.'

Isabela couldn't wait any longer.

'How do you both feel?! You are not *only children* anymore. You have each other.' she said, smiling.

'I had Antonio before I knew he was my brother.' Javier reminded her

'I feel the same.' Came the response from the phone. 'I always thought of Javier as my big brother. He's been there for me my whole life.'

Javier chuckled. 'Well, it's a good thing I was, now that I know it was always my responsibility. But after today, I'll be able to tell you what to do officially. Interfere in your life and impose my will. As the eldest.'

Antonio laughed, and it broke the tension.

'Your advice has always been something I have relied on.' he said. 'Now I know I'll always have it.'

John broke in.

'So, what now? Do you tell your families? I think Mateo will want to know. He's about to be a father himself.'

'What?!' asked Antonio, surprised. 'Mateo and Pen are having a baby?'

'Yes.' said Javier, smiling at John. 'They told us today. So, you'll be an uncle.'

'Wow. A lot is going on in Santiago. Here, Marta knows, and of course, all of you know. But we need to speak to my mother before we tell our children. I want to understand what happened from her perspective because they will have questions. How do I have the last name I have? Where did that come from? Why all the deception?'

'Agreed. If you don't mind, I would like to be with you when you speak to Ines. It will be easier for her if she doesn't have the conversation with you and then the stress of telling me. This situation is going to be very hard on her. We need to find a way to ease into it.'

'You are right.' agreed Antonio. 'When are you going back to Madrid? I don't imagine you want to be there long without speaking to her about it.'

'I can leave anytime. Tomorrow we can return to Madrid. Can you meet us?'

Antonio spoke to his wife while they waited.

'We will arrange for the girls here and speak to my boss. Then Marta and I will meet you in Madrid.'

'OK. I'll see you both in a few days.' said Javier

After hanging up, the three of them sat in stunned silence. Isabela spoke up first.

'I'm coming to Madrid. I drove here from Navarret. I don't have anything pressing to get back to at home. Pen and Mateo are taking the high-speed back to Madrid.'

Javier and John agreed it was the best thing. None of them would tell Pen and Mateo until after they had a chance to speak to Ines. Javier looked at his watch.

'We're late for dinner. We need to get to the lobby.'

They met their children in the old town for a meal and returned to the hotel.

'Well, that was almost painless.' said Isabela when they opened their door. 'Pen. She knew we were staying in the same room but chose not to comment. I think that is progress. Perhaps spreading her mother's ashes has allowed her to let go of feeling so responsible for you. To allow you to move on.'

'It's true. Pen is very protective of me.' agreed John, 'I can tell she's conflicted. She likes you, but it is difficult for her to see you with me. She'll get there.'

'It's all in the family, I guess.'

'In a weird way.' John smiled, 'You're right.'

It felt good to have Isabela in his arms, and he had nowhere else to be tonight — no set time to wake up in the morning. He didn't have to head out in the cold in less than 8 hours and dress for bad weather. But he knew he would miss the Camino. The predictability. The cadence. The fresh air. Each day, he had no idea what to expect. What would come, would come. It left him free to think, write poetry in his head, and imagine what Isabela was doing at the farm. The time to reflect on the previous 63 years. He had prayed in more churches in the last month than in his entire life. To whom? John didn't know, but he found it comforting.

'No more walking. No more harvest. We'll spend the day together driving to Madrid. I'm looking forward to road-tripping with you.'

'Road tripping?'

'It's an American thing. No one can burn more gas than Americans on a cross-country road trip. We can buy road food and take turns at the wheel. Like college students.'

Isabela laughed. 'We would be the oldest college students in history.'

John stroked her cheek.

'I feel like a college student when I'm with you.' Softly kissing her lips.

'I feel beautiful when I'm with you.' she sighed. 'You look at me like you think so, too.'

He smiled. 'Because you are. I have no idea how old you are, but I know how old I am. I'm not young anymore. I like you. Being with you makes me happy. I thought about you every day while I was walking. I wondered how you were and imagined what you might be doing. I missed you. I didn't think I would ever feel that way about anyone again.'

Isabela rewarded him with a radiant smile. 'I thought about calling you every day, but I didn't want to interrupt what you were doing. It was too important. And I was right, you know. You aren't the same man who started in Saint-Jean more than a month ago. I think you aren't the same man I met in Logroño. You seem calm and centered. Like you know what you want.'

John thought about it.

'All the bullshit is gone—all the anger I had. I'm not sure where it all came from, but it's finished. The anger towards Tess and Javier. Towards myself. All of it. I lived with it for so long that I didn't even realize how much it weighed me down. But now, I can hardly remember what it felt like. I'm just me—it's my life to live. No more living in the past. And I would like to spend a significant chunk of the future with you.'

Isabela led him to bed. They made love slowly and lay in the dark afterward, holding hands. John knew the conversation he needed to have with Isabela, and it nagged at him. Javier was right. He owed it to her. That old fear in the pit of his stomach churned. After revealing this secret, would another person he cared about leave him behind?

# Forty-Eight

## Déjà Vu

Breakfast the following day was a family affair. John noticed two women at the next table as the meal wore on. They looked familiar, but he couldn't place them in. When they finished, the women came over and said hello.

'Well,' said the taller of the two. 'You look much better than last I saw you in Pamplona.'

John leaped to his feet, wrapping her in a bear hug.

'Polly?! I didn't recognize you.'

She smiled and laughed.

'I barely recognized you. You look happy. I think the Camino worked its magic?'

'It did.' agreed John, smiling. 'You were right that day when you let me have it in front of the albergue. But I worked it out over the last month.'

He introduced Isabela and the others at the table. 'You already know Javier.'

'Ah yes, the ever-handsome Dr. Javier.' smiled Lucy. 'The last time I saw you two, it was 50/50 you would make it to the end without killing each other or innocent bystanders. I'm delighted to see you did. The black eye is gone.'

Pen frowned at Mateo.

'When did you get here?' asked Javier, changing the subject.

'We arrived in Santiago 6 days ago. We took a few rest days and then went to Finisterre and Muxia. It's gorgeous if you're up for it.'

'We're going to the service today and then heading to Madrid. Sadly, we'll have to do *The End of the World* another time.' said John.

Javier hugged each of them.

'I am happy we saw you.' said Javier.

'Us too.' said Polly, motioning to John. 'It's nice to see this caterpillar turn into a butterfly.' she teased.

The women said their goodbyes and left as Pen demanded an explanation.

'The last time we saw them was in Pamplona. That was the day Javier got his black eye.' explained her dad.

'So, Polly and Lucy were there?' asked Pen.

'Yes, they were.' said Javier, smiling at John.

'Something tells me there is more to this story than the simple, 'Javier fell.' observed Mateo.

John took a deep breath before admitting the truth of the deeply shameful incident. 'I punched your dad in the face.'

Their children's eyes widened. Isabela reached over and squeezed John's hand.

'What?!' asked Pen, confused. 'Why would you do that?'

'A couple of bottles of wine and some unfinished business.' said John, sheepishly

Pen looked from her dad to her father-in-law, who nodded and smiled.

'Did he hit you back?'

'No. Thank God, or I would have ended my Camino right there and been in traction this whole time.'

Javier laughed.

'Hardly. But your father was entitled to one good punch. We agreed, after that, he could expect me to hit back.'

John raised his coffee cup at Javier, who inclined his head. Pen shook hers.

'I swear.' Pen scowled at her father, 'It's like I don't know you anymore.'

'On the contrary.' said John. 'I think you finally know me. And I think *I* finally know me, too.'

Isabela leaned over and kissed his cheek. Mateo smirked, and Pen said nothing.

Later, they walked to the Cathedral for the service. Afterward, carrying his backpack to Isabela's car, John stopped and took one last look at old Santiago. After weeks of wondering why he was walking, he felt overwhelmed. His Camino was truly over. A part of him didn't want to return to real life. To face going back to Phoenix and an empty house. Spain was a noisy country, but John had become comfortable with loud voices and blaring music. It made him feel like he was a guest at the party of life.

As Isabela, Javier, and John drove out of the city, John craned his head to catch glimpses of the Camino when they reached AutoVia. Near the airport, he saw streams of pilgrims walking toward Santiago de Compostela in the same place he had walked just a day before. As they drove through Arzua, John thought of the morning when the boars confronted him and Javier.

By the time they reached Lugo, they rode silently with Isabela at the wheel. John tried to figure out when he might find the right time to talk to her about his affair. He owed her honestly and didn't want to leave it too long. But he also knew he could not have such a sensitive conversation with Javier in the car. He would have to wait until Madrid.

'You are probably wondering what I was doing at the sheep farm.' said Javier

Isabela looked over at John, then adjusted her grip on the wheel and returned her eyes to the road. John waited for him to say more.

'At the hotel in León, after the DNA test with Antonio, I called my father's lawyer—our old family lawyer. I needed to know what he knew. And he knew plenty.'

Isabela raised an eyebrow, looking in the rearview mirror at her cousin. 'Alright. So, out with it. What did he say?'

'He seemed reluctant to discuss the details but finally revealed he had sent some boxes up to *Tio* Javier after my father's death.'

'Boxes?' Isabela frowned. 'Filled with what?'

'Old wooden boxes nailed shut. It took me nearly a week to locate them. I searched everywhere but could find no trace of them. Then, *Brujita* helped me to discover their hiding place.'

Isabela laughed.

'A little witch helped you find your father's boxes. Really, Javier?'

'It's true. A kitten became trapped near the rafters of the barn. I had to rescue *Brujita*, my lucky charm. And in doing so, I found the boxes.'

'Tell her what was inside.' prodded John.

'Everything I needed to know, and then some. Eduardo's boxes are full of my father's journals. It appears he recorded his entire story for most of his adult life. And the journals began before he met my mother.'

'Interesting.' said Isabela. 'Filled with family secrets, I suppose.'

'Yes, and no.,' said Javier. 'Some of it wasn't so much a secret as a revelation. It seems my father married my mother because she was pregnant with me.'.

'What?' Isabela's eyes widened in the mirror. 'And you never knew this?'

Javier shook his head. 'No, I had no idea. I know my mother. She would bury this information in the deepest hole in the earth's molten core. But, after reading how it all came about in my father's journals, this revelation made me wonder if my father was my father. Did she trick him when she was pregnant with someone else's baby? Yes, we look alike in some ways, but I needed proof. The DNA test with Antonio helped to put that possibility to rest. But now, other things have arisen.'

'Like what?' asked Isabela, imploring her cousin to continue while she navigated them over the mountains, past Ponferrada and toward Madrid.

'Well. It seems my father was in love with another local girl in Navarrete — who was not Ines — before he met my mother. She was a girl with whom he went to high school and to whom Eduardo couldn't wait to return when his medical residency was completed. But my mother's pregnancy put an end to all of it. And that local girl married his brother.'

Isabela's face fell.

'Who was she?' asked Isabela. There were just four brothers.

'Your mother.' said Javier.

'No!' Isabela's eyes widened, nearly swerving off the road. 'Impossible!'

'It's true.' he assured her. 'I read it in my father's handwriting in the journals.'

'What are we doing?' she asked, excited. 'We should be heading for The Basque Country. We need those journals.' insisted Isabela. 'And we need them before we go to Madrid.'

Isabela turned the car off the A6 at the exit after Astorga and pointed them toward Logroño.

# Part VI

# Finding Grace

# FORTY-NINE

## HEADING FOR HOME

Things had changed between their fathers since walking the Camino, A seismic shift. It unsettled Pen to know her dad and her father-in-law had gotten into a fight on the Camino. Mateo seemed more interested in his father's trip to the sheep farm. He told Pen that he had heard from Isabela that his dad had skipped out on the Camino for more than a week to do something mysterious there. When they arrived in Madrid, he would pull him aside to ask his father what it was.

Pen and Mateo made the journey home on the high-speed train from Santiago in just over three hours. They were at the house waiting for their fathers to arrive by car with Isabela, but it was getting late, and there was no sign of the three of them. Pen wanted her father to take the train with her and Mateo so she could spend more time with him. He would be returning to Arizona soon, and Pen needed to maximize the rest of his stay before he flew back to the US. Now that she was pregnant, she felt the pull of family more than ever. Her father was the last of them. This baby needed to grow up with its American grandfather in its life. Pen needed him, too.

At nearly midnight, Isabela's car pulled up in front of the house in Madrid. Pen lay awake in the dark and heard the car door slam. Looking out the window, she watched as her father unfolded himself from the front seat and stretched before he went to the trunk to extract their bags. Javier emerged from the back seat, holding something fury. Was that a kitten?

Pen grabbed her robe as Mateo continued to snore and padded down the staircase just as the front door opened. Ines was also awake, offering to escort John to his room. He stopped to kiss Pen's cheek before following Ines up the stairs to a bedroom with their bags. The room held floor-to-ceiling windows and a large hand-carved bed.

'I hope you'll be comfortable here.' said Ines, drawing the curtains. 'Everything is ready for you. Please let me know if you need anything.'

'Thank you, Ines.' he said, putting his backpack on the chair by the door. 'Can I be upfront with you?'

'Of course, señor.'

'It's John, please.' he said. Formality seemed unnecessary. 'I don't want to pretend, and neither does Isabela. We prefer to stay in the same room.'

Ines stopped, stifling her surprise, then smiled.

'*Claro*. I prefer not to pretend, either. I will ensure there are enough towels in the en-suite bathroom for you both.'

'Thank you, Ines.' he said quietly before continuing, 'My wife, Tess. I didn't have an opportunity to speak with you at the wedding, but I wanted to tell you she spoke so highly of you when she returned from Spain. I felt I almost knew you. I'm glad we got a chance to meet.'

Ines blushed.

'Señora Tess was a special person. She changed everything around here when she and Pen came. I think I can say that Dr. Silva was broken before that. We were living in an apartment across town. This house was closed. Tess was the reason we moved back here. She is the reason your grand-children will be raised in this house. I was devastated when I heard of her passing. I went to church and lit a candle for her. I still say a prayer for her each time.' Ines reached out and squeezed John's hand. 'I will let you get settled and tell Isabela which room you're staying in.'

John went about unpacking. He hated knowing this lovely woman was in for the shock of a lifetime over the next few days.

It wasn't long before there was a commotion in the hall. John went down to see Javier carrying the boxes into the foyer. It was raining hard outside, and he was dripping wet.

'Let me help you.' offered John.

'No. I'm already wet. There is no sense in someone else suffering the same fate.'

He retrieved the final box and moved the car into their garage.

John helped bring the boxes into the great room and stacked them next to Javier's desk. Ines lit a fire in the enormous fireplace in anticipation of their arrival, so the room was cozy and warm on this autumn night.

Javier opened a bottle of wine as Ines returned from the kitchen with a tray of glasses.

'I don't know about you, but I can't sleep.' Said Javier as he poured the garnet liquid, and Isabela handed out glasses. Javier sat down on one of the couches with the others. 'This should warm us up.'

'It is good to have you all home.' said Ines, raising a glass. 'I heard from Antonio. He and Marta are coming tomorrow. I hope it won't be too inconvenient with everyone here.'

'Of course not.' said Javier, alleviating her concern. 'Antonio is family. He can come here and stay as long as he likes.'

'Where did you guys go?' asked Pen, concerned. 'What took you so long? I thought you'd arrive home just a few hours after us.'

Javier glanced over at John. 'We had something we needed to do at the farm. I remembered on our way back. So, we made a detour.'

He pulled the little black kitten from his coat.

'And you brought a kitten home with you?' asked Pen, smiling. She moved to sit beside Javier and gathered the kitten into her lap.

Javier smiled. 'Yes. She's an orphan, and she needs us. If it were summertime, I would leave her at the farm, but winter is coming. I am worried about her being exposed to the elements so far north. Besides, we could use a mouser in a house this big.'

Ines pulled a face. 'Do we have a mouse problem?'

'*Brujita* will help if we do.,' he assured her with a wink.

'Little witch?' Pen laughed. 'Who named her?'

Javier stroked the black fur ball.

'I did. *Brujita* is magic. You will see.' Javier said knowingly.

Pen stretched and yawned. It was nearly 1 am, so she bade them goodnight and returned to bed, taking the kitten upstairs with her.

John and Isabela kept Javier company after Ines returned to the kitchen to gather them something to eat.

'That was a little close to the bone, I thought.' Isabela pointed out to Javier.

'Was it? I want Ines to know that I already consider Antonio family. It doesn't change anything now that we know the truth.'

'I think you are being naïve.' she told him, 'It will change everything from how you and Antonio see each other to how Ines views herself. She is going to feel shame. It's unavoidable. She loves you like a son, Javier. And yet, she's been part of a deception that has lasted nearly your entire life. Having it come to light after all this time will be very painful for her.'

Javier satsilent for a moment. Isabela was right.

'I don't know how to soften the blow of this. Causing Ines pain is not the intent.'

'I might have a suggestion.' offered John. 'She's been an employee with your family for 40 years. After you tell her about the inheritance, she may want to leave.

'But I don't want her to leave. I just want her to know that no matter what, everything is alright.' said Javier, frowning. 'Why would she leave? She might have chosen to live at her parent's home in Ventosa long ago.'

'Yes, but she would have to be supported by Antonio. What mother wants to be a burden to her son? Except she may choose to go if it's too painful to stay here knowing you know about her affair with your father. Before Antonio gets here, you should tell her about the trust set up by your father. She has every right to it, and having some choices might ease her mind after you and Antonio talk to her about all the other stuff.' offered Isabela

Javier nodded.

'This is a good idea. I will speak to Ines tomorrow morning.' he said, just as Ines called them into the kitchen for a late supper.

The following morning, after a coffee, Javier shooed everyone out of the kitchen and invited Ines to sit with him.

'I wanted to speak to you about something important.' he began.

'Is everything alright?' she asked, her eyes narrowing. 'Did the Camino go as expected with John?'

Javier played with the cup in his hands, weighing his options on just how to broach such a delicate subject.

'Things are fine. It's something else. I should have known about this a long time ago, back when my father died. But I just discovered it in a box of old papers stored at the farm.' he said, looking up from the mocha liquid as Ines went white. He knew her mind must be reeling about what he might say next.

'When my father passed away, you were such a help to me, Ines. More than María.' Javier felt the stab of the memory. 'I had to handle all the arrangements with my father's estate. His *abogado* and the *testamento*. The *notaría*. Everything. My mother took to her bed for days, if you remember.'

Ines nodded, searching his face.

'Well, it seems my father left you something, and I have just discovered it. I apologize for that. If I had known, I would have informed you long ago. When Alejandra died, everything seemed to get muddled, and perhaps I didn't look as closely at things or keep track of them as I should have. But while walking with John, I learned about it, and I didn't want to wait any longer to tell you.'

Ines swallowed hard.

'If you remember, my father left money for Antonio's school fees and support until he graduated from university.'

'Yes, it was very generous of him.' she said, pulling her handkerchief from her apron pocket and wiping her mouth.

Javier cleared his throat. No less than the minimum a father would do for his son, he thought.

'Well, he also left something for you—an investment trust for when you stop working. So you won't need to worry about retirement. I was unaware of it, but the investment has been in an account in the Channel Islands for this entire time and appears to have been managed quite well. You have a tidy sum to see you into your old age.'

Ines's face turned bright red, and she cleared her throat before collecting herself.

'Do you want me to stop working in this house?' she asked, sniffing back tears.

Javier reached out and squeezed her hand.

'No. Of course not. If I could, I would keep you here with us forever. But I wanted you to know about the account and the investments. I want you to choose what *you* want to do. I don't want you to work if you want to travel, live in Tahiti, or climb a mountain.'

Ines nodded, rose from the table, and folded the dish towel by the sink.

'How much is the pension?' she asked, staring out at the courtyard as the morning sun began to reach over the roof and into the garden.

'Well. It has been invested and has grown substantially over the years. My father set up the account in 1985, which now stands at more than a million euros.

Ines froze. She turned slowly to look at Javier. Speechless.

'A million euros?' she whispered in disbelief as her hand covered her mouth.

Javier smiled. 'Yes. You can take it out however you like, but there are tax implications, so you must consult someone you trust. I can suggest some people if you like.'

She closed her eyes. 'A million euros.' she whispered again, as if afraid to say the words. 'Eduardo left me with a million euros.'

She hugged the dish towel to her breast as she sat in the chair again. Javier held his breath, waiting for her to say more. When she didn't, he added.

'So, you see, Ines. You can do whatever you want. The choice is yours.'

She straightened up and refolded the towel again. Then she cleared her throat and lifted her chin.

'Well, thank you for telling me. But I have the dishes to do before preparing lunch.'

Javier was unsure what to say next to reassure her.

'I hope you know you always have a home here, no matter what you decide to do. But I also know I'm being selfish in saying that. We love you, and we want your happiness. But I will admit that I'm calling all my friends today and bragging that I have a millionaire housekeeper. Only the best will do for my family.' he teased.

Ines laughed and hit him with the towel.

'Shoo. Get out of my kitchen. I have things to do.'

Javier did as bidden. He stood up, leaned over, and kissed Ines on the cheek. She held his face with tears in her eyes and smiled. Then she sent him on his way and turned back to the sink.

# FIFTY

## HE DIDN'T FORGET

A million euros, she thought, holding on to the counter. How did a girl from Ventosa, who left her village all those years ago to avoid the shame of having a baby with someone else's husband, have a million euros? What would her parents say now?

Ines knew there had always been rumors in her hometown. She heard whispers in the cafe and the *supermercado* when she visited her parents. She knew what people thought as she held her head high and ignored them. But when Eduardo passed away, Ines was left alone with their son. Expecting Eduardo to take care of her was out of the question. If she made a claim, his wife, María, would find out about their affair, and anything set aside for Antonio's education would be in jeopardy.

Besides, she had already moved to this house to care for Javier, Alejandra, and Mateo. Ines loved them all as if they were her own. She enjoyed caring for them, and when Alejandra died, she was glad she was there to help Javier. More especially Mateo. They needed her, and she needed them.

But now, she knew Eduardo had taken care of things. He hadn't forgotten her. She loved him with all her heart, and today, he reached out across time to show her how much he had loved her. She stood at the sink and sobbed quietly into the dish towel, but they were tears of joy, not pain. A man doesn't leave a woman, with whom he's fathered a son, a million euros if he doesn't respect her. If he doesn't truly love her. He had already provided for Antonio's education, so the money he left in the account wasn't for his son. It was for her.

Memories flooded back. Ines could see the blue cornflowers on her cotton dress the day she went to the clinic for a cough. Eduardo wore an expensive blue shirt, making him seem exotic. He smelled like fancy aftershave and coffee. The doctor was kind and listened to her. The sadness in his eyes spoke to her. He was lonely.

After a week, she had to return for a checkup, and that's when it started. At first, they met in the cafe by chance. Then he asked her if she would like to join him for a picnic on the *Ebro* riverbank, and she accepted. Of course, she knew he was married. Everyone in the village knew his wife was someone important in Madrid society. But she didn't care. She just loved him. His heart and hers could speak without words.

Sometimes, when she looked at her son, Antonio, she could see his father. For a brief moment, Eduardo would return to her. And then he'd be gone in a puff of smoke. Washing dishes was when she did her best thinking. She let the water run hot under her hand before squeezing the soap onto the dishcloth. Today, she had a lot to think about.

Javier returned from the kitchen to join the others in the great room.

'How did it go?' asked John.

Javier sighed.

'I think Ines is in shock. She had no idea she was left with so much money for her pension. At first, she seemed concerned that I wanted her to leave here. But after I assured her that we wanted her to stay forever, Ines settled down. I told her it gives her choices now. The money is hers, and she can travel or pursue an interest. I'm not sure that made her happy.' Javier frowned, worried about his friend.

'Give her time.' said John, 'It will sink in.'

In preparation for Antonio's arrival, Javier invited Mateo for a walk in the park. Since he left for the Camino, he had not had an opportunity to talk with his son. So much had happened, and he was concerned about how Mateo would react when the news of Ines and his father broke. He also wondered how Mateo would feel about not being told in advance. But another concern weighed on his mind since before he left for France.

'How are things?' Javier asked his son as they wandered through the Retiro, Madrid's largest park.

'I'm good. Things are good at the clinic. But I'm worried about Pen. She seems different lately. I don't know if it's the pregnancy or something else. And I don't know how to help her because she won't open up to me.'

Javier remembered when Alejandra became pregnant with Mateo. How scary and exhilarating it was at the same time. But he agreed with his son. Pen seemed more closed off. Pensive.

'John mentioned Pen is worried about her job. That she's not fitting in at work.'

This revelation seemed to surprise Mateo. It was more evidence that Pen wasn't talking to her husband.

'What do you mean?' he asked, confused. 'Pen works in Lola's department at the museum. You remember Lola from school. She's great.'

Javier chose his words carefully.

'Perhaps Lola is a good friend of yours. But how she sees Pen, an American, might be different. John says she feels ostracized at the office. Shut out from being part of the group. Pen is not invited to lunches or after-work gatherings. She goes to work and comes home.'

Pen was trying to adjust to the pregnancy. But, simultaneously, she was struggling to fit in at work.

'Think about it, Mateo. Who does Pen have in Madrid other than our family? When does she go out with a friend, even for a coffee? When you go out with your friends from school, does Pen connect with others who might reach out to her separately? Who does she have to talk to besides you, me, or Ines?'

Javier hesitated before revealing something more.

'Now that I am an old retired doctor,' he smiled. 'I often walk in the park during the day. I have seen Pen there — on her lunch break or walking home from work, and wouldn't have recognized her, but she often wears the old baseball cap that used to belong to her brother. Even in her suit from work, she has on the cap. I think it's a comfort to her. But she never wears it when she comes in the door at home. After walking the Camino, I noticed it was similar to the one John wore every day on the trail. Pen is always alone when I see her, and she looks sad. Heartbroken, even. It isn't easy to explain. I have never mentioned it to you before. Somehow, I thought it would pass. But now, that look, and with the pregnancy, I believe this is more than an adjustment to married life. It is something else. Something bigger. At the very least, I believe she is very depressed.'

'What should I do?' asked Mateo, stricken.

'Perhaps, sit down and ask her. And when she tells you how she feels, don't try to solve it for her or offer suggestions. Even if it doesn't make sense, just listen, Mateo. So she knows she's heard. Pen might not be able to articulate it, but I think she is hiding what is happening to keep from worrying you. That can become dangerous. Be patient with her. Whatever it is, I can see she is overwhelmed by it. If you look closely enough, you will see it too.' Javier told his son gently.

'I tried on the train to Santiago, but she wouldn't talk about it. What if Pen won't tell me?'

Javier sighed.

'Then, you keep trying. Pen is in pain. Somehow, we need to help her. John, you, me, and Ines. We need to find a way.' Javier went further than he planned. 'Think about it, Mateo. Pen has done everything to fit into your world here — your life. She has twisted herself in a hundred different ways to make things as smooth as possible for you. But it has cost her a great deal to do so. She needs a community of her own, her own people who understand her in ways we can't. And I think John moving closer to his daughter is one of the keys to that. But Pen also needs friends in Madrid, American friends who understand her, and you must be a part of that world, too. You need to bend to fit into a different culture for her, like she does for you. We must find a way to support her before the baby comes. Otherwise, I fear for her.'

Javier and Mateo walked back to the house, overwhelmed in thinking of ways to help Pen.

Around lunchtime, they heard a commotion in the hall. Antonio and Marta arrived.

'I hear congratulations are in order.' Antonio said, pointing to Pen's stomach.

'Yes, they are.' she said, smiling and holding her hands across her abdomen protectively.

'When are you due?' asked Marta.

'Not until Springtime. We don't know what we're having yet.'

Antonio walked through to the kitchen to see his mother while the others went back to the great room to sit down. It wasn't long before Ines reappeared with her son, holding a tray of coffee and cookies.

'Sit down, Ines, and visit.' said Isabela, getting up to play the hostess. 'I can hand these out.'

'Ines, did you tell Antonio about your pension?' asked Javier, grabbing a cookie.

Antonio's eyebrows went up as he looked from Javier to his mother.

'I haven't had an opportunity yet.' she said quietly.

'You can tell me now.' he said to his mother.

She shook her head.'I prefer to do it later.'

Her son hesitated before adding gently, 'Yes, that would be better. I have some things I want to talk to you about anyway.'

Ines appeared miserable.

After lunch, Javier pulled Antonio aside, suggesting that the conversation be sooner than later.

'She's struggling.' he whispered to his brother.

Pen rose to help Ines clear the table, but Antonio stopped her.

'I can help my mother. You're pregnant, and if you're like Marta was, you are probably tired.' he said, grabbing the plates from her hand and following his mother into the kitchen, setting them down on the kitchen counter.

'So, tell me about this inheritance.'

Ines froze at the sink—her back to her son. There was no other way to confront what was coming. They needed to do it head-on. Ines turned to him with her apron knotted in her hands. Antonio pulled out a chair for his mother and asked her to sit with him.

'Well?' he asked his mother, smiling.

'It is true. I have a pension.' whispered Ines.

'A pension? By whom?'

'By Javier's father, Eduardo.'

'Wow. That is surprising.' said Antonio, frowning. 'I suppose that makes sense. He paid for my schooling and expenses, so it only stands to reason that he would leave you some money for retirement. You've worked for the family for a long time.'

'Yes, I have.' she said, proudly raising her chin. Ines had worked hard, well beyond the remit of an average housekeeper.

'How much did he leave for your pension?'

Ines studied the well-worn table, picking at one of the knots in the wood. When she looked up at her son, it was with such anguish it took his breath away. Her eyes teared up, and her lips quivered. She was barely able to speak.

'More than a million euros.' she whispered.

Antonio's jaw dropped. He stared at his mother, speechless. This news changed how he would speak to her about what he and Javier knew. It changed how he viewed the man he now knew was his father.

'What? Why would he leave his housekeeper a million euros?'

Ines rose from the table and poured herself a glass of water. Her hand shook as she brought it to her lips. Antonio knew this was the one question she had feared. How would she answer? How could she do so and not lie to her son?

'Eduardo cared about us a great deal, Antonio. He considered you and I part of his family.'

He could see his mother fighting to keep her composure.

'Of course, he did. I practically grew up in that house.' Antonio reminded her. 'But that doesn't explain such a large pension.'

Ines sat down and buried her head in her hands. She cried into a dishcloth while her son put his arm around her and waited.

'Is there something you're not telling me?' he asked her gently.

She looked up at him and nodded.

'Can you please ask Javier to come in here?' she whispered. 'No one else.'

Antonio rose and returned with Javier, who shut the kitchen door behind him.

'Please sit down.' said Ines, 'I have something to discuss with both of you.'

Antonio exchanged a look with Javier. Ines's son was worried this was too much for his mother.

'You know I love you both. Antonio, you are my son. I would do anything to protect you.' she turned to Javier. 'And you. I have helped raise you from the time you were little. And I have been so happy to be part of your own family all these years. We may not share blood, but I consider you a son, too.'

Javier reached out, squeezing her hand. 'Ines, you were more mother to me than my own.'

She demurred, but Javier stopped her.

'You know it's true. You showed me love and affection and were there for me in the darkest times of my life. Mateo wouldn't have survived without you after Alejandra died. We owe you a great deal.'

At his words, Ines cried even harder. Both men waited for her to regain control before she continued. She wiped her nose with her handkerchief.

'Yes, but this is not why your father left me the money.'

'I know.' whispered Javier

'What do you know?' The blood drained from her face.

'I know my father loved you and Antonio.'

Ines agreed.'But that is not all.' she told them, 'I don't know how to explain it.'

Javier looked over at Antonio, who nodded.

'Mama. Maybe Javier and I can explain it for you.' he said, looking to Javier to start since he had uncovered the story from his time in Ventosa and the journals at the farm.

'A long time ago, there was a girl. She lived in a small village.' said Javier, 'One day, she met a doctor operating a clinic in her town. He was from the area, but he lived in Madrid. He was well respected.'

'And handsome and kind.' she finished – with a faraway look in her eye.

'Of course,' said Javier. 'She was the beauty of the village, and he was in a miserable marriage with a selfish woman. Sometimes, he would bring his son to his family's farm to escape the pressure in his house in Madrid. This is how they met.'

Ines stared down at the table as if in a trance. Antonio reached out and grasped his mother's hand, but she didn't react.

'They started to see each other, and a romance developed. The doctor would have liked to leave his wife, but he had a son and a life in Madrid. It would mean scandal for them both and their families. So, they carried on a secret love affair.' said her son.

Ines sat like a stone pillar. She had carried this secret for so long, and the story was being told back to her by someone she had protected from it for his whole life. She held her breath.

'One day, she discovered she was pregnant. She was concerned about telling the doctor because she feared losing him, but he was happy. They would have this child together, but she would have to leave the village and move to Madrid so he could take care of them. And they would have to keep it a secret.' Javier said gently. He reached into his pocket and withdrew the monogrammed handkerchief his father had kept all those years, placing it before her.

Ines picked it up and examined the fabric from decades ago. She held it to her nose as the memories and tears flowed out of her.

'The doctor set her up in an apartment, and she had the child, a son. The doctor would visit her as often as he could and see his son as often as possible—but times changed. After a while, it was a long time between visits.' she whispered. 'She was lonely then.'

Her bottom lip quivered.

'He was furious with her when his wife hired her as a housekeeper at his house. But, soon after, he decided the arrangement would work well. He could see her daily, and sometimes she would bring his son to his house.'

Ines stopped suddenly. The two men exchanged a look of concern, so Javier continued the story.

'The doctor introduced his older son to his younger son, and they got along well. Like the brothers they were, but neither knew it. The doctor began to attend events for the younger boy, sitting far in the back and paying for his school fees at the best schools in Madrid. He took care of everything. And then, one day, he died, and he wasn't around to take care of everything anymore. But he left money for his son and the beautiful girl he had loved so much – so she wouldn't have to worry. But it would be decades before she would learn of it.'

Ines looked up at them both. She wiped her eyes and straightened her back.

'So, you both have known this all along?' she asked.

'No.' whispered Javier. 'Only since passing through Ventosa this trip, walking the Camino. I went to check on your house, as you asked. Your parents' next-door neighbor said something about me looking like my brother and father. Since I thought I didn't have a brother, I was shocked. But then I started digging around. Isabela had heard the rumors, too.'

'And then I saw Antonio in León. We discussed it and had a DNA test. We didn't want to bother you with this. We just wanted to know the truth. You have always been family to me, Ines. And now, you really are family. The test came back proving we share a father.'

Ines searched her son's face for his reaction.

'I'm sorry I lied to you growing up. I didn't know any other way.'

Antonio squeezed her hand.

'Do not apologize. You made sure I grew up with my father. I saw him nearly every day after school. And he came to all my school and sports events. You did the best you could under the circumstances.'

'I did.' whispered Ines

'That is all we can ask of one person.' Javier assured her. 'And now that the secret is out, we can all live happier lives.' he stood. 'Of course, we will not tell the great martyr, María, unless we want the roof to cave in.'

Ines laughed and wiped her eyes.

'No, I will not be telling your mother. Besides, she is very old, and it would kill her. And it's not fair to her, Javier. This is mine to carry, not hers.'

Javier smiled at Ines.

'And this is why we love you so much. You have a kind and forgiving heart. I do think we need to tell Mateo and Pen. And your grandchildren. But for now, I will check on the others and leave you two alone for a bit.' he turned and left the kitchen.

Antonio rose and hugged his mother.

'*Ay hijo mío cuánto te quiero.*' she said, smiling into his face, so like Eduardo's.

# Fifty-One

## No More Secrets

The conversation had been exhausting. Javier slumped down onto the sofa.

'What was that all about?' asked Pen.

'I think I will wait until Ines and Antonio come out of the kitchen to explain.' said Javier to those assembled. 'Right now, I just want to close my eyes and rest.'

John reached for Isabela's hand, and she rewarded him with her best smile. In a few short months, everything had changed.

Ines and Antonio emerged at last and sat down.

'Well?' asked Pen, frowning. 'What's going on?'

The mother and son exchanged a look. Antonio encouraged Ines to tell her story.

'Pen, do you remember when you were here, before, with your mother?'

'Of course.' she said, encouraging Ines to continue.

'You had fought with Tess and returned to the apartment very upset.'

'Yes, I remember. You helped calm me down.'

'I tried.' she said. 'And do you remember I told you not to be so hard on your mother because good people sometimes do things we don't like or admire?'

'You told me the story of how you came to Madrid.' remembered Pen.

'Yes, I did tell you about that. But I left out one thing—the man in the story. The man I told you about is from the village where I am from. The man who brought me to Madrid, who was the father of my son, and whose home I worked in. That man was Eduardo Silva. Javier's father. And Antonio's father.'

Pen's eyes widened as Mateo turned white.

'What?' he asked his father, frowning. 'How can that be?'

Javier explained.

'My father ran a clinic on the weekends in Ventosa. Not far from the vineyard. He was unhappy in his marriage to my mother, and he would bring me up there with him. It's when he fell in love with Ines, and she became pregnant with Antonio and moved to Madrid.'

'How long have you known this?' Mateo wanted to know.

'Antonio and I just found out about it a few weeks ago. We decided to have a DNA test and got the results back in Santiago. Since we were coming to Madrid, we wanted to discuss it with Ines before we told anyone else.'

Mateo looked over at Ines like he had never seen her before. He rose and left the room as Ines began to cry. Pen moved over to Ines and hugged her.

'Don't worry. I will talk to Mateo. He's just in shock.'

'Thank you.' she said to Pen, patting her cheek before Pen went to find her husband.

'Everyone here knows the story, so we don't need to repeat it.' said Isabela, turning to Antonio and Ines. 'All it means is I have a new official cousin and a new *Tia*. You were always at the vineyard anyway, so this feels no different. Has anything changed, really?'

Antonio smiled at his mother.

'I think everything has changed—no more secrets. At last, I know who my father was, and I did know him. For that, I am very grateful. And I have a brother, a real one, not one who is just a brother-like friend. That's different.' he said, smiling at Javier. 'I think we should celebrate.'

Ines smiled weakly.

'Well, I agree.' said Isabela, smiling to reassure Ines. 'And I know just the wine. I'll get it.'

'Give me a moment.' Javier told his cousin, 'I want to speak to Mateo.'

Javier found his son and daughter-in-law in the dining room. Pen looked up when she heard him come in and shook her head.

'What's going on, Mateo?' he asked his son.

'I thought Ines was the most honest person I knew. She was there for us when Mama died. Now I find out she's been lying to us for years. I don't understand it.'

Javier glanced at Pen. This was a delicate situation; she had known about it longer than Mateo. Pen had enough going on without adding to her plate.

'Mateo?' they all turned. Ines stood in the doorway. 'May I speak with you?'

The hurt in his eyes told the story. As Ines walked over to where they were sitting, she appeared smaller than before. Diminished. This woman had helped each of them. She was there for Pen when she was in turmoil over her mother's illness and death. Even after they had returned to the US and after the Camino, Ines continued to write to them, keeping the connection between the families. She had been the glue that kept them all together when they were falling apart. She deserved their grace.

Javier pulled up a chair so she could sit next to Mateo.

Slowly, Ines began to tell her story as Mateo looked at the floor like he was a child again. One who needed her comfort when life had knocked him sideways. In the past, Ines had filled that role. Today, she was the cause of his pain, and Javier knew that was the hardest thing of all to bear.

'I know you are disappointed in me. I am not the person you thought I was. That no one thought I was. I have lied to everyone for nearly 50 years and paid a price for that lie. Your grandfather also paid the price. But I want you to know this lie was told out of love. Love for Eduardo, your grandfather, your father, and *Tio* Antonio. And even for your grandmother, María. Believe it or not.'

'But why?' he asked. 'I understand why you did it in the beginning, but you told Pen a long time ago. Why not tell us sooner? We're all adults.'

Ines nodded. 'It's true, you are grown now. But when you have told a lie for so long, you almost start to believe it yourself. Times were different back then. There were no single mothers. Divorce was impossible. Initially, there were questions about who I and my son were. Questions from neighbors and the school he attended about where we came from and why we had no relatives. I had to answer them, so I lied about what happened more and more often. But in the last few decades, no one has asked me anything about it, so it was easy to pretend to forget what I had done. After your grandfather died, I wanted to forget.'

'But you can't.' said Mateo, 'You have Antonio, and he had the right to know. We all did.'

Ines nodded. 'Yes, he did. You're right to condemn me. When I began working for your grandmother, I got to know your father.' she looked up at Javier, who smiled back. 'He was small for his age and lonely. He needed love. I wouldn't have hurt him for anything in the world. Exposing your grandfather would have disgraced his family. It would have hurt all of them. As much as I didn't enjoy María's company, she had given me a job and allowed me to bring Antonio to the house. I didn't want to see that house burn down.'

'I fell in love, not just with Eduardo, but with the family. And we became part of the family, Antonio and me. Then you came along, and there was more to love and more to lose. More people I cared about could suffer because of what I had done. I wouldn't allow that to happen. I wanted to protect you, too.'

Mateo took a deep breath.

'But I'm a man now. I have a family of my own. I can handle the truth.'

'I can see that. I should have told everyone sooner. Except I think María will still need to remain in the dark. It would kill her.' cautioned Ines, 'But you're right and deserved my honesty and trust. I should have told you. I apologize. It's the only thing I have ever lied to you about in your entire life, and now you know.'

Mateo glanced over at his wife, who nodded her agreement with all Ines had said. Then he turned to his father, who waited for his reaction. Ines held her breath, and when he reached out to hug her, she began to sob.

'You mean so much to me, Mateo.' she sniffed. 'I am so sorry I disappointed you.'

Mateo pulled back to look at her.

'You could never disappoint me. As you said, we are family.'

Pen rose and hugged Ines, and Javier squeezed her shoulder.

'Come.' he said. 'I think tonight we celebrate family. Isabela has gone to get the wine.'

Javier met John's gaze as they returned to the room and got a nod. Everything was alright. Mateo wiped his cheeks, and so did Pen and Ines, but they were all smiling. As Ines told Pen all those years ago, families heal.

Javier invited everyone to raise a glass.

'To family.' he nodded to Antonio, Ines, and Marta. 'Old and new. It seems this is the year our family just keeps growing.' smiling at Pen and John. 'May it continue to do so. Salud.' and the others responded in kind.

It had been an emotional day. After dinner, they retired early.

'Wow.' said John as he and Isabela got into bed. 'This is a family filled with emotion. Ours isn't quite as colorful.'

'Boring, you mean?' asked Isabela playfully.

'Perhaps. But I'm glad it's all out in the open. I think it's a relief for everyone.'

Isabela agreed.

'The cloud has lifted. Truth is a bright light.' she rolled over and hugged John. 'And the truth is, I like you very much.'

He hugged her back, but his bit of truth still nagged at him. Amidst all this, when would John find the right moment to discuss his biggest secret with Isabela? The moment had yet to present itself, and he was tired. They fell asleep until a commotion in the hall at 3 am. Javier stood outside the door, speaking to someone. John got up to find out what was happening and discovered a crowd. Javier stood deep in whispered conversation with Mateo, Pen, and Ines. They were surprised to see John awake.

'What's going on?' he asked when he saw the concerned looks on their faces.

'My mother has been taken to a local hospital. She has had a heart attack, and we need to go and see her.'

'Would you like me to get dressed and come with you?' he offered.

'No.' Javier shook his head. 'I think we'll go now. I'll get in touch later when we know more.'

They returned to their rooms to get dressed.

'What is going on?' asked a sleepy Isabela when he returned to bed.

'Javier's mother has had a heart attack. They're all leaving to see her.'

Isabela sat up.

'It's ironic that after everything that happened yesterday, María had a heart attack in the middle of it. Like somehow, it's all connected.'

She was right. It was as if María tapped into it. Yesterday, everyone agreed. María would die if she discovered the betrayal of her husband and Ines.

# FIFTY-TWO
## NOTHING LEFT UNSAID

Javier, Ines, Mateo, and Pen rushed to the hospital. They found María in the intensive care unit with tubes and machines surrounding her. She was ghostly pale. Javier took her left hand, and Mateo took the other. Their touch roused her, and she slowly opened her eyes to see her son and grandson gazing down at her.

'I knew you would come.' she whispered.

'Of course, Mother. We came as soon as they called us.'

María coughed.

'The doctors here are not as good as your father or Sebastian. But I suppose I'm old now, so no matter what they do, my time is up.'

'Don't talk that way.' said Ines from across the room.

María squinted her eyes, recognizing Ines for the first time. She coughed at the sight of her old housekeeper and requested help from her grandson to drink some water. Mateo held it to her lips before she waved the cup away.

'I would like to speak to Ines.' she said with sudden strength. 'Alone.'

They looked at each other, not sure what to do.

'Everyone else, please leave.' she ordered, pointing at the door with a bony finger and the spear of a glossy red nail.

Ines changed places with Javier and nodded as he herded the others out and shut the door behind them. But he remained in the corner, out of sight of his mother. After last night, he didn't want to leave Ines alone in the room with María.

'Señora, the doctors will do the best for you, and you'll be back home very soon.' said Ines

María coughed but batted away the comment like a fly.

'We both know that is not true, Ines. I will not be leaving this hospital. The doctor was honest with me about that. But I have some loose ends I want to tie up before I go.'

Ines braced herself. This woman, who had dominated so much of her adult life, could be brutal on her best days. María's imminent death would not soften her personality.

'Do not worry, Señora. Javier and Mateo will be alright. You know this.'

María studied Ines before she continued. 'I know. I have never doubted that. But this is not what I wanted to talk to you about.'

'*Claro.*' said Ines, and she waited as María closed her eyes, took a deep breath, and let it out.

'I always knew. Did you know that? I knew about you and Eduardo. About Antonio. I understood what was happening under my nose in my own home. I knew when I hired you.'

Ines went ashen, but she said nothing. The past twenty-four hours had depleted her strength.

'My husband spent every weekend up in that stupid village. A place that never accepted me. Once, I went up there to see what it was all about — where he took my son nearly every weekend like a moth to a flame. What was so special about that one-horse town? I saw you with him. You were younger and beautiful then, but I remember it like yesterday.

'It wasn't your youth and beauty that struck me. It was Eduardo's face when he looked at you. It was like a knife through my heart. I never got out of the car. I told the driver to turn around, and I returned to Madrid. Back to where I knew how to live in civilization, where there weren't naive village girls to entice my husband. Where everyone looked up to me, and so many men, even the husbands of my friends, thought me a prize.'

Ines looked away, awash in shame.

'But then you came to Madrid to live. I knew he had put you up in an apartment. I knew about the boy. He looked so much like Eduardo you would have to be blind not to see it, just like Javier. The Silva's have strong genes. At first, I pretended you didn't exist. But one day, I decided to take back control of the situation. I placed an advertisement in the newspaper. But that was not all. I directed my maid to speak to you about it in the cafe where you drank your morning coffee. Do you remember?'

Ines squinted, thinking back. She did recall the girl who told her about the position in a good house in the Salamanca neighborhood.

'You wanted a job. At first, even though it was my plan, I was angry with our audacity. You were shameless in coming to my house and asking to work. I wanted to tell you how unqualified you were and how you were not the quality of person I would have in my home. To crush you under the heel of my handmade shoes.'

María began to cough again, and Ines helped her with the water until she could compose herself. Two nemesis locked in a karmic battle.

'They say it's better to keep your enemies close, so I decided to hire you—the justice of seeing Eduardo's face that first night at dinner was worth it. And then I allowed you to bring the boy around. He was quiet and well-behaved. It might surprise you that I actually liked him because it surprised even me. And it was clear he had no idea that Eduardo was his father.'

'I felt like the puppet master. I held all the strings, and you danced before me, thinking I was blind. But, of course, I was the only one who could see the whole picture. It was like holding up a raw piece of meat to a starving dog. Just out of reach of its jaws, you watch them leap and snap at what they desire most, never quite able to grasp it while they salivate.'

Ines watched this woman as she spoke. The hatred María felt over the years spilled out of her like a leaky jug.

'But you know why I hated you both?'

'Because we betrayed you,' whispered Ines, choking back shame. 'we lied.'

María waved away Ines's explanation like it was smoke.

'No. That wasn't what it was at all. Men cheat. Every one of my friend's husbands had a mistress. *Es normal.* No. It's what I became because of your love affair. And it was a love affair. You weren't just his mistress – he loved you, and I knew it. He loved you more than he ever loved me if he loved me at all. And it ate me alive for all these years. I became a worse person than perhaps I already was. A worse wife and a worse mother, and I blamed you both for that.'

'I used to devise small tortures for Eduardo. Little things that I knew would cut him deeply. He missed birthdays for Antonio because I scheduled us to be elsewhere at events that could not be rescheduled. I called friends who sat on the boards at the schools he wanted Antonio to attend to ensure the boy wasn't accepted. My entire life became a game of chess, obsessed with making Eduardo's life and yours uncomfortable. And your sweet son suffered for it.'

As Ines looked down at María, her lip quivered. For decades, this woman stood between her and love, and in the end, Ines felt pity wash over her. María, who thought she had tortured them, had been the one who was tortured. Ines buried her face in her hands and sobbed as she felt a small, bird-like claw grasp her wrist, and she looked up.

'I am not telling you all this to exact my revenge, Ines. I have done that a thousand times over the years, and it has cost me dearly—the price was the love of my son, my grandson, and my husband. I am telling you this because I am dying. For my entire marriage and beyond, I was filled with the black tar of hatred, and it has eaten me alive. It's past time to stop it. I have just enough time left to forgive you and Eduardo.'

María squeezed Ines's hand, looking up into her eyes.

'You have been good to my son and my grandson. Because of my obsession, you have been closer to them than I ever was. I need you to promise me that you'll never leave them. They need your steady hand.'

'Of course.' Ines squeezed María's hand in response, 'I will take care of them.'.

At that moment, Javier stepped out of the shadows and approached the other side of the bed, taking his mother's hand.

'Mama. Do not worry about us. Mateo is happily married, and we were going to tell you tomorrow that he and Pen are expecting a child. You are going to be a great-grandmother.'

Tears welled in María's eyes.

'Don't cry. The doctors are going to give you the best care possible. I will make sure of that.'

María shook her head.

'It's not that.' she said, wiping her eyes. 'You haven't called me 'Mama' since you were a small child.'

Javier leaned over to kiss her cheek, and she wrapped her thin arms around his neck and held on. When they parted, he wiped his tears as she held onto his face.

'I have always been so proud of you, my son.' she said through rummy eyes. 'Now, I would like to see my grandson. And to speak with his wife. I have a lot of things to tell them before this baby is born. Family things. Perhaps a suggestion of a name or two.'

Javier chuckled, and Ines wiped her eyes.

'*Vale.*'

He and Ines left the room and sent the others in. Javier and Ines sat side by side in the hall, stunned by what they had just heard. How María had known all those years and tortured them, including herself, was unimaginable. Before long, the others came out.

'The doctor said she needs her rest.' explained Pen as they joined them in the hall.

'Take Ines and Pen home to have breakfast.' Javier said to Mateo. 'I'm going to stay here.'

He watched them walk down the hospital corridor toward the exit. Javier tried to sort through the last 24 hours — the revelations of his new-found family and all that his mother had said to Ines. In great pain for decades, María paid dearly for her anger and bitterness. She had sacrificed love for the cold companion of revenge. But she hadn't left it too late. And he would be with her to comfort her until the time came.

Javier drank a coffee in the lobby cafe and returned to check on his mother. The alarms went off at the door to his mother's room, and staff rushed in and out. As a doctor, he wanted to go in, but he knew they were working on her. He waited until the alarms stopped and the sound of her heartbeat on the monitor returned to normal. After a few minutes, it was clear it wasn't going to happen, so he went into the room and asked them if he could hold her hand while they came to the end of their life-saving protocols. The doctor nodded as the nurses began to shut off the machines, and the doctor ceased CPR.

Javier sat alone with María. A woman he felt he hardly knew but who had revealed so much on her final morning before the sun rose. He leaned over and hugged her.

'I forgive you, Mama, for all of it.' he kissed her cheek. 'It's finished. Rest peacefully.'

He went out into the hall and dialed Isabela to have her tell the others. Then, he called the funeral home and left a message. Javier had treated scores of geriatric patients throughout his medical career. He knew what to do.

# FIFTY-THREE
## GOD SAVE THE QUEEN

The day took on a surreal texture as they made the arrangements. Ines called the church and spoke to the archbishop, who had personally known María for decades. She would want church royalty presiding over her funeral.

Antonio and Marta arranged to stay in Madrid for the funeral, which would be attended by hundreds of people—an event unto itself.

Javier returned home from the hospital around lunchtime, and John met him at the door.

'I'm so sorry about your mother.' he said, embracing Javier, who looked exhausted.

'It was her time.' Javier sighed. 'Ultimately, she had a chance to make amends and ask for forgiveness, and she took it. Leave it to my mother; her timing was always impeccable.' he chuckled.

Javier embraced his son.

'I'm sorry, Papa.' he said, with tears in his eyes.

Javier led them all into the great room.

'What did your grandmother say to you when she spoke to you?' he asked Mateo and Pen.

They hesitated before recounting the conversation.

'She said we should name our child after Mama.' whispered Mateo

Javier's eyes widened.

'She said Mama was a kind and good person and deserved to have her grandchild named after her.' continued Mateo.

'That Alejandra was a patient person, something she had never been.' added Pen. 'María said she always admired her despite never showing it. 'Maybe this child will have blue eyes, just like you and your mother." she told Mateo.'

Javier leaned back and closed his eyes as tears poured down his cheeks.

'Why? Why did she wait until the end? Why did she never reveal to me who she really was?'

'Because of me?' came a voice at the French doors to the courtyard.

They all turned.

'Your mother was obsessed with Antonio and me, which hurt you. For that, I am very sorry.' Ines fought for composure.

'No.' said Javier. 'Not because of you. María had a choice, and she made it. She said as much when we spoke at the hospital. Your actions are not to blame for the choices she made. And she knew that.'

Ines sat down next to Javier, and he grasped her hand.

'You're being generous in what you say. But I know the truth.'

Javier shook his head.

'You loved my father. That is the only truth I care about. You made him happy. And I have a brother. It's finished now with all the secrets. Done. We can enjoy our family. María gave us that blessing at the end, and I intend to honor it.' He squeezed her hand and smiled at her through his tears.

Ines sighed, looking unconvinced. 'Lunch is nearly ready. I think it's still warm enough to eat in the garden.'

'I'll help you, Ines.' Isabela offered, and John followed, wondering when his secret might come to light.

# Fifty-Four

## The Funeral

Javier had been to many funerals for his patients and his family, but this one was different. Like John, Javier was indeed an orphan now. Both his parents were gone, and he was glad to have the entire family by his side.

The house overflowed with María's family and the children of her friends, who had preceded her in death. Javier and Mateo shook so many hands they lost count. Even Eduardo's extended family from La Rioja made the trek to pay their respects. They had never liked her, but she had been Eduardo's wife and Javier's mother. Certain traditions must be followed.

With Isabela's help, John purchased a suit at the Spanish department store *El Corte Ingles*.

'I don't know how I'm getting this home.' John told her, standing in front of the mirror. 'Nothing else is fitting in my pack.'

Isabela straightened his tie and smiled. 'I can keep it for you in my closet. You can take it back to America on your next visit.'

Through it all, Ines handled everything with the help of Pen, Isabela, and Marta. Mourners were fed, drinks served, and pillows fluffed. The last guest departed after the funeral reception, and they sat slumped in the sofas, exhausted.

'It's over,' said Javier, closing his eyes. 'It's finally over.' he reached up and loosened his tie.

Isabela turned to John. 'What's your plan now? Are you returning to the US immediately or maybe taking a little break?'

John shook his head. 'I need to go home. I've got places to visit to finish checking things off Tess's list. I'll be back in Spain very soon to be here for the birth of my new grandchild. But we'll keep in touch, Isabela. I'll make sure of it.' He squeezed her hand and kissed it.

Isabela remained silent.

# Fifty-Five

## Goodbyes

John stood outside security at Madrid airport and hugged his daughter. He knew she was in good hands, but he hated leaving her now that she was pregnant. With Tess gone, he felt he should stay and watch over her. But that wasn't his job anymore, and Mateo was a capable partner. Still, something nagged at him. Since he arrived back in Madrid, Pen seemed better than she had when he walked the Camino, but she lived in a culture with which he was unfamiliar. His advice no longer applied to her life.

For the next six months, John had a plan mapped out in his mind, and he was going to follow through on his promise to Tess before the birth of their first grandchild. Javier reached out his hand. John took it and pulled him in for an uncharacteristic hug.

'You changed my life on this trip, Javier. I can't thank you enough.'

Javier smiled. 'I'm glad we could help each other. I don't know what I would have done if you hadn't been here for the last few months. I don't think I gained just one brother. I have two now.'

John turned to Isabela, who struggled to put on a brave face.

'And you. What can I say about you?' he hugged Isabela fiercely and kissed the top of her head as Pen looked on, grasping Mateo's hand.

Isabela buried her face in his chest and hung on like she didn't want the moment to end. Eventually, she pulled back and looked up into his face.

'You'll come back soon.' It wasn't a question.

'I will be back,' he said in his worst Arnold Schwarzenegger impression. 'I've got a few things to take care of first.'

Lastly, he turned to Mateo. 'I know you'll take care of her.' he told him. 'Like you always have.' They embraced as John fought back tears, reaching over and embracing his daughter.

'You will call me night or day, right? Promise me, Pen. If you need anything, you call.'

'I will.' she nodded.

John picked up his pack and entered security. The last view from the other side was of Isabela standing with Pen. Both of them crying and waving goodbye.

# EPILOGUE

I t was a frosty drive through fields of *La Rioja* with the white knight
from his Camino perched on the dashboard for good luck. John arrived
in Madrid on a 6 am flight. He hadn't bothered to sleep before renting a
car and driving north. He wasn't exactly sure how to get there, but he had
some landmarks as his guide from his time on the Camino.

John awoke the morning before with no plans to be in Spain. The closer
he got to his destination, he wondered if he was crazy for jumping on a
plane on a whim.

After returning to Arizona from his Camino, John focused on Tess's
list. He went to the Pacific Northwest to check off those places that Tess
had requested, including sprinkling her at the grave of their son, Charlie.
He sent pictures to Pen at every location, and it got easier each time he
performed the ritual, leaving more of her behind.

Being home was distracting. His emotional time on the Camino slowly
faded from his everyday life. He felt a freedom he hadn't had before. But
eventually, the familiar won out over mystical pilgrimages and serendipi-
tous encounters. The healing and the lessons he had learned stuck, but the
drama he experienced while he was in Spain had overwhelmed him. John
needed distance and time to think. He spoke to Pen regularly, listening to
her describe her pregnancy. Marveling in the ultrasound photos she sent.
He even talked to Javier. Initially, John and Isabela had exchanged messages
and sent each other pictures of what they were doing. But they were both
busy, and time dwindled their communication. In moments alone, it made
him sad. And he knew it was his cowardice that kept them apart.

On a dark morning in late February, as the sun began to peek over the pink mountains in the distance, John stood alone in his house in Arizona. He drank his usual coffee and dressed for golf. His standing Tuesday morning tee time awaited. Over his coffee cup, John looked up at the fireplace. Above it hung a picture of him and Tess on their wedding day. But it wasn't the image of their younger selves that struck him. The morning light was just right, and he could see his reflection in the glass. But the man looking back was not him. He had the uniform, but he didn't fill it. No matter how hard he tried, he was no longer the guy in the wedding photo. Or the one who played golf with his buddies in the Arizona winter. Not anymore.

Lately, John had been dreaming of Isabela, awakening in the middle of the night, remembering their time at the winery. He had the urge to call her but never dialed the phone. Nighttime wasn't the only time she snuck into his thoughts. John began thinking about her during the day, too. Isabela's fury when he set her down after they stomped grapes in Logroño. And of her holding his hand and stroking his hair at the hospital. The mysterious goddess in the cave the night of the crush party, his joy at seeing her unexpectedly in Burgos, and the night together in her room.

Their lack of communication was his fault. If John followed his feelings for Isabela, he would have to tell her what he had told Javier. He dodged it in Madrid and didn't relish the thought of revealing his biggest secret. If they were to have a chance, he needed to bite the bullet. But Isabela scared him. It wasn't her strength or her beauty. It was how he felt when he was with her. Unsure of what would happen next. After María's funeral, he needed to escape Spain and had the perfect excuse with Tess's list. And he took it. He hadn't completed it yet, but John had no more barriers to traveling to Spain. His grandchild would be born in just a couple of months, and he wanted to be there to support Pen.

As he stood staring at his reflection in the old wedding photo, the ticking clock on the mantle grew louder. John picked up his phone and messaged his friends, begging off golf.

'Come on, man.,' wrote his friend on the group chat. 'What do you have to do that's better than playing 18 in perfect weather?'

'I'm going to a vineyard in northern Spain.'

John sent it before he thought about it.

'What?!?!' they all texted back.

He didn't reply. As with everyone he knew in the US, he had not spoken to them about his time on the Camino, and he wasn't going to start now. They wouldn't understand.

Sitting at his laptop, John Googled flights to Europe. At the last minute, the price was eye-watering. He could purchase a plane ticket or a small car, but now that he imagined going, he didn't care. He selected an itinerary and bought it before he could change his mind.

John stripped out of his golf clothes. He pulled out jeans and hiking boots, grabbed some dress shirts and T-shirts, and threw them into a bag with his passport. John didn't need to pack a suit, remembering the last time he needed to buy one in Madrid. Isabela had it waiting for him in her closet at the vineyard. Then, he threw on his dad's old *Cubs* hat, just for luck, and locked up the house.

That was yesterday. Bleary-eyed, John drove down what he hoped was the right dirt track. The acid in his stomach steadily increased as landmarks began to take on some familiarity. He hadn't called or messaged Isabela he was coming. If she wasn't there or if there was someone else in her life, he would quietly find a hotel in Logroño and head back to Madrid to see Pen. He had planned to surprise his daughter either way.

After several wrong turns, he drove down the driveway to the winery and parked in the area in front of the house. No one was around. Not even the fat orange cat that usually lounged on her terrace. When he rattled the iron gate to the courtyard, it was locked. John shook his head. It suddenly occurred to him that it was ridiculous to come all this way unannounced. February at a winery in Spain is not exactly the busy season. She might be in Tahiti.

John retrieved his yellow puffer jacket from the car, braced himself against the cold, and then walked down to the barns behind the house. A group of people stood together working on machinery. One of them in a green baseball cap looked up. It was Isabela.

She stood where she was with a wrench in her greasy hand, cocking her head like a puppy observing a curious human. John wasn't sure if she would throw it at him as she choked up on the handle, tightening her grip. Walking half the distance towards him, Isabela stopped.

'Look what the cat dragged in.' she said. She seemed more curious than happy to see him.

'I woke up yesterday morning and got on a plane.' he said honestly.

'I guess you did.' she raised an eyebrow. 'Why?'

'Well.' sighed John. 'I was all set to play 18 holes of golf with my friends.' he nervously pulled at the bracelet the Buddhist monk had given him on the Camino the previous autumn. 'We do that a lot in Arizona. Old guys play golf. That's what you're supposed to do when you retire. Hang out with other old guys and talk about your glory days while hitting a small white ball. So, I was going to do that.'

John took two steps towards her while Isabela tightened her grip yet again.

'Ah.' she said, as if bored by his nonsense. 'So, you were playing golf.'

'Well, I was going to play golf.' he said, walking a little closer to her. 'But then I was tired. Very tired because I have been getting no sleep.'

'And why aren't you sleeping?' she asked him, taking a tentative step forward. 'They have pills for that. You should see a doctor.'

John tried to look serious.

'I've been dreaming of a beautiful winemaker in Spain. Fortunately, they don't have pills for that. So, I thought I would get on a plane and see if she was real.'

Isabela stood her ground, searching his face. She was hurt when he left, and he knew that. But she said she understood why he had to go. Her pride kept her from chasing after him when his communication with her dwindled to nothing. He was sure he would pay a price for that.

'She was real then, and she's real now. But are you real, John? Are you ready to be real?' she asked him, raising her chin in defiance as the winter wind blew her hair from her face.

John studied this woman in dirty jeans and muddy boots. Her hair fell out of her braid, and black grease stained her hands. He was ready to be honest with her.

'I've never been more ready for anything in my life.'

Isabela started at him for a long moment, then turned to the men still working on the machinery and said something he didn't understand. She turned back to the man standing in front of her. The one who had traveled halfway across the world to see her. She walked closer.

'But there are a few things I need to tell you.' said John nervously. 'Before, well, anything else.'

Isabela nodded.

'How long are you staying?' she asked.

'After we talk, we'll see how long you'll have me.'

Isabela smiled.

'Okay then.' And she took his hand in hers, covered in grease, still clutching the wrench, and led John up to the house.

Sign up to be the first to learn about the launch date for *Book 3: The Impossibility of Time*. Read exclusive excerpts of the continuing story of the Sullivans and Silvas in *The Camino Family Trilogy* at kdfieldauthor.com or by scanning the code.

linktr.ee/authorkellifield

# ACKNOWLEDGMENTS

They say everyone has one book in them, so committing to a trilogy might seem like a fool's errand. The pressure! I am incredibly proud of the second book in The Camino Family Trilogy. But no writer does it alone, and I am no different. This book came together with the help of so many people who were generous with their time and expertise. And notes! There were so many notes! I read them all, and the note writers might just find some of their suggestions sprinkled throughout the story. I'm sure John and Javier are grateful. But there are a few people without whom you wouldn't be reading this story.

To my friend, Leigh Brennen, you're not only a Camino icon but also one of my fiercest supporters. Your enthusiasm and excellent suggestions are woven throughout. From the first read-through, your empathy for these characters and the story I wanted to tell has meant everything in moving this to publication.

To my friend, Matilde Rodríguez Vásguez, your advice on all things *español* is invaludable, as always.

To all the fantastic alpha and beta readers who slogged through typos and confusing sentence structure, you are my heroes. I am forever in your debt. David, Jordan, Lisa, Robert, Ginger, Jose Marie, Maria, Grace, Lauren, Joe, Marta, and Dora.

To my friends in Santiago and Valencia, who have encouraged me to keep writing. Without you, this book would never have been written. I am forever in your debt.

To the ladies in Melide: MariCarmen, Monica, Chus, Chusa, Carmela, Raquel, and Christina, your belief in me and my writing during the dark Galician winters has been everything. I would be lost without you all.

To Jeff for your unwavering support. You are still every man I ever write.

And finally, to the Pilgrims all along the Camino. I wrote this story for you.

# FOR BOOK CLUB DISCUSSION

1. Did the story of *The Weight of Fearsome Things* unfold like you thought it would after the end of *The Grief of Goodbye*?

2. Regarding John Sullivan, what were the most surprising aspects of his origin story? Did they make you more sympathetic to him over time or less so?

3. As Javier and John walk the Camino, they develop a relationship outside of that of Tess. What do you think were the key moments in that shift?

4. How do you see John as a husband and father as opposed to how you saw Tess after reading Book 1?

5. Isabela takes on a key role in the story. What are your thoughts on the intense winemaker?

6. In this book, Ines's story takes center stage. How did that unfolding impact the way you see her?

7. John's lack of religious faith comes up several times in the book. Why do you think that is, and how does that evolve by the end of his Camino?

8. Healing and letting go are key themes of the story. What are some moments that stand out when John starts to make that transition?

9. Caminos are about transformation and involve pain for all pilgrims, whether physical or emotional. How does pain play a role in this Camino for John and Javier?

10. Pen is going through a difficult time. She is not on a Camino but is still grieving and healing while transitioning to a new life in Madrid. How does her journey parallel that of walking a Camino?

11. What part do forgiveness and grace play in the story? How do we relate to that in our own lives?

# About the Author

K.D. Field is an American writer and blogger living on The Camino de Santiago in Galicia, Spain. *The Weight of Fearsome Things* is her second novel in *The Camino Family Trilogy*. She maintains the blog vivaespana movingtospain.com, chronicling the adventures of her and her husband, Jeff, from the decision to move to Spain after walking the Camino from Saint-Jean-Pied-de-Port in 2017 to the present day. Keeping up with the author is easy at kdfieldauthor.com – where she writes about her process and provides early previews of her upcoming books. Readers can follow her on all her social channels: @kdfieldauthor on TikTok and @kdfield. bsky.social on BlueSky.

**linktr.ee/authorkellifield**